# REBEL HEIRESS

When Henrietta woke, wondering for a
moment where she was, the little room was full
of dusk. Uncertain shadows hovered in its
corners and the noises of evening were
merging into those of night. Henrietta was on
her feet in an instant, remembering it all. She
was at the Swan Inn at Cumber, alone with
Cedric, whom she did not trust. Madness to
have stayed here for a moment. Outside, she
could hear sounds of bustle, Cedric's voice
and then the landlord's.

'No, no,' Henrietta heard Cedric say. 'Much
best let her sleep till morning. She had a sad
tossing of it and needs the rest.'

Was she being absurdly suspicious or was
there something uncomfortably pat about this
chapter of accidents? First the shortcut that
had proved so long a way round, and then that
Cedric, the admired whip, should have
contrived to overturn his curricle. Standing
there in the twilight, she began to wonder if
any of it had been accident at all. Could Cedric
possibly have risked her life, and, to be fair,
his own, so as to force her to spend the night
with him in these compromising
circumstances?

# Rebel Heiress

---

# Jane Aiken Hodge

**CORONET BOOKS**
Hodder and Stoughton

For my friend, Philip Evans

© 1975 by Jane Aiken Hodge

First published in Great Britain 1975
by Hodder and Stoughton

*CORONET EDITION 1978*
*Second impression 1978*
*Third impression 1980*

Printed and bound in Great Britain for
Hodder and Stoughton Paperbacks, a
division of Hodder and Stoughton Ltd.,
Mill Road, Dunton Green, Sevenoaks,
Kent (Editorial Office: 47 Bedford
Square, London, WC1 3DP) by
Cox & Wyman Ltd, Reading

ISBN 0 340 22292 1

# CHAPTER ONE

The black winter that began 1812 was the worst Henrietta Marchmont could remember. The snow began early, and lay long. The Charles River froze over and presented a lively spectacle as young men skated out from Boston to attend lectures at Harvard College in Cambridge. But for Henrietta it was a season of unrelieved gloom. Illness did not improve her Aunt Abigail's temper, and she was alone as nurse, companion and scapegoat. And then there was the news: War with England seemed increasingly certain and, if it came, would put an end once and for all to Henrietta's long dream of reunion with her English father. How often she had imagined the meeting, having recourse to dreams of it, as to a drug, when Aunt Abigail was more than usually bad tempered.

Spring came at last, unwillingly. Skunk cabbage showed green on the Common, sludge lay in the gutters, a raw wind blew off the harbour, and Aunt Abigail's strength dwindled as the days lengthened. Now, the long, angry fight with death was over and Aunt Abigail would scold no more.

As the funeral procession reached the little graveyard on the hillside, Henrietta pulled her pelisse more closely around her. It had begun to snow again and the faces of the few mourners were pinched with cold. Mr. Anderson, the young minister, looked enormous with an overcoat under his surplice. Bowing her head over her aunt's open grave, Henrietta watched the first flakes settling idly on raw earth. Above, the New England sky was bleak and grey as the hard soil. Her feet were ice-cold in their shabby boots and from time to time a slow trembling shook her whole body. Was it cold? Or perhaps, though she would hardly admit it, even to herself, excitement? Poor Aunt Abigail. Closing her eyes as Mr. Anderson began to pray, Henrietta thought how sad it would be to die so unlamented. She had tried, ever since she could remember, to love her aunt. Now, by her grave, she admitted defeat. The little group of polite mourners were muttering the Lord's Prayer, but Henrietta's prayer was different.

'Oh, God,' she breathed, 'forgive her for what she did to me, and help me to forgive her, help me to escape.'

Clenching her hands more tightly inside their darned gloves, she allowed herself just for a moment, as the prayer ended, to lift her eyes and glance down towards the harbour. Yes, the *Faithful* was still there, but from the bustle on the docks near her it was clear that the business of loading was proceeding apace. There was no time to be lost.

The short service was soon over. Earth began to fall hollowly on to the coffin that was narrow and dark and frugal like Aunt Abigail herself. Mr. Anderson shut his prayer book, came round the grave to Henrietta and took her arm.

'Come,' he said, 'my dear Miss Marchmont. You must not be lingering here in the cold.'

She let him guide her away to the gates of the graveyard, grateful for the convention that demanded nothing from her but docility. On her other side, Miss Jenkin, her aunt's only friend and relentless competitor in good works, had begun to talk again, taking credit for her devotion to her sick friend, her organisation of the funeral, and of the austere collation that awaited them now in Aunt Abigail's cheerless little house on the wrong side of Beacon Hill. There was no need for Henrietta to listen to her. Miss Cabot, on her other side, was providing the necessary chorus of approving monosyllables.

Mr. Anderson's grip on Henrietta's arm tightened. 'I must speak to you. Are you very cold? Could we perhaps take a turn on the Common before we go in?'

'Why, yes.' Henrietta had known that this explanation between them was bound to come, and at least it would postpone the dreary ritual of the funeral feast. 'I have no doubt that Miss Jenkin will do the honours to a nicety. And indeed,' she reminded herself rather than him, 'I have much to thank her for.'

She listened passively while he made their excuses to the other mourners, only rousing a little to think with a flash of her usual spirit what an advantage it was to be the minister. What other young man would have been able to detach her with such public calm from her chaperone: Yet there was Miss Jenkin smiling her approbation and then turning, as he led her away, to mutter something to Miss Cabot, who nodded with such emphasis that her black Sunday bonnet shook on her grey curls.

They were out of earshot now. Mr. Anderson turned to face her. 'Miss Marchmont, I do not know how to begin.' It was true enough; he stammered to a halt, his pulpit eloquence failing him utterly.

She managed a smile for him. 'Indeed, Mr. Anderson, you must not mind it so much. Aunt Abigail had every right to do what she would with her own. Her house will make an admirable minister's residence. And believe me, I beg of you, when I tell you that I do not want it.'

His face glowed still redder. 'It is like yourself to say so, Miss Marchmont, and I appreciate it, believe me, I do. But it is an iniquitous thing none the less; I would not have thought it of Miss Abigail. And yet I cannot refuse the bequest since it is made not to me myself, but to me in my capacity as minister. How can I reconcile it with my conscience to deprive my successors of so suitable a residence? But to have left you penniless and without even a roof over your head! When I think of all the donations I have accepted from Miss Abigail for her favourite charities — why, my blood boils. I thought her a good woman.' He paused, at a loss for words.

'Yes,' said Henrietta, 'I believe most people did.'

'But not you, Miss Marchmont, I know it. How many times I have blamed you in my heart for not being more loving to your aunt. I begin to understand it now. Tell me, what was there under that mask of virtue?'

'There was wickedness, Mr. Anderson, pure wickedness. I have long felt it, and now, at last, I know. The knowledge has made me happier. I used to feel so wicked myself because I could not love her when she had been so good to me. As I thought.'

'Well' — he made an obvious effort to be fair to the dead woman — 'the fact does remain that she brought you up when you were left alone in the world.' She made a move to interrupt him. 'No, let me speak, Miss Marchmont. There is something I have to say to you. You are alone again now, without a home, without means, and without, I fear, much hope of earning your bread. To go out as a governess or companion is what I know your proud spirit would reject, nor are there many families who can afford such a luxury these days. No, Miss Marchmont, you must hear me out and believe me when I tell you that I have long pondered this step. It may seem rash to you for a man so young as I am, with the world all before him, but I

7

have long believed it my duty as a minister to find myself a suitable helpmeet. And who could be more so than you, my dear young lady, brought up as you have been by your aunt, in the very odour of good works?' He paused here for a moment, embarrassed as he remembered the new and unlovely light that had recently been shed on her aunt, but then went on undaunted. 'Miss Marchmont, I am not a romantic man, but I have known you now these five years or more. I have watched you grow from a somewhat headstrong girl — you will pardon my frankness, I know — into a young woman I am proud to be able to call my friend. I have seen your attendance at your Sunday school class; so faithful, so patient even with the most ungrateful and disobedient of your charges. I have watched your devoted care of your poor aunt in her last illness — a care that was all the more praiseworthy because, as you have confessed, you found it impossible to love her as a niece should. Miss Marchmont, taking all this into account, I feel sure, young and inexperienced though you are, that I am doing the right thing in asking you to be my wife. Imagine the life of service we will lead together! I have always felt that a minister, more perhaps than any other man, with the many calls there are on his time and patience, needs the support and consolation of a devoted helpmeet, the comfort of the domestic hearth. All this, I am sure, despite your youth and some slight tendencies I have observed in you to frivolity, some hearkening after the things of the world, all this will make you, I am convinced of it, a wife I shall be proud to introduce to my faithful and, I think I may say, devoted congregation. Miss Marchmont, I am asking you to marry me. Will you be mine?'

Henrietta had listened to this remarkable speech with some astonishment. Now she turned to face him, releasing her arm from his. Their brisk walk and the cold wind had whipped up the colour in her cheeks; one dark curl had escaped from her mourning veil and blew against her face. Her blue eyes sparkled and for a moment his hopes soared, then plummeted as she spoke.

'You have not said you love me, Mr. Anderson.'

'My dear Miss Marchmont' — he was pained and showed it — 'I had thought better of you. I have often urged your aunt to forbid your reading those trashy novels. I blame Miss Edgeworth and Mrs. Radcliffe for this. If by "love" you mean that I would throw my bonnet over the moon, abandon all for your sake, then I must honestly confess that I do not love you. But as a sister in God, I may say that I love you most dearly and promise to care for you more tenderly than any hero of romance. Perhaps I have erred in speaking to you so soon. It is, I know, hardly fitting that we should be talking of love and marriage almost at the graveside, but I wanted you to know that, alone and penniless though you are, you yet have a friend who will care for you. Do not think you must answer me now. Treasure up what I have said in your heart, and remember, I beg, how truly I admire and respect you, how eagerly I look forward to your presence at my side. But come, our friends will be wondering what is become of us, and gossip is, as you know, what I in my position must of all things avoid.' He took her arm again and gently urged her up the slope to the far side of the Common.

'But I must answer you, Mr. Anderson, as much for my own sake as for yours. I fear you have been much mistaken in me, and when you know me better, will be grateful to me for this frankness. Do you truly believe that I want nothing else in life but to devote myself to good works? Why, I have had enough of Sunday school, of flannel and sewing bees to last me several lifetimes. I am about to begin to live, Mr. Anderson. But forgive me' — she softened at his hurt look — 'I am an ungrateful wretch. I have not told you how deeply honoured I am by your flattering offer, how grateful I am for it, how kindly I take it — but, indeed, I cannot accept it.'

He was walking faster now. 'I am grieved, Miss Marchmont, grieved and surprised. Has yours too been nothing but a mask of virtue? But I will not believe it; you are disturbed, not yourself; you will think more of this. Besides, how else will you live? What will you do? Have you seriously considered the position in which — I am sorry to have to say it — you find yourself?'

'What else do you think I have been doing since Aunt Abigail died and I found how I was placed? I have it all planned, only I need help. I had intended to ask it of you, for indeed, Mr. Anderson, I have always looked on you as my friend. But how can I ask you to help me now?'

'Help you? Of course I will. If you are truly convinced that you have no vocation for a clergyman's wife, why then (was there a shade of relief in his voice?) we will say no more about it and you must tell me how else I can help you.'

'Oh, if you only would! Mr. Anderson, will you persuade the captain of the *Faithful* to take me as a passenger when he sails for England? I know he does not usually take passengers, but if you were to make the request, perhaps he would accept me.'

'Go to England? And on an English ship? Have you taken leave of your senses, Miss Marchmont? Do you not realise that war between the two countries is now inevitable; that it is only a matter of time before it is declared? And, besides, what would you do when you got there: I would not wish to pain you, but surely you cannot intend to go to your father — to Lord Marchmont? You know only too well that he has ignored your very existence all these years. What hope have you that he will welcome you now?'

'The best. There is much that I must tell you. It will shock you, I fear, but I hope you know the story of my birth — it has provided enough talk for Miss Jenkin and her friends all these years. You know, I am sure, that my father came here from England as a wild younger son and met my mother (I am like her, they say), married her in haste and could not stay to repent it, for his elder brother was killed in a duel and his family sent for him to come home posthaste. My mother was not well enough to travel, and stayed here with her elder sister, my Aunt Abigail. She was to join her husband in England after her child was born. But — he never wrote to her. Of course, the posts were slow, but weeks passed and she had no word from him. Her health was affected, she pined and fretted, and died when I was born.'

'Yes, yes,' he said somewhat impatiently, 'it is an old story and a sad one; you will do yourself no good by reviving it now. I know only too well that your father even ignored the news of his wife's death and of your birth. After such heartless behaviour, what hopes can you have of him?'

'Heartless indeed it would have been had he done so, but only listen to me, Mr. Anderson. Since Aunt Abigail died, I have, of course, been going through her papers. There was one box, particularly, that I had never seen opened. You know how suddenly Aunt Abigail went at last. I am sure if it had not been for that, she would have destroyed the papers it contained and thus finished her wicked work. But she was not able to do so, and thus I found the letters from my father that she had kept hidden all these years. They were loving letters, Mr. Anderson, written to my mother from England, telling her of his reception by his family and how, after the first shock of surprise, they were prepared to welcome her as a daughter, and her child as the heir to the title. And then, a last, heartbroken note in answer to one from my aunt in which she had told him that mother and child had died together.'

'What? You mean she suppressed his letters to his wife?'

'Yes, and told him I was dead as well as my mother. Do you wonder I call her wicked? I do not know how I shall contrive to forgive her. All these years I have read of my father in the public prints: of the fortune he made in India, of his return to England and entry into politics; of his speeches, his successes, his position at last in the inner councils of their Tory Party. And always I have thought of him as my enemy, as having wilfully disowned me. But it was nothing of the kind. He thought me dead. Now do you understand why I must go to England?'

He had followed this passionate speech with deep attention. Now he sighed and nodded. 'You are in the right of it, Miss Marchmont. You owe a duty to your father; you must go and tell him the truth. Yes, I will help you to get to England. But what will you do for passage money? Captain Gilbert is a good man, I know, but no philanthropist, and gladly though I would help you, I fear it is much beyond my means.'

'You are too good. But there's no need. Before she died, Aunt Abigail gave me all the money she had. It was not much, and I fear it was but grudgingly given, but you know how she hated lawyers. She said it would save her the trouble of willing it to me. Of course, I did not then know about the house ... But at least it means that I have enough for my passage and a little to spare for my expenses in England. And after that, well, I can but hope for the best.'

'You have proofs of your birth?'

'Oh, yes, they were all there. Aunt Abigail may have been wicked, but she was a good woman of business. No, I shall have no difficulty in convincing my father who I am, If I can but get to him.'

'Then I will see Captain Gilbert on your behalf tomorrow. Fortunately for you, I know that though he is English he is no supporter of the iniquitous Orders in Council that have brought our two countries to the point of war. He will not hold your being an American against you.'

'But I am not an American. Had you forgot?'

'Indeed I had; you seem so much like one of us. Well, well, perhaps, after all, it is for the best.'

'Yes. It would hardly be fitting for a clergyman to marry a woman of the enemy, would it?'

'You are too quick for me, Miss Marchmont. I confess, though, that thought had passed through my head. But here we are' — his relief was obvious — 'at your poor aunt's house. Rely on me to do your business for you tomorrow.'

She thanked him and they went in to join the decorous party assembled over tea and cookies in Aunt Abigail's dark little living room. All conversation ceased at sight of them, and Henrietta was only too well aware that they had been its subject. She sat down next to kind, busy Miss Jenkin and parried as best she might her persistent and well-meant enquiries about her plans. Gradually, however, as she sipped lukewarm tea, she became aware that Miss Jenkin was leading up to something. She had made various angling references to Mr. Anderson: 'So fortunate for him to receive the house . . . but a responsibility for a single man . . . a minister really needs someone to take care of him,' and so on, which Henrietta had answered as neutrally as she could. Now she changed her ground.

'I hope you will not mind it, my dear,' she said, helping herself to another cookie, 'but dear Miss Cabot and I were speaking of you just now and wondering what the future holds for you. And — if some more eligible prospect should not open up before you' — here she paused archly for a moment, then continued — 'if, as I say, no more attractive alternative has presented itself, dear Miss Cabot was wondering if you would care to go and live with her for a while. She has that big house, you know, and neither chick nor child to call her own. You could do very much worse, my dear, left as you are. We will say nothing against dear Miss Abigail, but the fact remains that things have not come out just as we expected, have they my dear?'

'Have they not?' asked Henrietta. 'I do not know exactly what anyone did expect. But you are right; let us not talk about Aunt Abigail. And, dear Miss Jenkin, just for tonight, may we not talk about me either? I am deeply grateful to Miss Cabot — please tell her so. But I can decide nothing today.'

'My child, of course you cannot; so crushed with grief as you must be. We only wanted you to know that you had friends, however forlorn you may feel.' She pressed Henrietta's hand and Henrietta returned the pressure in the spirit in which it was meant. No need to admit that her only feeling at Aunt Abigail's death was one of heartfelt relief, her only anguish now her doubt whether Captain Gilbert could be persuaded to take her to England.

The party seemed to her to go on forever, but at last they had all gone and she could remember the encouraging pressure of the hand with which Mr. Anderson had said good-bye. He would do his very best to get her passage on the *Faithful* she knew, by way of easing his conscience over her aunt's bequest to him. In her cold and narrow bed that night she dreamed of her imagined father and of England, the unknown, the longed-for land.

She kept herself busy all next morning sorting through the rest of her aunt's papers. She had already found all those that concerned herself and laid them aside to be taken with her to England. For she would not let herself think that Captain Gilbert might refuse to take her. In fact, she found it best not to think at all. Instead, she opened the heavy black box in which Aunt Abigail had kept her family's letters and began to sort through these. It was a heartbreaking enough task, for both Aunt Abigail's brothers had died fighting the British, one at Bunker Hill and the other at Ticonderoga. Reading their last letters, Henrietta began a little to understand Aunt Abigail's fierce hatred of the British. No wonder she had been furious when her younger sister fell in love with what she must have considered an enemy. But still — and Henrietta began systematically throwing the letters into the fire — this did not excuse what her aunt had done.

She was interrupted by a knock at the door and hurried to admit Mr. Anderson.

'Well?' She hardly dared ask the question.

'Successful, I hope.' He shook a few flakes of snow off his heavy overcoat. 'Captain Gilbert will visit you this afternoon. He sympathises with your predicament, but is all too justly doubtful of the propriety of his taking you, a single girl, on a ship with no other female.'

'Oh, fiddlestick,' she exclaimed impatiently. 'What must I do? Dress up as a boy to ease his conscience?'

'No, no.' He coloured. 'He merely wishes to convince himself that you are the model of propriety I described. I only

13

trust, my dear Miss Marchmont, that you will not take him up so sharply.'

She blushed and laughed. 'I beg your pardon. And indeed, I cannot begin to thank you for what you have done for me. But where am I to see Captain Gilbert?'

'Oh, as to that, he has some business at the Capitol and said he would do himself the honour of calling on you here afterwards. Would you like me to give him the meeting?'

'Oh, no, I thank you. There is no need for that. If I can face him on his ship, I can face him alone here.' And indeed, she told herself, she would do better without Mr. Anderson's embarrassed presence. He protested a little, but finally acquiesced, admitting that he had business of his own to attend to.

When he had gone, Henrietta flew about tidying the house. All must be shipshape and businesslike to impress the captain with her competence to deal with any situation that might arise. For the first time in her life she found herself actually enjoying the familiar task of polishing up Aunt Abigail's collection of ugly old brassware. She even caught herself singing as she scrubbed down the already spotless front steps. She had just stopped, conscience stricken, at the second line of 'Jenny Sutton' when a sound behind her made her turn.

A square-set, solid-looking man, middle-aged and weatherbeaten, was considering her with piercing blue eyes. She stood up, blushing and trying at once to roll down her sleeves and take off her apron.

'Captain Gilbert?' she asked.

'Himself. And can you be the desolated Miss Marchmont?'

'Yes.' Furiously, she felt herself blushing. 'I had not expected you so soon. But will you not come inside?'

'Thank you. I finished my business at the Capitol more speedily than I had expected. We sail tonight.' He looked at her quizzically.

'Tonight?' She could not conceal her dismay. 'So soon?'

'Yes, I am warned that there is no time to be lost. I take it that settles the question of your sailing with us. You cannot possibly be ready.'

'On the contrary.' She was not to be put off so easily. 'I can be ready in half an hour.'

'Then you are a most unusual young lady.' He pulled out a large gold watch. 'But I can give you longer than that, if you are sure you wish to come with us. It will not be luxurious, you know. The living will be hard, the quarters rough, the society boorish. I do not know how your father's daughter will bear it.'

'My father's daughter?' She had never thought of herself in that light before. 'Oh, do you know my father?'

'In some sort. As much as a poor ship's captain can know a cabinet minister. To be frank with you, that is the only reason I will for a moment consider taking you with me. I understand — you will forgive my frankness — but there is no question but that you *are* his daughter?'

'Not the least in the world. Would you care to see my papers?'

'No, no. You will hear that I dislike most women, but I hope I know an honest one when I meet her. You could not lie without that colour of yours betraying you. There, what did I tell you?'

Infuriated by the recurrent blush, she nevertheless returned to the attack. 'Then you will take me?'

'Why, yes. I rather believe I will. But on conditions, mind you. Your passage will be paid in advance. I cannot trust your father for that. It is not the way I do business.'

'Of course not. Will I give it to you now?'

'No, no. When you come aboard will be time enough. As for your cabin, I shall give you the supercargo's, next to mine. You will be safe enough there. Fortunately for you, we are short-handed this voyage; my second mate is a Yankee and chooses to remain here. And that reminds me of the most important point of our agreement. You will not tamper with my officers. I'll not have a parcel of lovesick lubbers on my hands. Is that understood?'

'I will do my best, sir. To tell truth, I have not hitherto found myself irresistible to men.'

'Have you not? You surprise me. But so much the better. Very well then, that is the first article of our agreement. You will leave my officers alone. If you must have society, you may have mine. I will bear you company, if necessary, and tell you what you may expect of life in England. For I have no doubt you are full of golden dreams, are you not?' He barked the last question at her, a ferocious gleam in his blue eyes.

'Why, of course. I have dreamt of England ever since I was in short petticoats, and I do not propose to stop for you or any one. Only please take me there.'

'I will, never fear for that. But I warn you; it will be a

dangerous voyage. War will be declared, I have no doubt, before we are many days at sea. How will you like it if we are taken by one of your men of war?'

'One of ours, sir? I would have you remember I am as English as you.'

'Except, I take it, for a little matter of a Yankee mother, but well spoken just the same. Very well, we will flee the damned colonials together ... And that reminds me of another point of our agreement. You will not expect me to modify my language because you are aboard.'

'Why should I? My dear sir, I have lived with a maiden aunt all my life and when I hear myself cry "fiddlestick!" like her, I could cut my own throat.'

He laughed. 'We'll have you swearing more heartily before you get to England. Never fear for that. And so to the last point of our agreement. I have a young brother who longs to be in Parliament. When you have come into your own, will you speak to your father for him?'

'Of course I will.' Warmly. 'But I beg you will not hope too much from my influence. My father may not choose to acknowledge me. That is the risk I have to take. I cannot wait to write and ask his permission to come, for if war does break out, I shall be caught here.'

Captain Gilbert picked up his hat. 'No if about it, Miss Marchmont. I am told it is as good as settled in Washington. That is why we sail tonight. I will send for your boxes this evening. And I beg you will bring as little as possible. We carry a full cargo and all you bring must be stored in your own cabin. No need to bring provisions for the voyage; you will dine at my table. I nan best have an eye to you so.'

'Captain Gilbert, I do not know how to thank you.'

'Then do not try. I shall regret this piece of madness speedily enough without being badgered by your thanks. And so, I have no doubt, will you, when we meet our first northeaster. Have you ever been to sea before? No? I thought not. Well, don't expect me to nurse you, that's all. You'll just have to sink or swim with the rest of us.' He shook her warmly by the hand and took his leave.

For a moment, after he had gone, she panicked. How could she be ready by evening? Then she pulled herself together. She must be; there was nothing else for it. The rest of her aunt's long-hoarded collection of letters she burned unread on the dying fire, then quickly began to pack her few possessions in the strong black box that had held the letters. Her aunt had had rigid views about dress, and neither of them had ever had more than two stuff gowns, one for everyday, another exactly similar, but newer, for best. Henrietta packed her best, wondering how its severe lines would look in stylish England. A warm pelisse went to join it — she would wear Aunt Abigail's sable coat. It was not new, and she had to suppress a feeling of revulsion as she remembered how often she had walked meekly behind it to church, but it was good, and she knew she would be glad of it.

This part of her packing was soon finished. Then came the more difficult task of deciding what else to take. A miniature of her father and one of her mother, black-haired, blue-eyed and laughing, were tenderly wrapped in a pair of hand-knit woollen stockings. And, after a pause, the companion portrait of Aunt Abigail joined them. After all, those two were the sum of her American family; they must both come with her on this English venture. Then she turned to her books, which would fill a smaller box. She would be glad of them on the long voyage. Her Bible and her Shakespeare were soon packed, then she paused to consider what else of the family library she should take. Aunt Abigail had always frowned upon reading as a sinful waste of time, and the sight of her niece with a book had been the cue for her to produce some particularly repulsive piece of household mending. Now, Henrietta stood in the neglected little room that had once been her grandfather's study dazzled by the riches before her. To have so much time . . . She must be able to make the most of it. Boswell's *Life of Dr. Johnson* was an immediate choice: She had never had time to finish it. Her own treasured copies of *Clarissa Harlowe, Evelina* and *Belinda* went to join it: They had given her the only glimpses she had had of life in England. What else would be useful to prepare her for the Old World? The poems of Dryden and Pope, Lord Chesterfield's *Letters to his Son* and finally Burke's *Speeches* completed her little library. She must learn all she could about the complexities of English politics in which her father played so prominent a part.

She was cording the second box when a knock at the door announced the arrival of two red-faced English sailors. Grinning from ear to ear and swearing at each other amicably as they worked, they quickly loaded her boxes on to their hand barrow. 'Cap'n said as how you'd have all ready, miss, but us never believed 'un.'

Departing, they warned her to be aboard by seven o'clock at the latest: 'Cap'n sails with the tide and never waited yet for man, woman, nor child.'

Henrietta looked at Aunt Abigail's big old-fashioned watch which she had pinned to the lapel of her dress. It was five o'clock already. She had little enough time. But her farewells were soon said. Calling on Miss Jenkin, she found Miss Cabot with her and was relieved to be spared a visit. As for them, they were struck as near speechless by her news as they were capable of being. 'To England!' exclaimed Miss Jenkin, and 'Tonight!' chimed in Miss Cabot. They kept it up so faithfully with exclamation and counterexplanation that Henrietta found no need to explain what her Aunt Abigail had done. Grateful for the necessity of haste, she thanked Miss Cabot again for her kind offer, entrusted to Miss Jenkin the care of her aunt's elderly and repulsive pug dog, kissed them both warmly and left to hurry to Mr. Anderson's house.

To her relief he was at home, and to her still greater satisfaction insisted on accompanying her to the docks.

'It would be far from seemly for you to be walking through that part of the town in the dark, alone,' he said as he shrugged into his overcoat. 'Of course I will accompany you and lend what appearance of propriety I can to this venture. For I must tell you, Miss Marchmont, that I have been gravely troubled in spirit about you since we last met and have prayed ceaselessly for guidance. I only trust that what I have done may prove for the best, but indeed this seems a desperate enough undertaking of yours. To be going upon the sea, alone, among a parcel of rough and unruly sailors — and Englishmen at that, who are known the world over for their ribaldry. Miss Marchmont, I wonder whether even at this eleventh hour I should not urge you to turn back.'

'Dear Mr. Anderson.' She took his arm and encouraged him gently towards his own front door. 'I beg you will not trouble yourself about me. You have provided me with a most admirable protector in Captain Gilbert. I shall do very well, I promise you.'

But he continued his prophesies of doom all the way to the docks, so that Henrietta was heartily glad to see the *Faithful* at last, looking alarmingly small, at the dockside. Captain Gilbert was on deck, delivering an impassioned and blasphemous harangue to a group of sailors. Mr. Anderson began to go purple in the face. Henrietta seized his hand and shook it firmly.

'Mr. Anderson,' she said, 'I have just remembered something. I believe I forgot to extinguish the fire in Aunt Abigail's — I beg your pardon, in your house. I beg you will lose no time in going to ascertain that all is well. It would be a shocking thing if my last act in this country should be to commit arson.'

He was in agony. How could he leave her alone on the docks? And yet, to lose the house that would be such an improvement in his circumstances ... And all the time, Captain Gilbert's stream of language continued unabated. It was truly, Henrietta thought, a virtuoso performance, without a single repetition.

She tried again. 'Dear Mr. Anderson, I beg you will go. I shall do very well, I assure you. See, here comes one of the ship's officers.'

And indeed what appeared to be a schoolboy was approaching them along the dock, his uniform however proclaiming that he was in fact an officer on the *Faithful*.

'Miss Marchmont?' He saluted her smartly. 'Captain's orders, you are to come aboard at once. And no visitors allowed. We sail immediately.' And then, with a complete change of tone: 'I say, miss, isn't it a lark, your sailing with us? I only hope you won't be too damned — I mean deucedly — uncomfortable.'

Mr. Anderson drew himself up to his full height and swelled out his chest. He was about to make a speech. Henrietta knew the signs all too well and felt that it would be more than she could bear.

'Mr. Anderson,' she said, 'I must beg you will go. I feel more and more positive that I left the fire burning and the tinderbox near it. Pray, pray lose no more time, but hurry back there. I should never forgive myself ... And I shall do very well with this gentleman.' She took the young officer's arm and let him guide her up the narrow gangplank before Mr. Anderson could do more than bid God to bless her. Pausing once to turn back when she reached the deck, she could see him dodging his way through the crowd with unclerical haste. She turned with a smile to the young officer. 'I must seem very heartless to part so easily with my last friend.'

He was still young enough to blush. 'Not a bit of it, Miss Marchmont. We are all to be your friends. Captain's orders. I am Tom Singleton, and very much at your service.'

At that moment there was a furious roar from the stern of the ship where the cargo was still being loaded. 'Singleton! Goddammit, Singleton, where have you got to?'

'Oh' — she had not thought his colour could have been higher — 'I am afraid, Miss Marchmont, I must leave you.'

'Of course. I shall be very happy to stand here and say good-bye to Boston. We sail at once, you say?'

'As soon as the cargo is in and the hatches closed. It will be no time now ...' An even more furious — and to Henrietta quite unintelligible — roar from astern interrupted him and he turned and left her at a run.

She leaned against the rail of the ship and gazed up at the little town on the hill. Night had closed in now, and here and there a light showed already. Miss Jenkin and Miss Cabot would be sharing their frugal supper. It was Friday. There would be baked beans and brown bread. Oddly enough, this thought brought the first suggestion of tears behind Henrietta's eyes. She had not, she thought dismally, any real friends to leave — her aunt had seen to that. But to leave all one's habits ... It was a wrench, there was no doubt about it. On Sunday, the pew would be empty that she had occupied faithfully in King's Chapel ever since she was old enough for silence — and that, in Aunt Abigail's opinion was very young indeed. But this was no time to be remembering her aunt's tyrannies, minor or major. She was free, she was going to England, she was mistress of her fate at last. The thought was a formidable one, and she found herself shivering as she had at the graveside — with cold? with fright? Best not to enquire too closely.

But the chaos on the afterdeck had suddenly cleared itself. There was a new volley of orders from Captain Gilbert on the bridge, and then, miraculously, Henrietta saw the gap between the ship and the dock begin to widen. They were away ... she had escaped. It was good-bye, Boston.

# CHAPTER TWO

Much later, when the stars were all out in brilliant show, and the lights of Boston had dwindled in the distance, Captain Gilbert joined her at the rail.

'So you got here,' he said. 'I am sorry not to have welcomed you on board, but you will have seen that I was occupied. Now, I am to lecture you. Tonight is very well; it is natural that you should wish to see the last of your home. But from now on you will be below in your cabin when night falls, and stay there till morning. My crew are a good enough set of men, but they are no saints. I will not have them tempted.'

She coloured, grateful for the concealing darkness. 'I am sorry; it shall not happen again. But to tell truth, I do not know where my cabin is. Mr. Singleton was somewhat pressed for time . . .'

He laughed. 'I remember. Well, I will show you to your cabin myself. You will find that we do not stand on ceremony in the *Faithful*.' He led her down a steep companionway into stuffy darkness full of strange smells. One quavering lantern lit their way to the little cabin where Henrietta's boxes had been stowed.

'I trust you will not feel yourself too much confined,' he said as he left her. 'My cabin is next door; we will sup there in half an hour.'

This gave Henrietta ample time to stow away as many of her few possessions as the limited accommodation of the cabin would take. The rest would simply have to remain in the two boxes, piled in a corner. She then tidied her hair, added a clean white collar to her dark dress, and knocked timidly on the door of the next cabin. Captain Gilbert greeted her as formally as if she was attending a dinner party on shore and introduced her to his officers, a huge redheaded man called Frank Forster, and a fair-haired Henry Trenchard, who looked almost as young as Tom Singleton.

It was an oddly formal meal, despite the cramped quarters, for Captain Gilbert's cabin was not very much larger than Henrietta's own. Conversation lay mainly between Gilbert himself and Frank Forster, with Henrietta exerting herself to take at least some part. Luckily for her, Aunt Abigail's iron training held. 'You will not be thinking of yourself,' her aunt would have said, 'but of your duty to others.' Through many a long gathering of Boston elders Henrietta had acted on this precept and now she found it of golden use to her. As for the two younger officers, she could not make out whether they were tongue-tied out of deference to her, or to the captain, or both. Either way, she found that their bashfulness gave her courage and before the meal was over she was boldly questioning Captain Gilbert about the chances of war.

'Chances,' he said, 'there's no question about it. The resolution is taken by those damned warmongers in Washington. It is merely a matter of days before the declaration is sent. Not that I am surprised, mind you. Our Orders in Council are an iniquitous business — death to trade — should have been repealed long since. No, I don't altogether blame your people for acting on them. It's been a mismanaged business from the start, but you must remember that we have a tiger by the throat in Europe. Boney has kept Government too busy for cool thinking.'

'Bonaparte,' said Henrietta. 'It's hard to believe I may live to see him.'

Captain Gilbert laughed. 'I devoutly hope you do not. Unless it's in chains in Whitehall. The world would be a sorry place with him for its master. But you do not drink, Miss Marchmont.' He filled her glass. 'I hope you will take wine with me.'

She had heard about what Aunt Abigail called this immoral custom, but had never before touched anything stronger than sweet cider. Now, she bravely lifted the glass to her lips and drank. Although she was far from liking its taste, the rough red wine seemed to warm her heart. She found herself smiling as she emptied the glass.

'Good girl,' said Captain Gilbert approvingly. 'Your first taste, eh? We'll have you as good a judge of wine as your father before we land. But you must excuse me.' A sudden lurch of the ship had sent crockery chasing to the raised edge of the table. The light flickered wildly, Henrietta's hands held tight to the seat of her chair. 'I thought we were in for some rough weather,' said Gilbert as he left the cabin. 'You will soon find out what kind of sailor you are, Miss Marchmont.'

She did indeed. For the next three days, while the little *Faithful* tossed in the grip of the gale, she lay on the narrow bed in her cabin and wished she was dead. From time to time, a gruff voice from the door would ask whether she lacked anything, and she would groan out an incoherent reply. Hurried footsteps and shouts overhead made her wonder if their position was critical, but she did not really care. Shipwreck could not be worse than what she was already suffering.

On the fourth day, the ship steadied in her course and Henrietta gratefully swallowed a little gruel. Then, feeling suddenly much better, she fell into a deep and peaceful sleep. She was roused, much later, by a loud knocking on her cabin door and sprang from her bed with a cry of 'Who's there?'

'It is I, Captain Gilbert,' came the answer. 'May we speak with you for a moment?'

Much surprised by the sound of several voices outside, she hurried to smooth her dress and tidy her hair. As she did so, she realised that the motion of the ship had changed. Could she be lying to? What disaster could have struck them? At a renewed knocking, she abandoned her attempts at tidying herself and opened the door. Captain Gilbert stood outside with two uniformed strangers.

'Miss Marchmont,' he said formally, 'may I present Mr. Forbes and Mr. Clinton, both of the American Navy. They have boarded us for news and find themselves unable to believe my assurances that our countries are not yet at war. I told them we had an American citizen aboard who would assure them that I am in the right of it.'

'Why, of course.' Henrietta took the cue he gave her. 'There is no question of war yet, nor will be, I sincerely hope. Do you think,' she addressed the elder of the two Americans, 'that I would have risked travelling in an English ship if I had thought such a thing even likely?'

'Ah ...' The American smiled back at her. 'You're from Boston all right; I would know the accent anywhere. Whereabouts do you live, Miss Marchmont? I've a cousin there myself, a Mr. Anderson, a minister. Perhaps you may know him?'

'But of course I do.' Henrietta let her relief show. 'Indeed, he arranged my passage with Captain Gilbert.'

'Did he so? And is he as redheaded as ever?'

'Red?' She looked at him in surprise, then recognised the

trap. If she had not in fact known Mr. Anderson she would certainly have fallen into it. 'You must be speaking of another Mr. Anderson, sir. Our minister has dark hair — though I confess his face is often red enough.'

He laughed. 'My cousin to the life. Forgive me for cross-questioning you, Miss Marchmont, but we had to be sure. You will understand, of course, that should war have actually broken out between our two countries, it would be our duty to take the *Faithful*. I am only glad I have not been compelled to inconvenience a parishioner of Cousin Henry's. But are you sure you wish to go to England? My information is that war is very probable. You may find yourself in an awkward position over there. It would be a breach of regulations, but if you wish it we will take a chance on it and carry you home with us.'

Was this another trap? Henrietta knew she must take the greatest care what she said. Any minute the Americans might ask to see her papers which might well be fatal. She thought quickly, then: 'You are mighty good, sir,' she said, 'and in truth your offer is a tempting one. But I think I must continue with Captain Gilbert. This is no frivolous journey of mine. I have just learned that a relative has died in England leaving me heir to a considerable fortune. I must appear in person to claim it and you will understand my anxiety to do so before war does break out; though I continue to hope that it will be averted. The latest news when I left Boston was that the Orders in Council were likely to be repealed, and matters to come to an amicable settlement.'

Impressed at such knowledgeability in a female, Forbes did not pause to question the truth of what she said, but thanked her and turned to Captain Gilbert. 'Very well, I am satisfied, and must apologise for having doubted your word. But you must see that it might have been somewhat tempting to you to tell us a tall story, since you knew we had been at sea this month and more and were in no position to disprove it.'

'Of course, of course,' Captain Gilbert said, a hint of patronage colouring his voice. 'You acted like wise men, sir, and I have no quarrel with you on that score. Now, perhaps, you will come and drink a glass of wine with me before we part.' He led them next door to his cabin and Henrietta listened in an agony of suspense while they drank toasts to each other's countries and to enduring peace between them. Then, at last, a slight quickening in the motion of the ship gave them their cue to leave. Henrietta stayed cautiously below while Captain Gilbert saw them to their longboat. There was no use risking their suddenly thinking of her papers. It was only when she heard them pulling away from the ship's side that she dared go up on deck. The frigate *Constitution* from which they had come, lay alarmingly close to the little *Faithful*, whose entire crew were on deck, silently watching as Forbes and Clinton returned to their ship. Their freedom depended on how her captain received his officers' report. An anxious ten minutes passed, then a farewell signal was run up by the *Constitution*.

'Good,' said Gilbert laconically. 'Answer 'em, Forster, and we're away.'

With a sigh of relief, Henrietta saw the distance between the two ships begin to lengthen. She stood at the rail for a long time, watching the *Constitution* dwindling in the distance and thinking of the sang-froid of these Englishmen who had bluffed their way so calmly out of capture.

When he had the *Faithful* safely on her course again, Gilbert handed over to Forster and came down from the bridge to join Henrietta.

'Thank you, Miss Marchmont,' he said formally. 'You're a quick-witted lass and we all owe you our liberty. Your father has a right to be proud of his daughter.'

She blushed and changed the subject, but had to bear its renewal over dinner when the officers drank her health and even Singleton mastered his bashfulness sufficiently to pay her a stammering compliment. It was only as she was parrying it, and drinking the necessary glass of wine with him, that she remembered she had been feeling good for the last few hours and had not even noticed it. The excitement had cured her of her seasickness.

From that moment began her enjoyment of the voyage. The crew, who had begun by regarding her with suspicion as a possible Jonah, now took her to their hearts as a mascot. Wherever she went, there were smiles and greetings, while strange objects found their way to her cabin: a tiny model of the *Constitution* carved out of cork, a set of spillikens made from an old cask, and even a seagull with a broken wing. Somewhat to her relief, this poor creature came to a rapid end when the ship's cat paid her its next visit. The crew also discovered that she had brought her Aunt Abigail's well-stocked medicine box with her and was a very much gentler and more skilful surgeon than Henry Trenchard, to whom they had previously had to apply in case of sickness. She soon found herself unofficial ship's doctor, drawing out splinters, dressing wounds and doling out physic very much as she had in the old days among Aunt Abigail's poor. Captain Gilbert, finding her one day calmly lancing the infected foot of a large and moronic seaman, laughed and told her he would have to take her on the strength. As for Trenchard, he was delighted. It was a part of his duties he had always detested, and he handed over his store of laudanum and ipecac to her with a sigh of relief.

Perhaps as a result, he was the first of the officers to ask her to marry him, doing so abruptly, and immediately after breakfast, one fine morning two weeks or so after they had left Boston. She answered him as abruptly, though with more feeling than she had been able to spare for Mr. Anderson, and was relieved to find that her refusal made not the slightest difference to their good relations. It merely made her feel pleasantly at ease in his company, so that meals in the captain's cabin, which had begun by being something of an ordeal, became a positive pleasure to her. She had not realised how, under Aunt Abigail's wing, she had been starved for masculine company. Now she had nothing else, and enjoyed it immensely. The officers were busy teaching her how to behave in English society, and she proved an apt pupil, though the little cabin sometimes echoed with their laughter at her gaffes. She had so much to learn. She did not know how to behave when a gentleman asked her to take wine with him, nor what one said when offered a pinch of snuff, nor how one accepted a partner for the dance . . . Nor, indeed, could she dance the fashionable dances, since Aunt Abigail had frowned upon all such pastimes.

This discovery delighted her tutors. Mr. Trenchard got out his fiddle and strummed away at a rudimentary quadrille, while Mr. Singleton solemnly approached Henrietta, and with his best bow solicited the honour of her hand for the dance. Blushing and curtseying, she accepted it with a good grace and the lesson began. Luckily for her instructors' rather limited supply of patience, she was a quick pupil so that the lessons soon became a pleasure to everyone. The officers took turns to instruct her, and only Trenchard grumbled as he worked away on the fiddle.

When they were exhausted with laughter and exercise — for dancing on a small boat in mid-Atlantic is no mean acrobatic feat — they would pause to draw breath and cross-examine Henrietta once again on points of etiquette. How would she greet a duke? An archbishop? The Prince Regent? An elderly lady she disliked and distrusted? Her maid when she brought her up her morning chocolate?

'For,' said Mr. Singleton, 'you must expect to find your most rigorous critics in your father's servants. Now, again: I am the Prince Regent and we are meeting for the first time ... Admirable!' He took her hand and raised her as she swept him a magnificent curtsey. 'You will meet him, too, though you look so mutinous and unbelieving.'

'Yes,' said Trenchard, 'and you will take very particular care never to find yourself alone with him.' For her mentors made no secret of their anxiety about her. Her frank and open American manners were all very well with them, they explained, but she would find London society a dangerous jungle in which she must tread warily.

'Of course,' said Forster soothingly, 'we must hope that your father will find time to instruct and protect you, but he is a busy man — when I left England he was all in all to Perceval, the First Minister, and must have spent more time in the House of Lords than he did at home.'

'Yes, and will be busier still once this cursed war is declared,' added Singleton. 'I find it too much to hope that he will have a great deal of time even for the most charming of daughters.' He bowed elaborately. 'No, no, Miss Marchmont, the blush is well enough, but the slightest of curtseys will acknowledge such a compliment. Now, may I have the honour to offer you a pinch of my snuff? 'Tis a blend that Fribourg and Treyer keep for me alone.' He offered her his battered snuffbox with an elaborate flourish and smiled his approval as she placed a pinch professionally on the back of her hand and sniffed at it. 'No, no, if it's to be done at all, it must be done with an air. Thus —' He took an enormous sniff and they both exploded in a volley of sneezes and laughter.

'Oh, dear,' said Henrietta, wiping her eyes. 'I do not believe I shall ever pass muster as a member of the *ton*. Sometimes I find myself almost hoping my father will not acknowledge me. It all seems such monstrous hard work. I must ride in the park every day — but only in the afternoon and then only at a snail's pace — I must appear in society every night — my mornings must be devoted to receiving visitors. When shall I have such a pleasant life as this again? I wish this voyage would last for-ever.'

'And so do we,' agreed the officers. That night Forster and Singleton proposed to her, one after the other, having tossed a coin as to who should try first. They took their dismissals philosophically, Forster revealing that Trenchard had bet them a bottle of champagne — to be drunk to her health on landing — that they would be unsuccessful.

They were nearing Ireland now. The ship, which Henrietta had always found a model of such neatness as would have satisfied even Aunt Abigail, had been scoured and holystoned till she shone, and Henrietta had held an inquisition on her own and the officers' best clothes, all of which proved to have suffered severely from mildew.

'But never trouble yourself for that,' said Singleton, when he found her spreading her best stuff gown on the upper deck to air. 'Your father will doubtless fit you out from stem to stern in Bond Street. And indeed' — with a faintly reproachful look for the solid grey worsted Aunt Abigail had chosen — 'you will be well advised not to appear in public until he has done so. You will find the styles young ladies in London are wearing something of a surprise, I conceive.'

'I have no doubt I will,' said Henrietta, 'but how I should have survived this voyage in nothing but the muslins you de-scribe your sisters as wearing is more than I can imagine. Time enough when I get to London to be thinking of muslins and gauzes. Though I confess I shall be glad enough to see the last of this old rag.'

She shook out her skirts disdainfully, and Singleton burst into a peal of delighted laughter.

'Excellent, Miss Marchmont. You would not have done that when you came aboard. You will make a fine lady yet. I expect when we come to visit you in London you will freeze us with a look.'

She laughed. 'Never that. But you will come to see me, will you not? I confess I am more than a little frightened of what faces me. It will be such a comfort to see you.'

'Of course we will.'

He was interrupted by Captain Gilbert, who cast a quizzical look at Henrietta's best dress and told her that he hoped to sight Ireland that evening. 'It will not be long now,' he continued, as Singleton excused himself and left them.

'No,' said Henrietta. 'I confess, I almost wish we had the voyage to do over again. I never thought I should find myself so frightened.'

'No need to fret over that,' he said robustly. 'It is natural enough. But do not let those young idiots of mine frighten you with their talk of Almack's and the *ton*. You will find the world all before you, I am sure. If, by any chance, you should not, if your father should prove unwelcoming, which I find hard to imagine, why then, I beg you will go to my sister, who keeps my house for me, such as it is. She will advise you as to what would be best to do. I will give you her direction. It is in Russell Square, not the most elegant part of town, as I have no doubt those puppies have taught you, but you may be sure of a hearty welcome there, and good council, just the same. But what am I doing gossiping here! I very much hope that the French fleet is safe cooped up in Toulon, but just in case they should venture out, we are keeping a sharp lookout, and you would be well advised to go below at any sign of trouble. Though of course insofar as you are American the frogs are your dear friends.'

'True,' said Henrietta, 'but insofar as I am English, I would rather we did not encounter them. Indeed, I do not know how to thank you, sir,' she was beginning, when a cry from the lookout made him hurry away.

To her relief, it was an English merchantman like themselves that they had sighted, and its signals told them that the channel was clear to Plymouth.

'The frogs have learnt their lesson since Trafalgar,' said Singleton over dinner. 'We've beat them by sea and it's nothing but a matter of time till we beat them by land, now Lord Wellington's in command. He'll have Boney out of Spain and growling home to France in no time, if they'll just give him the support he needs from home. And if your American friends do not cause too great a diversion of troops. But I fancy there will be more talk than fighting in that quarter.'

Henrietta was not so sure, but forebore to contradict him and the discussion was soon forgotten in the lively performance of a quadrille, in which Singleton partnered Henrietta and Forster led out a reluctant midshipman.

To Henrietta's disappointment, they passed Ireland at night. Then the wind dropped and it was not until three mornings later that a cry of 'Land, ho' sent her hurrying up on deck with her hair still loose on her shoulders — no time for the intricate arrangement of plaits on which Aunt Abigail had insisted.

She found Singleton and Trenchard leaning on the rail, gazing ahead to where a long, green line lay low on the horizon.

'There you are, Miss Marchmont.' Trenchard made room for her between them. 'Home at last.'

'Home?' she said wonderingly. 'Yes, I suppose it is.'

She could hardly tear herself away from the rails as the wind freshened behind them and they approached near enough to see details of fields and woods, and here and there a miniature building, shining in morning sunlight.

'Well' — Captain Gilbert paused beside her — 'how do you like it, Miss Marchmont?'

'Like it?' To her dismay, she found her eyes full of tears. 'It's beautiful — beautiful. It all looks so tidy, so green; like a child's toy. But, do you know, it is the strangest thing: I do feel as if I was coming home.'

She hardly left the deck all day, watching as the trim fields slid by, straining her eyes from time to time as they passed some notable landmark — a red brick church on a hill or a vast mansion spread out in its park.

'It's so rich!' she exclaimed to Trenchard. 'It's like a dream of a country.'

He laughed. 'Ah, you should see some parts of London, Miss Marchmont, before you say that — or Glasgow, where I come from. You'd think that more like a nightmare, I'm afraid.'

They drank champagne on their last night at sea and toasted Henrietta as the future belle of Almack's. Once again she found herself near to tears, and it was a relief when Captain Gilbert urged her to bed early. If the wind held, they should make Plymouth at dawn. And indeed she was roused early by the excitement on deck and hurried aloft in time to see the *Faithful* slide gracefully into the little green harbour under the hill. For good or ill, she was home at last.

# CHAPTER THREE

In the hurly-burly of the landing, Henrietta found herself lonely for the first time since she had come aboard. Everyone was busy, preoccupied with thoughts of home and family. She stood about, trying hard not to get in the way, and waited for Captain Gilbert to order her ashore. At last he hurried up to her.

'Bad news, I'm afraid, Miss Marchmont. I had hoped to have the pleasure of escorting you myself to London, but I have received orders with the pilot. I am to take my cargo by sea to Southampton. I'll not suggest your coming too. Your best plan now will be to take the London coach. I have had inquiries made; you may get today's if you lose no time. Singleton shall see you safe on board.'

After that all was confusion. There were farewells, warmly friendly on their side, near tearful on hers, but hurried, hurried ... Her boxes were taken ashore; she tried for the last time to thank Captain Gilbert for all he had done, failed, gave it up and accepted his sister's address gratefully. Then Singleton was hurrying her through the little town to the coaching inn, steadying her with a friendly arm when she found the ground rock under her feet. When they arrived, the big coach was already loading; there was only time for Henrietta to pay her fare, see her boxes stowed away in the boot and shake Singleton warmly by the hand before the coachman was climbing to his box and she found herself shut in the dark and musty interior where she was to sit bodkin between an enormously fat woman in scarlet satin and a long thin clergyman with a dripping nose. Peering between them and out of the window, she saw Singleton looking anxiously in at her. It had all been so quick, but he had seen her start when the innkeeper had named the fare. He put his head in at the window and leaned across the woman in scarlet: 'Miss Marchmont, are you sure you have enough —' But the coachman had whipped up his horses; they were away.

Smiling reassurance as she waved good-bye, Henrietta

wished she was indeed certain that she had got enough money for the journey. The coach fare had left her alarmingly little with which to defray her expenses on the way. But it was too late to worry now; she would just have to manage as best she could. After all, it was only for a couple of days; if she must starve, she must. The woman in scarlet, producing a vinaigrette and beginning to complain dolefully of travel sickness, gave her her cue. She would just have to be too ill to eat, that was all.

But when they stopped, at last, for dinner, she was too hungry to resist the landlord's firmly worded suggestion that she eat his ordinary like the other passengers. It made an alarming hole in her diminished resources. Who would have thought that Plymouth would be so far from London? Slightly dizzy with fatigue, she leaned more heavily against the red satin bulwark beside her and fell into a fitful doze as the heavy coach lumbered on through wooded hills. She woke with a start. The coach had increased its speed and was rocking and swaying alarmingly as it bucketed along a narrow lane. Henrietta cast a nervous glance at her companions. The woman in red had also, it seemed, just waked up. The clergyman had given up reading his Bible and leaned anxiously forward to peer out of the window. A large, red-faced countryman facing them leaned forward confidentially to Henrietta.

'Told you so,' he said, 'young squire's got the ribbons now. Told me he would. Wagered his brother a fiver he'd drive this stage. I just hope we don't meet no one: young squire's a prime 'un all right, but damned awkward with his whip.'

'Do you mean to tell me' — the woman in red seemed to have swollen to twice her usual size — 'do you sit there and tell me that the coachman has handed over the reins to some unqualified person?'

' 'Deed and he has, ma'am, but for a consideration, I have no doubt. After all, coachman has to live same as you and me.'

An acrimonious discussion now broke out among the passengers of the coach, the younger ones maintaining that they had no right to interfere in a sporting venture of this kind, while the lady in red insisted that the coach should be stopped, and the clergyman looked anxiously at his closed Bible for guidance. As there was no means of getting in touch with the coachman, Henrietta soon realised that the discussion was entirely academic, and paid little attention to it, concentrating instead on steadying herself against the dizzying swoops and plunges of the coach. Suddenly, the noise outside seemed to be re-doubled, there was a confused sound of shouting from the box, then the coach lurched sideways, shuddered and turned slowly over. Within, chaos reigned. The lady in red screamed continuously on a piercingly high note. The clergyman, who had somehow fallen underneath her, could be heard grunting something between prayer and blasphemy. The countryman was upside down under the other seat, where Henrietta heard him exclaim, 'Told you so; told you young squire was unhandy with the whip. Now look what a's done.'

As for Henrietta, she was lucky; her side of the coach was uppermost. Shaken and bruised, she nevertheless contrived to get a purchase on the sideways seat and pull herself up to look out of the window, which was now above her. An alarming sight met her eyes. The coach had entirely left the road and was lying in the ditch. And on the other side of the road lay the cause of the accident, a light curricle drawn by two highly bred greys. Its driver lay motionless on the road beside it, his hands still engangled in the reins. He was, Henrietta saw at once, in danger of his life. If his horses should run away, he would be dragged along under the curricle. She looked down into the seething interior of the coach. The countryman was just extricating himself from under the seat; his broad back rising below her. She put her foot on his back, gave a spring, and pulled herself out through the open window. It was a narrow squeeze, and the coach rocked dangerously, but in a moment she had jumped clear and was on the road beside the curricle. A glance told her its driver was breathing, though unconscious. She moved quickly to his horses' heads, caught the reins and began to talk to them in the firm but soothing tones she had found efficacious with Aunt Abigail's bad-tempered old carriage horse. Soon the greys had stopped their nervous tossing and stamping and stood quietly enough, merely shivering from time to time. They had been driven far and fast, Henrietta could see, and exhaustion was on her side. Absentmindedly stroking a grey nose, she turned to look around her. The stage coachman, she now saw, was busy with the one outside passenger, doubtless the young squire, who lay unconscious in the ditch behind the coach. From inside the coach came a confusion of noises. The woman in red was still screaming, but intermittently now, and without much conviction. Beneath her treble came a ground bass of grunts, oaths and curses. From time to time an arm or leg would wave for a minute out of the window through which she had escaped, then disappear as suddenly as it had come.

On the road beside her, the unconscious driver of the curricle began to stir a little. Danger again. If he should twitch at the reins, it might startle his horses into flight. Henrietta began to tickle the ears of the near grey and at the same time called in low but firm tones to the coachman: 'You, coachman, leave that at once and come over here.'

He looked at her in surprise. 'But it's young squire, miss, he'm dead, seems like.'

'Not a bit of it, he's only unconscious, and no more than he deserves,' she said tartly enough. 'And will do him no harm to remain so. Come you here and hold these horses while I free their driver.'

He recognised authority in her voice, laid the young squire's head gently in a bramblebush and came over to join her, muttering something under his breath. She took no notice, handed him the reins and hurried over to the unconscious man in the road. He was stirring now, and muttering to himself: 'Charge,' he said, and then, 'damme, the devils have got me.' Blood trickled slowly from the side of his head. His hands were held fast by the reins, which seemed to be looped twice around them. After trying in vain to free them, Henrietta took out Aunt Abigail's little pearl-handled penknife, which, with her watch, she wore on a pin, and began to cut through the tough leather. She had just cut the last strand, when her patient suddenly twitched into life shouted, 'Got you!' and took her by the throat. A pair of very bright blue eyes blazed into hers, then the pale aquiline face flushed scarlet.

His hands dropped to his sides. 'I ... I beg your pardon.' He looked about him in confusion. 'I thought you were one of Boney's men. But now I recollect: This is England; there has been an accident. Of course, the coach. All over the road. You, coachman, what do you mean by it? If the greys are injured, I'll wring your neck.'

'The greys are well enough,' said Henrietta. 'Frightened, of course, but none the worse. But I fear you are hurt.'

He put his hand to his head. 'A mere scratch. Nothing to signify. But I think I owe you more than an apology. You have saved my life, or I am very much mistaken.'

'Oh, I do not think so,' said Henrietta, 'the greys were

calm enough. But I am afraid I was compelled to cut your reins to free you, which I am sure is what you will not at all like.'

'You are quite right.' He made a wry face. 'I do not. And it will teach me not to be such a cowhanded fool. If I had come down the hill at a proper pace instead of letting them out, I would have been able to stop when I saw that young fool was driving the coach. But — I was in a hurry. There is a boat sails tomorrow —'

He was interrupted by a shout from the coach; the countryman's angry face appeared for a moment at the window, then vanished again like a jack-in-the-box. 'I suppose we had better go to the assistance of these good people.' The injured man rose to his feet.'But first allow me to introduce myself: Charles Rivers, your most obliged servant.' He made her a courtly, if slightly dishevelled, bow.

'And I am Henrietta Marchmont,' she said, 'and you are quite right, we really must try to get them out. I am afraid that poor clergyman will be quite flattened by now.'

A confused and exhausting few minutes followed, but at last, by their united efforts, they managed to get the upper door of the coach open and help its bruised and furious passengers to crawl out. The young squire, too, had come to himself unaided and had come around the coach to face the vituperations of its passengers.

'Yes,' said Charles Rivers thoughtfully, 'that is all very well and I agree with everything they say, but we must be thinking what's best to be done. I am afraid neither my curricle nor the coach can be moved. Someone will have to ride for assistance. I would go willingly, but . . .'

It was perfectly evident that he was in no state to ride, and after some discussion, the coachman set out to ride back to the nearest village and summon help. The passengers resigned themselves in their various ways to the long wait before them. The clergyman settled down under the hedge with his Bible. The woman in red began for the third time to tell the young squire what she thought of him. The countryman fell asleep.

Rivers took Henrietta's arm. 'Come,' he said, 'we have something of a wait before us. Let us find somewhere a little more peaceful.'

He led her, unresisting, though a gate into a rolling field where sheep grazed peacefully in the warm sun. 'This is better.' He took off his blue greatcoat and spread it on the grass in the shelter of the hedge. 'We can sit here and rest in the sun while you tell me what an American girl is doing in this hostile country.'

'Oh,' She sank gratefully down on the coat. 'How did you know?'

He laughed. 'I trust you will not be affronted if I tell you that your accent is as unmistakable as it is delightful. Surely it must have been recognised before.'

'To tell truth, I am only just landed in England, so there has hardly been time, but I did wonder if the other people in the coach were not looking at me a little askance. That large woman in red kept making remarks about enemies in our midst.'

'Never mind; you have successfully established yourself as a heroine now, and I am sure they will sink the enemy in that. Not, I trust, that it will in fact come to war between our two countries.'

'But' — she felt it was time to protest — 'I am not an enemy; I am as English as you are — or almost.'

'Almost?' He looked at her quizzically.

'Well, my mother, it is true, was an American, but my father is English.'

'Is he so? I had wondered — forgive me if I seem impertinent — but you did say your name was Marchmont?'

'Yes. Oh! Can it be that you know my father?'

'If he is Lord Marchmont, I must certainly do. I am but now come from his house in town.'

'Have you really? Is he there? Is he well? Tell me everything about him. What is he like? Am I like him? Will he be pleased to see me, do you think?'

He laughed at the rapid flood of questions. 'Where would you have me begin: He is there, certainly, since Parliament is sitting, and well enough, save for a few twinges of the gout — and to tell truth he is seldom without those. As to being like him, no, I would hardly say that. His best friends would scarcely describe Lord Marchmont as a dark-haired beauty.' And then, as she blushed with pleasure for the compliment. 'But, Miss Marchmont, again I must risk seeming impertinent. I am but newly come from Marchmont House, as I said, and I heard no word of his expecting you. Indeed, to deal plainly with you, I did not even know that you existed.'

'No wonder for that,' said Henrietta, feeling better every moment. 'No more does my father.' And she went on, sitting there in the warm spring sunshine, to tell him her whole story. He made an admirable audience, interjecting just the right amount of question and comment, and she found herself wonderfully at her ease, sitting there among buttercups and talking to this complete stranger about Aunt Abigail and then about the voyage, Captain Gilbert and his officers.

He laughed with her at her descriptions of the lessons in deportment. 'Not but what you will live to be grateful to them, I am sure. You will find the London world a strange and formidable one, and I am afraid there will be many people who will make it their business to find fault with Lord Marchmont's American daughter. I must tell you, you may well find your father First Minister when you reach London.'

'My father First Minister? But what has happened to Mr. Perceval?'

'He was assassinated a few weeks ago in the lobby of the House of Commons.'

'Good heavens! What a shocking thing. And you say my father may succeed him in office?'

'It might well be. There were all kinds of rumours going about town when I left. If the Regent does not take this chance to send for his old friends the Whigs, it seems most likely that he will send for your father, who has long been Perceval's right hand. And if, indeed, Lord Marchmont is to be First Minister — why, it will behoove you to walk warily and give people no handle to abuse him with talk of an enemy in his house. But your own good sense will be your guide, I am sure, and, of course, you will have a most admirable adviser and friend in your stepmother.'

'In whom?'

'Why, your stepmother, Lady Marchmont. Did you not know that your father had married again?'

'Indeed I did not. Why, this is famous news. Tell me all about her! To think that I am to have a mother at last!'

'Well, as to that' — doubtfully — 'I am not sure that Lady Marchmont will be exactly a mother to you, but a sister and a dear companion, that I am sure she will be.'

'Oh, she is young then. Better and better. But has she no children of her own?'

'Not of Lord Marchmont's. She has one son, by a previous marriage, Cedric Beaufrage.'

Again Henrietta exclaimed with delight: 'A mother and a

brother at one swoop; how lucky I am! But tell me about them; shall I like them? And — oh dear' — she looked down at her crumpled gown — 'will they like me, do you think? Are they very fashionable? Is she a patroness of Almack's and he a pink of the *ton*? But I am being absurd; if Lady Marchmont is so young, then of course her son is but a boy. Does he go to Eton? Shall I be able to go to Montem? I have always wished for a younger brother.' She paused for breath and found that his blue eyes were regarding her quizzically, but surely with something like embarrassment.

'I have misled you, I fear,' he said. 'It is true that Lady Marchmont is the most beautiful, the gayest, the wittiest creature you can imagine, and very much in the swim of society, but her son is, as a matter of fact, grown up and very much a young man of the town. I hope you will like him well enough' — he did not sound at all sure of it — 'but as for her, there can be no question. You will love her the minute you see her. Who, indeed, could help it? Ah, Miss Marchmont, how I envy you. If only I could accompany you to London, which, indeed, I have left most reluctantly.' He stopped. 'Shame on me to say so, for I am on my way to rejoin my regiment in the Peninsula. I beg you will not repeat it.'

'Of course I will not. But is this the first time you have served abroad?'

'No, indeed. I was with Graham at Walcheren — and a deuced mismanaged affair that was — and again in Cádiz, but a plaguey wound I got at Barrosa has kept me at home ever since — that and the lack of a commission. But I have that at last, and your father to thank for it.'

There was something she did not quite understand in his voice as he said this. In fact, ever since her father and stepmother had been mentioned, she had felt that she was only understanding the surface meaning of what he was saying. It was a relief to be on more certain ground.

'Will you be serving under Wellington, then? Oh, how I envy you. If I had only been a boy, I should have gone into the army.'

He laughed. 'And been ready to fight against us by this. God knows how this wretched American war will affect the course of events in Europe if it does break out. They say that already the Peer is complaining that he does not receive the drafts he needs.'

'The Peer? Who is that?'

'Why, Wellington. The Iron General. His setdowns are enough to make a man shoot himself, they say. I am to serve on his staff.' The blue eyes flashed. 'He shall have no chance to set *me* down. I mean to come back a colonel, at least. Then we shall see ...' He stopped, as if conscious that he had said more than he intended, then continued on a lighter note. 'What a strange conversation! Here we are, just met, and talking about our lives and plans as if we were old and dear friends. Well' — his smile sent a little tingle of pure pleasure throbbing down her spine — 'you have saved my life today. That makes us dear friends, does it not? But here comes help at last. You will understand now why I am so eager to be on my way. There is a ship sails tomorrow for Lisbon. If I do not catch her, I may miss much of the summer's campaigning. Who knows? Wellington might be in France before I caught up with him. If I had not been in so great a hurry, I would not now be indebted to you for my life. Lucky for me that you know horses or I think my commission would have been void almost as soon as signed.' Rising to his feet, he reached down a warm hand to help her up, and once again she felt that extraordinary thrill of pure excitement, a kind of madness throbbing through her veins. Angrily, too, she felt herself blushing, but, if he saw, he gave no sign of it, picking up his greatcoat and taking her arm to lead her back to the road. 'Let us see how those good people are contriving for our repair. Perhaps a financial inducement might urge them on. Do you find, in America, that the lower classes react better to ha'pence than to kicks?'

His curricle, it turned out, was but slightly damaged, and was soon ready to take the road again, but repairing the coach was to be a longer business. When he was ready to start, Rivers came over to take his leave of Henrietta, who was standing somewhat forlornly at the side of the road. 'I need not wish you success,' he said, 'for I know what a warm welcome you will receive in London. Who knows? When we next meet, you will most likely be the toast of the town, and I, I hope, a colonel.' He pressed her hand. 'Give my grateful duties to your father, and tell Lady Marchmont' — he hesitated — 'tell her I have not forgotten.' And with that he swung himself up into his curricle and was away.

Henrietta stood for a moment looking down at the hand that still seemed to feel the warmth of his touch. Everything was changed. Everything was different. She had a young and beautiful stepmother and a full-grown stepbrother. This was surely matter for rejoicing. But why was it that after her talk with Charles Rivers, her father, who should surely have seemed more approachable, had become somehow infinitely remote and formidable? And what, she kept wondering, was it that Rivers had not forgotten? But the coach was ready at last and its weary passengers took their seats with relief, and a good deal of grumbling. Henrietta was dismayed to learn that the accident had cost them so much time they would be one more night on the journey. How was she to manage for money? She must eat, however frugally. None of her fellow passengers seemed sympathetic enough to be asked for a loan. Indeed, their first suspicion of her as a stranger had obviously been exacerbated by Rivers' attentions. The woman in red now made frequent and grating references to 'some people with ideas above their stations'.

Only too aware of her own travel-stained appearance, Henrietta hardly blamed her, but this undercurrent of ill will towards her made any request for aid impossible. No, she would just have to manage as best she might. At least she had learned from Rivers that Marchmont House was within walking distance of the London inn where the coach stopped. She therefore decided to spend the small sum she had been reserving for London expenses and trust to luck that she would be able to leave her boxes at the coaching inn and make her way on foot to her father's house. If he was out, surely either Lady Marchmont or her son would receive her. It was, at any rate, the greatest comfort to know that they were in town.

When the coach finally rattled on to the first pavingstones of London early on a fine Friday morning, Henrietta had a grumbling headache from lack of food, and nothing in her pocket. Leaning dizzily back into the corner that the woman in red had vacated the evening before, she thought wryly of how often she had imagined this moment. The streets of London, the sights and cries she had so often read about — it was around her at last, the noise, the bustle, the confusion of the greatest city in the world. And all she wanted to do was lie back and shut her eyes. She hardly opened them when they crossed the Thames, and only managed to rouse herself when a bustle among the other passengers warned her that they were nearing their destination. Then, with a hand that would not stop shaking, she smoothed her braided hair and shook out the folds of her dress, which, alas, was almost beyond shaking. The coachman, when she had asked him, when they stopped for dinner, to get out her box from the boot so that she could change into her carefully hoarded best, had made it all too clear that this could only be done for a consideration. For a moment, confronted by his cockney churlishness, she had hated England and wished herself back home — but what was home?

The coach turned into a crowded yard and stopped. The steps were let down; the passengers began to push their way out, chattering excitedly, calling greetings to friends, and orders to the coachman and to the men who were already unloading the boot. Henrietta, alighting last, found the air blessedly fresh and sweet, and stood for a moment taking deep breaths to steady herself while she looked around at the animated scene. On the steps of the inn itself stood a portly red-faced man whose air of consequence proclaimed him the landlord. Henrietta went up to him.

'I beg your pardon.' She was beginning, herself, to be conscious of her accent. 'Would it be possible for my boxes to remain here until I can have them fetched from Marchmont House?'

'From Marchmont House?' The man looked down at her, unsmiling. 'And what would the likes of you be doing at Marchmont House, Miss Yankee? Lord Marchmont has not turned traitor yet that I know of, nor yet a host to enemies. But the boxes may lay here as long as you wish, so long as they are paid for — in advance.'

'That is precisely my difficulty.' Henrietta refused to be cowed by the man's rudeness. 'The journey has taken longer than I expected, owing to an accident on the way, and I am without funds. I will send round from Marchmont House as soon as I get there. Lord Marchmont is my father.' She had not intended to play this card, but needs must. 'I assure you that there will not be the slightest difficulty about it.' She could only hope, passionately, that this was true.

'Ho, no.' The man had decided she was negligible. 'Not the slightest difficulty in the world. Lord Marchmont your father, indeed, and I suppose Liverpool is your uncle and the Duke of Devonshire your cousin! And I am to let you disappear and leave me with your boxes full of trash as if I had not enough rubbish on my hands as it is. No, no, I'm not to be caught with that kind of chaff. Jem,' he shouted to the man who had now reached Henrietta's shabby boxes, 'throw them there in the street. I won't have 'em here.'

Henrietta's angry protest was interrupted by a voice from behind her. 'I beg you will not disturb yourself, ma'am,' it drawled, 'there is nothing more unbecoming in a female than passion!' She turned in surprise to see a slim, middle-aged man who had just alighted from a sedan chair. Dressed in the most quiet of taste, he yet gave, even to her inexperienced eye, an impression of extraordinary elegance. He bowed to her and smiled with surprising sweetness. 'You find yourself in a difficulty of some kind, I collect. Allow me the pleasure of assisting you. Sykes' — his voice took on a note of steel — 'I had not thought you given to insulting your guests.'

The man had started at sight of him. 'Why, Mr. Brummel, I am sure I had no idea the young lady was a friend of yours! If I had but known, it would have been quite another pair of shoes. But arriving unattended on the public coach, and without funds, too; you must admit it has a damned havey-cavey look about it. But in course if she is a friend of yours that's another story. Jem' — he raised his voice again — 'them boxes in the front parlour and look slippy about it.'

'And now' — Henrietta's rescuer was considering her gravely — 'let us consider what is best for you to do. First, I must beg your pardon for having listened to your most interesting conversation with the landlord here. You are, I collect, Lord Marchmont's American daughter arrived most unexpectedly to visit him. You will forgive me if I admit my surprise. I thought I knew everything that went on in London and I confess I never heard Lord Marchmont had a child.'

'It is all the kinder in you to have come so quickly to my rescue,' said Henrietta, 'but believe me, I *am* Lord Marchmont's daughter, only he does not as yet know it himself. It is a long story, sir . . .'

'And this is neither the time nor the place to be telling it.' He took her arm and led her towards the sedan chair from which he had just alighted. 'Miss Marchmont, you shall promise me the full story when I do myself the honour of calling on you tomorrow morning. In the meantime, I beg you will make use of my chair to carry you to Marchmont House. You will, I think, be sure of finding your father at home. Pray give him my regards, and my felicitations on so precious an acquisition.'

'You are too good, sir.' Sinking gratefully back against the white fur that lined the chair, Henrietta heard her new champion tell the men to make sure that she was admitted to Marchmont House. Luckily for her peace of mind, she did not hear his last order to his servants, which was that having seen her safely admitted, they were to take the chair straight home for a thorough cleaning.

She leaned back in the chair, giving way to the unfamiliar jerking movement as it was carried down a succession of crowded streets. She hardly noticed the gay figures on the pavements, nor heard the unceasing cries of 'Sweet lavender', 'Scissors to grind' and 'Ripe oranges'. Her mind was busy on the problem of how to greet her father. Suppose he refused to recognise her: But she would suppose no such thing, for that way lay despair.

Her porters turned sharply in at the gates of a large house, stopped and set down the chair on the gravelled sweep. One helped her to alight while the other beat a resounding tattoo on an imposing front door, set in a handsome grey stone façade. It was far and away the largest house she had ever seen, let alone entered. For a moment her courage failed her. But the heavy door had swung open, revealing a massive footman in full livery. There was a quick interchange between the two servants as she reluctantly mounted the flight of shallow stone steps that led to the door. Her reluctance, she soon saw, was matched by that of the footman, but Mr. Brummel's servant had obeyed orders and the door was held wide, then closed with a soft thud behind her. She stood in a lofty entrance hall from which a red carpeted stair rose in a graceful curve.

'Miss Marchmont?' the man could not quite keep the question out of his voice, any more than he could entirely avoid a glance at her shabby skirts. Then he suddenly became human. 'I am sure I do not know what to do for the best,' he said, and then, with inspiration: 'I will fetch Mr. Masters to you.' And opening the door of a small saloon, he ushered her inside.

It was all too clearly a room in which people of no importance might be left to await the pleasure of their betters. Spindly gilt-backed chairs discouraged sitting. A glass-fronted bookcase held a drab collection of religious and political treatises. The pictures on the walls appeared to have been selected because their gilt frames matched the inhospitable chairs. A high, elegant window, revealing a prospect of the gravelled sweep Henrietta had just left, made her wonder if she would soon find herself back there. And who, she asked herself, was the omnipotent Mr. Masters?

The door, opening again, revealed him as the butler, majestic in his garb of office, dignified, unbending, and, at the moment, sorely puzzled.

'Miss Marchmont?' His voice, too, held a question. His eyes took one comprehensive sweep of her appearance before they fixed themselves in honest doubt on her face. 'James tells me that you are his lordship's daughter, come unexpected from America.' His voice committed him neither to belief nor disbelief in her story.

'Yes. And I wish to see my father. At once.' This was no time to be timid.

'Of course you do. It is most natural. Only, you see, there is a difficulty.' He dwindled to a stop and stood looking at her with what she suspected of being compassion.

'A difficulty? My father is not then at home? Mr. Brummel was positive that he would be.'

'Ah ... Mr. Brummel.' Masters sighed. It was all, he seemed to suggest, too difficult for him altogether. 'He was in the right of it, of course. My lord is always at home at this hour — when he is in London, that is.'

Henrietta was getting impatient. 'Well, and is he then *not* in London? I had understood that Parliament was sitting.'

'Quite so. You are entirely right, Miss' — he paused — 'Miss ... Marchmont. That, in fact, is the heart of the difficulty.' He stopped again, then went on in a rush. 'The truth of the matter, miss, and there's no use beating about the bush and making a long story of it; the truth of it is, he came home from the House yesterday in one of his tearers, and it's as much as any of our place is worth to disturb him.'

'A tearer?' The word was new to Henrietta.

'A passion, miss, a regular ripsnorting rage, if you'll pardon the expression. Well' — he was suddenly human — 'can't blame him, can you? We'd all hoped, in the servants' hall, that he'd be First Minister, now poor Mr. Perceval's been killed ... And to be passed over for Lord Liverpool! No wonder he's neither to hold nor to bind. But when he's like that, miss, we don't go near him.'

'Nobody?'

'Not my lady herself. Not till he rings, you see.'

'I do see. And when is that likely to be?' Henrietta pulled off a shabby glove.

'Well, miss, you can never tell. It might not be till he was ready to go down to the House again, and then, of course, there would be no stopping him. All's at sixes and sevens, you see, miss, since poor Mr. Perceval was killed. First it's to be a Whig government, then Prinney changes his mind and it's the Tories after all. Yesterday my lord was to be First Minister, but today lord knows why, it's all to do again and I believe Liverpool's the man after all. It's no wonder if my lord's in a passion: I'm sure it's very disrupting in a genteel establishment.'

Henrietta pulled off the second glove. 'I think I begin to understand. It is politics, then, that have put my father in his tearer, as you call it. Well, I am sure I do not blame him for that. It sounds an ill-managed business enough. But perhaps the sight of me will be a distraction. At any rate, we can but put it to the proof.'

His ruddy face paled. 'Miss, I dare not, I tell you.'

'Very well then. If none of you has the courage to announce me, I shall just have to make shift to announce myself. He is awake, I take it?'

'Oh, yes, miss, he has been in his study these two hours past. But I'm sure I do not know whether I should let — '

'I do not precisely see how you can stop me. Where, pray, is the study?' This, she realised, was the crucial point. Suppose he were to refuse to direct her? But she had contrived, in the course of their brief conversation, to achieve a mastery of the man; there was something about her quiet voice that he had to respect.

He led her, then, out into the hall again and pointed to a door at the far end. 'There it is, miss, and I'm sure I hope I'm doing right.'

She smiled at him. 'Never trouble yourself, Masters. If the worse comes to the worst, I will say I found it out by myself.' She walked steadily down the hall, knocked once on the door and opened it without waiting for an answer.

'What the devil?' came a furious growl from the far end of the room.

It was twilight in here, for heavy blue velvet curtains were drawn across the high windows, and only an occasional glint suggested the morning sunlight outside. Henrietta advanced slowly, threading her way among chairs and tables. 'I am

45

sorry,' she said, 'to break in on you so unceremoniously, but my errand is urgent, and your servants, for some reason, were reluctant to admit me.' She could see him now, sitting hunched up in a big armchair, by the embers of a fire, an older man than she had expected, with grizzled hair, strong bones, and dark-shadowed eyes in the half light. 'I am sorry if I do not find you well, sir.'

'I'm well enough, only blue-devilled. But who in God's name are you? I'll dismiss the whole pack of them for this.'

'Pray do not, sir. They could hardly help themselves. You see, I am your daughter, come from America.'

'*My what?*' He was on his feet now. 'What lunacy is this? I have no daughter, nor any son either, as those who sent you doubtless know. You'll have time to regret this conspiracy in the Bridewell.'

In the half-light, she saw his hand go out towards a bellpull and put her own on it to stop him. Strangely enough, she found herself not in the least afraid of him. 'Stay a moment,' she said, 'before you do something you will regret. Have you no picture of my mother?'

'Of whom: Of my dead wife, you would say? What's that to the purpose?'

'Only that they say I am much like her.' She withdrew her hand from his and moved over to the window where she pulled the heavy curtain cord so that light flooded into the room. 'Look at me, sir, and listen to me, and if you still say I am not your daughter, send me to the Bridewell, or where you will.' She turned to face him, her hand still among the soft blue velvet, the sunshine glancing across her strong, fine features and bringing out red lights in her dark hair.

His hand dropped to his side as he gazed at her. 'Who in the devil's name are you: Your voice — the accent — I remember it so well ... And those eyes, blue with dark hair. But I have no daughter; she died when she was born.'

'No, sir.' Henrietta knew the battle was as good as won. 'My Aunt Abigail told you I had died. I only learned this spring when she herself died, what she had done. She told me you had disowned me, but among her papers I found your letter about my death, and also, I must tell you, your letters to my mother. She never had them. Any of them. From the time you left. It was only then that I knew I had a father. I have come a long way to find you, sir.'

'A dangerous one, if what you say is true. But why should I believe you? And yet ...' He was gazing at her now as if he almost wanted to be convinced. 'It's true, you have something of her. The voice ... the eyes ... the smile. Mercy ... my beautiful Mercy. Can you really be her child?'

'Here is your letter, sir. About our deaths, my mother's and mine.' She had got it out ready for him as she waited in the glum little reception room.

He took it with a hand that shook. 'Yes.' He moved over to the window to read the faded handwriting. 'God, that was a black day. When I got Abigail's letter. Both dead. Mercy and the child.' He put out his left hand to tilt her chin gently and gaze long and deeply at her. 'It was you?'

'Well' — now she could afford to smile at him — 'yes and no. Because I'm very much alive, as you can see, sir.'

'And feel.' He put down the letter and took her hands in both of his cold ones. 'By God, perhaps my life is not such a wasted business after all. I never needed a happy surprise more, nor ever had a better one. But, come sit down and tell me all about yourself. Damme, when I think of that hellcat Abigail keeping you from me all these years, I could ... Well, best not think of that. So you're Mercy's girl, are you? And almost as beautiful as she was. What did she call you, hey? It was to be Henry, you know, for a boy. I was bound it would be an heir — but I'm not complaining, I'm a young man again for sight of you, my dear. What am I to call you, eh?'

'Henrietta, if you please, sir. My mother named me before she died.'

'Henrietta, is it? So Mercy must have forgiven me, for all that harpy's meddling. But, come, tell me all about yourself. How did you get here, in the teeth of this damned war that's coming? And which are you, Yankee or Englishwoman? Damme, that's a rum touch, to have an enemy for a daughter! But we'll not quarrel ... Henrietta, indeed. D'you know what I was thinking, when you came in? That my life was over, my day done. Now I'm a man again, thanks to you. But come,' he said again, 'tell me about yourself.'

'There is not much to tell, sir,' Henrietta was beginning, when she was interrupted. A door at the far end of the room opened to reveal a vision in a blue velvet riding habit. As she glided towards them, this blonde beauty looked sharply at Henrietta, summing her up from braided hair to bedraggled

47

skirts. Her own hair, extravagantly curling, hung around a small sharp-boned face. At the moment, the face showed surprise.

'But where is Mr. Brummel?' she asked, ignoring Henrietta.

'Mr. Brummel?' Her husband — for this was clearly Lady Marchmont — echoed her surprise.

'Why, yes. I saw that ridiculous chair of his turn in at our gates and thought that if he had the courage to beard you in your den, my lord, I would not be behind him in daring.'

He looked at her quizzically under bushy brows, one hand still firmly clasping Henrietta's. 'I regret to disappoint you, my lady, but I have seen nothing of Mr. Brummel today. Your visit is well timed, however. Here is a charming surprise for you: my daughter, Henrietta.'

'Your *what*?' Arched brows rose sharply.

'My American daughter, my love.' There was nothing loving about his voice. 'I know how happy you will be to welcome her to our home.'

'What madness is this? You know the child died at birth. Are you in your dotage so soon, my lord, to allow yourself to be imposed upon thus? And by who knows what draggletailed American female: As if your position was not unhappy enough! Do you not see that this is but a plot to embarrass you still further in the House? An American daughter, arriving so pat — 'pon honour, my lord, it would make me laugh if I did not pity your gullibility.'

Henrietta was angry now. She withdrew her hand from her father's and looked her challenger up and down, noting, with the pitiless eye of youth, the fine lines about eyes and mouth that betrayed the beauty's age. 'I am sorry, madam, that you choose to receive me so. I had hoped for a different welcome. But here' — she put her hand into the deep unfashionable pocket of her dress — 'my father has not even asked me for these, but I have them: my mother's marriage lines, the certificate of my birth. You will find all in order. And here' — she turned back to her father — 'my mother's miniature, my Aunt Abigail's, and yours.'

He took the miniature with a hand that trembled. Breathing heavily, he was making a visible effort to control his fury. His wife's taunts about dotage had hit him hard. 'I thank you, my dear, but there is no need for proofs between you and me. Your own looks and that letter are enough. As for you, my lady, you will, I think, wish to apologise to Henrietta for the wrong you have done her.' There was steel in his voice.

Lady Marchmont had been glancing rapidly through the papers Henrietta had given her. Now she dropped them casually on a table and swam towards Henrietta, arms held out, an exquisite smile lighting up the beautiful, empty face. 'Henrietta, I know, will forgive me,' she said. 'It was but natural, after all, that I should wish to protect you against what I could hardly be blamed for thinking an imposture. After all, I am not familiar, as you are, with the appearance of Henrietta's mother.'

'No,' growled her husband, 'I recollect that you banished her picture to my study when you first came to live here.' He took Henrietta's hand again and led her across the room to a picture that hung on the far wall. 'You can see why I could be in no doubt,' he said.

Looking up at the picture, Henrietta swallowed tears. She had never seen her mother, nor, till now, any other picture of her than the tiny miniature. Looking up at the gentle, smiling face under dark curls, she was painfully aware of the likeness to herself — and the difference. She had often wondered, thinking about it all on the *Faithful*, how her mother had let Aunt Abigail bully her into despair. Now she understood. This gentle creature would have been no match for Aunt Abigail. She looked from the picture to her father. 'I am glad that I am like you too, sir.'

He smiled down at her. 'You have my temper, I can see. How else did you force your way into my presence? I wager Masters and the rest are shaking in their shoes for fear of the consequences. But, tell me, what magic did you use to gain admission in the first place?'

She smiled back at him. 'Ah, there, I confess, sir, I was lucky. I met a Mr. Brummel at the coaching inn and he was so good as to send me here in his chair. I think he told his servant to make sure that I gained admission. And in fairness to Masters, I must tell you that it was with the greatest reluctance that he told me which was your study.'

'I'll warrant it was. So Mr. Brummel sent you in his chair, did he? There's the explanation of your mystery, my lady. I can see my daughter has the gift for making friends. I wonder who was the last lady to be honoured with a ride in Beau Brummel's chair.'

A confusion of emotions chased each other across Lady

Marchmont's beautiful face, while Henrietta watched and wondered. So far, Mr. Rivers' 'angel' had shown herself in no very amiable light. But she had herself well in hand now. 'It was vastly kind of Mr. Brummel,' she said. 'I must write and tell him how deeply I feel myself in his debt. For the compliment was, of course, to me — and to you, my love.' And with a ravishing smile for her husband: 'Mr. Brummel is too truly our friend to let any connection of ours be wandering about London unprotected.'

'No need to write Mr. Brummel,' said Henrietta cheerfully. 'He said he would do himself the honour of calling on me tomorrow morning.'

Lady Marchmont almost lost control of her temper again. Her high colour and a tightening of the hand that held her gloves betrayed her. But she kept her voice calmly patronising. 'Well, in that case, my dear creature, we must set about making you fit to be seen.'

## CHAPTER FOUR

From time to time in the course of that endless afternoon Henrietta almost found herself regretting that she had ever left Boston. Her father had handed her over to her stepmother with a warm, wine-flavoured kiss before he left for the House of Lords, where, he told her, the Orders in Council were to be debated.

'It makes me happy,' he said, 'to see you two friends before I go.'

Neither Henrietta nor Lady Marchmont said anything to disillusion him. If he could ignore the feeling that still ran high between them, so much the better. And, indeed, it seemed that Lady Marchmont was ready to strike a truce. She certainly devoted herself with the greatest enthusiasm to the task of outfitting Henrietta for her first appearance in society. But then, as Henrietta was well aware, this was largely because she would feel herself disgraced if her stepdaughter should appear as anything less than a young lady of the highest fashion. As soon as Lord Marchmont had left the house, she hurried Henrietta up to her own boudoir and rang violently for her maid.

Fenner, a dried-up little person with a prim mouth and incredible auburn curls, must have already heard all about Henrietta in the servants' hall. She listened impassively as Lady Marchmont explained the problem: Mr. Brummel to call tomorrow; the news undoubtedly all over town already. 'No wonder Mr. Brummel took you under his wing, my dear, your coming is a veritable gold mine of gossip to him. He will dine out on it these many weeks to come. But of course he will come here tomorrow to see what we have contrived to do with you. Fenner, send for Pierre this instant. He is my hairdresser,' she explained to Henrietta, 'a French émigré with a perfect genius for the latest styles. I shudder to think what Mr. Brummel must have thought of those braids. And, Fenner . . .' She proceeded to enumerate a long list of mantua makers, milliners and so on who must also be summoned urgently to Marchmont House. 'Of course, it would be more entertaining to visit them in their warehouses,' she explained to Henrietta, 'but how can we venture forth with you looking as you do? Ten to one we should meet some old cat or other, and then good-bye to your chances of a voucher for Almack's, or, indeed, of recognition of any kind.'

'What?' said Henrietta, amused. 'Merely because I am dressed something out of the mode?'

'Out of the mode!' Fenner had taken her cue from her mistress by now. The line was to be amused patronage. 'Why, Miss Marchmont, they are more elegantly dressed in Bedlam. That sleeve has been dead as mutton these ten years past, and as for the collar — well, only look at my lady.'

Henrietta had already been looking, or rather trying not to. Lady Marchmont had given up all thoughts of riding and changed into a muslin housedress whose low neck and clinging lines showed her slender figure to rather too much advantage. Resolving to have her own gowns cut more discreetly, Henrietta said nothing, surrendering herself silently to Fenner, who began to comb out her long hair ready for Pierre's arrival. When he came, he too, exclaimed in his broken English over mademoiselle's bizarre appearance and went straight to work to remedy it. Soon, however, he was exclaiming again, this time with pleasure over the natural curl of her dark hair. 'We will attempt something a little daring, shall we not, my lady?' He turned to Lady Marchmont. 'You have seen Milady Lamb, with her curls à la Milord Byron? With mademoiselle's hair to work on, we shall leave her crying *miséricorde!*' And he went to work with a will, cutting and shaping while Henrietta suffered in spellbound alarm. At last he stood back and handed her a looking glass. '*Voilà*, mademoiselle, what you think, no?'

She looked, and gasped. Instead of the neat braids that had given her, always, a look of the schoolroom, a multitude of unruly curls clustered over her head and around her face. 'There!' Pierre stepped back, satisfied at her exclamation of amazed delight. 'It is just to add a bandeau, so, and we are ready to conquer the world. My felicitations, mademoiselle, in one little half hour we have made a beauty of you.'

It was true. Her fine firm features that had made Mr. Anderson, once, liken her to a Greek goddess, were offset by the mass of curls. No need anymore to look up Pallas Athene in a classical dictionary. Her likeness now was to a very much more frivolous inhabitant of Olympus. She put out an impulsive hand to Lady Marchmont. 'Indeed, ma'am, I am much indebted to you.'

'Tush, child, it is nothing.' Lady Marchmont did her best to conceal her dismay at having her goose turn so suddenly into a swan. Luckily, both Fenner and Pierre knew her well enough to guess what she was feeling.

'Naturally,' said Pierre, 'mademoiselle cannot expect to hold a *bougie* to milady — the great ones of fashion are not grown in a day, but with such an example before her, ah' — he kissed his fingertips — '*qui sait*? I would say, who can tell? But I hear milord; I am gone, I vanish, I take to myself wings.' And he collected up his tools with surprising rapidity and bowed his way obsequiously out by way of an antechamber, just as the main door of the boudoir was thrown open to reveal a young man dressed in what Henrietta could already recognise as the extravagant height of fashion. But while Mr. Brummel had worn his elegant clothes with ease, this young exquisite looked as if he hardly dared turn his head for fear of disturbing the intricate folds of his cravat. His fair, small, boned handsomeness was marred, in Henrietta's opinion, by a petulant turn of the lip, and there was nothing endearing about the look of haughty surprise with which he favoured her through his eyeglass.

For her part, she had expected her father, and turned to Lady Marchmont in blushing surprise at this intrusion, gathering the folds of the loose morning gown her stepmother had lent her more closely about her as she did so.

Lady Marchmont merely looked bored. 'Cedric,' she said. 'But how delightful. I had thought you fixed at the Pavilion this sennight or more.'

She did not, Henrietta thought, look particularly delighted as she held out a languid hand to be kissed.

'Why, to tell truth, so had I, ma'am,' said the young man, coming forward and taking the hand with an air. 'But —' Here he raised it to his lips, paused, considered for a moment and then continued: 'A new perfume, I see and a delicious one. Your taste, as always, ma'am, is flawless. But I beg you will make me known to your charming companion.'

'Why, of course. How could I be so shatterbrained? I have a most delightful surprise for you, Cedric. This is your new sister, Henrietta Marchmont. Henrietta, my love, you must allow me to present my son, Lord Beaufrage.'

Lord Beaufrage let fall his glass. 'This is a surprise indeed. I need hardly add a most charming one. But you must bear with my stupidity, ma'am, and explain while I admire.' He sketched an elaborate bow to Henrietta, then turned back to his mother. 'Miss Marchmont is, then, some unexpected relative of my lord's?'

'Unexpected, indeed, but more than a relative. I said a *sister*, Cedric.' Why was there a warning note in her voice? 'She is my lord's daughter, come all the way from America to find him. 'Tis a most romantic story and we must do our possible to make her happy in her new life.'

He bowed again to Henrietta, this time more deeply. 'It will be a pleasure, as well as a privilege. Miss Marchmont is but newly arrived, I collect.'

'But this morning. We are still recovering from the shock. For,' she turned with a pretty gesture to Henrietta, 'in course, it *is* a shock, though a most delightful one. To find myself once more a mother!'

He laughed. 'Best sink the mother at once and be a sister to her, ma'am. I wager it will suit you both the better. But how does my lord take this surprise?'

'Why, with tears of joy, as you would expect. He has been too long without an heir. Even a girl — you will forgive me, my dear, I know — even a girl must be better than nothing.'

Henrietta listened in silence. There was something about this interchange that she neither liked nor understood. Doubtless, she told herself, this was merely because of her ignorance of the language of fashion, but still she felt uncomfortably aware of hidden depths in the conversation and longed for an excuse to escape. Cedric Beaufrage might be her stepbrother, but to her mind that was no reason for appearing before him in what was little better than a dressing-gown. What on earth would Aunt Abigail have said: The thought cheered her. After all, it was to escape Aunt Abigail and all she stood for that she had come here. She must not boggle at her first fence. If Lady Marchmont found nothing out of the way in this interview, why should she? But still, she was relieved that they had turned away from her, thus giving her a chance to take a firmer hold of her gown.

'But why then are you come?' Lady Marchmont was asking. 'I had thought you fixed for these three weeks or more.'

'And so had I, ma'am, but to tell truth, I have had such a devilish run of luck that I have had to retreat for reinforcements.'

'Oh, Cedric.' For once her voice registered a genuine emotion: fright. 'You are not in debt again?'

'In debt!' He gave a wild laugh that Henrietta was too ignorant to recognise as an inferior imitation of Lord Byron's. 'Oh, no, nothing like that. I am merely rolled up, undone, disgraced — unless you can come to my rescue, ma'am.'

'But, Cedric,' she began, 'you know too well,' then changed her tone. 'But why should we be troubling Henrietta with these dreary trifles? You must know, my love, that my Cedric is a shocking wild young man, who thinks nothing of sitting up all night with the Prince Regent. He is "undone", as he calls it, every week and I come to his rescue as often. Indeed, Cedric, I am angry with you, but we will talk more of that later. Now you must advise us how best to dress this poor Henrietta so she may face the world tomorrow. What dress of mine do you think she could best wear?'

'Of yours, Ma'am? What are you thinking of? It would be the talk of the town. No, no, you must do better than that. It is but to pay a little more and they will sit up all night to make for you. You have sent for Madame Bégué, surely?'

'Naturally. I expect her instantly. You shall stay and advise us, Cedric, and perhaps with a little of your charming she will indeed make for us overnight.'

'Damme, of course she will! Tell her she has no hope of recovering what you owe her else.'

Not for the first time Henrietta was aware of some sort of warning sign passing from Lady Marchmont to her son. He turned to her now with a light laugh. 'You will have much to learn, my new sister, of the ways of the fashionable world. You must know that a lady of the *ton* would no more pay a bill the day it arrived than she would ride down St. James's. But here, if I mistake not, is Madame Bégué.'

And indeed the door now flew open to admit a round little red-faced woman who burst at once into a torrent of French. She seemed to be protesting about something, and Lady Marchmont answered her soothingly, also in French. It might as well have been Greek, so far as Henrietta was concerned. Aunt Abigail had disapproved of the French so passionately that she had never allowed a word of their language to cross Henrietta's lips. Recognising her plight, Lord Beaufrage laughed and took her hand. 'You are no linguist, I see. Well, no more, to tell truth, am I. I could never get my tongue round those frogs' lingo. We shall have much in common, you and I, besides a mother. But come, tell me how you like England and what we are to show you first.' He led her to the other side of the room where a window looked out over the gardens into the Marchmont House, which ran down without a break into the park.

Henrietta stood there for a moment, looking out at the smooth lawns, the exquisitely swept gravel of the paths, the clipped yew hedges that bordered them. 'It's so beautiful,' she said. 'I had not imagined anything could be like this. Why, there is not so much as a leaf out of place.'

He laughed. 'I should rather hope not, or Briggs, the head gardener, would have something to say. But if you are an amateur of the romantic, we must take you to Vauxhall Gardens.'

He was interrupted. The conversation at the other side of the room had come to an amicable conclusion and Lady Marchmont came over to them, her face all smiles. 'Well' — she took Henrietta's hand — 'that is all settled. Madame is only too delighted to have a hand in launching the newest society swan. I explained to her, my love, that we had no time to discuss with your father the question of your allowance, and she is happy to do her best for you in the meanwhile. Now, Cedric, away with you. We have work to do.'

Lord Beaufrage laughed and lifted Henrietta's hand to his lips. 'I thought I was to stay and advise you, ma'am. But I can see you have no need of me. You can contrive most admirably for yourself. Farewell, my new sister. May I call you Henrietta, and will you call me Cedric?' And, still laughing, he left the room without giving her time to answer.

Henrietta crawled into bed that night more tired, she thought, than she had ever been before. It seemed an age since she had arrived at Marchmont House, and she was dazzled by a confusion of first impressions. Her stepmother, after her first outburst, had been uniformly kind, Lord Beaufrage everything that was welcoming. Why, then, did she still retain a feeling of discomfort about them both? Through all their surface kindness they had seemed, somehow, to be watching her, considering her, planning about her. It had, of course, been a disappointment that her father had not returned from the House of Lords before exhaustion had made her give in and go to bed.

Lady Marchmont had explained that it was often so. 'Unless we have a dinner of our own, that is. Otherwise, he is too busy to return; he will have dined at White's, with Lord Liverpool and the rest ... You must not mind it, my dear.' She pressed Henrietta's hand. 'It is not that he is not dearly glad to see you, but he is a man, busy with a man's affairs. It was the same even when I was a bride. All my friends said he neglected me shamefully.'

Henrietta, who had, in truth, been minding it, found herself at once on her father's side. Naturally his business in Parliament was infinitely more important than even a newfound daughter. It was not, however, entirely consoling that Cedric for his part had made a particular point of remaining at home all evening to entertain her. She liked him well enough, but his endless chatter about the bets he had won, the parties he might at that moment have been attending and the conquests he had made, finally gave her such a headache that she was compelled to give up all thought of saying goodnight to her father, admit fatigue and retire to the unbelievable comfort of her room.

Lady Marchmont came up too and fluttered about her for a little while to make sure she had everything she required.

'Tomorrow,' she said, 'we must find you a maid, but for to-night, I will make shift to help you. After all, you are to be my daughter.' She insisted that Henrietta drink a cup of hot milk and even made as if to unfasten her dress for her, but Henrietta, all New England rising in her, declined her help, explaining that she was too tired to talk. Much to her relief, Lady Marchmont accepted the rebuff with a good grace and glided from the room, adjuring Henrietta to sleep as long as she could in the morning. 'We are not early risers, you know.'

Alone at last, Henrietta struggled out of her clothes as quickly as she could. She was quite incredibly sleepy. The hot milk had had a strange taste. Had her stepmother perhaps added some soporific to it? She almost collapsed on to her bed, then forced herself to struggle up again. The papers that proved her birth were still in the pocket of the dress she had worn. Some instinct compelled her to totter over to where it lay across a chair, secure the papers and tuck them carefully under her pillow. Then she fell into a deep and dreamless sleep.

She was roused by morning sunshine across her face. The curtains had been drawn and a cheerful-looking young maid stood by her bed holding a tray.

The maid bobbed a curtsey, tray and all. 'If you please, miss,' she said, 'I'm Rose, as is to be your maid, if you'll bear with me, miss, as I ain't had much training, but willing as can be, I'm sure, miss. And will you have your chocolate now?'

'Yes, please.' Henrietta pulled herself up among her pillows and made a lap for the tray. 'But what time is it? I have slept very long, surely.'

'Why, no, 'tis but eleven, miss. My lady said you were on no account to be disturbed before. Besides, your new clothes are but now come home. And stunning, too, miss, if you'll forgive the liberty.'

Henrietta glanced across to the chair where she had left her old dress and saw that it had been replaced by the elegant confection of striped muslin for which Madame Bégué had fitted her the day before. 'But my clothes,' she asked, 'what has become of them?'

'Lord, miss, no need to be thinking of them,' said the girl. 'Lady Marchmont said you'd have no more need for such trash — excuse me for saying so, I'm sure — and I'd best take them out and have them burnt.' She coloured anxiously at the look on Henrietta's face. 'Was that wrong, miss?'

'No, no.' Henrietta recovered her composure. 'It was quite right, Rose, if my lady told you to do so. And since I have my fine new clothes, what is there to complain of?' But there was a cold feeling about her heart. Suppose she had not got out of bed the night before and rescued her papers from the pocket of the dress? They would have been burned by now and with them would have gone her only means of proving her birth. And, she realised with a new pang, her father had never even looked at anything but his own letter and the miniatures. Only her stepmother had read her birth certificate and glanced angrily at her mother's marriage lines. Supposing she should choose to deny having done so?

The girl was still looking at her anxiously. 'I only acted for the best, miss, I'm sure.'

'Of course you did, Rose. Now run along, like a good girl, and let me drink my chocolate while it is hot. I shall need your help when it comes to putting on these fine new clothes of mine.'

Rose curtseyed her way from the room, leaving her new mistress deep in thought. The hot milk *had* tasted strange the night before ... Suppose she had let her stepmother help her to undress. Would she have removed the papers or merely stayed beside her until she was too fast asleep to remember them? Either way, their fate would have been the same. They would have been burned by 'accident'. Or was she being unfair? She might easily be imagining the whole thing. Her dress had been old and soiled with voyaging and might well have offended Lady Marchmont's delicate sensibilities. The accident might have been genuine enough. But she must see to it that another one did not happen.

She finished her chocolate and rang for Rose. The new muslin was certainly ravishing and the sight of her reflection in the long glass gave her a fresh accession of courage. She might be entirely wrong in her suspicions, but she would not take any chances. She smiled kindly at Rose, who was also admiring the finished effect in the glass, and asked casually whether it would be possible to send a packet to an address in London.

'Why, of course, miss, one of the men will carry it for you.'

'But this is something out of the ordinary, Rose. Can you arrange for it to be taken without anyone's knowing? I cannot explain the whole to you, but it is a secret commission I have undertaken for the captain of the ship I crossed in. The packet is to go to his sister. It is no treason, you know' — she had seen the girl's look of alarm — 'Captain Gilbert and his sister are as English as you.'

'Oh, in that case,' Rose said with obvious relief, 'there is not the least difficulty in the world. My brother Jem is under-footman and he shall carry your packet for you without anyone's being the wiser.'

'Admirable.' Henrietta sat down and wrote a brief note to Miss Gilbert, asking her to hold the enclosed papers until she should call for them in person. After some thought, she did not send the three miniatures, but hid them instead among her books.

She had hardly done so when there was a light tap at her door and Lady Marchmont appeared, devastatingly casual in a pink silk negligée. 'What, up and dressed already, my love? You put us all to shame. I had come to warn you to be dressed betimes since we shall doubtless be overrun with morning visitors. But I see there is no need. How elegant you look in your new gown, my dearest creature.'

Had a quick glance gone to the chair on which, last night, Henrietta had thrown her old dress? She could not be sure. She had already decided not to mention its burning, but to act as if nothing was amiss — as, indeed, was very likely the case. So she merely returned her stepmother's compliments and asked if her father was up yet.

'Why, to tell truth, my dear, I do not know. I hope you do not think me so out of fashion as to share a bedchamber with my husband. But we can find out easily enough.' She rang the bell and told Rose to ask whether my lord was stirring yet.

Learning that he was indeed up and had just sent for his breakfast, Henrietta excused herself and went to join him. 'You do not mind?' she asked timidly as she entered the break-fast room.

'Mind! Damme, it's the best thing that's happened to me in years!' He gave her a hearty kiss and seated her beside him. 'I shall expect you every morning at this time to pour my tea and tell me your news. And first, tell me how you think you will like living here?'

Henrietta deduced correctly that this was a tactful way of asking how she expected to get on with her stepmother and answered in a hearty affirmative which he greeted with gruff approval, and a compliment on her appearance. 'No doubt about it,' he said, 'you can't fault my lady's taste in dress. You'll not go wrong if you listen to her, my dear. And that reminds me, I have business to discuss with you.'

Henrietta's heart sank. Was he going to ask to see her papers after all? But to her relief he was merely anxious to fix the size of the allowance he intended to give her. It seemed to her an immense sum, but he laughed and told her she would get through it quickly enough. 'With my lady for adviser, you will hardly find yourself devoted to economy. And that puts me in mind of something else. I have one request to make of you: This allowance is for your own use, my dear, and I shall not question what you do with it, but I should much prefer that you make no loans to anyone.'

'Loans? But why should I? I have no acquaintance in London, you know, Father.'

'You will, soon enough. But that was not exactly what I had in mind.' He seemed relieved to be interrupted by a footman, who requested Miss Marchmont's presence in the morning room, where Lady Marchmont awaited her.

'Ha!' Her father laughed a shade wryly. 'Go, my dear, the world of fashion awaits you. And remember, I shall be here when you tire of it.'

'Indeed, sir, it frightens me already.' Henrietta screwed up her courage, kissed him quickly and left him. She had not thanked him nearly enough for the munificent allowance, but consoled herself with the thought that there was already between them an understanding that made words unnecessary.

Her stepmother was in the morning room talking animatedly to Mr. Brummel. She was dressed now in a morning gown of lilac-sprigged muslin that took years off her age. For Mr. Brummel's benefit, she was all surprise and delight over Henrietta's arrival. There was no hint of yesterday's doubts and questions. Smiling at Mr. Brummel, Henrietta decided that she had been unjust in her suspicions. The near burning of her papers had been merely an accident. Full of contrition for her doubts, she exerted herself to return Lady Marchmont's affectionate speeches, and was disconcerted, presently, to find Mr. Brummel's sharp grey eye fixed somewhat quizzically upon her.

'So the prodigal has been welcomed as a prodigal should be,' he said. 'It quite restores one's faith in human nature, Lady Marchmont.' Then, apparently changing the subject. 'I hear Lord Beaufrage is returned to town.'

'Yes. Is it not delightful? He is come just in time to welcome his new sister. He and dear Henrietta are to be such friends.'

'Are they indeed?' What was going on behind that shrewd, impassive face? 'But, Miss Marchmont, I am come to claim a debt. You promised, yesterday, when I was so fortunate as to be of assistance to you, that you would tell me the whole story of your adventures.'

Henrietta looked at her stepmother in some doubt, wishing she had thought in advance of consulting her about the propriety of this. But she was saved the necessity of replying by the appearance of another group of visitors. Lady Marchmont had been right. All of London seemed to have heard of her arrival and to have come, on one pretext or another, to have a look at her.

Mr. Brummel waited at her side for a minute or two, then, as she was constantly interrupted by her stepmother's bringing someone else to be introduced, gave it up. 'We shall talk again, you and I?' He took her hand in farewell. 'You owe me a debt of honour, and they must always be paid. And, meanwhile, remember that you must count on me as your friend.'

'Did you hear that?' said a gushing young lady after he had left. 'Mr. Brummel's friend. Indeed, you are the luckiest creature in London.'

'Why?' asked Henrietta, puzzled. 'He is most delightful, it is true, and has already been a friend indeed to me, but I do not quite understand —'

'Not understand!' the other interrupted her. 'Only listen, Mama, here is Miss Marchmont who does not understand why she is so lucky to have made a friend of Mr. Brummel.'

Her mother, a formidable dowager in purple satin and a turban, considered Henrietta with kindly scorn. 'You must remember, my love, that Miss Marchmont has much to learn about London society.'

The morning seemed to go on forever. Henrietta talked, laughed, was questioned, was introduced over and over again to more and more gushing women and quizzing young men, and found herself increasingly furious at their air of patronage. So far as they were concerned, she was, she could see, little better than a barbarian. They giggled behind their hands over any little difference in her speech and congratulated her step-mother over and over again on her appearance. 'So much better than one might have expected,' she heard one dear old dowager remark in clarion tones, and heard with repressed fury, Lady Marchmont's laughing reply.

At last, with a final fluttering of ribbons and wafting of snuff and perfume, they were all gone. Lady Marchmont sighed luxuriously. 'A most successful beginning, my dear. I think we are safe enough for Almack's. But of course you will not know what I am talking of.'

'On the contrary,' Henrietta said. 'I was well aware when Lady Cowper was so kind to me that she is one of the patronesses. You think, then, that I shall receive my voucher?'

'I am sure of it. But how come you to be so knowledgeable about London life, child? Surely you did not see the fashionable journals in that New England wilderness of yours?'

'Oh, sometimes.' Henrietta felt reluctant to tell Lady Marchmont about the lighthearted coaching she had received from the officers of the *Faithful*.

'Ah well, so much the better.' Lady Marchmont rose to her feet and drifted to the window. 'What a beautiful day. I think perhaps I will go for a ride in the park and blow away the cobwebs of all this talk. What a pity that you do not ride, my love.'

'Not ride? But of course I do.'

'Oh, how delightful.' She did not sound at all delighted. 'Then, naturally, you must accompany me. How could I have been so stupid as not to have thought of it yesterday so we could order a habit for you. But, for today, I am sure there will be no objection to your borrowing one of mine. And we must see if Cedric can escort us.'

Cedric was only too delighted to do so, and Henrietta presently found herself riding sedately through the park at his side while her stepmother rode on ahead in the midst of a laughing group of young officers. Watching her turn to flirt first with this one, then with that, Henrietta found herself wondering, not for the first time, just what kind of a woman her father had married.

# CHAPTER FIVE

To Henrietta's well-concealed relief, Lady Cowper did indeed send the coveted voucher for Almack's and she was able to make her debut there the following week, ravishing, Cedric told her, in silver gauze over white satin. Mr. Brummel danced with her, and a Royal Personage was heard to enquire who she was. *The Mirror of Fashion* called her The Boston Beauty and *La Belle Assemblée* hailed her as The American Heiress. Her success in society was assured.

She plunged into her new life with an enthusiasm that amused and amazed Lady Marchmont and her son. But Cedric was her devoted slave and she even persuaded him to rise somewhat earlier than his accustomed hour of noon in order that she might take advantage of the unfashionable morning hours to explore the sights of London. Laughing and protesting that he had not worked so hard since he left Eton, he nevertheless acted as her guide as she plunged further and further into the heart of London, insisting one day that she be taken up the dome of St. Paul's, the next that they visit the menagerie at the Royal Exchange. If she sometimes wished for a more congenial companion, or found herself dreaming of an encounter in a country lane and a pair of piercing blue eyes, she kept these thoughts to herself, bore with Cedric's inevitable boasting and bets, and congratulated herself on his faithful attendance.

Meanwhile, the season was in full swing and she was in the thick of it. She attended a breakfast at the Duke of Devonshire's Chiswick house and refused an offer of marriage in the conservatory. She went to the opera and refused another offer in the lobby. She went to the play and to a succession of balls, each one more crowded than the last; and all the time Cedric, who seemd to have given up all thought of returning to Brighton, remained her squire, while his mother was constantly surrounded by a fluctuating group of officers and young men about town. Henrietta, brought up in a sterner society, could not help but be shocked at the way she flirted with them, though she had to admit to herself that it all seemed quite impartial: None of them was more of a favourite than the rest. There was, after all, safety in numbers. Besides, they all sooner or later proposed to her. She was not The American Heiress for nothing.

As for Lord Marchmont, he and his wife hardly ever seemed to meet except when they entertained in their house, when he always put in an appearance but tended to talk almost entirely to his political associates. If he noticed Lady Marchmont's flirtations, he gave no sign of it, and when they were together she was all pretty deference to him and all affection for Henrietta. Indeed, they were in appearance a perfect model of a family, and Henrietta was puzzled to find that her only moments of real ease were the breakfasts she made a point of sharing with her father. She might not creep into bed until four in the morning; she was always up at eleven to pour his tea and hear how things had gone the day before in the House of Lords. He made no secret of his surprise at her understanding of English politics and delighted her by making her his confidante and often his secretary. She knew that she had done much to help him resign himself to his failure to achieve supreme office. Instead of being First Minister himself, he was rapidly becoming Lord Liverpool's right-hand man, as he had been Mr. Perceval's, and many of his most successful speeches were rehearsed to her over the breakfast table. His wife, it seemed, cared nothing for politics, or rather cared only, as she did for so many things, in terms of society. She would exclaim as loudly as anyone at the iniquity of the Whigs or the shameless manoeuvrings of Mr. Brougham, but it was in exactly the same tone in which she would condemn a social climber or an ill-made dress.

And there was worse than that. Henrietta learned a bitter lesson when she happened to mention to her stepmother on their morning ride that her father intended to take a particularly strong line in the House about the question of supplies to the army in Spain. To her horror, she later heard Lady Marchmont broadcasting this information to her callers, among them a few notable Whig ladies. Fortunately, Lord Marchmont had not yet left for the House. Henrietta excused herself, hurried to his study and told him, almost in tears what had happened. There had not been time for her to think what an unpleasant accusation she was bringing against her stepmother as well as against herself and it was only as she told her story that she realised this. But her father merely smiled and thanked her.

'You have learned a useful lesson, my dear. In politics, trust no one.'

She swallowed a sob. 'You mean you will not talk to me anymore. Oh, I know it serves me right . . .'

'I meant nothing of the kind. I said you had learned a useful lesson and I know you will remember it. As for today's business, put it out of your mind. You have given me warning. I shall get Harrowby to make the speech instead of me and the gossips will be confounded. Now, had you not best return to your guests? I have no doubt you have enough of them. But first tell me, my dear, are you happy here?'

'Happy?' She thought it over for a minute. 'I am happy when I am with you, Father, but to tell truth I am beginning to find this business of society a little tedious: One seems to have the same conversation so often and to do the same things so regularly. I wish it was possible for an elegant female to *do* anything.'

He smiled at her very kindly. 'I was afraid you might find it so. But do not despair. It will not be for long. When you are married, you will be able to make a life of your own. In the meantime, remember that you are indeed doing something: You are being the greatest possible comfort and help to me. I do not think I had realised, before you came, how lonely I was.'

From that time on, Henrietta's understanding with her father was closer than ever. But Lady Marchmont was furious.

'I thought you said my lord was to speak in the House yesterday,' she scolded over the morning paper next day. 'A pretty fool you have made me look to the world. It was Harrowby, you see, who spoke about supplies for Spain. What gave you the idea that it was to be my lord?'

Henrietta, who was learning rapidly, merely smiled and excused herself. She must, she said, have mistaken something her father had said. From then on, she never referred to their breakfast-table conversations. But she received another shock when Madame Bégué sent in her bill, which was for more than the whole of her first quarter's allowance. She took it at once to her stepmother, who was busy examining satins and gauzes.

Lady Marchmont greeted Henrietta with enthusiasm. 'The very person. I am choosing my gown for the Birthday and you

shall give me your advice, for' — she sounded rather surprised — 'I must tell you that I find your taste quite admirable.
Now: Which is it to be — the rose-coloured satin with silver
gauze or the scarlet with blond?'

Henrietta voted at once for the rose colour and gauze, wondering as she did so at a certain vulgar tendency in Lady
Marchmont's usually impeccable taste. 'But, ma'am,' she went
on, 'it is about clothes I am come to speak to you, or rather
about Madame Bégué's account, which I find myself quite
unable to understand.' She took out the note and handed it to
her stepmother. 'You see this first item, of two hundred
guineas I cannot rightly comprehend it. The rest is clear
enough: the dresses she made for me, the extra charge for
speed, and the riding habit we commissioned afterwards. But
why this two hundred guineas?'

Lady Marchmont had been looking increasingly embarrassed. 'Why, my dear creature, how could I have forgot to
explain it to you? But indeed I was quite sure I had. Do you
not remember that first day, when all was such confusion and
Madame Bégué arrived in so ill a humour? And how long I
took to soothe her down? Why, she positively refused to make
for you until I had settled my own account. Of course it was
the grossest impudence, and ordinarily I would simply have
sent her about her business, but you had to have the dresses,
my love, did you not? So there was nothing for it but to promise you would pay off my arrears with your first bill. After all, it
makes not the slightest difference, does it? It is all your dear
father's money; it is but a question of which purse it comes
from. And to tell truth I have not a feather left to fly with this
quarter. But, come' — she made a gallant effort to change the
subject — 'what are you to wear for the Birthday? Cedric told
me yesterday he expected you to be the belle of the day and we
must not disappoint him, must we?'

There was much in this speech that was unpleasant to Henrietta, but little that she could do about any of it. If her stepmother had promised in her name that she would pay off
Madam Bégué, of course she must do so, while inwardly resolving to change her dressmaker. But it was the reference to
Cedric that really discomposed her. She had noticed with increasing discomfort Lady Marchmont's tendency to make
these coy remarks about Cedric, and found them disturbingly
difficult to laugh off. It was not that she had the slightest feel-

ing beyond a tolerant friendship for him, nor indeed had he ever given her cause to suspect anything more on his part. But to listen to her stepmother, one would have thought an engagement imminent. It troubled Henrietta; sometimes it almost frightened her. Still, she consoled herself, nobody could force her into an engagement, and her father had certainly never given any hint that he had such a project in mind. As for her, she was still haunted, dreaming and awake, by the memory of a strong handclasp, blue eyes and friendly talk in a country lane. Compared to Charles Rivers, Cedric Beaufrage and his friends were merely negligible. Indeed, now that the first dazzle of life in society was wearing off, she was increasingly aware that the people who visited Lady Marchmont were not quite the ones she herself would wish to make friends of, let alone consider marrying. That they were gay, and charming, and in the first rank of the *ton* there could be no question — or could there? Too young and too inexperienced to be quite sure on this point, Henrietta had nevertheless noticed that although her father's political associates always came to her stepmother's parties, they usually came without their wives. And though their sons hung around Lady Marchmont's carriage, their daughters stayed at home. The Harrowby girls had had the best of reasons for not attending the ball Lady Marchmont had given for Henrietta, but the fact remained they had not come. Henrietta had noticed, and minded, this particularly, because she had taken such a liking to Susan Harrowby when she had met her, once, in the Ladies' Gallery of the House of Lords.

But her stepmother had returned to the serious question of her Birthday dress. 'I said white, my dearest creature, with just the merest *soupçon* of silver. It will make an admirable foil for my rose colour.'

'But I am afraid I shall not be able to attend the Birthday,' Henrietta said. 'Or at least not if I cannot go without a new gown.'

'Not attend the Birthday! What madness is this! Of course I admit it is little better than mockery, with the poor old King as mad as Mahomet, but the fact remains that to stay away would be ruin. And of course you must have a new dress. Depend upon it, there will be plenty of eyes to see if we are stinting you. You would not wish to cast doubts on your dear father's generosity, would you?'

'But that is the whole point,' said Henrietta. 'When I have

settled this bill of Madame Bégué's, I shall be penniless until I receive my next quarter's allowance.'

'Fiddlestick,' said her stepmother. 'What a monstrous Boston miss you are yet, to be sure. Madame Bégué does not expect to have her bill settled all at once; she would much liefer make you a fine new dress. She has told me already that your appearance at Devonshire House last week was worth several good commissions to her. No, no, leave me alone to deal with her, and do you be choosing between white and the cream coloured satin. This is your province. Leave high finance to me, who am expert at it.'

But Henrietta, who did not like her kind of expertise, stood firm. The bill must be paid at once, and indeed, the money was sent off that very day, much to the amazement of Madame Bégué. As for the Birthday, she would go gladly — in her twice-worn white satin, which she and Rose would retrim with blond. To her surprise, Lady Marchmont gave in without further protest. It was so unlike her that Henrietta felt puzzled and faintly anxious. Could she really have been vanquished so easily?

A few days later she learned her mistake. Joining her father at the breakfast table she found him silent and glum. Her questions about his speech the night before were met with grudging monosyllables; her description of her own evening met with no better a reception. Her father said, 'Oh,' and 'Yes,' and 'Very true' and returned to his perusal of the *Morning Post*.

At last she poured out his second cup of tea, put her elbows on the table and looked at him steadily over the newspaper. 'Father,' she said.

'Yes?' There was no 'my dear' today.

'Something is wrong. What is it?'

Thus directly attacked, he put down the paper at last and looked at her. 'Yes, something is wrong indeed. I am disappointed in you, Henrietta. I had meant to sign my will this morning. I thought I knew, at last, what to do with my property. I thought I could have confidence in you. But now what am I to think?'

'About what, sir?' She continued to gaze at him steadily, in honest bewilderment.

'Why, about you, to be sure. I had thought we trusted each other. Fool that I am, I thought I could treat you as the son I never had. I suppose I should have known better. Women are all the same. It is not the extravagance I mind so much, though that is bad enough, but to commission your stepmother to approach me on your behalf! Am I so formidable that you cannot face me yourself? I — I am an old man this morning.'

It was true; his face was as drawn and grey as it had been on the day of Henrietta's arrival. A great light had dawned on her as he spoke, and now she was too angry to consider her words. 'I think you must explain yourself more fully, sir.'

'Explain myself? I hardly see the need.' He was angry too and glared back at her across the table. It struck her as a great improvement on his previous remoteness.

'Do you not? Well, then, pray tell what is this "commission" I have given Lady Marchmont?'

'Why, to ask for an advance on your allowance, of course. For a Birthday dress, of all fripperies. Oh, I know I was not to mention it to you. It was to be a surprise, a spontaneous gesture of affection. Spontaneous gesture!' He spat out the words. 'Pah!'

'And you believed all that?' She was angrier than ever. 'I think it is I who have a right to be disappointed. Had you not enough confidence in me to ask, before you flew into a passion, whether I had really done such a thing? I, to ask Lady Marchmont to intercede with you! Father, you should have known me better.' She was sorry the moment she had said it. She had never meant to let him see the distrust she felt for her stepmother. But it was too late now.

He thought for a moment, then reached across the table to take her hand. 'You are right. I owe you an apology. Forgive me.'

'Of course.' She was close to tears.

'And the less we say about it, I think, the better,' he went on. 'Though the fact remains, my dear, that you have got through a most remarkable deal of money since you have been here. I wonder . . . But did I not ask you particularly not to make any loans!'

'Yes, Father.' This was coming uncomfortably near the bone. 'Believe me, I have not done so. At least — ' She paused. How could she explain without seeming to accuse her stepmother?

'At least not voluntarily, perhaps? Ah, well, best leave it alone. I will not ask you for an accounting this time, and you shall have your advance even if you did not ask for it. I cannot have you looking shabby at the Birthday. Your stepmother is in the right of it there. We have had enough of rumours as it is.'

'Rumours, sir?'

'I fear so, my dear, and not pleasant ones. We could hardly have expected that the world would take your sudden appearance quite without question. Luckily, you have had a good friend in Mr. Brummel, and, of course, a champion in me. But why did you think your Cousin George appeared so unexpectedly to visit us the other day? Did you not know that until your appearance he had considered himself my heir? No, no, never trouble yourself about him; he had no grounds for doing so. I earned my fortune too hardly to leave it at a milksop's disposal. You must know, my dear, that my title is about the sum of what I inherited from my father. What I have, I made, and consider myself free to dispose of as I please. Until you came, I had thought of making Cedric my heir. He is a butterfly, it is true, but an honest enough one. And, I confess, my good opinion of him has been confirmed by the way he has taken your coming. Both he and his mother have been ... You know well enough how good they have been to you. You should have heard the setdown Lady Marchmont gave your Cousin George. "Papers?" said she. "And what right have you to be asking to see Henrietta's papers? If her father and I are satisfied, what is it to you?" I was pleased with her, I can tell you. But just the same, my dear, it puts me in mind that it would, perhaps, be best if I were to have those same papers to show to Stevenage, who is coming today with the draft of my will. You do not have to convince me who you are, but he will be the happier for the sight of them.'

Henrietta had been thinking quickly. 'Of course,' she said. 'And perhaps he will be so good as to keep them for me. They are, at present, with a friend, for safekeeping. I will fetch them for you this morning.'

'With a friend?' He looked his surprise.

'Yes.' The less she explained, the better. She had cast more than enough doubt on Lady Marchmont already today. No need to let her father know that she suspected Lady Marchmont herself of having put Cousin George up to enquiring about her papers. Easy enough, then, to acquire merit by seeming to scout his suggestions. The plan had failed because of her father's confidence in her. But suppose her papers had been destroyed, as Lady Marchmont doubtless thought they were, and suppose he had indeed asked for them to show to Cousin George? Well, it would have been unpleasant enough in all conscience. As it was, she excused herself quickly and sent for a sedan chair. It was high time, anyway, that she paid a visit to Miss Gilbert, who had written her the kindest of notes on receipt of the packet.

She found her as warmhearted and much more eccentric than her brother. Her house was full of stray cats who had made their home with her, and lived, it was easy to see, in the lap of luxury. She seemed to find nothing out of the way in Henrietta's either sending or reclaiming the packet and was much more interested in discussing the latest scandal. Was Princess Charlotte really in love with her illegitimate cousin! After they had disposed of this entrancing possibility, and a glass of ratafia, Henrietta reluctantly took her leave. It was strange to find herself so much more at home in this undeniably shabby, untidy and catridden house than in her stepmother's elegant apartments.

Back at Marchmont House, she went straight to her father's study and handed him the packet of papers. 'There,' she said, 'I am glad to be rid of them.'

He gave her a shrewd look. 'You do not, I collect, intend to tell me what you had done with them, or why?'

'But of course. They were with Miss Gilbert, Captain Gilbert's sister. She is the most remarkable old lady you ever saw.' And by describing Miss Gilbert and her menagerie she hoped to distract her father from the other half of his question, the why. At any rate he did not press it, but told her instead that he had had, that very day, news of the parliamentary opening he hoped, at her request, to obtain for Captain Gilbert's young brother. 'We are almost sure of a dissolution before autumn. That will be the time for him to make the attempt. As for these' — he tapped the little bundle of papers with a snuff-stained forefinger — 'Stevenage shall take charge of them for us when he brings my will for me to sign. I want all right and tight about that, and no chance of trouble for you when I am gone. It's a heavy responsibility I'm leaving you, but I know you will bear it gallantly. Besides' — he smiled up at her — 'I don't intend to die for many years yet, and hope to see you married first, with a husband to take care of you. Ha!' His sharp eye had noted her blush. 'So there *is* someone?'

'No, sir.' She put all the conviction she could into it.

'I'm sorry for it. I wish . . . Oh, well, what's the use . . .'

Henrietta made her escape with a sigh of relief, and much to think about. It was an eventful day altogether. That evening Cedric asked her to marry him. They had been engaged to go to Almack's, but at the last moment Lady Marchmont had cried off. She had a splitting headache, she said. Her friend Mrs. Quatermain would have to chaperone Henrietta in her stead. This meant, to Henrietta's dismay, that she and her step-brother set out, alone together, in Lady Marchmont's carriage to call for Mrs. Quatermain, who had put down her own carriage for reasons of economy since her husband's death. Lady Marchmont pooh-poohed Henrietta's scruples, calling her, as she habitually did on such occasions, a nonsensical Boston miss. And indeed, Cedric's conduct remained entirely brotherly throughout the evening until they had taken Mrs. Quatermain back to her elegantly tiny house in Mount Street. Having escorted her courteously to her door, Cedric said something to the coachman, climbed in beside Henrietta and took her hand.

'At last,' he said as the coachman whipped up his horses, 'we are alone.'

'Indeed?' Henrietta withdrew her hand, and herself, to the farthest corner of the coach. 'Pray, why is the coachman turning down Park Lane?'

'Because I must speak to you, Henrietta. I can no longer play the comfortable brother. Have you not realised how passionately I love, admire, adore you?'

'Why, no, since you ask me, I cannot say that I have, Cedric.'

'Oh, Henrietta.' He followed her into the corner of the carriage and tried to seize her hand again. 'How can you be so cruel? Why, I have given up everything for your sake. I have not been to Waiter's this sennight, nor had a decent game of cards since I remember. My friends are quizzing me already and now you say that you have noticed nothing! Did you not know that Gully was fighting a newcomer at Moulsey Hurst last Tuesday when I took you to the British Museum? Why, I am a veritable Benedict, and all for love of you.'

'Love?' She looked at him thoughtfully. 'Are you sure, Cedric?'

'Sure? Deuce take it, how am I to convince you? Have you not seen that I have eyes for no other woman when you are in the room? Have you not heard me fighting your battles?'

'My battles? What would you have me understand by that?'

'Why, dammit, I was nearly at swords' point with your Cousin George only yesterday. If your father had not intervened, it would have been Wimbledon Common for us — and a deuced good shot he is too.'

'What a fortunate thing, in that case, that my father *did* intervene. I have no wish to be fought over, Cedric. Nor, to tell truth, do I find myself inclined to believe in this passion of yours. Come, Cedric, I beg of you, forget it and be a comfortable brother to me again; you suit me very much better so.'

'Impossible.' He had her hand by now and looked over her, smelling faintly of snuff and the scent she had always suspected him of using. 'You cannot ask it of me, Henrietta. If I cannot be everything to you, I will be nothing. Dammit, I'll join the army.'

'And a very good notion too,' said Henrietta approvingly. 'I have often wondered how you could bear to live so idly here when men are dying every day in Spain.'

'Idle! You call my life idle! I, who have danced attendance on you daily since you arrived! Dammit, I would sooner be in the treadmill than spend so much time at musical evenings and Almack's. And all for nothing, for no thanks, merely to be "a comfortable brother". Henrietta, you must think again of this.'

'Must? 'Tis an odd word, surely? Come, Cedric, if we are to continue friends, let us speak no more of this. I am most excessively fatigued; tell the man to drive straight home, I beg. We have lost too much time already; your mother will be growing anxious.'

To her relief Cedric obeyed her, though something in his behaviour made her wonder whether his mother would, indeed, be anxious, or whether the whole thing had not been arranged between them. Lady Marchmont's headache had certainly been a convenient one for her son.

# CHAPTER SIX

In the course of a restless night, Henrietta decided to say nothing to anyone about Cedric's proposal. If he wanted to tell his mother, that was his affair. She would most certainly not speak of it to her father, who could hardly help but come to the same conclusion as she had — that Cedric's proposal was the direct result of the new will making her his heiress. She had been as much pleased as surprised by her father's approving comments on Cedric and his mother's reception of her. Why should she do anything to disturb his approval of them? Her arrival had done enough already to disrupt the family's at least superficially good relations.

She joined her father at the breakfast table that morning with a nagging, anxious headache. He knew her too well, already, for it to be easy for her to keep anything from him. But to her relief, she found that he had a topic of his own to discuss. Lord Liverpool had asked him to take his place at the forthcoming review at the new Military Academy at Sandhurst, and had suggested that he might like to bring his family.

'The compliment is to you, my dear,' Lord Marchmont said. 'It will give you the chance you have wished for of a look at the royal family, for this is to be something of a family affair. I expect it will be damned dull, at that, but it will make an outing in the country for you. We will shorten the day by sleeping afterwards at Marchmont Hall, which I know you have wished to visit. Indeed, I am half inclined to suggest that you and Lady Marchmont stay there for a few days. You look a trifle fagged this morning, if you will forgive my saying so.'

She laughed. 'I hope I am not such a fine young lady yet, Father, that I cannot be grateful for your noticing it. Yes, it is true, I should be very glad of a few days in the country, if it did not interfere with Lady Marchmont's plans.'

He looked at her shrewdly. 'If you wish to go, my love, Lady Marchmont must change her plans.' And he rang the bell and told a footman to find out if her ladyship was up. Learning that she was, he went directly to her room to broach his plan. He found her in an unusually ill humour, and, not knowing of her son's rebuff the night before, ascribed this, too, to the exhaustion of the London season. He urged, therefore, with all the more emphasis, that they should spend at least a weekend at Marchmont on their way back from Sandhurst.

Lady Marchmont cheered up at once on hearing of the invitation, which she took as a compliment to herself, and was soon enthusiastically planning the party. Yes, certainly, they would stay a night or two at Marchmont afterwards if he wished it. He was right, she had noticed that dear Henrietta was not quite herself. A day or two in the country would do them all good. 'And as for Lady Allen's rout, why, we shall just have to ask to be excused.'

Henrietta was amazed at the energy with which her stepmother threw herself into plans for their country visit. They were to picnic on the way to Sandhurst and this seemed to entail more preparations than would have been needed for an evening party: An English picnic, it seemed, was a highly complex affair. The excursion required an entirely new suit of clothes, too, so that Madame Bégué was called in, and Henrietta found her resolution to employ another dressmaker already broken. But she did do her best to impress the volatile little woman that in the future all their dealings must be directly between themselves. 'I am sorry my French is no better,' she said, breaking down into English at last, having done her best to make this clear by signs and frequent references to a phrase book she had found in her father's study.

To her astonishment, Madame Bégué burst out laughing and answered her in perfect English. 'You must forgive me, mademoiselle, and promise to keep my secret. I am no more French than you are, but if her ladyship and her friends were to know it, why good-bye to my success as a modiste. For them, I chatter in the French I learned from my aunt's husband, who was indeed a French émigré, and made a very good thing of it too. I know you won't betray my secret, miss, for you're a young lady as *is* a lady, unlike some I could name, but won't. Not to make a long story of it, miss, my conscience has pricked me many a time about that bill I sent you, but how was I to get my money from her ladyship else? And lord knows your father can stand the shot well enough, but you can hardly blame him for drawing the purse strings something tight with her ladyship. Why, I could tell you things — '

75

Henrietta interrupted her. 'I beg you will not; I would much sooner not hear them. And as for the bill, that is all settled, and to be forgotten. Only, in future, we will make our own arrangements. I must confess it is a great relief to find you speak English. And as for your secret, it is safe enough with me.'

Thus reassured, Madame Bégué turned to with a will to make for Henrietta, who was amazed to find how much less expensive her work was if paid for in cash. 'But naturally, miss, I have to lay it on thick when they aren't going to pay me,' explained Madame Bégué, or rather, as she confided to Henrietta, Miss Jones — 'But whoever heard of a modiste called Jones? *Ah, mais Mademoiselle a une taille superbe, à fair ravir ...*' She was off into French ecstasies as Lady Marchmont entered the room to complain, as she now frequently did, that madame was giving all her attention to Henrietta.

The day of the review dawned clear and fine, with that hint of mist in the air that Henrietta had learned to recognise as the herald of one of England's rare, delicious, hot summer days. Even Lady Marchmont was down to breakfast, full of last-minute orders that must, Henrietta thought, be creating chaos and despair in the servants' hall. She paused for a moment in her stream of instructions to admire Henrietta's costume of sage green trimmed with black. 'You look exquisite, child. Lord Marchmont, you will have to keep a close eye on Prinney and the royal dukes. I do not trust one of them with anything so pretty as our Henrietta.'

Lord Marchmont smiled at her over his newspaper. 'Well, at least, my love, no one will take you for her mother.'

And, indeed, Lady Marchmont, in royal blue and swansdown, looked, even to Henrietta's ruthless eye, hardly a day over thirty. She smiled and blushed for the compliment, then returned to her plans for the day. 'It is so fine,' she said, 'that I have urged Cedric to take his curricle. We shall all be the better for a breather in it, after the closed carriage.'

'An excellent idea, my love,' Lord Marchmont said. 'And he will be glad of it, no doubt, if we decide to stay longer at Marchmont. Though we shall miss his company on our way down.'

Henrietta surprised a sharp glance in her direction. Was he suspecting her of an interest in Cedric? It was all too possible. She had soon learned how acute he was where her feelings were concerned, and he must have noticed a certain shyness in her manner to Cedric since the night of his proposal, and might well have drawn the wrong conclusions from it. For herself, she was glad enough that Cedric was to be on his own in the curricle. He had not joined the army, nor had she ever seriously believed that he would. Instead, he had gone on dancing attendance on her more assiduously than ever. She liked it less and less and was beginning to realise to what an extent he succeeded in making her seem his property and thus keeping other young men at arm's length. Gently bred, and unused to society as she was, she found it very difficult to protect herself against his monopoly and was increasingly perplexed as to what to do about it. If she spoke to her father, it would mean a row, and it hardly seemed worth that. After all, there was no young man in London that she cared about. If she read the news from the Peninsula assiduously, that was her own affair. But she was glad that they were to be spared Cedric's company on the long drive down to Sandhurst.

It began as a halcyon day. They picnicked on a hill near Bagshot, and Henrietta, contentedly washing down cold chicken with champagne, thought she had never seen anything so beautiful as the trim countryside that rolled away below them. Except for excursions to Chiswick and Richmond, this was the first time she had been out of London since her arrival and she was amazed all over again at the garden appearance the country presented. Her father laughed when she remarked on this, and agreed with her.

'Yes, I remember thinking your America a damned untidy place when I first arrived there. But remember how long we have been working on our landscape. In a few hundred years, no doubt Massachusetts will rival Berkshire.'

Henrietta looked doubtful. 'I am not so sure. I do not believe people in America care in the same way for their countryside.'

Lady Marchmont smiled over her wine glass. 'Heartless girl. You do not sound to be at all homesick.'

'Nor am I. Though I should like to go back there one day.'

'Oh, never think of it!' Her stepmother pantomimed horror. 'Now you are used to live somewhat in comfort, you would find it nothing but barbarous squalor, I am sure. Why, they are little better than savages, if you ask me, and as for giving way to them and suspending the Orders in Council — I am sure I

77

think Lord Liverpool must have taken leave of his senses. Now, if only you had been First Minister, my love — '

Much to Henrietta's relief, her father cut short this incipient tirade by announcing that it was time for them to be moving on. Henrietta was never sure which irritated her the more, her stepmother's harping on her husband's failure to achieve supreme office, or her attacks on America. It was one thing to admit, as she herself now did, that life in America had lacked some of the civilised graces, another to hear her one-time compatriots contemptuously dismissed as savages. Anxious to hear no more of the subject, she agreed with a good grace to Cedric's suggestion that she drive the rest of the way in his curricle. It was, indeed, too fine a day to be cooped up in the carriage.

The rest of the drive was beautiful, the wind on her face refreshing, and she arrived at Sandhurst very ready to enjoy the review and her first near look at royalty. This proved, in truth, disillusioning enough. Her father had warned her what to expect, but just the same, it was hard to believe that these large, red-faced men, who showed every sign of having dined lavishly, were royal dukes, the dowdy ladies they escorted their sisters the princesses. It was true that there was something courtly in the Prince Regent's air, despite his corpulence, and something majestic about his bad-tempered-looking mother, but as for his blowsy daughter, who was romping about the parade ground like an overgrown schoolgirl, her petticoats too short under her ill-chosen violet satin, Henrietta found herself for the first time tempted to believe the rumours she had heard against her.

The ceremony was short, and Henrietta soon found herself walking about the newly laid-out grounds of the academy with Cedric, who had a passion for landscape gardening and architecture and became unusually interesting on the subject. When they returned to the marquee in which refreshments were being served they found Lady Marchmont standing by herself in a corner drinking a glass of iced punch and looking furious.

'It is enough to provoke a saint,' she said. 'Cannot he leave his affairs of state for half a day without being sent for like a truant schoolboy? I am out of patience entirely, and have a good mind to go back to London myself.'

Henrietta had been looking around for her father. 'Why, what's the matter?'

'Matter indeed! Your father has been summoned back to Whitehall. Your Yankee friends have declared war after all. They are rioting in Derbyshire. All's amiss and of course your father must set it to rights.' She took it as a personal affront. 'Well enough for him to send us off to ruralise at Marchmont while he lives in comfort at White's — and Lady Allen's ball tomorrow too. I declare, I do not know when I have been so vexed. And he has taken the carriage without so much as a by your leave, as if I was to be jaunting about the countryside in a curricle at my time of life.'

Tired with journeying and champagne, she looked, for once, almost her age and Henrietta forgot in pity her own dismay at the American news. It was hard, she could see, for Lady Marchmont to find herself suddenly abandoned in this gathering of royalty. The situation was not eased by the Duke of York, who had taken a sudden fancy to Henrietta and now came up, greeted her enthusiastically as his Beautiful Savage, and carried her off to drink a glass of punch with him, talking all the way about Military training and the best uniforms for cadets. After twenty minutes of yeses and nos to this, Henrietta was relieved when he was peremptorily summoned to his mother's side and she was able to return to Lady Marchmont.

She found her amazingly back in spirits. Instead of receiving a setdown for abandoning her for such exalted company, she was greeted with wreathing smiles and rebuked lovingly as a 'dear giddy creature'. She soon discovered why. Lady Marchmont had discovered that Mr. Croker of the Admiralty was planning to drive back to town that night with his wife and her sister and had prevailed upon them to come, instead, to Marchmont, and take her with them. They were to leave almost immediately. 'But there is no need for you to be hurrying yourself, my dearest love, for Cedric will not be ready to leave for this hour or more, I am sure. He has met that creature Nash and is talking porticoes nineteen to the dozen.'

Henrietta began at once to protest. She had no mind to drive the ten miles to Marchmont in the gathering dusk alone with her stepbrother. But she found herself overruled. There was, it seemed, no help for it. Mr. Croker's barouche normally held two. It was only by stretching a considerable point that they were prepared to accommodate Lady Marchmont as well as Mrs. Croker's sister. As it was, she would be sitting bodkin. 'Which you know, of all things, I detest.' Henrietta would be much better off in the curricle. 'Why, what could be more delightful than to drive though this delicious air? I do hope, my dear creature, that you are not going to play me one of your scenes of Boston prudery. I had thought we had contrived to rid you of those crotchets.'

This was a kind of attack that Henrietta always found it difficult to counter. And it was reinforced by Mr. Croker himself, who now joined them and apologised for being unable to offer Miss Marchmont a seat in his barouche. There was nothing for it but to submit with good grace, merely insisting that she and Cedric set off at the same time as the other party.

Her stepmother acquiesced at once. 'Why, very well, my dear, if you wish it. I know Cedric too well to think he would dream of running counter to a lady's whim — and most particularly one of yours. It is but to find him and give him his orders.'

But this proved more easily said than done. Mr. Croker, who disliked driving in the dark on strange roads, had already sent for his carriage and had begun to grow restive at the delay when Cedric finally appeared. He agreed at once to drive Henrietta. They would start immediately. He would send for his curricle . . .

Here a slight hitch occurred. The Queen had chosen this moment to announce her intention of returning to Windsor, and the royal carriages had been summoned. Mr. Croker, whose carriage was already awaiting him, was politely requested to remove it from the sweep. Lady Marchmont shrugged and smiled apology at Henrietta, kissed her effusively in a waft of patchouli and got into the barouche, adjuring Cedric to take the greatest possible care of her.

It took a long time for the royal cortege to get itself formed up and ready to leave. Princess Mary had left her gloves behind in the marquee and Princess Charlotte had contrived to lose one of the many scarves that were wreathed untidily about her plump person. A great deal of abortive bowing and curtseying went on before they were all safely loaded into their carriages and driven away, and it was half an hour or more before Cedric's curricle was finally brought round and he handed Henrietta in.

'Not much chance of catching them.' He gathered up the reins. 'But I know a shortcut by which we can beat them to

Marchmont for all that. Croker is a deuced slow driver, I know. What do you say that we race them there?'

Delighted with this plan, Henrietta did her best to encourage Cedric in it by complimenting him on his skill as a whip. He had, indeed, a neat, firm pair of hands and was known to be a hopeful candidate for the Four in Hand Club. But today his skill was less marked than usual and as he whipped up his horses and took a sharp corner very much too fast for comfort, Henrietta began to wonder whether he, like the royal dukes, was not somewhat the worse for wear. She had suspected that something rather stronger than fruit punch was being served in one corner of the marquee, and it was only to be expected that Cedric would have found his way there. Well, all the more reason for getting to Marchmont Hall as quickly as possible. She certainly did not wish for a renewed proposal from Cedric in his present loud-voiced and fuddled state.

He seemed to pull himself together for a while and they tooled along comfortably enough through a pleasant country of rolling hills, high hedgerows and inconspicuous grey stone villages. Cedric was concentrating on his driving and Henrietta let herself relax. The shadows of the trees were growing longer and the fierceness had gone out of the sunshine, leaving the evening bland and pleasant, fragrant here and there with the scent of new-mown hay and many other country smells that were strange to her. Enjoying them to the full, she did not, for a while, notice that Cedric had begun to pause and consult milestones. But at last he drew up abruptly in the main street of a small village and shouted at a labourer who was making his dusty way home from work.

'Hey, you there! What village is this and which is my road for Marchmont?'

'Marchmont?' The man stopped and scratched his head with an earthy forefinger. 'I reckon you's lost yoursells, mister and lady. This is Imber village and I did hear tell Marchmont is dunnamany miles thataway.' He gestured vaguely with his pitchfork back in the direction they had come. Pressed, he could add nothing to this unsatisfactory bit of information. He was sure that Marchmont was 'back thataway', but when Cedric tried to cross-question him about the shortcut he had intended taking, the man disclaimed all knowledge of it. Henrietta had listened to this exchange with increasing alarm. So far as she could make out from the man's vague estimates, they were now rather further from Marchmont than they had been when they left Sandhurst. And by now the brightness had quite gone out of the air.

The man summed up her fears: 'Happen you'd best hurry yoursells if 'e don't wish to be benighted. And no inn nearer than Swan at Cumber, neither.'

Henrietta wished to question him further, but Cedric threw him a coin and whipped up his horses into a graceful turn around the village green. 'That will teach me,' he said cheerfully, 'to believe in any shortcut of Alvanley's describing. He was always a shatterbrain. No man is to be trusted who puts out his night candle by shying a pillow at it.'

Henrietta was not to be distracted by this interesting bit of information. She was growing both anxious and angry. 'Do you mean to tell me that this shortcut of yours is one you have never taken before?'

'But of course, my dear creature. Where would be the sport in it if I knew the way? Alvanley bet me a pony I couldn't find it the first time, and deuce take it, unless you let me spring the horses, he'll win his money. Come, what do you say? Shall I let them out? If that lobby's to be trusted, we've more than twelve miles still to Marchmont, and I bet Alvanley we'd get there in two hours even.'

'You have lost your bet then,' Henrietta said. 'But let us by all means make haste. Your mother will be growing anxious.'

'Not her,' Cedric said, comfortably ungrammatical. 'She knows you're in good hands, don't she? Besides, she'll be too busy doing the pretty to those Crokers to notice whether we are alive or dead. Come, my dearest creature, relax and enjoy this beautiful evening, and trust me to get you to Marchmont as fast as I can.'

There was a change in his tone during this last speech that Henrietta did not at all like. She had never been his 'dearest creature' before and did not wish to be so now. But this did not seem the moment to protest and bring in, perhaps, some further demonstration of the feeling he claimed to have for her. Instead, she did her best to distract him by keeping up a flow of talk about the events of the day, sounding, to her own ears, uncomfortably like the kind of babbling female she particularly despised. But at least, as she chattered on about Princess Charlotte's dress and the Duke of York's manners, the miles were rolling away behind them and she flattered herself that the discovery that they were lost had had a sobering effect on Cedric. His driving had improved, and he was handling his horses to a point when they swept down a long hill into a slightly larger village whose church tower Henrietta had been able to see, over the woods, for the last few miles.

'Cumber at last,' said Cedric with satisfaction as he coiled his whip neatly around the ears of the leading horse. 'Now we are but ten miles from home, my love, and you may quiet your fears and that tongue of yours. If I did not value every syllable you utter, I vow I would have been praying for a merciful deafness this half hour past. Why, you have outdone Silence — my Lady Jersey — herself.'

This was too much. 'Lord Beaufrage —' Henrietta began in her most quelling tone, when Cedric interrupted her with a sharp oath. His last flick of the whip had startled the lead horse, and now, as the light curricle bucketed from side to side of the increasingly steep hill, she realised that both the horses were out of control.

'Hang on for your life, my love!' shouted Cedric above the rattling of the carriage, but the advice came too late. At the bottom of the hill the road turned sharply round a cottage. He wrenched hard at the reins, but without avail. The horses turned, but not enough to allow for the carriage behind them, which struck the cottage a glancing blow, reeled giddily, and fell on to its side. Henrietta was thrown clear and landed dazed but unhurt in a bed of strawberries. A noise of shouting from the road told her that Cedric, too, had survived, and was apparently being helped with the horses. She rose dizzily to her feet, removed an all too ripe strawberry from the back of her neck, and looked over the hedge. The horses had come to a shuddering stop just round the corner, and the curricle was still lying on its side, while Cedric and a couple of villagers were trying to disentangle the traces and right it.

He looked up. 'Thank God you are unhurt. I was this instant coming to look for you.'

That seemed to Henrietta very much too late in the day. She might have been lying dead for all he seemed to have cared, but she forebore to comment and merely asked whether the curricle was badly damaged.

'Oh, the merest trifle,' Cedric replied cheerfully. 'A shattered splinter bar is the worst of it. You are my luck, my love, there is no doubt about it. Why, such a tossing and it might have been a dead loss, but this is nothing that a morning's work will not repair.'

'A morning's work!' said Henrietta in horror. 'But what are we to do for tonight?'

'Why, what but put up at the Swan Inn, which, if I remember rightly, is just around the corner.'

'Put up at an inn? Have you taken leave of your senses, Cedric? How can I spend the night here with you?'

'What else can we do, my dear creature? These good people tell me there is no carriage to be had this side of Farnborough, so we must make the best of a bad job and stay here. I'll have you home safe and sound in the morning, never fear, and no one a penny the wiser. Besides, you are shaken. He took her arm and guided her solicitously towards the inn, whose sign she now saw by the roadside. To her dismay, it was a tiny place, little more than a cottage, and the hopes she had been nourishing that there might after all prove to be a carriage they could hire died at sight of it. But it was just across the road from the church, and she looked eagerly for the vicarage. Surely help would be forthcoming from there?

Cedric swept the hope away with a casual remark. 'Admiring the church? A crying shame, is it not, that they should have no vicar? Only see how the vicarage is falling down since the incumbent of Marchmont has added this cure to his own.'

So there was no vicar and no hope from him. And Cedric was right; although she had broken no bones, she had been badly shaken by her fall. Angry and anxious though she was, she could not help leaning more heavily on his arm. 'My head,' she said, 'it aches so . . .'

All solicitude, he guided her tenderly in through the open door of the inn where the landlord was hospitably awaiting them. At sight of Henrietta's pale face, he shouted for his wife, who came bustling out to offer sympathy and cold compresses. Henrietta accepted her attentions gratefully. Her headache was growing rapidly worse and when the landlady ushered her volubly into a cool little back room she almost collapsed on to its narrow bed. The woman hovered over her anxiously for a few minutes, then left her with the assurance that a good sleep would put all to rights.

A bee buzzed outside the window; further off, doves cooed and a herd of cows lowed their way home to be milked. Henrietta turned once, anxiously, on the hard pillow. She ought to *do* something. Then, worn out, she slept.

## CHAPTER SEVEN

When Henrietta woke, wondering for a moment where she was, the little room was full of dusk. Uncertain shadows hovered in its corners and the noises of evening were merging into those of night. Outside the window, a bat swooped against the darkening sky. Henrietta was on her feet in an instant, remembering it all. She was at the Swan Inn at Cumber, alone with Cedric, whom she did not trust. Madness to have stayed here for a moment. She moved on silent, stockinged feet over to the bedroom door and paused there. Outside, she remembered, was the main room of the inn and she could hear sounds of bustle, Cedric's voice and then the landlord's and his wife's. A meal, she gathered, was preparing for Cedric, but he seemed to be rejecting a suggestion of the landlady's that she would take something to 'the poor young lady yonder'.

'No, no,' Henrietta heard him say. 'Much best let her sleep till morning. She had a sad tossing of it and needs the rest.'

Henrietta's first instinct was to open the door, tell Cedric she was better and insist that a messenger be sent at once to Marchmont to fetch help. But something held her back. Was she being absurdly suspicious or was there something uncomfortably pat about this chapter of accidents? First the shortcut that had proved so long a way round, and then that Cedric, the admired whip, should have contrived to overturn his curricle. Of course he *had* taken a good deal of drink, but she had never known that to affect his driving before, and indeed had often heard him boast that he never judged his corners with such nicety as when he was, as he put it, a trifle bosky. Standing there in the twilight, she began to wonder if any of it had been accident at all. Could Cedric possibly have risked her life, and, to be fair, his own, so as to force her to spend the night with him in these compromising circumstances?

As for his promise that no one should know; what reason had she to trust him? And if it did get out, the story would destroy her socially; or rather, and here was the heart of the matter, it might compel her to marry Cedric. This, no doubt, was his intention. She shivered. If so, he must be desperate. She had never flattered herself that he loved her, and various interchanges she had witnessed between him and his mother had made her suspect that they were both of them in very much graver financial straits than they admitted. No doubt they had counted on her father's money to extricate them from their difficulties, perhaps had even borrowed on their expectations. Now, they must have it, even if it meant having her too.

Or was she imagining things? Of course she was. Cedric was a lightweight but no villain. She was being absurd. Her hand was on the latch, ready to open the door, when she heard the landlord's rumbling voice. 'Could send a message easy enough,' he was saying. 'The lad can take it if you'll lend 'un one of your horses. 'Tis but five miles if you take the ferry at Barnsley and ferryman will mind the horse while he goes up to the hall.'

Cedric's voice cut him short. 'No need for that. There's no one there to be fretting over us. If there were, I'd ride over myself, only, as I told you, I do not like to leave my sister in case she should wake in one of her fits. And as for sending the boy, thank you just the same, landlord, I'll not risk one of my horses in the dark with a stranger for no need. Now, where's this capon you promised? I'm famished.'

Henrietta had heard enough. Her suspicions were all too well justified. Cedric had no intention of their plight becoming known before morning. She moved silently away from the door and over to the window. No use to appeal to the landlord and his wife. Cedric had taken care of them with his story of her fits. Doubtless they would ascribe anything she might say to her being 'queer in the head like' as she had heard the landlady murmur sympathetically. 'And such a pretty young lady, too.' No, if she was to get out of this fix, she must do so by herself. She sat down on the bed and put on her shoes, then went back to the window and opened it to its fullest width. It was a narrow squeeze, but she just managed to slip through, and found herself standing, quickly breathing, among hollyhocks.

She stepped off the flower bed on to a little path that ran round the side of the house. The air was heavy with the smell of roses, and a rambler dropped its petals down the back of her neck. Passing a lighted window, she looked in and saw Cedric taking the wing off a chicken. His back was towards her, but she hurried past and round to the front of the house. To her relief, there was no side gate to betray her with its creak. Her path led straight out on to the road. The village was quiet now; candles glimmered here and there in cottage windows, people were home for the night.

A signpost stood in the centre of the village green and she hurried towards it, the landlord's words echoing in her ears: ' 'Tis but five miles if you take the ferry at Barnsley.' Soon she was walking quickly down a green lane, turning from time to time for an anxious backward glance. Suppose Cedric should change his mind about leaving her to sleep till morning and find her gone? Would he risk following her? She very much hoped not, but quickened her step just the same, grateful that her deep sleep, and now the evening air, had cured her headache. She still felt stiff and shaken from her fall, but perfectly capable of walking five miles, or more if need be. Her only anxiety was lest it grow quite dark before she reached the ferry, and she rejoiced as never before at the long English twilight. In Boston, it would have been full dark by now, but here she reckoned that she had at least an hour more of dusk, and after that might well be able to find her way by the light of the moon.

She walked on briskly for a while, soothed by the evening noises and savouring the comfort of being alone. The lane led up a small hill, through sweet-smelling meadows, and then into a little wood, where, to her dismay, it split in two. This time there was no signpost and no house in sight. She paused for a moment, irresolute, then took the slightly wider of the two branches. But as she started along it her courage began to fail her. Suppose she should be benighted before she reached Marchmont Hall? What a story that would be for gossip to feed on. But she was committed now and there was nothing for it but to go on with a good heart, if a slightly lagging step. Her shoes, new for the day's outing, had worn a blister on her left heel, and she paused for a moment to try and ease it, and heard, as she did so, the sound of a carriage approaching rapidly from the way she had come. Could it be Cedric? Dared she risk being seen? As she hesitated, uncertain whether to stand her ground, to dive into the hedge and hide, or to try to beg a lift, the carriage swung into view and rattled past. Then, at a shouted order, it pulled up a little way ahead.

She had her shoe on again by now and limped forward. The coachman had gone to the horses's heads while a man's figure leapt lightly out of the door on her side of the carriage. He came towards her through the dusk.

'You are like to be benighted here, ma'am. Can I have the honour of assisting you?'

She started at the voice, so well remembered. But how could it be? Surely she was imagining things. And yet ... 'Good heavens!' she said. 'Mr. Rivers?'

'Himself. And very much at your service. But have I had the pleasure?'

It was no surprise, if no satisfaction, to find that he did not recognise her. 'Why should you remember me?' She made it casual. 'We met but once, and briefly, on the Plymouth road.' Extraordinary, and extraordinarily painful, that while he had forgotten her, she remembered him with every fibre of her being.

'The Plymouth road? Why, it cannot be ... Miss Marchmont?'

'Yes. We seem fated to meet under strange circumstances, sir. I cannot begin to tell you how glad I am, this time, to see you. Is it hoping too much to think you on your way to Marchmont Hall?'

'That is certainly where I am bound.' No wonder if there was a note of reserve in his voice. 'Am I to have the pleasure of driving you there?' He handed her into the carriage, and once again she felt that strange, betraying thrill of pleasure at his touch.

'Shall you think me very impertinent' — he took his seat beside her and the carriage began to move forward — 'if I say that I find this encounter still more surprising than our last one?'

'I cannot blame you for anything you think of me.' Her voice *would* tremble. 'I only wish I knew how to explain — '

'Oh, explanations ...' He shrugged it off. 'Naturally, you can rely on me to say nothing of this encounter. Only' — he paused for a moment — 'if I do not know how you came to be walking along the King's Highway in the dark, I shall find it the more difficult to explain our encounter when we reach Marchmont.'

This was all too true. She sighed. 'It is not, I fear, a very edifying story, but if you will bear with me, I think I will tell it you.' After all, what better did Cedric deserve of her?

'I am your most obedient audience. We have, by my reckoning, half an hour at least before we reach your home where, I have no doubt, you are most eagerly-awaited.' And then, seeing that she was having difficulty in getting started, he went on. 'Do young American ladies often go out for moonlight walks? I cannot believe that your Aunt Abigail would have approved of it.'

She was so delighted to find that he had actually remembered what she had told him about Aunt Abigail that she had to pause again to collect herself. But he had given her her opening. 'I was not out for a walk. We were driving, Cedric Beaufrage and I, back from the review at Sandhurst, when we met with an accident.'

'You surprise me, Miss Marchmont.' His voice was dry. 'Whatever else might be said of Lord Beaufrage, he is generally reckoned a pretty crack whip.'

'Yes, it surprised me too. He took a corner too fast coming into Cumber and broke his splinter bar.'

'And what happened to you?'

'I fell into a strawberry bed. I fear I must look as if I had done so, though I am none the worse, save for a shaking. But the curricle was beyond repair until morning. And Cedric said there was nothing for it but to spend the night at the Swan in Cumber.'

'You surprise me more and more. Was there no one could be sent for help?'

'Yes.' She was committed now to telling him the whole of it. 'That was just what made me begin to wonder. You see, at first I felt so shaken that I was glad enough to lie down for a while, and to tell truth I fell asleep for an hour or so. When I woke up I heard the landlord telling Cedric he could easily enough send a boy to Marchmont. And Cedric said there was no need, we would do well enough where we were. So then, of course, I began to think something was amiss.'

'As well you might. So what did you do?'

'I climbed out the bedroom window — it was on the ground floor, most fortunately — and came away. I was looking for the ferry at Barnsley when you found me.'

She sensed his smile, warming in the darkness of the carriage. 'I am sorry to have to say it to so heroic a young lady, but you had missed your way. You were on the main road for Marchmont, which goes five miles further round. I fear you would have been sadly weary before you reached home. As it is, we shall be there shortly, and I think I know what story we shall tell. You and Lord Beaufrage met with the accident exactly as you describe it, but most fortunately, just as you were wondering what to do, I came past and, of course, offered to take you up with me. Lord Beaufrage, equally of course, could not leave his beloved curricle, and has stayed at the Swan until it is repaired. So here we are, you and I, driving pleasantly together through the dusk.'

'Admirable. But what of Cedric, and your man?'

'Oh, James does what I tell him, and as for Lord Beaufrage ... Well, in the morning, I will very kindly volunteer to ride over to Cumber and find out how he goes on. I think when I return I can promise you that he will tell the same story as I do.'

'Oh.' She considered this for a few minutes. 'I ... I beg your pardon, but you will not *fight* him, will you?'

'I? Fight Beaufrage? I'd as soon call out a mayfly. No, no, never fear for that, I'll frighten him enough without having recourse to pistols. I — well, have my reasons for not wishing to go out with my Lord Beaufrage.'

She was still wondering what these could be when the carriage turned in at a pair of ornamental gates and up a noble sweep of driveway. They wound their way through shadowy parkland and came to a halt in front of the long, black bulk of a house. Rivers leapt out quickly and gave her his hand to alight. As he did so, big doors swung wide and Lady Marchmont's figure appeared on the threshold, illuminated by light from within.

'Rivers,' she said, 'at last.'

'Yes, at last it is.' He led Henrietta up the steps. 'And only see who I have brought with me.'

Lady Marchmont peered out through the gathering gloom. 'Why, can it be — Henrietta? What does this mean? Where is Cedric?'

'Quite safe. At Cumber.' Rivers launched at once into the explanation he had suggested to Henrietta.

Lady Marchmont listened with the proper exclamations of alarm and sympathy as she ushered them indoors. Henrietta, she cooed, must be quite exhausted. She had best go at once to her room. The housekeeper would show her the way and Rose would bring her a cup of hot milk. Henrietta fell in gratefully enough with this plan and followed the housekeeper up the wide stairway after the briefest of grateful goodnights to Rivers. Her last sight of him was as he turned to follow her stepmother down the long hall to an open doorway glimmering with fire and candlelight. Sinking gratefully back against soft pillows, a little later, Henrietta paused on the threshold of sleep to consider Lady Marchmont's appearance at the door. She had never seen her father greeted thus. And where, she wondered, were the Crokers? But she was too tired to puzzle it out; sleep enveloped her and she dreamed, confusingly, of Cedric Beaufrage and Charles Rivers.

She woke to find the house filled with sunshine and cheerfulness. The Crokers appeared at ten o'clock breakfast, explaining to Henrietta that they too had retired early and exhausted. Astonishingly, Lady Marchmont was also down, pouring tea for the party as if she did it every day. Rivers, beside her, handed cups and explained that he had got no further than Ushant on his voyage to Portugal. They had been caught by contrary winds there, and had finally, after much beating about the Channel, been forced back to Plymouth.

'And a good thing too,' said Lady Marchmont. 'I thought all the time 'twas a shatterbrained scheme of yours to go back so soon. But you are safe home with us now and shall stay here till we have you fully recovered. Charles is my lord's ward' — she turned to explain to Henrietta — 'so naturally I feel almost as concerned for him as I would for my dear Cedric.'

Rivers made her a gallant bow of acknowledgment. 'And that puts me in mind,' he said, 'that I promised Beaufrage I would ride over this morning and see if I could be of any assistance to him.'

Lady Marchmont made some objections on the grounds of his health but he soon scouted these, insisting that the doctors prescribed fresh air and exercise as the best specifics for his complaint. He bowed once more over Lady Marchmont's hand, combined a less formal farewell with a reassuring smile for Henrietta, and took his leave.

Carrying on a polite conversation with Mrs. Croker about yesterday's review, Henrietta wrestled with amazement. How had it happened that she had never known that Rivers was her father's ward? Natural enough, perhaps, that Rivers himself had not mentioned it in that first conversation of theirs on the Plymouth road. Looking back on it, she thought with discomfort that she had talked so much he had hardly had a chance to get a word in. The wardship explained, of course, the warmth of his references to Lady Marchmont. And, after all, why should she have heard of it? Having failed to do so on the day of her arrival, she herself had never, somehow, mentioned her encounter with Charles Rivers. And now, looking back, she did remember two brothers called Charles and Simon, young men in whose careers her father had interested himself. Her father had mentioned Simon's brilliance at St. Andrews; her stepmother had been anxious about Charles' health. How could she have known? But Mrs. Crocker was repeating an enquiry about the accident the night before. She collected her wits to reply.

Rivers and Beaufrage rode up to the house late in the afternoon, apparently on the best of terms, and, as Rivers had predicted, Beaufrage confirmed their story at every point, apologising prettily to Henrietta for the accident and thanking Rivers for coming to the rescue. The curricle would be repaired tomorrow. The incident was over.

Henrietta sighed with relief, and, a little, with puzzlement. Rivers' conquest of Beaufrage seemed almost too easy. She wished she knew whether Cedric had told his mother the truth about the previous night's adventure. She thought not, but if he had it would help to account for the feeling of tension in the household that became increasingly apparent after the Crokers had left for London. Or was it all her imagination? Very likely. The previous night had been enough to overset the strongest nerves.

Lady Marchmont had carried Rivers off to her boudoir to render, she said, an account of himself. Wishing at all costs to avoid Cedric Beaufrage, Henrietta escaped to explore the garden, with its ornamental water and Palladian temple. Ridiculous to let herself wish Rivers had been free to accompany her and be properly thanked ... Naturally, he had a duty to Lady Marchmont.

She had just made the circuit of the ornamental water and was wishing she had brought bread for some very exotic ducks, when she was surprised and delighted by the sight of her father's carriage rolling up the drive. She ran to meet him at the front of the house, and he jumped quickly down to embrace her. 'The news is all too true, I fear.'

His first words puzzled her for a moment, then she remembered that he had left on the unwelcome tidings of the American declaration of war. It amazed and shamed her to think that she had forgotten about it for so many hours. Now she recollected herself and cross-examined him eagerly about the news, which was scant and discouraging enough.

'And I fear,' he concluded, 'that I can only remain here overnight. I came but to see whether you and my lady wish to remain or to return with me to London. What do you think, my dear? Can you bear to miss Lady Allen's rout or will you be glad to have a few days of country quiet, even if I cannot share it with you?'

She hesitated a moment. 'For myself, Father, I believe I would rather return with you, but I think Lady Marchmont may wish to stay, for Mr. Rivers' sake.'

'Rivers?' There was surprise, but not much pleasure, in his tone.

'Yes, he arrived last night. His ship has been beating about the Channel these weeks past, and the confinement has brought on a recurrence of his Walcheren fever. But, Father, you never told me he was your ward.'

'Why should I? He and his younger brother have been in my charge for years. Simon is studying for the ministry; a promising boy. As for Charles, nothing would suit him but a pair of colours, which I was glad enough to buy. Nothing about either of them that should concern you, my dear.' And then, on a sharper note: 'Arrived last night, did he? And how long does he intend staying?'

'Why, till he is quite recovered, I collect. Lady Marchmont says he went back too soon last time and she will see to it that he does not do so again.'

'Oh, she does, does she?' He was walking, as he spoke, briskly towards the house, and as Henrietta's arm was linked with his she had no choice but to accompany him. By now the news of his arrival had spread, and the doors were thrown open as they approached. The butler advanced with a speech of welcome, which Lord Marchmont answered, Henrietta thought, with unusual curtness. Lady Marchmont had appeared at the head of the wide stairway.

'My lord! What a delightful surprise.' She hurried down to greet him.

He, on the other hand, had paused, and was considering her

from the foot of the stairs. 'Yes,' he said dryly, 'I had hoped to surprise you, and have succeeded, I collect, better than I had intended.'

'And most happily.' She held up her exquisite cheek for his kiss. 'And I have a surprise for you, too, my lord.'

'A pleasant one, I hope.'

'Oh, exceedingly. Charles is returned from the wars.'

'Rivers? I did not even know he had returned *to* them.'

'Why, nor had he. That is why it is so delightful. But I can see that Henrietta has played traitor and stolen my thunder. So in return I will tell you a story of her, my love, that will make you raise your eyebrows. What do you think of her returning here, alone in his carriage, with Rivers last night?'

'With Rivers?'

'Yes. I was like to sink with surprise. But I must tell you the whole story. It is most romantic, I assure you, with Henrietta for the damsel in distress, Rivers for the gallant knight, and my poor Cedric, I fear, for nothing better than the clown. Only think of his contriving to overset Henrietta in his curricle on their way back from Sandhurst. Did you ever hear of such a looby? If it had not been for Rivers' coming to their rescue, I do not like to think what would have happened. But I can see you are exhausted. Come but upstairs to my boudoir and I will tell you the whole.' And she led him away, every inch the loving wife, with an affectionate, apologetic and at the same time conspiratorial smile that effectively dismissed Henrietta.

## CHAPTER EIGHT

To Henrietta's surprise, they went back to London after all. Her father announced the decision over dinner in tones that brooked no discussion, but suggested that Rivers might wish to remain in the country for the sake of his health. 'The house is at your disposal as always. Or will you run down to Oxford to see how Simon is getting on with his studies?'

'Oh, I think not, sir. Young Simon gets along very well without me, and, to tell truth, I do not find his Oxford friends quite in my line.'

'No,' said Lord Marchmont dryly. 'I imagine not. From what I hear, he is what you would doubtless call a grind. His tutor spoke highly of him in his last letter.'

'I am delighted to hear it.' Rivers' warm tone was in marked contrast to his guardian's. 'I must write old Simon. He always *seems* older than me,' he explained in a laughing aside to Henrietta. 'But as to visiting him ... Well' — he shrugged — 'I believe I would liefer give myself the pleasure of accompanying you back to town. I have my old rooms, sir. There is no need for me to be a trouble to you or to Lady Marchmont.'

So they were in town, after all, for Lady Allen's ball, and Henrietta learned with delight that Rivers was to meet them there. To her pleased surprise, her father also joined them there for a short time after the House of Lords had risen, and when they left it was he who handed his wife into her carriage while Rivers followed with Henrietta. To her profound relief, Lord Beaufrage had finally left for Brighton. There had been no explanation between them about the accident at Cumber, and indeed he had studiously avoided being alone with her. She was only too happy on her part to forget the whole incident and soon did so in the excitement of the season's end, to which Rivers' constant escort added a new delight. They all went to the races, where Henrietta was happy to watch her father and stepmother parading the course arm in arm, like Darby and Joan, as Lady Marchmont said, while she herself followed happily with Rivers. A few days later they saw Mrs. Siddons' last appearance at Covent Garden. Henrietta wept herself weary at her performance as Lady Macbeth, and the management was forced to ring the curtain down after her last exit. The season was waning now and people had begun to drift out of town. Lady Marchmont talked, from time to time, about the heat, about Marchmont Hall and country air. But Lord Marchmont was still fixed in London. There was talk of a dissolution; the war news was bad; the cost of living was rising and the Derbyshire riots had left an unhappy aftermath. He must stay in London, and while he stayed, it seemed, his wife would too. So, to Henrietta's silent pleasure, did Rivers.

Henrietta, who went frequently to the House of Lords to hear her father speak, was puzzled, on two occasions, by seeing her stepmother's familiar blue chariot drawn up near Rivers' door in Curzon Street as she passed the turning. On the second occasion, she felt bound to remark on this to Lady Marchmont when she returned, but was greeted with an amazed stare.

'My chariot? In Curzon Street? My love, you must have been daydreaming. Fenner will tell you I have been confined to my room all day with one of my megrims. As for the chariot, no doubt Harriette Wilson or one of that sisterhood has thought fit to copy my colours. Best not mention it to your father, my love, I fear he is prejudiced enough against poor Rivers as it is. Anyone would think the poor boy took ill again on purpose, but you and I both know, do we not, love, how he longs to be back at his duty? To tell truth, my lord has never had much patience with those two boys. I think he was not best pleased to be named their guardian when they had a grandfather still living.' She laughed. 'And if you ask me, Lord Queensmere, the grandfather, was not precisely enchanted either. Naturally he blamed my lord for this new idiocy of that silly boy, Simon.'

'Oh?' Henrietta knew that her father had flown into one of his rages after receiving letters from Oxford.

'Oh, indeed! The silly young fool must needs decide he wants to go into politics. A younger son with a family living in keeping for him and he pleads religious scruples! I will say for Charles that he has always seen his duty and done it. I've no patience with his brother. An obstinate palefaced boy, always sitting in corners with a book, and I fear he is like to prove as obstinate a man. Well, if he refases to take orders he'll have his own fortune to seek, and so I told my lord to warn him. As for Charles' — her tone warmed — 'leave me alone to scold him for keeping petticoat company, but let us not trouble your father with it. He has enough on his mind as it is.'

It was true enough. Lord Marchmont looked tired to death, but July turned dustily to August and still they lingered in town. Lady Marchmont complained prettily about the dearth of Society, but consented to venture so far as Covent Garden to see the young Roscius, now a personable young man and an infant prodigy no longer. Henrietta found him disappointing, and was glad when her father arrived and insisted on taking them home before the farce. Henrietta, he said, was looking fagged. He hoped they would all be able to leave town next week.

It was true. Henrietta was extraordinarily weary. The strain of the season and of her new life had begun to tell, and besides, there was a deeper cause of unhappiness, one she hardly admitted even to herself. She could neither control her own feeling for Charles Rivers nor pretend that he felt anything more for her than friendship. And yet, he came constantly to the house and escorted them on most of their parties of pleasure. It was maddening,unsatisfactory ... She would be glad when they went to Marchmont where, as she understood it, he was not to accompany them. Alone there, she would fight it out with her unruly heart. For the moment, she must live as best she might from day to day.

As a distraction, and to salve a guilty conscience, she visited kind old Miss Gilbert one hot afternoon and found her welcoming and eccentric as ever among her cats. She had had recent news of her brother the captain, who had just brought the *Faithful* into Southampton and enquired kindly, she said, after Henrietta. She herself was about to leave London for her younger sister's school at Shrovebridge and expressed her surprise that the Marchmonts had lingered so long in town. And she, too, commented tactfully on Henrietta's changed appearance. 'I hope Lady Marchmont takes proper care of you, my dear.'

Returning home, Henrietta found Marchmont House strangely quiet. Fenner met her in the upstairs hall with her finger on her lips. 'My poor lady,' she said. 'Another of her megrims. His lordship sent a message to say he'd sleep at Chiswick with the duke so I've told the poor lamb she's not to leave her bed.'

Henrietta was surprised at her own relief. Why did she find it such a strain, these days, to dine alone with her stepmother: She rang for Rose and ordered a light dinner to be brought to her room. She would spend a peaceful evening writing to Miss Jenkin in Boston. Miss Gilbert had said that despite the war it might be possible for her brother to get a letter delivered for her — best not to ask how.

Time passed peacefully and Henreitta had just rung for candles when a quick tapping on her door heralded Fenner.

'Miss Marchmont.' She was breathing fast. 'You must come to her ladyship at once.'

'Why, what's the matter?' Henrietta jumped up in alarm.

'Matter enough if you do not hurry. Thank heaven you are dressed still. Come, there is no time to be talking here.' And she whisked Henrietta along the corridor to her stepmother's room.

Passing the head of the stairs, Henrietta was aware of bustle below; footmen were hurrying about, shrugging themselves into their livery jackets as they went; somebody must be arriving; the message would have come up from the gate. But Fenner had ushered her into Lady Marchmont's boudoir, where, to her astonishment, she saw Rivers leaning against the mantelshelf.

'There you are at last, my love.' Lady Marchmont was seated at her spinet. 'What an age you have been, to be sure. I sent Fenner for you this half hour since, did I not, Rivers? We have been waiting for you to practise your song. But come, let us begin at once. I must have you perfect at it before we leave for the country.' And she struck up the opening bars of the air.

'My love is fair, my love is false,' began Rivers in his pleasant baritone, and Henrietta was about to chime in with her part when the door was flung open and Lord Marchmont appeared, still in his greatcoat, his hat under his arm.

He took in the scene with a glance. 'A charming domestic interior, my lady. I came to enquire about your megrim, but I see it is better.'

'Quite better, I thank you, my lord. You see I have roused myself to practise these children in their duet. But what a delightful surprise that you are come home after all. I thought you fixed with the duke for the night.'

'Yes. I thought you would be surprised.' There was something in his tone that Henrietta did not like. 'So you are singing duets, are you? A charming pastime. And how long, I wonder, have you been doing so?'

'Oh, this age. My fingers are worn to the bone. I have been making Charles practise his part while we waited for dear Henrietta. But I have a surprise for you, my love. I hope you will think it as delightful as I do.'

'Oh?' He did not sound as if he expected to.

'Yes. I must tell you at once why Charles sought me out so late. He wishes our consent to pay his addresses to dear Henrietta and hoped I would put in a word for him. And now' — she smiled playfully up at Rivers — 'I can see he is angry with me for blurting it all out at once like this, but I am no believer in secrets. In truth, it has made me so happy I could not keep it to myself.'

Henrietta was so amazed at this speech that she did not know where to look. Rivers a suit for her hand? It was impossible, and yet equally impossible not to feel her heart leap at the idea. She dared not look at Rivers, but turned, instead, to gaze imploringly at her father, who seemed to have been struck dumb by his wife's announcement. Still without a word, he advanced deliberately into the room, taking off his coat as he did so and laying it with his hat on one of Lady Marchmont's pink satin ottomans.

'You have indeed surprised me, my dear,' he said at last. 'It is the young lady's part, I know, to say, "This is so sudden", but I confess I am half inclined to do it myself. So you wish to be considered as a suitor for Miss Marchmont's hand?' He turned suddenly to Rivers, who stood motionless, his hand still on the back of Lady Marchmont's chair.

There was a tiny pause, then: 'If you will not consider me too presumptuous, sir,' said Rivers.

'Oh, I! It is no matter what *I* think; it is for Henrietta to decide, and we will not embarrass her with the question now. This has been an ill-managed business enough. We will sleep on it. Henrietta, my dear, it is time you were in bed. We will talk more of this in the morning.'

Henrietta accepted her dismissal with relief, dropped a blind and indiscriminate curtsey to the three of them and retired to her room with her head in a whirl. There was no ordering her thoughts. Rivers wanted to marry her. Surely that was happiness enough? Why, then, should she find herself so absurdly distressed because he had first broached the subject to her stepmother? After all, what could be more natural, especially as his relations with her father were all too obviously not of the best? She would have to change all that now. They must be friends. As for her answer, there could be no doubt about that. If her father had asked her, she would have given it at once. She had loved Rivers from the first moment she had seen him and was even prepared to forgive him for having come somewhat more slowly to caring for her. Thinking how she would tease him, later, about this, she fell asleep and dreamed of white satin and Valenciennes.

Alone with her over breakfast, Lord Marchmont was disappointingly grave. In her happiness, she wanted all the world to smile, but he would not, even for her. It was, he said, a good enough match, though far from being an extraordinary one.

Rivers, it was true, was heir to a barony, but his grandfather, Lord Queensmere, was a hale and sober old man of sixty odd. It might be years before Rivers inherited. In the meantime, his prospects were hardly better than those of a younger son. As for marriage, it was out of the question so long as Rivers continued in the army. 'And a long engagement is the devil, my dear. I beg you will think more of this. Indeed, I confess, I am surprised at Rivers' effrontery in asking you, but it is all of a piece — '

'Of a piece with what, Father?' Henrietta asked. 'Tell me,' she went on, suddenly bold, 'what is it you have against Rivers? How can you help but love him?'

He smiled at her at last. 'Does it seem so strange to you that I should not? My poor child, I see it is useless to be talking of reason to you. Very well then, an engagement let it be, but promise me that if you should ever change your mind, you will tell me at once.'

It was not exactly an enthusiastic assent, but at least it was one. It was only afterwards that Henrietta realised he had not explained his prejudice against Rivers. And by then she was in such a daze of happiness that she dismissed it from her mind. There were better things to think about. To her relief, they had no morning visitors that day. Town was so empty that this was no cause for surprise, but reason for much delight: She could wait in peace for Rivers' arrival. He came at last, with a bouquet of exquisite hothouse flowers for Henrietta and a tiny bunch of violets for Lady Marchmont. The hothouse flowers, he explained, were, with her fondest love, from his grandmother's conservatory at Wimbledon. Henrietta had just time to wonder whether he was not taking her acceptance somewhat for granted when her father appeared and carried him off to his study.

Lady Marchmont was taking deep breaths of the violets' perfume. 'My favourite flowers,' she murmured. 'So thoughtful, always. But, my dear, you are looking quite fagged. Why do you not walk out into the garden? Never fear, I will send Charles out to you when he leaves your father.'

Henrietta obeyed the suggestion gratefully enough. If she felt she was being somehow a little managed, it was very much in the right direction. She ran upstairs past the silent study door, amazed Rose by insisting on arranging her bouquet herself, collected a shady chip hat and wandered out into the sun-drenched garden. She paused for a minute on the terrace, but her father's voice, rumbling and irascible from the study window, drove her on through the rose garden. She paused here and there to pick a late bud — Rivers, too, should have his nosegay — but then, feeling herself too conspicuous in such clear view of the study window, wandered on into the shrubbery that concealed the park fence. Rivers would find her here and they would meet for the first time as lovers in this comparative privacy. She settled herself on a shady bench to dream of it, looking up now and then with a quick start. Was he coming at least? Impossible not to consider the picture she presented; to rearrange herself from time to time; the big hat first in her lap, then impatiently back on her head; the flowers now in her hand, now on the bench beside her.

But time passed. The shadows moved, and she found herself caught in fierce sunshine. The rosebuds began to droop in the heat. Surely Rivers' interview with her father was taking too long? Could something have gone wrong between them: At the thought, she was on her feet at once. But her father had promised his acquiescence, if not quite his approval. He could not, at this eleventh hour, have seized on some pretext for breaking off the match. She stood for a few minutes, irresolute, thinking, then moved with a quick step towards the open lawn. Perhaps Rivers was this minute looking for her. Or, horrid thought, perhaps Lady Marchmont had been prevented, by the arrival of company, from telling him where she was. She was hurrying now, but the lawn, when she reached it, was empty. Again she stood for a moment, hesitating, the tired flowers drooping in her hand. Then, decided at last, she walked quickly towards the house.

On the terrace, she paused for the briefest instant outside the study windows. But there was no sound from within; the interview must be over. She passed on to the big doors that stood open into the main hall. Entering, she found herself half blind, for a minute, after the brilliant sunshine outside. The footman in waiting there had sprung to attention at her approach. It was Jem, she noticed, Rose's brother.

'Lord Marchmont?' she asked. 'Is he in his study still?' Impossible to ask about Rivers.

'Why, no, Miss Marchmont.' The man sounded surprised. 'He went out this half hour since. Did you not hear the carriage?'

'Oh,' She paused for a moment, irresolute. But it must be asked. 'And Mr. Rivers?'

'In the morning room, I believe, miss, with her ladyship.'

'Oh,' she said again. 'Thank you, Jem.' What to do now? And what could have kept Rivers so long with her stepmother? Absurdly, it seemed quite impossible to walk down the hall and open the morning room door — equally impossible not to do so. Worst of all, though, would be to be caught lingering here. She was conscious, suddenly, of the roses drooping in her hand. 'Here.' She handed them to Jem. 'Have these put in water for me, would you?'

He took them. 'You've scratched your hand, miss.'

'Why, so I have.' Here was the pretext she had needed for action. She turned and hurried, almost in flight, up to her room, where she made a business of bathing and having Rose bind up the wound. While doing so, she was able to keep watch over the garden below. At last she saw Rivers walk out across the lawn towards the shrubbery.

'There,' she said, 'that will do very well. I thank you, Rose.'

'But, Miss Henrietta, there's blood on your gown,' protested Rose as she turned towards the door.

'No matter for that. 'Tis but a tiny stain and will pass for the figure in the muslin.' There was no keeping her now. She hurried down the stairs only to encounter her stepmother hovering, as she herself had earlier, in the hall.

'Why, there you are, my love,' she said. 'Rivers is but this instant gone to seek you in the garden. Did you think him an unconscionable time in coming? It was my fault; I could not let him have anything so precious as my child without some commands of my own. It is all settled, my dearest creature; all but the date of the wedding, and I am sure we shall contrive, in the end, to persuade your father that it is not reasonable you should have to wait for peace. Why, it might be years.' She sounded remarkably cheerful about it. 'But what am I doing delaying you here while your lover is searching for you in the garden? Away with you, and make him the happiest of men.'

But as she spoke, the footman who had been lurking in the shadows at the far end of the hall sprang to open the front door and admit, of all people, Lady Marchmont's toadies, the three Miss Giddys. They advanced on Lady Marchmont and Henrietta with little crows of delight.

'Why, my dear Lady Marchmont,' said the first, standing on tiptoe to kiss the lacquered cheek.

'What a delightful surprise,' chimed in the second, reaching even higher to kiss Henrietta.

'To find you still here in August.' The third had been patiently waiting her turn at Lady Marchmont's cheek.

'We did not think Lady Marchmont could have left town without saying good-bye to her devoted friends,' said Miss Giddy.

'And yet it seemed strange enough that you should be still lingering here,' added Miss Letitia.

'But of course there is poor dear Lord Marchmont and his politics to be considered.' Miss Patricia made them sound like an infectious disease.

'So altogether,' summed up Miss Giddy, 'we hoped we might not be too late to come as petitioners to you.'

By this time they had all been swept, in a wave of muslin and orrisroot, into the morning room, where two chairs, close together by the window, spoke to Henrietta of the interview that had just taken place. And, still, Rivers was seeking her in the garden. But how could she escape?

Miss Patricia had her by the arm. 'So you see,' she was explaining earnestly, 'we feel ourselves compelled to ask it for poor dear Fanny's sake. And dear Lady Marchmont is so kind . . . so good; we knew we should not ask in vain.'

Henrietta, who knew all too well that Miss Fanny was the fourth and invalid Miss Giddy, in whose name her sisters would ask anything, turned to listen to the request the eldest sister was making. It was prefaced by an alarming list of Miss Fanny's new symptoms.

'And Sir Henry Halford says,' Miss Giddy concluded triumphantly, 'that she must have country air to build up her strength for next winter. Poor dear Fanny; if you could but see her, dear Lady Marchmont, you must pity her; so thin, so wan, so languid. "Do not trouble yourselves for me," she said this morning. "I am nothing but a burden to you; let me pine away and die as the good Lord intended." '

'But *we* said' — Miss Letitia took up the tale — 'we said: "Lady Marchmont would never forgive us if we did not tell her Sir Henry's verdict." '

'So often as she has urged us to consider Marchmont Hall as our own," that is what we told Fanny,' explained Miss Patricia.

'So here we are, humble petitioners,' concluded Miss Giddy. 'Not for ourselves, of course, but for our poor dear Fanny who must have country air or die. And to think that you have not yet left for Marchmont! Why, it seems like the hand of Providence.'

'Yes, indeed,' said Miss Patricia.

'Perhaps there will even be some corner in one of the carriages where we could put our poor dear Fanny,' said Miss Letitia.

'Of course, as for *us*,' said Miss Giddy, 'you know us, Lady Marchmont. We are old campaigners; the public coach is good enough for us.'

'Though perhaps,' suggested Miss Patricia. '*One* of us should go with poor dear Fanny in case she has one of her seizures.'

'Just the tiniest corner of a carriage,' said Miss Giddy. 'You know how slender poor Fanny is.'

At last they all paused and three pairs of large brown eyes, in three thin brown faces, were directed eagerly at Lady Marchmont.

'I collect,' she said, 'that you wish to accompany us when we go to Marchmont.'

'Dear Lady Marchmont,' said Miss Giddy.

'Always so quick,' said Miss Letitia.

'Always so *generous*,' said Miss Patricia.

The door of the room swung open. 'I have looked everywhere,' began Charles Rivers. 'Oh. I beg your pardon.'

They were upon him. 'Dear Mr. Rivers,' said Miss Giddy.

'We have not seen you this age,' said Miss Patricia.

'But "Here's metal more attractive," ' sighed Miss Letitia.

'Yes, indeed,' said Miss Giddy. 'Who are we to complain that we have not seen you this month or more? What are our poor evenings compared with dear Lady Marchmont's soirees?'

'But perhaps,' said Miss Patricia, 'we shall be so fortunate as to have your company in the country.'

'Yes,' said Miss Letitia. 'Only think, Mr. Rivers. Dear, dear Lady Marchmont has invited us all — yes, four miserable spinsters that we are — '

'To bear her company to Marchmont,' said Miss Giddy. 'Of course, Lady Marchmont knows that any attic will do for us.'

'Any garret,' said Miss Patricia.

'Some nook under the tiles,' said Miss Letitia.

'Though of course,' said Miss Giddy. 'We must not forget poor dear Fanny's palpitations.'

'No,' agreed Miss Letitia, 'stairs are death to poor Fanny.'

'And if she *were* to have one of her spasms,' added Miss Patricia.

'It would be best if one of us were within call,' concluded Miss Giddy.

Lady Marchmont rose to her feet. 'Well, that is settled then. We leave for Marchmont on Friday. It is but this morning decided, so you are arrived most happily.' Her voice was dry. 'And naturally you will have your usual rooms. As for the journey, we must see what can be managed. Charles, you bring your carriage, do you not? But in the meantime, Henrietta and I must beg you to excuse us; we are expected this moment in the park. Henrietta, my love, you must make your best haste to change into your habit. Charles, you will accompany us, of course.'

He bowed a silent acquiescence while Henrietta said the quickest farewells she could to the voluble Miss Giddys and retired, with somewhat mixed emotions, to change. A ride in the park with Rivers was hardly a substitute for the private interview she had hoped for. But her immediate disappointment was lost in her pleasure at the news that Rivers was to accompany them to Marchmont. In the country, surely, there would be time to talk.

## CHAPTER NINE

Henrietta's dream of country solitude with Rivers at her side was doomed to disappointment. She arrived to find Marchmont Hall full of the bustle preliminary to a week-end party. The house, her stepmother told her, was to be full to capacity. Lord Liverpool was coming down with several other members of the Ministry. Doubtless they wished to discuss the news of Bonaparte's invasion of Russia, which had set all political London in a whirl. And indeed, all week-end, the house was full of currents and crosscurrents, of interrupted conversations and suspended sentences. Some new arrangement or combination seemed to be afoot, though Henrietta had no idea what it could be. Questioned, her father laughed and put her off.

'No, no, child. You attend to your romantic affairs and leave my politics to me. This is too secret even for your ears.'

She could tell, however, that it was something that very much interested him, and the atmosphere of the house, all weekend, was full of a greater excitement than could be accounted for simply by the news of her engagement, about which, of course, each guest, as he arrived, had said all that was proper to her. Smiling and thanking them in turn, she wondered why she was not happier. True, she had still to await a proposal in form from Rivers. It was odd enough to have been officially engaged for several days and still not to have had the opportunity of accepting her lover's hand. And yet, she told herself, it was not so surprising after all. They had never been alone together for longer than a few minutes at a time. With the four Miss Giddys in the house, their chances of more seemed slight indeed.

But — and here was the rub — she was beginning to wonder whether Rivers really wanted such an opportunity. He behaved to her with all the attentions of an accepted lover: there was nothing to trouble her there. But on one or two occasions, when chance had seemed to be on their side — when she had really begun to hope that they might be alone for a while, whether in conservatory, library or shrubbery — it seemed that he himself, as if by accident, threw away the opportunity. She was shivering, he must fetch her shawl; the sun was too hot, he would get her hat ... It was absurd; she must be imagining this; and yet the week-end passed and still there had been no *éclaircissement* between them.

And on Monday her father made his announcement. Lord Liverpool had done him the honour of asking him to go on a mission to the Czar, who had now become an ally, willy-nilly, on being attacked by the French. He was to leave at once. For a while all was forgotten in the bustle of his departure. It might be months before he returned, and he was to travel through the very heart of Europe at a time when Bonaparte seemed all-powerful there. All thoughts of her own affairs forgotten, Henrietta hung constantly about him, insisting on helping with his packing, and getting, as he laughingly told her, very seriously in his way.

He left with Lord Liverpool next day. Henrietta had begged to be allowed to accompany him back to town, but he would not let her. He was to drive with Lord Liverpool and they would be discussing the line he was to take in St. Petersburg. Henrietta would not be able to go with them. And besides, she had Rivers to consider. For the first time there was a faint suggestion of warmth in her father's voice when he referred to her engagement.

'I confess, my dear,' he said, 'it is something of a relief to me that I leave you an engaged young lady. If anything should happen to me — which I do not in the least expect — I have no doubt that Charles Rivers will take good care of you.' As so often, the criticism of Lady Marchmont remained unspoken between them. Both were aware that as a guardian she would leave a good deal to be desired. 'I shall not have time to change my will again,' Lord Marchmont went on. 'Nor, indeed, do I think it necessary. After proper provision for Lady Marchmont, I have left you my heiress unconditionally.'

But Henrietta did not want to talk of wills, nor even, for once, of Charles Rivers. It was her father's journey that exercised her mind. It seemed so soon, after finding him, to lose him again. She cried, unashamedly, when he actually left, and, shamed at last more by Lady Marchmont's crystal calm than by her own emotion, hurried into the garden to recover herself. Charles Rivers had ridden a little way with the London party and when she heard a horse coming up the drive, she thought with pleasure that he must have returned, so soon, to comfort her.

But the horseman, when he appeared, was not Rivers but Beaufrage, who came up the drive with a face of thunder. When he saw her, he reined in his horse.

'The very person I wished to see.' He did not sound pleased. 'Henrietta, what madness is this of yours?'

'Madness? I do not understand you, Cedric.'

He jumped from his horse, looped the reins over his arm and turned to walk beside her, back the way he had come. 'I have but this morning seen Friday's gazette with the announcement of your engagement. Need I say more?'

'You could congratulate me, I collect.'

'Congratulate you: I'll see you damned first. I beg your pardon' — he recovered himself — 'but this news has near maddened me. What can you have been thinking of? And as for my mother: I knew she was shatterbrained enough, but this is more than folly.'

Henrietta was growing angry. 'I do not understand,' she said, 'what affair my engagement is of Lady Marchmont's.'

He laughed harshly. 'You do not understand! Truly, Henrietta, you are even more of a ninny than I had thought. You do not think my mother needs concern herself with your engagement to Rivers! I always took you for a green girl, but this passes everything. Is it possible you do not know?'

'Do not know what? You are talking in riddles, which I neither like nor comprehend.'

He laughed again. 'I am sorry to seem so mysterious, but it is hard to believe you ignorant of what all the world knows. I had thought at least the Miss Giddys, or even your own common sense would have enlightened you.'

'About what?' She was nearly at the end of her patience.

'Why, that Rivers and my mother have been lovers this age. Why did you think that your father looked so sourly on him? And that he haunted the house so? Not for the sake of your *beaux yeux*, I can tell you, though it may have suited my mother to let it seem so. But to carry it to the point of engagement: that is really the outside of enough, and so I shall tell her. Why do you think she gave in so gracefully on your arrival, but that she saw your presence would provide an admirable screen when Rivers returned, as, you will note, he soon did, with his convenient bout of "Walcheren fever"? Did you not think it odd that he should arrive so pat when we were down at Marchmont the last time? Did you not wonder how he knew where to find us? Have you never noticed, though he does his best to conceal it, how much he knows of our affairs, and how much, equally, my mother knows of his? They have been in constant correspondence for years, ever since she left my father for his sake. You did not know that, did you? Nor that when my father died my mother would have married Rivers if either of them had had but a feather to fly with? But my father had run through everything. The only kindness he ever did my mother was to die when he did and so save her the disgrace of a separation. And then my Lord Marchmont comes along, with his nabob's fortune, fresh home from India, and almost as innocent as you, and, hey presto, they are married, and the world's mouth is stopped. But it was touch and go, for a while there, with my mother's reputation, I can tell you. She saved her bacon well enough then, but this, this using you as her screen — well, I tell you, it is too much, and so I shall tell her too.'

Henrietta had listened to this tirade in shocked silence. At first she had striven to disbelieve him, but it was impossible. The whole thing, appallingly, made sense, and she even realised that she could, if she had wished, have added to Cedric's indictment of his mother. Now, at last, she understood the scene that had led to her engagement. How could she have been so blind? But how, on the other hand, could she have suspected anything so sordid? Now it was all agonisingly clear. Lady Marchmont, thinking her husband safe at Chiswick that night, had sent for her lover. And then suddenly she had heard belowstairs the bustle that heralded Lord Marchmont's return — or, Henrietta wondered, did the ubiquitous Fenner act as look out on these occasions? At any rate, Fenner had been despatched, posthaste, to fetch her and thus give the assignation an appearance of innocence. Had Lady Marchmont planned all along to play the trump card of the engagement? Henrietta doubted it. She remembered her father's stony face as he entered. His wife had been frightened, as well she might, and had decided to risk all on a bluff. As for Rivers, no wonder if he had seemed silent and embarrassed. It must have been the first he had heard of it. At this point, Henrietta's thoughts became too painful to be borne.

'You must excuse me,' she said to Beaufrage, 'I am not well. Thank you for what you have told me. I admit I needed to know it. Now, I beg you will leave me.'

But he had seized her hand. 'Henrietta, I have hurt you, and I could kick myself for doing so. But as you say, you had to know. How could I let you be sold into such a mockery? Now, but recollect yourself; remember how I have always loved you and take your revenge on Rivers by announcing your engagement to me. Only think what a laugh the world will have at his expense then.'

Henrietta snatched away her hand. 'Lord Beaufrage, if you ever wish me to speak to you again, say no more of this. I have had enough, too much . . .' She turned from him and made her way, almost running, through a shrubbery path to the house. Her thoughts were in a whirl of shame and pain; her only idea to get unobserved to her room. She went in, therefore, through a side door into a conservatory from which a convenient stair led to her bedroom. But as the door shut with a soft sigh behind her, she heard Lady Marchmont's voice, a tearful whisper: 'I can bear no more,' she said.

And now, through the warm green half-light of the conservatory, Henrietta was aware of two figures, intertwined, their backs towards her. Lady Marchmont's head was on Rivers' shoulder, his arm around her waist. And even as she looked at them, Rivers, alerted perhaps by the sound of the door, turned and saw her. He started and dropped his arm from Lady Marchmont's waist. She in her turn raised her head from his shoulder to stare steadily at Henrietta.

They all remained speechless for a moment; then Henrietta spoke: 'Do not trouble yourselves to say anything. I know it all. I have heard it this instant from Lord Beaufrage.' She advanced towards them, pulling the ring off her finger as she went. 'Here' — she held it out to Rivers — 'here is your ring.'

He did not take it. 'Miss Marchmont — Henrietta, you must hear me.'

She looked at him steadily, still holding out the ring. 'I do not see that there can be anything for you to say to me, Mr. Rivers.'

'But there is. You do not understand.' And then, passionately, to Lady Marchmont: 'Lavinia, leave us. Have you not done enough harm already?'

She looked up at him for a moment in silence, her large eyes aswim with tears, then turned, still silently, to glide away. Henrietta, too, was silent with the new shock of hearing Rivers call her stepmother by her first name. She made as if to leave him too, but he caught the hand that still held his ring.

'Henrietta, you must listen to me.'

'I do not see why. I think I have heard too much already.'

'But you do not understand.'

'On the contrary, I do understand, at last. What an innocent fool you must have thought me, Mr. Rivers! How you and Lady Marchmont must have laughed at me, so gullible, such an easy mark. Oh' — she put her hands to her face — 'I cannot bear myself.'

'Henrietta —' There was no mistaking the appeal in his voice. 'You must try to understand. Here —' He took her hand and led her, only half resisting, to a seat under a giant fern. 'You cannot think me such a scoundrel as to have wooed you merely as a cover for my affair — to which I must plead guilty — with Lady Marchmont. Henrietta, say you do not believe that.'

'What else can I believe? And, besides,' with a flash of her usual spirit, 'you did not woo me. Lady Marchmont most kindly did it for you.'

'And I tamely submitted? Is that how it looks to you? Do you really think I would stand by and let my mistress choose me my wife? How little you know me.'

'You have not given me,' she said, 'much chance to know you better.'

'Oh . . .' It was almost a groan. 'You are in the right of it, of course. But how could I, circumstanced as I was, take the privileges of an accepted lover? Henrietta, I know what you must be suffering, but think a little what I have suffered too.'

'You? I should have thought all had gone swimmingly for you. What more could any man want?'

'Only what I begin to fear I have lost: your respect, Henrietta. But you must let me try to explain. And first, here, take my handkerchief. I cannot bear to see you sit there and cry.'

She accepted it and dried her eyes. 'I do not much like to cry either. I promise you I shall not do so again.'

'I know, you mean to forget me, and I cannot blame you. What a shameful figure I must cut in your eyes. To allow myself to be plumped into an engagement merely to avoid the embarrassment of discovery. But, I tell you, it was not like that at all. You *must* have known how truly I was falling in love with you. God knows, it was apparent enough to —' He paused.

'To Lady Marchmont, you would say?'

'Yes. Oh, God, how am I to explain without hurting you more?'

'Well' — she looked up at him — 'you might try telling the truth.'

'I will, I promise you. Only, I do not know how they look on these things in Boston.'

She jumped up in sudden heartwarming fury. 'That is enough, Mr. Rivers! If you are to take a leaf out of Lady Marchmont's book and start twitting me with Boston, I will take leave to leave you.'

But again he had her hand. 'Henrietta, please . . . I did not intend it like that; you must know I did not. But you are too fine, too innocent, for our sordid way of living. Oh, God, how often I have cursed myself since I first met you, and more especially since I have come to know you better.'

'You have not, I collect, carried your contrition to the point of breaking off your affair with Lady Marchmont.'

'Breaking off? If you but knew how I have tried. But I can see there is nothing for it; you must bear with me while I tell you the whole. It casts, I fear, no very happy light upon me, nor — which is what I mind the more — upon your stepmother, but it is too late to be thinking of that now. I do not know how much Lord Beaufrage thought fit to tell you in these revelations of his, but I, if you will but hear me, will start from the beginning.' With gentle firmness he drew her down to sit once more beside him. She had never been so close to him before and there was dangerous excitement, despite everything, in his touch. But a moment before, he had been still closer to Lady Marchmont. With an effort, she withdrew her hand from his.

'But where shall I begin?' He reached up to grasp the huge trunk of the fern, his arm warm across her back. 'If I tell you that I was an orphan, much alone in the world, you will think I am making excuses for myself, and I shall not blame you. And yet, it is to the point. For when I first came to London, a very young man of eighteen, I was, I cannot tell you how shy, how ill at ease in society. Simon was still at Harrow. I was quite on my own. Lady Marchmont was Lady Beaufrage then; her husband, who was twice her age, had been a friend of my father's. It was natural that I should spend much of my time at their house. It was inevitable that I should see that Lavinia — Lady Beaufrage — was not happy. Her husband was a good enough sort of man, but he cared nothing for the things that amused her. They had been married for ten years or so at that time. Cedric was a boy at school, Lavinia had nothing to occupy her. She took me up; she made a man of me. Your father, my guardian, was in India still; if it had not been for her, I do not know what would have become of me.'

She was struggling against sympathy, against the hinted caress of his arm. 'And your grandparents? Where were they?'

'Oh, Henrietta . . .' He gave a half-despairing sigh. 'But I do not blame you: I have given you cause enough for suspicion. My grandfather was in Scotland, seriously ill, my grandmother absorbed in nursing him. My father, you must know, had defied their wishes to marry my mother and they had washed their hands of us all. It is only in the last few years, since they have been living in Wimbledon, that I have come to know and love them. Besides (ruefully), they always liked Simon best. He and my grandfather used to spend hours together in the study. And I . . . I was alone indeed, with the world before me, and no one, if it had not been for Lady Beaufrage, as a guide. She taught me everything: how to dress, how to behave, when to talk, when to be silent. She persuaded me to join the army and got me my first commission.'

'How?' asked Henrietta.

'Why, by introducing me to the Prince Regent at Brighton. Lord Beaufrage was a Whig, you know, and those were the golden days of Whig society. Oh, if you could but have known it, you would be able to understand! In London, there was Devonshire House: the parties, the talk, the friendship. And at Brighton, of course, the Pavilion. It was so gay, so easy, so friendly . . .'

'So wicked?' suggested Henrietta.

'Well, in a way, I suppose so; but it did not seem wicked when we became lovers. At least, not at first.'

'And what of Lord Beaufrage?' Henrietta asked.

He coloured. 'That was when the shoe began to pinch. You see — you must understand — I had accepted the whole affair as a natural part of the world we lived in. Lavinia — Lady Beaufrage — had given her husband an heir; it seemed the understood thing that she might do as she pleased. After all, there was Lady Melbourne, and the Duchess of Devonshire . . . it was all around us, Henrietta; it was in the air.'

'But just the same, I collect, Lord Beaufrage was so unreasonable as to dislike it.'

'Well, yes. When he found out, there was the devil to pay. He sent Lavinia away. War had broken out again by then, so she could not go to Europe, but had to make the rounds of the watering places, from Bath to Cheltenham and from Cheltenham to Harrowgate, and deuced bored she was too, poor thing. You must see that I could not give her up then.'

'I can see that you were in some sort committed.'

'Of course I was.' He seized upon it gratefully. 'And then my regiment was in camp near Bath, so of course Lavinia stayed there, and Lord Beaufrage was angry with her anyway . . .'

'So it went on?'

'Yes. It went on. And then, all of a sudden, Lord Beaufrage died.'

'And you did not marry her?'

'That was another shock to me. Of course I took it for granted I would marry her as soon as she was out of black gloves.'

'And what did she say?'

'She laughed at me. She told me that I was very well as a lover, but that she did not propose to live on love in a cottage. Lord Beaufrage, you see, had tied up every penny of his money for Cedric — what he had not spent, that is. I think towards the end of his life he spent his fortune simply so that she should not touch it after his death. At all events, she was left in sadly straitened circumstances, and would have none of me. She sent me away, and, to my relief, just then my regiment was ordered aboard. When I returned on leave, a year later, I found her married to your father.'

'Whereupon it began all over again.'

'You speak like my conscience. I cannot tell you how often I have reproached myself on that very point. But she was so unhappy.'

'Unhappy? Why?' She tried to move a little away from him, but his hand fell gently on her shoulder to keep her where she was.

'I was afraid I should never make you understand. But she *was* unhappy, Henrietta, truly she was. You may think the less of her on that account, but the fact remains, it was not a happy match for her.'

'Not for either of them.' If only she could keep her pulse as steady as her voice.

'My God, no. You are in the right of it there. I suppose your father was dazzled by her, fresh back from India as he was, and I am afraid she did not give him time to know her better. It was, from a worldly point of view, an admirable match for her.'

'And I collect that she might have had some difficulty in finding so good a one again.'

'It is true, of course. Her separation from Lord Beaufrage had been public knowledge. That was why I had urged her so strongly to marry me.'

'But she still thought she could do better for herself?'

'I am afraid you could put it that way. And as it proved, she was right — in worldly terms at least. But I do not believe they were ever happy together. Your father, as you know, plunged at once into politics, and was soon high up in the councils of the Tory Party. Lavinia, for her part, had never cared much for politics, and, worse still, her friends were all Whigs. I am afraid your father soon learned that it was best not to talk to her about what most interested him. And what remained? He cared no more for her balls and masquerades than she did for his affairs of state. By the time I came home they had agreed to go their own ways.'

'But she had not given him an heir.' Henrietta had learned enough of the conventions of London society to know how important this was.

'Nor ever will,' said Rivers. 'But that — no, damme, we'll not talk of that. Only, believe me, you cannot accuse me more bitterly than I have done myself. And when I think that it was through me that she met him —'

'Through you?'

'Yes, did you not know? When he came back to London, the talk of the day, Lady Beaufrage sought him out for my sake. I was his ward, remember.'

'Oh.' It was all she could say.

'Yes. It all started with that.'

Henrietta thought for a moment, then: 'One has to admit that she is a very capable woman. And still you loved her?' She could not resist the question.

'I was besotted with her. I promised to tell you the truth and I will do so. She is — do not ask me to describe what she is. Only believe that I have learnt my lesson now, most bitterly.'

'And why should I believe that?'

'Only because it is true. That first time I saw you, on the Plymouth road, I was shaken, I cannot tell you how much. You talked to me, so frankly, so freely, about yourself, your life, your hopes. And they were such *true* hopes. They were real: no schemings, no connivings, no plots. It was like a breath of fresh air, of the spring itself, to make me realise in what a false and sordid atmosphere I had been living. On the boat, afterwards, beating up and down the Channel, I dreamed only of you, of how we might meet again, of how I might make myself worthy of you. Oh, I was to do such things. I would join Wellington; cover myself with glory; return with I do not know how many eagles, and win your hand like a hero of old.'

'It has hardly worked out that way.'

'As if you needed to remind me! Instead, I became ill on that

cursed, fever-stricken tub of a boat, and had to return, in-
gloriously, a sick man. And still all might have been well. That
night when I met you, walking, alone, on the road to Marchmont, I thought fate was on my side at last. We were destined
for each other.' His hand was moving gently now, warmly, just
inside the neckline of her dress, as if it, too, were speaking,
pleading with her.

'And what went wrong?' It was an effort to keep her voice
cool.

'Why, everything! Oh, I was a fool, a coward, a craven. Tell
me, if I had asked you to marry me, that night in the moonlight, would you have said yes?'

Why deny it? 'Of course I would,' she said.

His hand bruised her shoulder. 'Oh, God, I thought so. But,
fool that I was, I thought I must wait, must make all straight
with Lady Marchmont before I was free to speak to you. And
in the meantime —' He paused, at a loss for words.

'In the meantime it all began again. Is that what you would
say?' Gently, reluctantly, she pulled away from him.

'Curse me, yes. She was so pleased to see me, so concerned
over my health. I told her about you: our meeting, what I felt.
She was delighted, or pretended to be. It would all arrange
itself. She would be my spokesman with your father, but in the
meantime she was so lonely, so unhappy, she had missed me so
much ... But I swear to you, Henrietta, that of this plan of
hers, this idea of using you as a screen for a continuing liaison
with me, of that, so help me God, I had no idea. When she
spoke so suddenly to your father the other night, I merely
thought that, driven into a corner, she was protecting herself as
best she might. I could not blame her; I know what he is like
when he is roused, and although he has had his suspicions this
long time past, he had never —' He faltered.

'Never seen them proved before.'

'No. And, Henrietta, for his sake, not for ours, he never
must. He is a proud man; too proud to bear it. Suspicion is one
thing; proof might kill him.'

'I believe you,' Henrietta said. 'I only wish you had thought
of it sooner.'

'Oh, God, do you not think I do too? But you must understand. I did not know him. To me he was merely the unloving
figure behind Lavinia, the cruel, the captious, the jealous husband.'

'That was what she told you?'

'Of course. When he was kind to me, as, at first, he often was, I thought it was but his pride, his sense of duty. He would not show to his ward the harsh side he displayed to his wife. It was only when I saw him with you, Henrietta, that I realised how much I had been mistaken in him.'

'Or misled?'

'Yes, if you like, misled. But do not blame poor Lavinia too harshly; you must realise that she did not understand what she was doing.'

'Did she not?'

'Poor girl, how could she? Her father, you must know, was a timeserving country parson. Her mother — well, the less said about her the better. She made her husband's fortune by marrying him, and taught her child nothing but the principles of expediency on which she had always acted. With such parents, how could poor Lavinia be other than what she is?'

'Poor Lavinia,' Henrietta said reflectively. 'Well, sir, I have listened to you now, very patiently, you must admit, and for longer than I intended, and you have said nothing to dissuade me from giving you back this ring. Please, let us not speak of it further. I cannot pretend I have not cared for you. I will not pretend I am not suffering. But there is nothing, in this world, for us. We must part, and the sooner it is over the better.'

But once again he refused to take the ring. 'Henrietta, have you understood me so little? If you will not for my sake, I beg you to think a little of your father. Imagine what he will feel if he hears, far away as he will be, that our engagement is at an end. Think what he will suffer, for himself as well as for you.'

The hand that held out the ring sank to her lap and she gazed at him, horror-struck. 'I had not thought . . .'

'Then think now. It will be confirmation of all his worst fears.'

'And it will be true,' Henrietta said austerely, as she rose to leave him.

'Oh — truth . . .' His hand on hers detained her. 'Have you not yet been long enough in this world, Henrietta, to know that the greatest truth may still be the greatest selfishness? Stop thinking, for a moment, of yourself, and think of him. For his sake, only, I beg you will continue publicly engaged to me until he returns from Russia. I will be not trouble to you, I promise, in the meantime. I have my orders at last. I had been waiting the opportunity to tell you. I leave tomorrow for London. The next day, I hope, I shall be on my way to Spain. If I can get myself killed — gloriously if possible — in the coming campaign, I promise you I will do so. If not, at your leisure, when your father is returned, you may jilt me how you please. But for now, for all our sakes, keep my ring, Henrietta.'

She was crying too much to speak. Silently, his handkerchief to her eyes, she let him put the ring back on her finger and kiss her hand. Then, with a smothered exclamation, he pulled her to him and his lips sought hers; pleading, demanding, commanding. She could not help it. For a moment, she was all his, her lips answering him, her whole body shuddering in helpless ecstasy towards him. Then, memory returned. Half an hour ago he had held Lady Marchmont thus.

She pulled away. 'Good-bye, Mr. Rivers.' Half blinded with tears, she left him.

CHAPTER TEN

Alone, at last, in the sanctuary of her room, Henrietta sat for a while, quite still, hands close folded in her lap, defying the tears to fall. It was all too horrible for their easy solace. Charles Rivers and Lady Marchmont. Lady Marchmont and Charles Rivers. It had been there all the time, so obvious that she could not see it. Such an easy dupe as she had been; led by the nose; a convenient screen for their amours. How could she not have guessed? And yet, how could she have imagined anything so sordid? And, all the time, throbbing below her own pain and shame, exacerbating them almost beyond endurance, was her anguish for her father.

As she sat there, hating herself, she could hear carriages rolling away down the drive. Now that Lord Marchmont had gone, his political friends were leaving too. No wonder they did not stay; no wonder they tended not to bring their wives and daughters. How much did her father know? How much suspect? Something, of course. Why else had he returned home so unexpectedly only the other night and thus precipitated her disastrous engagement. If only she could hurry after him, catch him before he left, tell him the whole wretched story and beg him to take her with him, away from it all.

She could not do it to him. He had already refused, on good grounds, to take her with him. Nothing she said would change him now; it would merely mean that he went on his dangerous mission haunted equally by anxiety for her and by rage with his wife. It was all misery, all wretchedness together, and, in many ways, the worst of all was that try how she would she could not quite bring herself to hate Charles Rivers. When she reminded herself of how he had betrayed her, of how, even today, he had pretended to set her father on his way and then crept back to keep his shameful assignation with Lady Marchmont, she could not help remembering the warm pleading of his arm around her, the intoxication of his kiss. Admitting, now, that she had loved him at first sight, she could not resist the seductive argument that it must have been mutual. 'Whoever loved that loved not at first sight?'

He had flung it at her that he would do his best to get himself killed. She could not bear it; could not imagine facing the news, and her own responsibility for it. If it happened, she would never forgive herself. So — what to do? Having abandoned the thought of writing to her father, she began instead to compose a letter to Charles Rivers and found it just as impossible. The fifth illegible and much-crossed sheet had just joined its fellows in her waste-paper basket when a little scratching on her door heralded Lady Marchmont.

She was pale, but composed. 'I know.' She recognised Henrietta's instinctive recoil. 'You do not wish to speak to me; nor do I blame you, but, Henrietta, we must talk. You must do something, or they will fight.'

'Fight?' But she saw it at once. How could she have been so stupid? Plunged in her own private hell, she had not thought of this hazard. Cedric had been angry enough for anything, and Charles — Charles had promised to get himself killed. Horrible. And horrible, too, to remember that he had once told her he had his reasons for not fighting Cedric Beaufrage. Now she knew all too well what they were. 'I think you will have to stop them,' she said.

'I cannot. Charles refuses to speak to me, and Cedric is neither to hold nor to bind. Everyone is gone but the Miss Giddys, and they are no help! I don't care what you do,

Henrietta, or how you do it, but something must be done if you do not wish to have their blood on your hands.' And then, as Henrietta still sat mute. 'Oh, God, I wish my husband was here! He would not sit, consulting his own pride, when my son's life was at stake.'

'Pride?' Was it true? Was she really so far gone in self-pity? Or — was not this the excuse she needed for doing what she wanted to do anyway? 'Where are they?' she asked.

'Oh, God bless you, Henrietta! Cedric is in the billiard room. Charles is in the study, writing a letter. To you, I have no doubt. Henrietta —'

'No. We will not discuss it. Any of it. Now, or ever. Not if I am to continue in the same house as you, and, for my father's sake, I see that I must. Have I your promise?'

'Yes. Anything! Only, hurry, Henrietta. I think they are only waiting for the changing bell to ring and the Miss Giddy's to go upstairs, and then it will happen, somehow . . . anyhow.'

'Then you had best go down and keep Cedric company until I have changed and can relieve you,' said Henrietta drily. 'They will hardly quarrel in front of one or the other of us.'

'I pray God they won't. But, later, over their wine . . . They will be alone.'

'Yes.' It was the obvious time. An 'accident' with a glass of wine, a word, a blow, a challenge, and an early morning meeting from which only one would return, and he to face exile. 'I will speak to Charles,' said Henrietta.

She found him in the study, with the same sort of pile of scribbled paper beside him that she had left in her own room. 'Henrietta!' He jumped to his feet at sight of her and came forward eagerly. 'I had not hoped . . . I have been trying to write to you. This is like you; this is goodness indeed. Can I . . . Henrietta, may I hope?'

It was incredibly more difficult than she had imagined. 'No . . .' She hesitated. 'I do not know. Nothing now. Mr. Rivers, I am come to you on Lady Marchmont's entreaty. She is afraid . . . afraid of what you and Lord Beaufrage may do.'

'And she had the impudence to come to you!'

'She says you will not speak to her.' Impossible not to find this heart-warming. Impossible, too, not to hate herself for doing so.

'How can I! She who has ruined all my hopes of happiness with her wiles. Henrietta, only give me a breath, the merest hint of hope! Tell me that I may come back to you in a year . . . in two years . . . when this war is over. I will do anything . . . anything you say.'

She stood silent, looking up at him, twisting his ring on her finger. 'I cannot,' she said at last. 'Not now. Not yet. Perhaps not ever. How can I, now, so soon, after such a — ' She paused, at a loss for words. And then, as his hand closed over hers. 'No! Not that way, Charles.' She pulled away from him. 'I must think; I must recover; try to see my way. Only, Charles, promise me you'll do nothing desperate. Not now . . . not later?'

'I promise.' He stood there, very straight, the blue eyes seeming to read her heart. 'You're right, Henrietta. I have no right, after what has passed, to ask you for more than the pretense of an engagement, for your father's sake, but whatever you may feel, you cannot prevent me from looking on myself as engaged to you. Whatever happens, I am your man. And, one other thing: You'll let me write to you? Please? After all, it would be — expected.'

'And to her?' She could not help it.

'No!' Explosively. 'To you; for you only. Damnation!' The study door had opened behind her.

'Oh, my gracious me.' The oldest Miss Giddy started dramatically at sight of them. 'What have I interrupted! How could I be so wanting in tact? But it is for dear Fanny,' she explained as she advanced into the room. 'The second volume of *The Wanderer*. Dear Madame d'Arblay. Such an improving writer, even if her husband is French. Dear Lady Marchmont said it was in here; on the desk, she thought. My goodness, what a monstrous deal of paper you have used, dear Mr. Rivers. You must have been so occupied' — here an arch look for Henrietta — 'that you quite failed to hear the changing bell. It will be dinner time in ten minutes.'

'Thank you for reminding me, Miss Giddy.'

She was behind him now, and for a moment his eyes met Henrietta's in the old, shared amusement. 'I think you will find your volume here.' He moved swiftly between her and the desk before she could lay her birdlike hands upon her papers. 'You may rely on me,' he told Henrietta across her. 'Always.'

'So gallant.' Miss Giddy took the book. 'So romantic.' As he left them. 'So mysterious.' Hopefully.

'So nearly dinner time,' said Henrietta, and made a life-long enemy.

Cedric did not appear at dinner, his mother reporting, with a meaning smile for Henrietta, that he had decided to ride over and dine with a friend beyond Cumber. So, after all, Henrietta thought, making a pretence at eating, that scene with Charles Rivers had been unnecessary. How like Lady Marchmont to have double-ensured herself against disaster. And yet, she could not but be grateful to her. Indecisive though it had been, and unsatisfactory in its interrupted conclusion, the brief scene with Charles had left her feeling less wretched than she would have believed possible in the disaster of the morning.

They had no further chance to speak alone together before he left. The Miss Giddys saw to that. As soon as one of them decided that the poor young things must be left to their farewells, and tiptoed knowingly from the room, another would appear, as if by black magic. Rivers seized one brief opportunity to mutter: 'I have told no one of what has passed. Do not you either.' His emphasis meant Lady Marchmont. Henrietta was grateful, and promised. Knowledge of their feigned engagement at least they shared alone. Lady Marchmont, she could see, was puzzled, and this, too, was some meagre, painful satisfaction.

Her stepmother must inevitably have expected the engagement to be broken off; to find it apparently continuing was a shock to her, and many times afterwards Henrietta was to see her walking warily round the subject, trying tentatively this way and that to peer through the mask of her reserve. The strain of this was particularly evident when one of Rivers' letters arrived for Henrietta. In each, he carefully sent his kind regards to Lady Marchmont, as if to emphasise the fact that he did not write to her. Each one was signed, simply, 'Your Charles.' Beyond this, he did not plead with her, nor even refer to their pretence engagement, and she was grateful to him. Instead, he wrote entertaining, diary letters, making light of the dangers of the campaign, and stressing absurd details of his daily life: the wolf hunt when the hounds followed a cart-load of salt fish; the dressing down Lord Wellington had given one of his officers who put up an umbrella on the field of battle. Wellington was his constant theme, and combined with his note of admiration was the unmistakable one of ambition. 'I mean to make myself noticed,' he wrote, and Henrietta sighed with relief. They were not the words of a man who meant to get killed.

In his first letter, he had begged for an answer. 'I shall indulge myself by writing whenever I can; may I hope for an occasional word from you?' She was glad to think it within the terms of their agreement, and worked hard to compose answers that should tell him everything, and nothing. She told him of the autumn election and subsequent state opening of Parliament; she reported the Miss Giddys' gossip about the Prince Regent and his impossible wife. Where he signed himself 'Your Charles,' she replied with 'Yours, Henrietta.' Each letter was draughted and redraughted many times before it was finally fair-copied and sent; it was so hard to keep her anxiety for him from creeping in. The weather at the siege of Burgos was bad, he had told her; did he take proper care of himself? The question was angrily scratched out and a flippant comment substituted.

Her letters to her father were hardly easier to write, for in them she must keep up the pretence of her happy engagement. Her comfort was that in them at least she could talk freely about how much she missed Rivers, and show some of her loneliness and misery, while disguising their true reason. She longed for and yet dreaded her father's return, for how, to his face, would she be able to keep up a pretence of happiness? But time passed and the question did not arise. His letters came from further and further afield, and at last from St. Petersburg where he described the bitter winter, the problems of housekeeping in Russia the news of Bonaparte's disastrous retreat from Moscow. He was soon on the best of terms with the Czar and his ministers; they had urged him to join them in their forthcoming march against France and he had seen nothing for it but to agree. Lord Liverpool, meeting Henrietta at the opening of the new theatre in Drury Lane, took her aside to tell her how delighted Government was with what her father was achieving. This was her happiest moment in a dark and gloomy winter.

Public misfortunes exacerbated her private sorrow. After the triumphant news of Wellington's entry into Madrid came the damper of his retreat. The long, unsatisfactory and at last unsuccessful siege of Burgos roused her anxieties for Rivers, and it was small satisfaction to her that he was mentioned in despatches for his gallantry on the occasion. In her heart of hearts, she blamed herself for this. Was he after all fulfilling his promise to her and trying to get himself killed? This time, it was true, he had come off without a scratch, but what of the future? Her bedroom fire, those cold winter nights, consumed many an attempt at a letter which should at the same time convey her complete unconcern for his safety, and beg him to take care of himself for her sake.

For the public, good news from America was some counterbalance to failure in Spain, but for Henrietta it was the last straw. How could she rejoice in the news of Wadsworth and Hull's surrender to the Canadians, or, worse still, at the burning of Niagara? A school friend of hers had married a minister in Niagara. What would her fate have been? Unfortunately, she met the Miss Giddys at the opera when the news was still fresh and sore in her mind. They began by offering their congratulations on Rivers' gallant conduct.

'You must be very proud,' said Miss Giddy.

'But somewhat concerned,' added Miss Letitia.

'Mr. Rivers should remember,' put in Miss Patricia, 'that he has more than himself to consider. Such foolhardy daring is very well in a single man.' And then, seeing Henrietta's heightened colour, she changed the subject. 'What splendid news from America, is it not?'

'You find the burning of a peaceful town splendid?'

'I most certainly do.' Miss Letitia took up the challenge. 'Those upstart colonials must be taught a lesson, and the sharper the better.'

Henrietta always saw red at this use of the word 'colonial'. 'The lesson does not seem to be succeeding so well by sea,' she said.

Miss Giddy bridled. 'You refer to our recent losses, I collect. I have it on the best authority that they are due entirely to the mistaken gallantry of our captains. Dear Mr. Croker tells me that what the Americans call a frigate is practically a ship of the line. Naturally ours are no match for them, and they are to be instructed to keep clear of them in future.'

'I take it,' said Henrietta drily, 'that you do not find it entirely sporting of the Americans to have better ships than yours.'

'Hoity-toity, Miss Marchmont.' Miss Giddy lost her temper. 'It is as well your father is not here to listen to you talking so like a rebel. But I hear our carriage announced. Come, Letitia, come, Patricia.' And taking an arm of each, she swept them away with the curtest of farewell nods for Henrietta.

Conscience-stricken at what she had let herself be teased into saying, Henrietta derived little consolation from the fact that Lady Marchmont was close beside her and had heard the whole exchange. One of the worst things about that dismal winter was the fact that she had to go on living with Lady Marchmont. Indeed, in the black depression of a foggy February, she seriously began to consider defying the proprieties and setting up her own establishment. But Mr. Brummel, to whom she mentioned this project one night, disposed of it effectively and, oddly enough, on lines very similar to Rivers'. 'What?' he said, 'and have your father ruin his career by hurrying home to save your name for you?'

It was unanswerable. So Henrietta and her stepmother lived on together in a state of uneasy truce. Except when Rivers' letters arrived, they never mentioned him, nor, though Henrietta suspected that Lady Marchmont would have rather enjoyed an hysterical scene about it, had either she or Cedric ever referred to that fatal day at Marchmont. She and Henrietta made the minimal necessary public appearances together. For the rest, they lived in the same house as strangers. And Henrietta had grown sick of society. If she rode in the park, it was to see Lady Marchmont surrounded by her latest crowd of young officers on too long leave from Spain. If she went out in the evening, it again meant accompanying her stepmother, watching her flirt, and having all too ample time, herself, to reflect on the unhappy position of an engaged young lady without her fiancé, compared to that of a married woman without her husband. Lady Marchmont paid only the merest lip service to the idea that she missed her husband. It was obvious that she missed him very pleasantly. Henrietta, on the other hand, finding herself suddenly without the throng of charming fortune hunters who had been wont to hang on her every word and vie with each other for her favours, felt that she had the worst of all possible worlds. The fact of her engagement put her on the shelf, and only she knew what a bitter pretence it was.

No, society was no pleasure to her that winter, and, fleeing from it, she began to spend more and more time with Miss Gilbert in Russell Square, or, better still, with her sister Patience at her school in Shrovebridge. Henrietta had always loved children, and now, with all her plans for happiness in dust about her, often thought that when her father returned she would persuade him to let her go into partnership with Miss Patience Gilbert. But time passed and still he did not return. Winter yielded to her first English spring, the grass was green again in Hyde Park and primroses bloomed in Kensington Gardens. Lambs frolicked beside their mothers in the Green Park and lovers walked arm in arm under its trees. But for Henrietta life stood still. Her father wrote from Berlin now. The Russians had taken the city in March, and he was hopeful of an early march against France. Perhaps, he said, the autumn would see him home.

It seemed centuries off to Henrietta, reading his letter in the privacy of her bedroom while the birds built under the eaves and spring rain pattered against the window. And meanwhile the London season had begun. Each morning the Row was fuller of riders showing themselves on their return to town, comparing notes on the winter, the hunting, and, of course, the news. The Miss Giddys had returned in full tide of volubility from the country house where they had succeeded in planting themselves for the winter, and renewed a systematic teasing of Henrietta, who was at a loss to understand what made them dislike her so. She was not wise enough yet in the ways of the world to realise that they merely expressed the dislike that their patroness, Lady Marchmont, concealed so skilfully.

On the surface, Lady Marchmont was all smiles as usual, but with the opening of the season, her demands on Henrietta began to increase. Through the long, dull winter, she had seemed glad enough to go her own way and let Henrietta go hers, but now, as the invitations began to pile up once more on the table in the hall, she began to press Henrietta to accompany her. And to make matters worse, Cedric had just returned from a round of hunting visits and seemed inclined to recommence his pursuit of Henrietta. Suddenly, one morning, it was all more than she could bear.

Lady Marchmont had looked up with a sigh of satisfaction from her letters. 'Ah,' she said, 'the invitation to Lady Liverpool's dinner. I had begun to fear that she had forgotten us. The Miss Giddys had their cards these three days past. Cedric, you will not be able to go to Brighton tomorrow. We must have your escort to Combe Wood on Friday. I do not intend to be lost and dragged in the mud like Madame de Staël. But what will you wear, Henrietta? You have not had a new gown this age. Had you not best send for Madame Bégué: The new sleeve should suit you to a marvel.'

Henrietta looked up from her embroidery. 'I thank you, ma'am, but I believe I will not go.'

'Not go? What foolishness is this? Not go to Lord Liverpool's! Truly, Henrietta, sometimes you betray your upbringing. These country notions may do well enough in Boston, but I hope that now you are in London you will conduct yourself with more propriety. To refuse the First Minister, when your father is presently engaged on a dangerous mission for him! How do you think that will look in the eyes of the world? Indeed, I have been meaning to speak to you on this very subject for some time past. Miss Giddy, who is a true friend to us all, gave me the hint only the other day. There is beginning to be talk, Henrietta, about these odd notions of yours. Cedric tells me they call you The Rebel now at White's — and not kindly, either. The world is quick to sense a slight, and you have been absent from too many occasions of late. To cut Lady Porminster's rout for no better reason than a school prizegiving: It was bound to cause comment, and, which is what I most complain of, the gossip is as unfavourable to me as to you. Dear Miss Giddy warned me in no uncertain terms: the world is saying that you and I have quarrelled. It will be in the scandal sheets soon if you do not look about you, and then how long do you think it will be before it reaches your father — and Charles? I do not think that you and I can afford to have it said we are not friends, my dear. I am sure it is very high-minded of you to wish to live like a recluse while Charles is away, but, I must tell you, it is not at all the thing. Do you see Lady Wellington pining at home? Or me, for the matter of that? Who knows what I suffer in your father's absence? But I put a brave face on it for the world, and the world respects me for it. No, no, I shall send Lady Liverpool a grateful acceptance on your behalf as well as on my own, and you had best send for Madame Bégué at once. That muslin you wore to Lady Harrowby's last week was scarce fit to be seen.'

And with this clincher, she hurried out to the park, to conceal, as Henrietta bitterly thought, her grief at her husband's prolonged absence by an animated flirtation with four young men at once. Nevertheless, she left Henrietta with much to think about. For all its selfishness, there had been an obvious grain of truth in what she had said. It could not help but be damaging to Lord Marchmont to have his daughter gossiped about in such terms. With a heavy heart, Henrietta decided that she had best pocket her pride and accompany her stepmother to Almack's that night to see if the world was indeed so little her friend.

Lady Marchmont's congratulations on this decision were hard to bear, and a cool reception from Mr. Willis, the guardian of the rooms, was disconcerting, but it was the Miss Giddys who showed her how the land lay. She found them on a sofa, drinking lemonade.

The eldest inclined her head slightly: 'Dear Miss Marchmont,' she said, without conviction.

'You are quite a stranger,' said Miss Letitia.

'Positively a hermit,' added Miss Patricia.

'You find our amusements trivial, I collect,' said Miss Giddy. 'But I see dear Lady Marchmont. Come, Letitia, come, Patricia, we must pay our respects to our friend.' And with a whisper of muslins they rose and left her.

Digesting this slight, Henrietta looked up with a wry smile and caught the eye of a young man who was gazing at her steadily from the other side of the room. For a moment, her heart stood still. That head held high, those piercing blue eyes — it was Rivers. But, no, she looked again. Of course it was not. This man, who was now making his way towards her through the crowd, was slighter, younger, darker than Rivers, his carriage less assured, but his eyes as formidable.

'Miss Marchmont?' He had reached her side. 'I am taking a great liberty in making myself known to you like this. Will you forgive me?'

'Of course.' She held out her hand to him warmly. 'And there is no need for you to introduce yourself. I knew you the minute I saw you. You must be Mr. Rivers' brother, Simon. He never told me you and he were so alike.'

Simon Rivers laughed. 'It flatters me to have you say so, Miss Marchmont, for you must know that I have always been the runt of our family. To have Charles to live up to is quite a task for a younger brother.' It was lightly spoken, yet she was aware of feeling behind it as he changed the subject. 'I have been lamentably remiss in paying you my respects upon the happy occasion of your engagement, but, as perhaps you will have heard, I have been a prisoner of the universities.'

'Yes, you have been at St. Andrews, have you not, and are now at Oxford?'

'Exactly. Charles is to be a general and I am to be a bishop. My grandfather has it all planned.' No mistaking the bitterness in his voice now. 'But, Miss Marchmont' — again he changed the subject, colouring as he went on — 'I am to speak to you, if you will permit it, like a brother, and claim a brother's privilege to defend you from the slanders I have been hearing. Since Charles is away, you must allow me the right.'

'Oh dear.' Henrietta sighed. 'So you have heard them too? Was that why you were looking so monstrous angry when you first approached me?'

'It was indeed. And now, with your good leave, I will return to Mr. Peveril and Mr. Stanmore and make them eat their words.'

'Mr. Peveril and Mr. Stanmore, was it?' They were two of her stepmother's most devoted slaves. 'What were they saying, pray? Do not try to spare my feelings; I am beyond that.'

'Had you thought them your friends? No, I will not tell you what they were saying; it is not of the slightest importance. But I promise you I will make them sorry that they spoke.'

'Mr. Rivers — Simon — I beg you will do no such thing. You have spoken to me, and I thank you for it, like a brother; let me answer you as frankly. Your championship warms my heart, but do you not see that to have you fighting on my behalf would only make the talk about me ten thousand times worse? And, besides, what about your chances of a mitre?'

He laughed. 'You could not think of an argument, Miss Marchmont, that would more encourage me to fight. And as for the rumours, they are intolerably bad enough already. I'll not allow it: my brother's future wife to be called a traitor and I to stand by and do nothing. No, I am your very humble servant, ma'am, and will do myself the honour of calling on you tomorrow with their apologies.'

'Mr. Rivers, I beg of you . . .' As she put her restraining hand on his arm she noticed a neat figure approaching them. 'Mr. Brummel.' She greeted him with a sigh of relief. 'The very person. I beg you will persuade Mr. Rivers he can do me no good by fighting on my behalf.'

Mr. Brummel paused and bowed. 'My dear Miss Marchmont, and, I collect, Mr. Rivers? You are presenting a very dramatic scene for the world's delectation. Surely, Mr. Rivers, you were not thinking of offering a challenge *here*?'

Henrietta dropped her hand from Simon Rivers' arm, while he coloured, his impetus lost. 'I . . . I had quite forgot.'

'Then you had best recollect yourself,' said Mr. Brummel. 'Nothing could do you — or for that matter Miss Marchmont — more harm than a challenge on her behalf issued in these rooms. And if you are thinking of seeking out your adversary elsewhere, I beg you will think again. Miss Marchmont is in the right of it. This is a matter for more delicate weapons than swords or pistols. Presently, you may dance with her, which, I collect, will be very much more to the question than all your untidy early-morning heroics. But first, pray cool your valour with a turn about the room, while I give Miss Marchmont a scold.'

Simon Rivers coloured more deeply than ever, bowed to Henrietta, and left them as Mr. Brummel took her arm and continued: 'I am but this morning returned to town and what do I find is the latest *on dit*? Why, that my protégée, Miss Marchmont, is a rebel, a traitor, and I do not know what else besides. I do not like it, Miss Marchmont. It is an affront to me — to Brummel.'

She laughed. 'I do not like it either, Mr. Brummel, but what am I to do about it? I have been foolish, I admit, and, I suppose, I have enemies. I am lucky to have so good a friend.' And then, as he bowed his thanks for the compliment: 'But come, advise me, I beg. What must I do to make my peace with society?'

He smiled. 'You might begin by taking another turn about the room with me. I can see the Miss Giddys changing their minds already. And then, perhaps, some amiable eccentricity? A pet monkey perhaps? A tame bird? Carried everywhere on the wrist?'

She made a face. 'Dear Mr. Brummel, must I?'

'Not if it appals you so. But, stay — I have a better idea. What would you say to a new friend?'

'I should like one of all things.'

'Good. I will make you known to her straightaway. For I believe that you have not met Miss Jenkinson?'

'Miss Jenkinson? I do not recall her. Is she, perhaps, some connection of Lord Liverpool's?'

'He calls her cousin. She is rich, Miss Marchmont, much,

much richer than you are like to be. She is but recently come to town, on the providential death, I collect, of her manu-facturing parents in — I cannot recall and it does not signify, some metropolis of the north: Birmingham, Manchester — it makes no difference. She stays with her newfound cousin, Lady Liverpool, and the world is at her golden feet. Had you not noticed that you had lost all your lovers?'

'I have missed them very pleasantly.' But for the first time it occurred to her that not even Cedric had asked her hand for the dance tonight. She saw him now, at the far side of the room, bending solicitously over a short, buxom girl with a weather-beaten face and a dusting of freckles down her nose.

Mr. Brummel had seen them too. 'Lord Beaufrage has been paying her his court these three weeks past. They are betting heavily on his chances at White's.'

'And she is to be my friend?'

'If you will be ruled by me. I have no doubt that she eats cabbage and talks about taking tea, but she is all the rage, and if you will not have a monkey, then it must be Miss Jenkinson.' And so saying, he led her across the room to where Cedric was apparently trying to persuade the new heiress to dance with him. She laughed a great good-natured laugh as they ap-proached, and rapped him over the knuckles with her fan.

'You think because I talk somewhat broad,' she said, 'that my wits are all abroad too.' There was indeed more than a hint of the Midlands in her voice. 'But flatter away, Lord Beau-frage,' she continued, 'you do it purely and I adore it.'

'Ah, Miss Jenkinson,' said Cedric, who had his back to Brum-mel and Henrietta, 'if you could but see my heart.'

'On the contrary,' she said, 'I rather think I see your stepsister. Mr. Brummel, you are my true friend, you are going to make me known to Miss Marchmont at last. Miss March-mont, you are to forgive me for stealing something of your thunder. You can see that I am plain and freckled, your rival only in fortune. If you will but forgive me for that, I promise in my turn to forgive you your beauty, which is very much more handsome of me, I can tell you, and we shall be friends and laugh at Lord Beaufrage together.'

Henrietta could not help a smile at this odd speech. 'With all my heart,' she said.

'Good,' Miss Jenkinson said approvingly. 'And we will begin by sending Lord Beaufrage away. Mr. Brummel, I see, has had the sense to go without being bidden, but you, my lord, will be so good as to fetch us some lemonade. I am as dry as the Sahara and almost as hot. And,' she added to Henrietta as Cedric bowed and left them, 'if my mama could but have seen me ordering a lord about like that she would have fainted with shock — as indeed she did often enough at me and my papa both, for what with my ideas and his language, she had but a sad life of it, poor thing.'

'Your ideas?' said Henrietta, amused despite herself. 'And what were they, if I may ask?'

'You may ask me anything, dear Miss Marchmont. I have been longing this age to meet you, and I mean it when I say I intend we shall be friends. I can see you have heard nothing about me — and why should you have? But I know great plenty about you, and all I have heard I have liked. You are weary of society, are you not, and want to live in the country and run a school? Well, I have lived in the country, *and* run a school, and a very good one too, and very happy I was until dear Papa made so shocking much money out of this war and I had to turn young lady to please him. And now he has died and left me to my prunes and prisms, and if you will but try to teach me how to behave like a young lady, I will tell you a thing or two about schools. But here comes Lord Beaufrage. Will you dance with him, or shall I?'

Henrietta laughed. 'I think you had best.'

'Very well. And here is that delightful young Mr. Rivers making sheep's eyes at you, so let us go down the dance together. For I tell you' — she took Henrietta's hand and drew her out to the centre of the room where the set was forming — 'I am to be your champion now, and we'll have no more gossip.' And then, as Henrietta coloured angrily 'Now, pray, do not fly out at me. We are to be friends, remember, and you must just get used to my free tongue and how it runs away with me. Come, love, kiss and make up, if only to make the old tabbies stare.'

And indeed as she laughed and complied, Henrietta was aware of the Miss Giddys goggling at them with all their eyes. After that, what had begun so gloomily proved a happy evening indeed. Though not such a polished man of the world as his elder brother, Simon Rivers surprised Henrietta by proving a better dancer and an admirably considerate companion. Miss Jenkinson used her privilege as the toast of the day to keep the four of them together for much of the evening and they dined, danced and supped together. When at last Simon Rivers handed her into the carriage in the cool first light of morning, Henrietta told herself she had forgotten what it was like to be so simply happy.

Waking late next day, she was instantly aware of a new brightness about life. It was a heartwarming thing to have made two such friends as Miss Jenkinson and Charles's brother in one evening. Rising at once, she dressed with unusual care and found various reasons for staying at home as long as possible. Surely Simon Rivers would call upon her this morning, though not, of course, with news of a duel. But she might have spared herself the trouble. He never came. No doubt, she told herself wryly, he had had quite enough of her last night. Now that he was honourably excused from flying to her defence, he had gone back to Oxford and forgotten all about her.

She did, however, receive a call from Sally Jenkinson, who came, as she cheerfully announced, to cement their friendship and to engage Henrietta, her stepmother and Cedric to remain at Coombe House for the week-end after Lady Liverpool's party. All three accepted readily; Henrietta with honest pleasure, for she found herself increasingly drawn to forthright Sally; Lady Marchmont and her son with one of their quick, silently exchanged glances.

The dinner itself was like all the dinners Henrietta had sat through: formal, dull and incredibly long, but she derived considerable amusement, later, when the gentlemen had rejoined the ladies, from watching the skill with which Cedric shared his attentions between Miss Jenkinson and herself. The heiress was in tearing spirits. This was, she confided to Henrietta, the first big dinner Lady Liverpool had given since she had come to live with them.

'It is vastly tedious, is it not? I had rather hear a parcel of brummagem businessmen talking cotton than all this gossip about the princess and her lovers. And, talking of lovers, what do you think of mine? Shall I have Lord Beaufrage — and you for a sister? It is a mighty inducement, I can tell you. But, come, advise me, I beg, for by all the signs he will make me an offer before the week-end is over.'

Henrietta laughed and did her best to evade the issue, but Miss Jenkinson was bent on having an answer. 'No, no, you shall not dodge me so. I know he is your brother, but he has not been so for long. And besides, if you cannot speak up for him, who will? To deal plainly with you, what I most want is to know the extent of his debts. Are they as bottomless as I have heard said? Lord knows I am resigned to having to pay something for a title, for who would marry me but for my money and who would want it if he were not in Queer Street? I do not mind debts so much: It is the habit of debt that I fear. Do you think your brother has it?'

To Henrietta's relief, they were interrupted by Cedric himself before she had time to try for an answer. He stayed with them until candles were brought, turning the pages of her music for Henrietta when she played, and admiring Miss Jenkinson when she sang. There was no more private talk that night.

## CHAPTER ELEVEN

The younger members of the party rode out into Richmond Park next morning and Henrietta was surprised to find herself once more the main object of Cedric's attention, but somewhat less than flattered when he lost no time in leading the conversation first to the subject of his financial embroilment, and then, by an all too logical connection, to Sally Jenkinson.

'Tell me,' he said, reining in his horse to a walking pace as they passed the Pen Ponds, 'as my sister, what chance do you think I have with the heiress?'

Somewhat taken aback by this direct question, Henrietta nonetheless answered him with tempered encouragement, but warned him of her new friend's feelings on the subject of debt.

He pulled a wry face. 'It is all very well for you to preach, Henrietta. You do not know what it is to be a young man of fortune — without the fortune. You are well enough, with your expectations, your allowance from your father, your living free, and no calls upon you. I wager you have the whole of your last quarter's money untouched to this day.'

'Well, not quite.' Henrietta began to wonder just where the

conversation was leading. And, looking up, she saw that the rest of the party had already vanished into the wood at the top of the hill. She made as if to spur on her horse and catch them up, but Cedric leaned over and put a hand on her reins.

'One moment, Henrietta. I have a favour to ask of you. Or, to be exact, it is on my mother's behalf.'

'For Lady Marchmont?' Henrietta did not try to conceal her surprise.

'Well, yes, in a manner of speaking for her. It is a debt — a debt of honour, you might call it — which must be paid. And she and I, alas, are both penniless. We must throw ourselves on your mercy.'

'But' — she looked around her, puzzled, at the peaceful park with its grazing deer — 'why now? Why today?'

'Because it is urgent. It has been left too long. It is but to leave the party for ten minutes. We can easily explain it away. You wished to look at the White Lodge . . . or Ham House . . . or what you will. The house is just outside the park gates, in Richmond. Henrietta, you would not let a child suffer?'

'A child?'

'Yes. Come, I will show you.' And before she had time to collect herself, he had turned his horse's head towards Richmond and whipped it up to a gallop. Hers followed suit, and an exhilarating five minutes brought them to a group of poverty-stricken cottages on the Richmond edge of the park.

Cedric reined in his horse at last outside one cottage that was somewhat neater than the rest. Some attempt had been made at tidying the little garden and in it stood a strapping, red-faced young woman hanging out shabby half-washed children's clothing on a makeshift line. She stopped when she saw Cedric and ran over to the gate.

'Mr. Smith,' she said 'is it yourself at last? We began to think you was never coming. And where is the madam? This ain't she, I know, and little miss has been pining for her something cruel. And as for Ma, she's fit to be tied, 'twould have been bread and water, and no mistake, for missy if you had not come today. "We're no charity house," says Ma, "and so I'll tell 'un if he ever comes back, and if he don't, so much the worse for miss." You'll be sorry, sir, when you see her, and no mistake. They don't thrive here, when they ain't paid for, and can you wonder? But you'll be wishful to see the child, no doubt. Bill!' She raised her voice to an eldritch shriek. 'Come you here and hold the gentry's horses. I won't be more than a minute,' she added as she left them. 'It's but to change her smock and make her half-way decent for the lady.'

And she disappeared round the side of the house as a gangling boy of thirteen or so appeared to take charge of the horses.

'I forgot to warn you,' said Cedric as he helped Henrietta alight, 'that when I come here, I am Mr. Smith. You had best be nameless, as my mother is, and the less you say the better. But first tell me how much money you have with you. They drive a hard bargain here.'

More and more puzzled, Henrietta took out her purse and counted its contents.

He sighed with relief. 'Excellent. Six guineas will keep them quiet for some time to come. Best give it me now. I do not know what the old harridan would do if she saw how much you have. But, come, let us walk round into the garden. I had as lief not be seen here.' He took her arm and led her round the side of the house into a bedraggled-looking back garden, where two pigs and five shabby children were routing about under a few gnarled old fruit trees. The only difference between them seemed to be that at sight of Henrietta and Cedric the pigs ran squealing away while the children came tumbling forward and began to beg in wheedling cockney.

'Give us a penny, miss,' said the oldest, a boy of seven or eight whose scarred face and knees bore witness to a series of neglected accidents, or fights.

'Or some sugar plums,' chimed in a slightly younger girl, whose face, Henrietta thought, might have been pretty if it could have been seen for the dirt, and whose black hair hung in filthy collops on her shoulders.

'I'se want an apple,' appealed a very small creature of indeterminate sex. 'I'se been hungry all morning.'

'Burnt porridge,' explained the oldest.

'And not much of it, either,' added the girl.

Henrietta, horrified at these revelations, was reaching for her purse when she was interrupted by the appearance of an old crone in a rusty black dress and a cap of dubious whiteness. 'Damme if it ain't Mr. Smith,' she said from toothless gums. 'And come without warning too, which he knows is what we hates here. How are we to have the little dear fit to be seen if we don't know you's coming? "Rough and ready's" our motto here, as you well know, and I hopes you's brought the ready, Mr. Smith, for we's been awaiting on you too long already and rough it's been for poor miss. I tell you it quite made me sad to see the little darling crying for her crust last night when the others had theirs, but "Can't have what ain't paid for," said I. "Business is business" is our motto here, as I've told you often enough, and the sooner the little angels learn it the better. "This world is a vale of tears," says I, "and you might just as well start crying now as later." And blessed if she don't stop there and then and look at me with those big eyes of hers in that scrap of a face. Damme if she's long for this world, Mr. Smith, and who's to say it wouldn't be a blessed release from toil and trouble? But, see, here she comes, the little darling, and if she ain't quite apple pie, blame yourself for coming unbeknownst, and bringing a fine young lady, too; and if a future customer, so much the better.'

Henrietta left off puzzling over this speech at sight of the buxom young woman who now reappeared from the house leading a little fair-haired girl by the hand. The child was so thin and small that Henrietta first thought she could be little more than two years old. Her face was red with a recent and vigorous washing which had not, unfortunately, extended as far as her filthy neck. Her hair, too, which was fine and plentiful, had been smoothed out over what Henrietta suspected of being a perfect rat's nest of tangles. Two large tears, still trembling in the corner of her eyes, bore witness to the vigour with which this operation had been conducted. But it was the shape of the thin little face that caught and held Henrietta's attention. The fine bones and delicately pointed chin combined with her fair hair to produce a speaking likeness to Lady Marchmont. Concealing amazed horror, she held out her hand to the child.

'What is your name, my pretty?' she asked.

The child merely shrank closer to her guide, put a dirty finger in her mouth and stared up at Henrietta.

'It's Caroline, miss,' said the old lady. 'She don't speak nohow. Had the doctor to her and all, we did, after the last time my lady come, and his bill not paid yet neither, and all the good he did was to say it was nought but the sullens and she could talk as well as you or I, if she but cared to try. But not a word we've had out of her since. Only tears, which don't rightly count, to my way of thinking, though at least it shows she's got enough sense to know she's in disgrace. But we'll have her speaking yet, never you fear, sir,' she told Cedric, who had by now handed over Henrietta's six guineas.

'Course it's the sullens,' said the girl. 'Talked all right, she did, last time my lady come. Found her begging on her bended knees, I did, to be took away from here.'

'The ingratitude of it,' said her mother. 'After all we've done for her. I never did see the like. Now, these others know their manners, don't you, me little dears?'

'Yes, Mrs. Muggeridge,' answered the ragged band in a dutiful chorus.

'You know who's good to you, and gives you apples when the pigs don't get 'em, and an egg when they're to spare.'

'Yes, ma'am, Mrs. Muggeridge,' they said again.

'And brimstone and treacle in the mornings, and prayers at night, for all the world like their mothers would, and still this little vixen won't speak. And girls who don't pray go to hell direct, as I've warned her often enough.' And the old lady lowered down on little Caroline with such effect that the child suddenly let go of Miss Muggeridge's hand and made a dive for Henrietta, catching and clinging desperately to the skirts of her habit.

'Well, damme,' said the old lady, 'if she ain't took a fancy to you, miss. I never did see the like; it almost makes one wonder, don't it?' She shot a sharp glance from Henrietta to Cedric and back again.

'You are not paid to wonder, my good woman,' Cedric said angrily. 'And now we must be taking our leave. I am sorry you have not a better report to make of the child, but we must hope she will make some progress before we see her next.'

'Oh, yes,' said the old lady, 'she'll make progress all right, either in this world or out of it, never you worry for that. I knows my job and don't you be thinking different, sir. And honoured, I'm sure, by the visit, Mr. Smith and miss, and commend us to my lady when you see her and tell her the child's cared for like my own, and I can't say handsomer than that, can I, my love?' And she leered at her daughter, who returned the look with one of such loathing that Henrietta shuddered involuntarily and put a protective arm round the thin shoulders of the child, who still clung to her skirts.

But Cedric had taken her arm. 'Come, we must be going, or we will be missed and perhaps looked for. You would not wish that, I collect.'

'No, no. But, Cedric — '

'Hush!' He interrupted her. 'No names, I beg of you. Come, we will talk of this later. Miss Muggeridge, I must beg you will remove the child.'

And Henrietta had to watch, in agony, while the child was roughly picked up and carried off, sobbing with the quiet of despair, under Miss Muggeridge's arm. At the same time, Cedric said a curt good-bye to Mrs. Muggeridge and hurried Henrietta to her horse.

'We have been too long already,' he said as he helped her to mount. 'But my mother was frantic for news of the child and I fear it is true enough that old Madam Muggeridge knows how to make them suffer if their shot is not paid. But Caroline's all right now, for some time to come, so do not you be fretting about her. I am sorry to have exposed you to such a sordid scene, but there was no help for it. To have rode off by myself would have been to court exposure.'

'And besides,' Henrietta could not help remarking, 'you had to have the money for the poor child's board, did you not? But, Cedric, if she is what I assume she must be, how can your mother bear to leave her in that dreadful house?'

'Why, what else can she do?' Cedric asked, surprised.

'I don't know,' Henrietta said mechanically. The whole scene had shocked her inexpressibly and she was desperately trying to sort out its implications. That the child was Lady Marchmont's she could not for a moment doubt, but: 'Cedric?'

'Yes?' He had pushed his horse to a trot and turned back impatiently to answer.

'I must ask. The Father?'

'No one you know.'

'You swear it?'

'Cross my heart. The child's older than she looks. It was a long time ago and best forgotten. You'd do my mother untold harm by stirring it up, asking questions. She never did have any luck. No call to look so missish, Henrietta. You know it happens often enough. It was all very well before the war, when a lady could retire to Europe and rusticate there till her time was out, but in England, I tell you, it was no joke. Dodging about from one watering place to another, trying to avoid discovery! I was dragged along too, from pillar to post, from Cheltenham to Buxton; from Buxton to Harrogate, always out of season, and still someone would turn up and we had to pack our traps and move on again. And in the end the brat had to arrive unexpectedly, and when least convenient, and the upshot of it all is that my mother will never be able to give your father an heir.'

'Did she tell him?' Henrietta did not try to keep the horror out of her voice.

'What do you think?' He was impervious to it. 'The brat had lost her my father . . . Oh, yes, that was what finished things for him. She wasn't going to take another chance, was she? That's why the poor little beast has to be farmed out with those Muggeridges.'

'The father doesn't help?' It was an effort to make herself ask.

'I tell you she lost touch with him years ago. He refused to help when the child was born. Why should he now?'

The casual answer laid to rest a horrible fear that had been creeping through Henrietta's bones. The child could not be Charles Rivers'. 'Poor Lady Marchmont,' she began, and was relieved to have the conversation ended by the sight of the rest of the party still loitering near the Pen Ponds. Miss Jenkinson, it seemed, had conceived an invincible desire to feed the swans, and had sent Peveril and Stanmore to beg some stale bread from a keeper's cottage. Now they were standing anxiously by, talking of powerful wings and broken legs while she lightheartedly threw crumbs to a miscellaneous conclave of birds.

'There,' she said to Henrietta, as she skilfully threw an enormous crumb to a timid duck on the outskirts of the crowd. 'Am I not a true friend? We have been so busy with these tedious birds that I truly believe no one but I has so much as noticed your absence. But, come' — she raised her voice — 'it is time we started homewards. Lady Liverpool will be giving us up for lost.' And then, lowering it again. 'You shall tell me later what you meant by carrying off my beau so shamelessly.' She turned to Cedric. 'Here, Beaufrage, a wager for you. A riding crop to a pair of gloves I beat you to the park gates.' And she set off full gallop across the park, scattering deer and swans alike. Having assured herself a good start, she won by a head, and spent the rest of the ride home teasing Cedric about the French gloves she expected to be given. She pooh-poohed his talk of the war. 'Do not tell me you have not a smuggling friend who sneaks to and fro with brandy and news. But, remember, I beg, that my hands are something of the largest. Do not use your sister's for a model, I beseech you, or I shall have to use my gloves for fingerstalls.' And having thus neatly established that Henrietta was at least technically Cedric's sister and therefore entitled to loiter with him if she wished, she led the cortège home to Coombe Wood.

Later, however, when Henrietta was changing, Miss Jenkinson came to her room. 'I am to beg a favour of you,' she said. 'Will you be so good as to let your Rose instruct my poor Phyllis in the secrets of your coiffure? To tell truth, my poor girl is little better than a millhand on her promotion and, as you see, can no more dress my hair than she can tell a lie, poor innocent. Let her practise on you tonight, Rose, I beg, and perhaps tomorrow I may appear half-way decent. In the meantime I will take your place here and hand pins to your mistress, who, I am sure, is very capable of performing her own toilette.'

Since this was perfectly true, Henrietta had no option but to dismiss Rose, who was delighted to show off her own newfound skill with the curling tongs.

'There,' said Miss Jenkinson with satisfaction, 'now they will be busy primping each other this hour or more, and you and I, my dear creature, may have a comfortable coze. And first, tell me — have I not mastered the lingo to a miracle? If my mother could hear me calling you "my dear creature", she would say a thing or two, I can tell you, and more worth the hearing than your "fiddlesticks" and "gracious me's". She was a millhand herself to start off with, and never quite forgot it. Lord, how she'd have frightened my poor Beaufrage! But, come, my dear, sit down, stop looking so scared and admit I saved your bacon for you with a vengeance this morning. I am to scold you, I think. I am supposed to be the hoyden who knows nothing of society's ways, not you. To ride off alone with a young man might pass for country manners in me, but it will not do for *you*, my love. Most particularly not when he is *my* young man. That story of his being your brother was well enough for the time, but do not think I am to be caught with my own chaff. Come, confess. Have you changed your mind and decided to have Lord Beaufrage after all? If you have, it is but to say so, and I and my millions will find ourselves another market. I know he was yours in the first place, and will never have it said I poached on another girl's preserves, but, to tell truth, I had it from himself he had received his dismissal and in no uncertain terms either. And, besides, if I am to quiz you, what of poor Mr. Rivers, languishing there in Spain?'

Pausing at last, she fixed Henrietta with a pair of shrewd brown eyes. 'Lord,' she went on after an uncomfortable pause, 'you make me feel like my own grandmother. Come, speak up; it cannot be so bad as all that. If you want him, say so and have him. I won't pretend I had not toyed with the idea of having him myself; he's well enough, and will know how to ease me into society, where, now I am begun, I mean to succeed. But do not think that if I lose him I will pine and die like a romantic heroine. We Jenkinsons were not bred that way. So stop your blushing and tell me who it is to be. I confess, from what I have heard of him, I had thought Mr. Rivers a very much more likely *parti* for you, but who am I to say? If you wish to let him die of disappointment in Spain, that is your affair.'

At this point, Henrietta, not surprisingly, burst into tears. 'Oh,' she sobbed, grasping the cool, firm hand her friend held out to her, 'if I could tell you all. But I cannot. Dear Miss Jenkinson, believe me when I tell you that I cannot. And believe me, too, when I say that Lord Beufrage will never be more to me than a brother. If you can really bring yourself to marry him, it will be the best day's work you ever did for me in your life. As a brother, I could love him; as anything else — oh, no, impossible.'

'Good.' Miss Jenkinson drew a large clean pocket handkerchief out of her reticule and handed it to Henrietta. 'So we are come down to cases at last. Mr. Rivers is to be the man after all. Well, I can only say, my dear, that you go a mighty strange way about it. Having caught such a prize, for by all reports, he is a perfect Lancelot, why do you go so roundly about to throw him away? I tell you, even without this morning's work, there is enough gossip about you in town to make the most gallant cavalier blench. I had it from Mr. Willis himself that if Mr. Brummel had not spoken up for you, he would have been in two minds about admitting you to Almack's tother night, and you know what *that* would have meant. It is lucky for you that you have so good a friend in Mr. Brummel, for, trust me, you have some bitter enemies, and some of them rather nearer home than you might think. And to give them such a handle as you did this morning — why, my dear creature, it is mere madness.'

'I know it.' Henrietta handed back the handkerchief. 'But if you knew all, you would see that there was nothing else I could have done today. I can only tell you I am glad I went and thank you from my heart for your help. And as for Lord Beaufrage, take him with my blessing if you really feel you can face his burden of debt.'

Miss Jenkinson laughed. 'I have told you already, my dear, that it is not the debt itself I mind so much as the tendency to it — and I have thought of a way to wean him from that. You saw my wager with him this morning? He was just as happy racing with me for a pair of gloves as he would have been if five hundred pounds were at stake. He is merely a schoolboy, that is all, and must be treated as such. Besides, when he is busy running my mills and minding my money he will have no time for such frolics. I blame his mother for much that is amiss with him. With such an example, how could he be other than he is? But I am quite an example too, and once he has swallowed my vulgarity, which seems to go down easily enough sweetened with my money, I think we shall deal admirably together. Besides, do you know, I begin to think I am a little bit in love with him. I tell you frankly when I saw the two of you dodging away behind the trees in the park this morning, I was neither to hold nor to bind for a minute. It's lucky for you my father brought me up so strict. "Never let that temper of yours run away with you, Sal," he used to say, "for if you do, you'll be sorry for it, and being sorry never helped anything." And he was in the right of it, too. But it was touch and go there for a minute this morning. So be warned by me, and if you really do not want him, keep your hands off my Cedric in future, for mine he is to be. And now, come, we shall be keeping Lady Liverpool waiting and you know she hates that almost as much as she hates a Whig.' And so, arms lovingly entwined around each other's waists, the two girls went down to the big drawing room where, indeed, Lady Liverpool was beginning to fidget with her embroidery frame and glance at the big clock on the mantelshelf.

Next morning, Rose came to Henrietta with an oddly anxious expression. 'If you please, miss. There's a young person belowstairs who says she must speak to you.'

'A young person? Who can you mean, Rose?'

'Why, it's hard to say, miss, for young lady is what she ain't, and why she should be wanting speech of a real young lady like yourself is more than I can imagine. But sitting there in the servants' hall, she is, and vowing she won't budge till she's seen you. And the butler in the fidgets, and the footmen not best pleased, and passing nosey, miss, if you'll forgive my saying so. I don't half like it, and that's the truth of the matter. And when I asks her what she's come about, she sticks her nose into the air (and very dirty it is, too) and says, "Tell her it's Miss Muggeridge to see her and if that don't fetch her then throw me out as hard as you please." And there she sits, miss, bold as brass. And what they're saying about us in the servants' hall, I don't like to think.'

'Miss Muggeridge? Rose, I must see her. Come, dress me quickly and bring her up. Tell them belowstairs that she is come about a private charity of mine and let them mind their own business for a change.' And so saying, Henrietta ran a comb through her short curls, settled the skirts of her cream-coloured muslin, cast a quick, appraising glance at the reflection in her looking glass and finally almost pushed the protesting Rose from the room, promising that she herself would set all to rights before she returned.

As she quickly straightened her bed and hung her dressing gown in the closet, she wondered what this visit could mean and how Miss Muggeridge had learned who she was. Could it be a blackmailing request for more money or was there something wrong with poor little Caroline? At any rate, she could not possibly take the risk of refusing to see Miss Muggeridge, whatever servants' gossip might result.

Rose returned quickly and ushered Miss Muggeridge into the room with an expression of sour disapproval. Dismissing her maid, Henrietta turned to her visitor. The girl was clearly ill at ease and, despite Rose's remarks, had tried hard to make herself presentable for the visit. Her coloured gown was very nearly clean, her checked apron little less so and a cap with cherry coloured ribbons hid the worst tangles of her hair. She stood awkwardly just inside the door, looking about the room with quick darting glances.

'Lord, miss,' she began at last, 'ain't you fine here, and begging pardon for the intrusion I'm sure, but I thought you'd be wishful to know, seeing as how you took such a fancy to the poor child. And her to you, too. Lord, you should have heard her carry on after you left. Sobs and tears and hystrikes and I don't know what all, and if you ask me that's really why Ma made up her mind, 'cos I can tell you, miss, if one of the little varmints takes to acting up, it starts the others off something cruel. But anyway, what with one thing and another, and six guineas, excusing me, miss, for saying so, not doing much more than cover what we've been out of pocket already and so Ma'd have told you and the gentleman, if you'd only a' given her time ... But of course he had to fly into one of his panics, thinking you'd betrayed his name. Lord bless you, miss, do you think we'd a' kept the child so long if we hadn't a' known who she belonged to? But enough's enough, my Ma says, and she knows well who'll be pleased with the news when it comes, she says, the child being nothing but a trouble and a shame, not to mention an expense, which is where it pinches most, if you ask me. But I says to myself there's one person as'll cry for the child, or I ain't got eyes in my head, which I have, and better than my Ma's a long chalk, she being sand-blind these many years past. Yes, and one who might gladly pay for the news I've got for her, being a freehanded young lady as I'se seen for myself. So I just puts on my best gown, locks the children in the hay barn, and here I am, miss, hoping you'll be grateful to me.'

'Why, I am sure it is very good of you to have taken the trouble to come and see me.' Henrietta had listened to the girl's speech with increasing bewilderment. 'But I am afraid I still do not rightly understand why you are here.'

'Why, because of the accident, miss, to be sure.' The girl seemed puzzled that Henrietta had not yet taken her meaning.

'The accident?' Henrietta was more and more confused. 'Oh, you mean to tell me that some accident has befallen poor little Caroline?' Quick suspicion flashed through her mind. It seemed this was a blackmailing expedition after all. The girl had come to plead additional expenses on Caroline's behalf and ask for more money to cover them.

But the girl's next words undeceived her. 'No, no, miss, there's been nothing happened to the child — yet. It's the accident that *will* happen I'm talking about. Course it's more difficult when they're grown like her. Babies — well — anything can happen to *them*. There's overlaying, of course, and strangling their poor little selves in their own ribbons (lucky to have them, says Ma) and just plain pining away, which is easy enough if you don't feed the little dears, and a great saving, too. But with a big girl like Caroline, Ma says, it takes a bit of thinking for. There's the well of course, but she's a timid little soul and keeps away from it, nor she won't try to climb trees either, but, "Leave me alone to think of a good new way," Ma says to me this morning, and that's when I puts on my Sunday best and comes to see you, miss, suspicioning you wouldn't rightly like it. And besides, it's a funny thing, but I've grown fond of that child meself, and that's why I come to see you, and if I was mistaken, well then I'm sorry I've wasted my journey and will go back home again and let what will happen. Only don't you come blaming me afterwards!'

She stopped at last, and Henrietta, who had been too horrified to interrupt her sooner, forced herself to ask the direct, appalling question. 'You mean the child is to be murdered? Little Caroline: In cold blood?'

'Oh, well, miss.' The girl sounded affronted. 'I wouldn't want you to go saying nothing like that about my Ma. I never said nothing about murder, did I now? Or blood, neither. I just said I was afraid the poor little lamb might meet with an accident, as others have before her, who were nothing but a plague and an inconvenience to them as shoulda loved them, and nobody more regretful than me, no, nor my Ma neither. Sobbing and crying, I've seen her many a time when she's grown fond of the poor little varmints, as I must confess she ain't of Caroline. And that's why if you *are* mindful to do something about it, I wouldn't recommend your leaving it too long. Better safe than sorry's a good motto and I can tell you I'll be just as glad to see that child safe away from my Ma's, and the sooner the better.'

Henrietta was pacing up and down the room. 'My God, what shall I do? I cannot possibly come today to take the child away. We are to go home to London, and besides, what am I to do with her when I have got her?'

'Well, I suppose that's rightly your worry, miss,' the girl said, 'but one thing I'll promise you, if you like — and if you felt like making it worth my while, naturally. Something for nothing is what we Muggeridges never did fancy nor never will, and so Ma will tell you any day.' She paused, watching Henrietta expectantly.

Henrietta actually found herself wishing she had Cedric to support her. How much did the girl want? And, more important still, could her frightful story really be true? Impossible to take a chance on it. She opened her reticule and took out a guinea. 'There,' she said, 'that is to show you I am indeed grateful for the information you have brought me, and there is as much for you again if you will undertake to keep the child safe until tomorrow.'

'Spoke like a lady.' Miss Muggeridge snatched the guinea. 'I thought from the first you was a right 'un. And as for today, you ain't to trouble yourself about that, for accidents on a Sunday is what my Ma would never allow, being a pious woman and a churchgoer, and polishes the brass in the sanctuary something beautiful. So the little dear's safe enough till the morning, but I'd get there as soon as you can then, if I was you, 'cos there's the copper on a Monday, and water from the well and I don't know what all. But I tell you what I'll do, since you're so freehanded, and maybe, *if* I do you might think it worth two more guineas for my trouble — *and* the risk of Ma's catching me, which is what I don't like even to think of. But how would it be if I was to lose Caroline, first thing after breakfast? Then you could come along and find her when you chose, and Ma would just think the child had strayed and saved her dear knows how much trouble and fret, for she don't *like* the accidents, don't Ma, being a God fearing woman, as I've told you already. But how you've got to look at it, as she's told me many a time, is she's doing the little angels a kindness, sending them to heaven direct, and no more wailing and gnashing of teeth in this vale of tears. Though I never could think it was quite the same, meself. So how about it, miss — is it a bargain?'

'Indeed it is, and you shall have your two guineas. But how will you contrive to lose the child where I may find her?'

'Bless you, miss, that's easy enough. She minds me all right, has learned better than not to. I'll just take her over into the park first thing in the morning. There's an old keeper's hut in the wood above Pen Ponds. Nobody goes there no more, she'll be safe as houses and I warrant you she'll stay there till you come.'

Henrietta did not altogether like this plan, but could not for the life of her think of a better one, and finally agreed, and gave Miss Muggeridge her additional two guineas, since, as the girl pointed out, they would not be meeting next day. 'But you can count on me, miss, cross my heart, and I count on you not to tell Ma.' She left at last after swearing Henrietta to secrecy and trying without success for a fourth guinea.

Left alone, Henrietta paced up and down her room in an

agony of indecision. Of course little Caroline must be rescued, and she did not for a moment regret the arrangement she had made with Miss Muggeridge. But what next? Her first instinct was to go to Lady Marchmont with the whole story. But then she remembered a sinister, significant phrase of Miss Muggeridge's. There would be some, she had said, who would be pleased to hear of the child's 'accident'. Who else could she mean but Lady Marchmont? So — horrible, but no help there. Well then: Caroline must be taken down to Miss Patience Gilbert's school at Shrovebridge, where she was sure of a hearty welcome. But how to get her there? Henrietta had a healthy enough respect by now for her old enemies, the conventions, to realise that she could not possibly drive so far unaccompanied. Who could she ask to go with her? The elder Miss Gilbert was the obvious person, but she was out of town for the week-end. There would be no help from her. Cedric, then? He was in the secret already which was a great argument for employing him in the business. But could she trust him? If he was actually engaged to Miss Jenkinson it would be something else again. Then, as she had told her friend, she would be able to regard him as a brother. But, as things stood, to ask for his escort seemed a chancy enough expedient. Besides, there was Miss Jenkinson's own warning to be considered. What would she think if, after so positively claiming Cedric as her own, she should learn that Henrietta had gone jaunting about the countryside with him again?

For a moment, Henrietta was tempted to take Miss Jenkinson herself into her confidence. She could, she was sure, be certain of her enthusiastic support, and there would be nothing improper about their making the journey to Shrovebridge together. But this would entail betraying Lady Marchmont's secret, which she had no right to do. No, it was no use. Everything pointed to Cedric as her companion. She must merely count herself fortunate that he had given up all idea of paying his addresses to her.

She hurried downstairs in hopes of finding him and making her arrangements for the next day, but there was no sign either of him or of Miss Jenkinson. Peveril and Stanmore who were lounging in the billiard room, greeted her with their usual elegant langour and told her that Lady Marchmont was out in the *vis à vis* with Lady Liverpool. Cedric and Miss Jenkinson had, they believed, accompanied them on horseback. 'For my part' — Peveril stifled a yawn — 'I'd as soon dance attendance on a hearse. Your play, I believe, Stanmore. Servant, Miss Marchmont.'

Feeling herself dismissed and having, indeed, no inclination to remain, Henrietta found her way to the morning room where she occupied her fingers with her embroidery while her mind fretted round and around the subject of tomorrow. She was soon interrupted by her hostess and Lady Marchmont who returned, she thought, not in the best of charity with each other. Lady Marchmont, who was not used to going about unescorted, complained of heat and headache. Lady Liverpool showed all the signs of a gentlewoman whose patience has been sorely tried. Of Cedric and Miss Jenkinson there was no sign.

They appeared at last just as the covers were laying for luncheon, and one look at Miss Jenkinson's pale and Cedric's triumphant face told Henrietta that they must have come to an understanding. As he handed Miss Jenkinson upstairs Cedric turned and caught Henrietta's eye. 'There,' his look seemed to say, 'so much for you!'

She had no opportunity to speak to him during luncheon, for he never left Miss Jenkinson's side. Afterwards, there fare-wells to be said, for the party was breaking up that afternoon. Miss Jenkinson kissed Henrietta warmly, called her 'her dearest creature', winked to underline the phrase and told her she would visit her next day. 'I have a thousand things to tell you, my love.'

Blushing and stammering, Henrietta begged her to postpone the visit until Tuesday. 'Tomorrow —' She stopped, boggled and began again: Tomorrow, I am most unfortunately engaged.'

To her relief, Miss Jenkinson only laughed, called her a teasing mysterious creature and allowed Cedric to hand her into the carriage in which she and her cousins were to return to town. If he had hoped to be invited to go with them, he swallowed his disappointment and accompanied his mother and Henrietta with a good grace. He could not have told his mother about the engagement Henrietta was sure must exist, for if he had, Lady Marchmont could not possibly have concealed her triumph. As it was, she grumbled all the way home about the heat, the dull week-end and her dislike of politics. When they arrived, she went straight upstairs to her room, announcing that she intended to go to bed at once.

Henrietta paused beside Cedric in the hall. 'I believe I am to congratulate you.'

He was delighted to have his secret guessed. 'So you spotted it, eh? I bet Miss Jenkinson — Sally, I should say — a snuff-box that you would. She won't bet money with me. Ain't she an odd girl? But rich as Crassus or whoever it was that turned things to gold, and besides, you know, Henrietta, she's as game as they come. But it's to be a secret, mind, till she's talked to her cousin. I'll say it for you, Henrietta, I know you won't blab, but my mother's another story. Tell her and you might as well tell the world, so mum's the word till I give you the office.'

'Of course I'll not speak of it, unless to Miss Jenkinson herself, who, I collect, may choose to tell me. But, Cedric, I have a favour to ask of you.'

'Oh?' He did not sound best pleased. 'Don't tell me you're in Queer Street now, Henrietta, and don't think I can do anything for you if you are. If I don't get Sally to the altar damn quick, the Jews'll ruin me and no mistake. But she's a Trojan. I told her just how I stood, and she laughed and said it was nothing. I'm a lucky man and I know it. I'm turning over a new leaf today: No more betting, no more horses, no more cards. Do you know, she has three cotton mills and a shipping business? And lord knows what in real estate. That's worth a few good resolutions, don't you think, Henrietta? I bet you a pound to a pocket handkerchief I'm the soberest Methodist of them all by next year.'

'No more betting, Cedric?' asked Henrietta.

'Oh, well.' He coloured. 'You must give me time, you know. And Sally doesn't mind so long as it ain't money. I should have said a pouncet box to a pocket handkerchief.'

'Of course. I think it's a capital notion of hers. But now for my favour. I must ask you to accompany me to the country tomorrow, Cedric.' And she hurriedly outlined the story Miss Muggeridge had told her and the plan they had made between them.

He whistled between his teeth when she told him of the 'accident' that was to befall little Caroline, but when she came to the end of her story, with a final 'So you see, she must be taken away at once, and I am counting on you, Cedric,' he looked grave.

'I am sorry to disappoint you, Henrietta, but I do not see

how I can come tomorrow. Sally has arranged for me to meet her man of business and, perhaps, to talk to Lord Liverpool. It cannot be so urgent as all that, and indeed I think the girl was probably making it up out of whole cloth to get money from you. 'Yes' — he was convincing himself — 'it sounds like a mare's nest to me. Trust you to be taken in by a sharper, Henrietta. You should have sent for me; I'd soon have sifted her.'

She protested in vain. He had made up his mind that the story was a fabrication and nothing would shake him. At last she gave it up and retired despondently to her room to cast about for expedients. She had finally decided that there was nothing for it but to go alone, when Rose knocked at her door to announce that Mr. Simon Rivers was below asking for her. She jumped to her feet. It seemed a miracle. She had liked Charles' younger brother immensely when they met at Almack's, and had been surprised at her own disappointment when he failed to call on her next day. Now, he came most timely. So far as the world was concerned, he was her fiancé's brother, and, equally important, like Charles he was Lord Marchmont's ward. What better ally for this strange venture of hers?

She moved quickly to the glass, patted a curl into place, pinched a little colour into cheeks pale with anxiety and hurried down to find Simon Rivers in the morning room. He came quickly to meet her, an apology on his lips. To call at this unseasonable hour, and on a Sunday too, was, he knew unpardonable. But he was returning to Oxford immediately and must enquire first for news of his brother.

She had indeed found a letter from Charles awaiting her and was able to report that he was well, but that from hints he threw out she thought he expected a major action shortly. 'He promises us glorious news,' she concluded. 'I only wish it was safely over.'

'Never fret yourself for Charles,' Simon Rivers said robustly. 'He bears a charmed life, always has. Trouble passes him by. Now if it were me, you'd be in the right of it to be worried; if there's a scrape going, I'm for it; always have been, always will. Look at me now, condemned to Paley's *Evidences* when I would give my eyeteeth to be in Spain with Charles, or at the last of it here in London with my way to make in the world. But as for Charles, do not you be worrying yourself about him; he will come out with glory and a whole skin too, I promise you.'

Henrietta took the plunge. 'Mr. Rivers, you are come most happily today. I was in despair until you arrived and now I am to ask a favour of you.'

He looked surprised but spoke out roundly. 'I am yours to command, of course.'

'It is a somewhat delicate matter, and you will, I know, forgive me if I do not go into it too much in detail. But the long and short of it is I have to go out of town tomorrow on an errand to Shrovebridge and would be most grateful if you would accompany me. I have my carriage, and see no reason why we should not be back by nightfall, but I do not think I should go alone.'

'Go alone! I should rather think not. Of course I'll go with you. It is but to climb into college once more.'

'Oh.' This was a new idea to Henrietta. 'You cannot get permission to come?'

'Well, hardly,' he said cheerfully, 'since I have overstayed my leave already. But that's nothing: I climb in as often as not, there's more sport that way. Tell me when I shall call on you in the morning.'

'Why, as to that' — she had already considered this point — 'I think perhaps it would be best if I were to call for you at your lodgings.'

'Call for me in St. James's! I may not be quite up to snuff yet, Miss Marchmont, but I hope I know the world better than to let you do that. No, no, if you do not wish me to give you the meeting here, you had best pick me up by the new pagoda in the park. There are always enough idlers there so that I may pass unnoticed. You will, I collect, wish to make an early start. I will be there, awaiting your arrival, at ten o'clock.'

Henrietta sighed with relief. Here was help at last. Simon Rivers might not have his brother's elegant good looks, but there was something wonderfully solid and reliable about him. As at their first meeting, she found herself wondering why Lady Marchmont and, indeed, her father, seemed to think of him as negligible. But they had not seen him for some time. No doubt they still thought of him as the awkward boy he must have been. Now he was a man, and one to be trusted.

# CHAPTER TWELVE

Henrietta was up betimes next day and contrived easily enough to leave the house without encountering either Lady Marchmont or Cedric. She had told Rose that she was going to visit Miss Patience Gilbert, and hoped it would be assumed that the elder Miss Gilbert had accompanied her. If her coachman thought it somewhat odd to be ordered to drive to the pagoda in Hyde Park, he was much too well trained to show it. As they approached the pagoda, Henrietta was relieved to see Simon Rivers loitering unobtrusively at the side of the road, and ordered the coachman to draw up. Quick as a flash, Simon was in the coach and the astonished coachman had received his orders to drive to Richmond. 'To Richmond?' Simon lifted one eyebrow in a way so reminiscent of his brother that for a moment Henrietta's heart stood still.

She hurried to explain: 'Yes, first to Richmond. There is a child there we must take to Shrovebridge with us.'

Too well bred to show his surprise, Simon changed the subject. 'Have you heard the news, Miss Marchmont?'

'No. Is it a battle, at last?'

'No, no, nothing like that. Only that there has been an escape from the Tower.'

'From the Tower? Impossible. Why, the prisoners there are guarded night and day.'

'One of them has escaped just the same, and there is the devil to pay, I can tell you. The word is that it was planned from France. I would not be in his guards' shoes for all the tea in China.'

'It is one of the French prisoners, then?' Henrietta asked, as the carriage turned out of the park.

'A frog? What gave you that idea? No, it is a Yankee spy. Oh' — appalled recollection struck him — 'I cry your pardon, Miss Marchmont, I had quite forgot.'

She laughed. 'I am only too delighted if anyone can forget for a moment that I am partly American. But tell me more of this escape. It is an American, then?'

'Yes, a noted spy — you must have heard of him — he passed for a while as an officer in their navy and went to and fro between here and France with advice, encouragement, and, it is said, money to aid their cause. What is his name? My cursed memory: Clacton, perhaps, or Frinton? No.' He shook his head. 'But something like that.'

'Not Clinton, surely?'

'The very man. Good God, Miss Marchmont, you are not acquainted with him!'

'Not exactly.' And she told him how, when she was coming to England, the *Faithful* had been stopped by the U.S. *Constitution* and boarded by two American officers. One of them had indeed been called Clinton. 'A little dark man, with a pair of eyes very much too sharp for my comfort at the time. I remember thinking he was not just what I would have expected one of our ship's officers to be.'

'Ours, Miss Marchmont?' Once again he raised an eyebrow too like his brother's for Henrietta's peace of mind.

'Of course "ours",' she said crossly. 'I would be a very wretched Englishwoman now, Mr. Rivers, if I had not had some feeling for America when I lived there.'

He begged her pardon so disarmingly that she was bound to forgive him, and they conversed on indifferent subjects until they reached Richmond Park, where the coachman stopped for instructions. For the first time on this odd expedition, Henrietta found herself seriously embarrassed. If only she could tell Simon Rivers the whole story . . . But that was impossible. Instead, she merely asked him to tell the man to take them to the Pen Ponds and stop there.

'He don't half like it.' Simon settled himself once more beside her. 'He says this track's only fit for horses, not a good carriage like his.'

'I cannot help that,' said Henrietta with unusual sharpness. 'I have no doubt that we shall have to walk the last bit of the way, but we must have the carriage as near as possible. The child is far from strong.'

'Surely you do not expect to find a child in this wilderness?'

'Why, yes; as I told you, that is exactly why we are come. I only wish the man would hurry; the poor little thing may be in terror all this time.'

Simon lapsed into a puzzled silence until the carriage drew up at last at the side of the wood above the Pen Ponds. Refusing to notice her coachman's grumblings, Henrietta alighted and led the way quickly up the rough path that led to the wood.

'There is a keeper's cottage in the wood,' she said. 'This path must lead to is, surely.'

'I should think it most likely.' Simon took her arm to help her over a rough bit of the path. 'But what is that?' He stopped for a moment to listen, a hand raised for silence. Borne on the fitful breeze came the intermittent, desolate sound of a child's hopeless crying.

Henrietta began to run. Brambles caught at her legs, a trailer of wild rose whipped across her face and tore her hand as she pushed it aside, but she took no notice and hurried on, breathless now, up the little path. Simon Rivers was close behind her, but the path was too narrow for him to pass her and she was the first to come out into the little clearing where stood a derelict hut, its windows boarded up, its door shut. From inside, quieter now, but no less hopeless, came that desolate sound of crying.

Hurrying to the door, Henrietta found to her horror that it had been effectively wedged from outside. Miss Muggeridge had made sure that little Caroline would wait until she was collected. No time for explanations, but she was grateful for Simon's help in removing the wedges, which had been rendered even firmer by frantic pushing from within. As they worked, Henrietta called soothingly to the child but got no answer except the continued desperate sobbing.

'She does not speak,' she said as the door opened at last, revealing the sordid interior of the hut, and Caroline, curled up on a pile of old sacking, her face filthy with tears, her eyes huge with terror.

'Oh, my poor lamb!' Henrietta took the unresisting child in her arms. Worn out with crying, Caroline was beyond recognising her, but at least made no attempt to struggle as she picked her up and carried her out of the musty, ill-smelling hut. Once outside, she sat down in the long grass and did her best to soothe the child, stroking the wild fair hair away from the high forehead, gently wiping the worst of the dirt from the ravaged face, murmuring words of consolation and encouragement all the time.

Simon stood by, puzzled but heroically unquestioning, until at last, with an anxious look at the sky, he said, 'Deuced sorry to interrupt you, Miss Marchmont, but if you really mean to get to Shrovebridge and back before night, we had best be moving.'

'Of course. You are quite right.' Henrietta stood the child gently on her feet. 'We must be going, Caroline,' she said. 'We are taking you to a find new home, where no one will hurt you ever again.'

But the child was beyond reason, and, deprived of the immediate comfort of Henrietta's lap, burst once more into anguished sobs, clung to Henrietta's skirts and refused to move.

'Best let me take her.' Simon said. 'Here, missy, up you come.' And before Caroline had time to protest, he had swung her up on to his shoulder, steadying her there with one arm. At first she screamed with terror, but as he began to walk steadily down the hill, taking no notice of her cries, she paused, glanced sideways at his face, and then, to Henrietta's amazement, smiled at him and put her arm round his neck. By the time they got back to the carriage, she had fallen fast asleep and he managed to lay her gently on the seat without waking her.

'Well?' He turned to look at Henrietta. 'Is it to be Shrovebridge, then?'

'It must be. I only hope we have not lost too much time. But I cannot take her back to Marchmont House.'

'No, I should rather think not.' He helped her into the carriage, gave the order to the coachman and got in beside her. 'I only hope you know what you are doing, Miss Marchmont. I am not so green that I cannot see who the child is, but what you are doing with her is more than I can understand.'

Henrietta coloured. She had hoped against hope that Simon would not realise who little Caroline was. Now she would have to revise the version of the truth that she had meant to give him. 'I know it must seem strange,' she said, 'but if you had seen the place where the child was, you would understand. I am taking her to a school run by the sister of a friend of mine. I am sure she will take her in for my sake. I shall say that I found her in the park — which is true enough — and took too much of a fancy to her to leave her straying there. And that is true, too.' She paused and looked at him almost defiantly. If she could avoid telling him about the plot against the child's life, she would do so. It reflected too frightfully upon Lady Marchmont.

To her relief, Simon seized upon another problem. 'And your coachman?'

'Thank you for reminding me. We will stop presently for some refreshment and I will teach him the story he is to tell. Briggs has served my father ever since he came back from India and is devoted to him, and, I really think, to me. He will not betray me.'

Simon still looked doubtful and said again 'I only wish I was certain you knew what you were doing. Do you not realise what the world will say if this day's work gets out?'

Henrietta laughed. 'That is why it must not. But come, Mr. Rivers, be reasonable. Even the tattling world can hardly claim that the child is mine, when everybody knows I only came to England this spring.'

But he only shook his head and turned, very gently, to settle little Caroline more comfortably on the seat and spread his greatcoat over her. 'She is exhausted with fright,' he said. 'We had best obtain a little brandy and milk for her when we stop. And for you, too, Miss Marchmont. This has been no sort of an experience for a young lady.'

Henrietta laughed. 'I know I should be grateful to you for the compliment,' she said. 'But you must know the world has long since decided I am insufficiently genteel, and I begin to think it is true. I do not see why I should go into spasms because we have been through some rough country, though I am afraid I must present but an odd appearance.' She put up her hand to her face, realising for the first time that it had been badly scratched and was bleeding.

'I wish you would let me tend to that for you,' he said as she began to dab at the cut with her handkerchief. 'We got plenty of practice at that kind of thing at Harrow, and you would prefer, I know, to arouse as little comment as possible when we stop.'

This was such obvious sense, that Henrietta submitted with a good grace as he cleaned up a deep scratch across her cheek and a still worse one on her left hand with his spotlessly clean white handkerchief. 'There,' he said at last, 'I fear you will be seeking for explanations for a few days to come, Miss Marchmont, but at least it is clean now.' Henrietta thanked him, did her best to tidy her hair, which had also suffered from the thorns she had hurried through, and then turned to look aghast at a great tear in the skirt of her habit.

He was looking at it too. 'I hope you are genteel enough to carry a supply of pins,' he said, 'for if so I think I can make shift to cobble you up, if you will allow me. Has Charles ever told you about our amateur theatricals? I was always wardrobe master, being the youngest, and have become quite an expert at running repairs.'

Speechless now, Henrietta produced the paper of pins she carried in her muff and sat rigidly still while Simon pinned her up. 'There.' He sat back to survey his handiwork. 'I flatter myself your maid could have done no better. But look, the child is waking.'

Grateful for the distraction, Henrietta turned to Caroline, who was indeed stirring in her corner. She woke up all at once, as a child will, and gazed for a moment from Simon to Henrietta and back. Then, apparently satisfied with what she saw, she wriggled over so that she could put her head in Henrietta's lap and fell asleep again.

He looked at her with compassion. 'She does not speak, you say?'

'Never, they told me. Except once, when Lady — when somebody she loved was leaving her. But at least it means she can, if she wants to. I would have kept silence in that place myself.' But the less she told him about the Muggeridges the better. She changed the subject, questioning him instead about his life at Oxford and his plans for the future. It proved a painful topic. He had come to London, it seemed, in a last attempt at persuading his grandfather that he was not cut out for the church, and had failed dismally.

'It is not his fault.' He was twisting and untwisting the handkerchief he had used on Henrietta's face. 'He is old. He does not understand. He is still living in the last century, when younger brothers went into the church as a matter of course. There is a family living I can have, and that settles it.'

'But what do you want to do?'

'Why, at the moment, join the army, of course. How can I stay at Oxford with a parcel of mother's darlings when lives are being lost, and glory won, on the Continent?'

'But the war will not go on forever, I hope.'

'No, indeed, and that is just what I have been trying to explain to Grandfather. If I do not get there soon, it will be all over and I shall have lost my chance.'

'And never be a general. Oh, poor Mr. Rivers.'

'You are laughing at me and I do not altogether blame you. But the fact is I do not so much wish to be a general. Charles will, I am sure. He has the ruthlessness it needs, but I do not believe I could bear the responsibility of all those lives. No, you do not understand Miss Marchmont. It is not so much that I pine for a military life — I sometimes think I should detest it — but — do not laugh at me — it seems to me my duty to go. Besides,' he added with a touch of honesty that pleased Henrietta, 'I think it would be advantageous to me afterwards.'

'Afterwards?'

'Yes, when I take up my career, if only I ever manage to.'

'What, as a clergyman?'

'No, no. I do not mean to give in so easily. There is no making my grandfather see reason now but when your father comes back from Europe, I am sure he will understand and speak for me. My grandfather is not obstinate, really, he is just old. When he understands, he will let me have my way. And in the man's world I mean to enter, it will be necessary, I am sure, to have played a proper part in this war.'

'I am afraid you go too fast for me,' Henrietta said. 'What is this man's world you have your eye on?'

His laugh, surprisingly, was deeper than Charles'. 'If only I knew! Politics would be my choice, but there is a difficulty there. Our family has been Tory time out of mind; I do not know what would happen if I come out as a Whig. And yet, I cannot reconcile it with my conscience to do anything else. I hope you will not construe it as a criticism of your father, Miss Marchmont. He and his friends have been in the right of it, I think, in their conduct of the war. I do not carry my Whiggery so far as to join the extremists of the party who cry for peace at any price. No, no, we must fight Bonaparte to a finish, but when we have done so, as, please God, we soon will, why, then, believe me, new men and new measures will be needed. We shall have the whole world to put to rights! A mangificent opportunity and, forgive me, I do not think the Tories, with their vested interests and their cut-and-dried thinking, are the men to take advantage of it. There is a something stirring in the country that will not, I think, be long denied. Politics must cease to be a family preserve, like the church. We must have a new law and a new justice, equal alike for rich and poor — oh, there is so much to be done — but forgive me, Miss Marchmont, for boring you with such a lecture. I cannot think what has possessed me to run on so.'

'But I am not bored in the least,' she said. 'On the contrary, I am delighted to hear what you say, for I must confess that I have found much in England to make me uneasy, though I beg that you will not tell my father I said so.'

He laughed. 'I will promise to keep your secret if you will do as much for mine.' Then, more bitterly, 'You can see how impossible it is for me to dream of entering politics as a Whig when I dare not even let it be known that I am thinking of it. I truly believe it might kill my grandfather, whose health is precarious enough as it is. No, I have abandoned all thought of a political career, but that does not mean I will let myself dwindle into a Sunday-only clergyman. I have seriously considered going into business. Many of the fellows are doing that now, and, do you know, society may turn up its nose at it, but at least it is real. If I cannot make two blades of grass grow where one did before, perhaps I may contrive to make a better bolt of cloth — and to keep my workpeople happy too. I have a friend, Matt Gurney — you should just hear him talk about conditions of work in the Midlands. It would make you weep, Miss Marchmont. And he says it is people like us who are needed to go in and improve things. I think he would help me to a place in one of his family's businesses, or even in their London bank, if only grandfather would approve, and if this cursed war was but over. And would not that be a better life than prosing once a week to a parcel of sleepy villagers about things they do not understand?'

Henrietta laughed. 'It is but too plain that you are not cut out for a clergyman. I wish for your sake that my father was at home; I am sure he would sympathise with you, for I have heard him say very much the same thing himself. But, look, the child is waking and, if I remember rightly, there is a tidy little inn in this village. Tell the man to stop here, will you, and we will give her the brandy and milk you advise. I am afraid her diet so far has been something of the most frugal, poor little creature. Did you ever see anything so thin and frail?'

As the carriage drew up outside the inn Henrietta gathered Caroline into her arms, murmuring to her soothingly as she did so. The child, who had been stirring restlessly, opened wide blue eyes and stared in alarm at her for a moment, then began again her soft hopeless wailing. Simon, who had jumped out to speak to the coachman, returned and held out his arms for her.

'Come, come,' he said, 'soldiers don't cry like that, you know.'

The child hushed at once at the sound of his voice and held out her arms to him, managing a watery smile for his benefit.

'You seem to have made a conquest,' said Henrietta as she handed her over.

'Yes, I am flattered.' A quick, questioning glance for Henrietta.

The child cheered up over a bowl of bread and milk, generously laced with brandy, and smiled impartially at Henrietta and Simon, but still maintained her impenetrable silence. Henrietta, too, dutifully swallowed the brandy Simon had ordered for her. Back in the coach once more, she found herself overwhelmingly drowsy. She had returned home late from Coombe House the night before and made an early start today. The brandy, on top of the excitement of the morning, was too much for her. With an apology, she leant back in her corner of the coach and closed her eyes. She dreamt fitfully: of Simon, storming a breach at the head of his men; of Charles in a bishop's mitre. Then, suddenly, she was awake. Her head was pillowed on Simon's shoulder and he was very gently shaking her.

'We are nearly there,' he explained as she started upright and put up a hand to her dishevelled hair. 'You have slept well, both of you.'

Caroline was still fast asleep in her corner, and when the coach came to a halt outside the plain front of Miss Patience Gilbert's school, Simon managed to carry her indoors without waking her.

To Henrietta's deep, unspoken relief, Miss Patience was at home and welcomed her warmly, accepting her story of finding little Caroline straying in Richmond Park with a politeness that totally masked her inevitable incredulity. If this was to be Henrietta's story, she was too well bred not to accept it as it stood, and, equally of course, she would accept the child as a member of her little school. She shook her head when Henrietta described Caroline's refusal — or inability — to speak, but said they must hope for the best.

The light was beginning to fade, and Simon to look anxious, when Henrietta arose to take her leave. But her farewells were interrupted by a maid who hurried in to tell her mistress that the little girl had awakened and was carrying on 'something dreadful, if you please, 'm.'

Miss Patience hurried away and returned to say that the

child was hysterical. She suggested that the sight of her rescuers might help to calm her. Grateful for the excuse, Henrietta followed her to the room from which the child's hopeless screams were coming, but tried in vain to soothe her.

At last the door opened. 'May I try?' said Simon.

'Of course. Why did I not think of it sooner? See,' she said to little Caroline, 'here is Mr. Rivers come to say good-bye to you. He will think you do nothing but cry.'

'Yes.' Simon took the child's hot little hand. 'I had been thinking of coming to see you again soon, and bringing you a doll, perhaps, with golden hair and blue eyes just like you, but what is the use of a doll to a girl who does nothing but cry?'

The child stopped crying and gazed at him, her question written in her large, beseeching eyes.

'Yes, indeed I will come, not this week, or next, because I am at a kind of a school, like you, and cannot always get away, but as soon as I can and if they tell me you have been a good girl, you shall have a doll with the bluest eyes and the yellowest hair in all of London.' And with that he handed Caroline gently to Miss Patience and led Henrietta from the room.

'Well.' She settled herself gratefully in the coach. 'I do not know what I should have done without you today, Mr. Rivers. But are we very late? Will you be able to get back to Oxford in time, do you think?'

'In time for breakfast,' he said cheerfully, 'if I ride all night as I propose to.'

'I do hope I have not got you into trouble,' she said, conscience stricken. 'Will it be very bad if you are found to be absent?'

He reassured her convincingly enough, but as the shadows began to draw in she realised that the last delay had cost them more time than she had thought. A new anxiety added itself to her worry over Simon. They would be returning over Putney Heath very much too late for comfort. Suppose they were to encounter one of the highwaymen who lurked there? It was true she had hardly any money on her, having given all she had to Miss Patience in earnest of Caroline's school fees, but that might be so much the worse. She had heard alarming tales of what the highwaymen did if disappointed of their booty.

She mentioned her fears to Simon, who scouted them with his usual cheerful common sense, but, seeing that she was genuinely anxious, volunteered to sit on the box with the coachman for the rest of the journey.

'The sight of two of us will make them think again, I promise you. I will hold my hand inside the pocket of my greatcoat as if I had a gun there, and any rascals will give us a wide berth.'

To Henrietta's relief, they crossed the heath unmolested in the gathering dusk, though Simon reported when they stopped to put him down that he had seen at least one doubtful figure skulking in the bushes as they passed. He brushed aside Henrietta's thanks for his escort and laughed at her anxiety over his ride to Oxford that night. It would be full moon. He would enjoy every minute of it. 'Only mind you do not mention having seen me today,' he concluded. 'I have been back in college ever since last night, remember.'

Henrietta laughed and gave him her promise: 'I do hope I have not got you into trouble.'

'Not the least chance in the world. And besides, what could they do but send me down? And that would be doing me the greatest possible kindness. But it will not come to that, I promise you.'

It was dark now and Henrietta drove the short distance to Marchmont House anxiously enough. If only her stepmother were out, so that she could creep in and to bed unobserved. It would be so much easier, in the morning, to invent some story to account for her late return. But as the carriage turned in at the gates of the house, her heart sank. Every room on the ground floor was brilliantly lighted. Lady Marchmont was most certainly at home, perhaps entertaining, though Henrietta was sure she had had no such plan for tonight. Well, there was nothing for it. Henrietta dismissed as cowardly a temptation to tell the coachman to take her round to a side entrance where she might enter unobserved. Best get it over with.

There was no hum of voices as she stepped into the lighted hall. 'Lady Marchmont does not entertain tonight?' she asked the footman who admitted her.

'No, miss.' What was the matter with the man? He seemed about to speak again when the door of the small saloon opened and Lady Marchmont appeared.

'Well.' Her colour was high. 'There you are at last, Henrietta! Where in the world have you been? I have been in the greatest anxiety for you these hours past. I tell you, to be jauntering about the countryside to all hours by yourself is very far from being the thing. I only hope it is no worse. But I will not believe that! When you have taken Miss Gilbert with you on these excursions, I have forborne to comment, because, though her company does you no particular credit, it does, I suppose, count as chaperonage. But today, the Miss Giddys tell me, she is out of town. Henrietta, I am shocked at you, and what your father will say, I hardly dare to think. As for the other thing — but that I will not believe . . .'

Henrietta was hardly listening. In the lighted room behind Lady Marchmont she had seen a man's figure.

'Rivers,' she breathed.

'Yes. Mr. Rivers is returned with glorious news. We have won a great victory at Vittoria.' And then, in a lower voice, 'I fear he is not best pleased with you, my love. I have been trying to make your peace with him this hour past. But, good God!' She raised her voice again as Henrietta advanced into the light. 'What has happened? Have you met with an accident?'

In her fatigue and anxiety, Henrietta had forgotten her scratched face and dishevelled appearance. Now, advancing into the light, she was miserably aware of it all. 'Not precisely an accident,' she said, and then, everything else forgotten: 'Charles! I am most happy to see you safe.'

He took her hands in his and looked down at her gravely, both of them much aware of Lady Marchmont, who still hovered in the doorway. 'I wish I could return the compliment. But it was not thus that I dreamed of finding you, Henrietta!' He swept her, just the same, half-resisting, into a long embrace, then, his hands still warm on her shoulders, held her at arms' length for a long, considering look. 'Thank God, she's gone,' he said at last. 'I am afraid I am to scold you, Henrietta.'

'Oh, come!' Happiness at his return would not be denied. 'This is no time for scoldings, Charles. I am sorry indeed that I was not here to greet you, but it has been a long day.' Even to him, she had already realised, she could not tell the real reason for her journey. To speak of little Caroline was to betray Lady Marchmont. 'I have been down to Shrovebridge,' she went on, 'but what's that to the purpose! I am so *glad* to see you, Charles. Has it been a splendid victory? Is Lord Wellington safe? Shall we be in France soon? But how comes it that you are returned so quick? You are not hurt?' She looked him up and down anxiously. 'Your fever is not returned?'

'No, no, nothing like that. I am afraid I must be plain with you, Henrietta. I had hoped for more time to put it to you gently, but there is none. I return tomorrow. It is already late. I beg you will be seated.'

She let him place her in a chair, aware all over again of her scratched face and the long tear that Simon had pinned up in her skirt. She looked beseechingly up at Charles. 'Do not be angry with me, I beg. You cannot be so sorry as I am that I was not here to greet you, but in truth I could not help it. Besides' — her spirits were rallying — 'how could I know you were coming?'

'It is not that.' He took her up almost brusquely. 'I am sorry to have to lecture you, Henrietta, but Lady Marchmont is in the right of it this time. How can you be so lost to any sense of your own position as to go rambling about the countryside with no protection but an old rascal of a coachman? Do you not realise that the gossip about you has reached even to the Peninsula? I made a special appeal for permission to carry these despatches so that I might have an opportunity of a word with you — and what do I find — that you are off on who knows what treacherous errand?'

'Treacherous? What in the world are you talking about?'

'Why, about the American prisoner, Clinton.'

'Clinton?' She remembered something Simon had told her that morning. 'Oh, yes, the man who has escaped from the Tower. Do you know, it is a most remarkable thing, but I met him once. He and another man whose name I have forgot boarded the *Faithful* when I was coming over, and a very bad half hour they gave us. But what has his escape to say to me?'

Rivers was looking at her anxiously. 'Can you truly swear to me that you were not concerned in it?'

'Who? I?' For a moment she was dumb with astonishment, then broke into an almost hysterical peal of laughter. 'Good gracious, Charles! No wonder you were looking so grave. Did you really think I had contrived his escape from the Tower? And spent today driving him into the countryside, disguised, no doubt, in cap and apron, as my abigail? Oh, Charles, you must forgive me, but I really believe I shall die laughing.'

But he would not join in her mirth. 'I am greatly relieved if I have been mistaken, Henrietta, but, I ask you, what else could I think? I come home to remonstrate with you about the rumours I have heard of your unpatriotic behaviour and am greeted with the news that you and an escaped American prisoner have both mysteriously disappeared. It is no laughing matter, I can tell you. It will be all over town tomorrow, and if the Bow Street Runners are not on the doorstep first thing in the morning, I shall be very much surprised.'

'I see.' Henrietta was beginning to see a great deal. 'And to whom, if I may ask, am I indebted for this rumour of my disappearance? I have yet to learn that to drive down into the country and visit a friend is to disappear.'

'Yes, but to go alone, Henrietta. What have you to say to that?'

'Oh, of course. Lady Marchmont has been conferring with the Miss Giddys. I had quite forgot. No wonder the story of my "disappearance" is all over town. This is really most unfortunate.'

'Unfortunate! I should rather think it is. Of course I believe you implicitly, Henrietta. If you tell me that you have had nothing to do with Mr. Clinton's escape, that is good enough for me. But I am afraid the Runners will not be so easily satisfied. What are you going to tell them? Henrietta, how *could* you go so far unattended?'

'But I did nothing of the kind, Charles. Thank God, there is no reason I should not tell *you*. Simon was with me.'

'Simon?'

'Your brother. I knew I ought not to go alone, and, truly, Charles, I had to go. So, as he happened to visit me yesterday, I asked him to be so good as to accompany me. And I must say, he was the greatest comfort and assistance to me. I think your brother does you credit, Charles.'

'Oh, he is well enough.' Carelessly. 'But he is at Oxford, or supposed to be.'

'Now you have hit on the exact difficulty. He had overstayed his leave already and has ridden back tonight hoping that his absence will not have been noticed. I promised him faithfully that I would not mention he had accompanied me. I cannot possibly betray him, so what am I to do!'

He was frowning. 'Really, it is too foolish in you, Henrietta. What on earth was the use of having him go with you, if you knew you could not mention it?'

This was an aspect of the situation that had not struck her before. 'Well,' she said, 'he was the greatest comfort to me, and sat on the box across Putney Heath and frightened off a highwayman. But I see what you mean: You are concerned about what the world will say, not about my safety.' She stopped, horrified at what she had said. For how many sleepless nights had she thought of this meeting, and now they were wasting the precious minutes in quarrelling. 'Charles,' she went on, 'forgive me. I did not mean it, and nor, I know, did you. To tell truth, I am so weary I do not rightly know what I am saying. Let us talk of this again in the morning. You cannot really mean that you have to leave again tomorrow?'

'I am afraid so. But not, I hope, till the afternoon. The despatches I am to carry can hardly be ready before then.' He took her hand. 'Sleep well, Henrietta, and forgive me if I seemed to speak sharply. I love you too well not to be anxious for you sometimes.' And on this note of half reconciliation they parted.


## CHAPTER THIRTEEN


Henrietta woke to sunshine, and happiness. Charles had been angry the night before, it was true, but he was home, even if only for a day. And he had come because of his anxiety for her. There was great comfort in this. She knew well what a coveted honour the bringing of despatches was; it must have taken the greatest solicitude on her behalf to make him ask for it as a favour. No wonder then he had been put out when he found her so mysteriously absent. And then, to have her return, looking such a hoyden. Of course he had been displeased. She would not have blamed him if he had spoken to her more sharply still. Anyway, there was happiness in the thought that his chidings had been those of an accepted lover. In her heart she had never been able to stop thinking of herself as engaged to him; now, to her infinite relief, the breach had been tacitly healed. If it had taken a quarrel to do it, thank God for quarrels.

Her only anxiety, as she urged Rose to lose no time in putting her into her most becoming muslin, was for Simon. Suppose the Bow Street Runners really did come to question her?

How should she clear herself of suspicion without getting him into trouble? But this anxiety was soon allayed. Rose, handing pins, was talkative as usual. She dealt first with Mr. Rivers' unexpected arrival and then turned to the news of the day.

'Only to think, miss, of that poor American gentleman being catched so easy. My heart bleeds for him, truly it does. Fancy escaping from the Tower and then being caught by a parcel of bargees.'

'What? Is he caught then?'

'Why, yes, miss. He had hidden himself on a barge in the Thames, hoping, I have no doubt, to find some means of getting over to France, but his foot stuck out of the sacks and they spotted him — and back he is in the Tower, this very minute.'

'Oh, the poor man.' But Henrietta's heart sang. She hurried downstairs in the hope of finding Charles alone, but the footman on duty in the hall told her that Mr. Rivers had already ridden out, to Whitehall, as he understood. He had said he would return shortly.

And, indeed, Henrietta had hardly finished her second cup of tea when Charles joined her. Mindful of the man in waiting, he bent low, respectfully over her hand, but his eyes told her of the kiss she should have had.

'I can see you are none the worse for your long day.' He had an approving glance for Rose's handiwork.

'Not the least in the world. But tell me, what news in Whitehall?'

'Why, a reprieve, I am glad to say. I do not leave till tomorrow. And good news, too, from the Tower.'

'Yes, so I have heard. Poor Mr. Clinton. I cannot help but feel sorry for him.'

'Hush,' he said warningly. 'Have you not learned your lesson yet, Henrietta?'

'Oh, come, Charles, let me at least be myself with you. Good God, how I have missed you, and now you come home only for one day. It is too much to be borne.'

He accepted a cup of tea and smiled warmly at her. 'I owe it to a good friend of yours that I do not have to return today.'

'A friend? Of mine? I did not know I had any.'

'Now it is I who must say, "Oh, come," to you, Henrietta. Of course you have friends, and good ones too. I referred to Miss Jenkinson, whom I met at Lord Liverpool's today. It was she who persuaded her cousin that he could not possibly make up his mind what to say to Lord Wellington until tomorrow. And, to complete her kindness, she has invited me to accompany you to their house tonight.'

'Of course. It is Lady Liverpool's rout. I had quite forgot. And you are to come too. Oh, that is delightful news indeed. And I owe it all to Miss Jenkinson. Yes, I was wrong, she is a true friend. Did you not find her delightful, Charles, in her odd way?'

He laughed. 'Anyone with so much money has leave to be odd. She means to call on you this morning, by the way.'

'Oh.' Henrietta made a moue. 'I had hoped that we might have this day at least to ourselves. Can we not escape before she comes, Charles? Let us, for once, be wicked and go riding in the park together.'

For a moment his hand touched hers. 'If we only could! But it will not do, Henrietta, as your own good sense, I am sure, will tell you. Miss Jenkinson is too valuable a friend to be lightly affronted. I cannot tell you how pleased I am to find that you have formed so eligible a connection. I must confess that I had some anxious moments when the gossip about you began to reach me. You will forgive me, I know, for referring to so painful a subject again, but talk of any kind is what I must of all things avoid, and you also for my sake. I have long wished for an opportunity to talk to you about our future. Let us go out into the garden. There, at least, we can with propriety be alone.' And he handed her out through the French windows on to the terrace, pausing merely to tell the footman in attendance that if Miss Jenkinson called, Miss Marchmont was to be found in the garden.

Henrietta could not help feeling that it would have been more gallant to have omitted this precaution, but, at least, here she was at last, alone with her love. He led her across the lawn to a seat under an arbour and installed her there, solicitously. Was it shady enough for her? Should he fetch her a hat? She longed to suggest that they would be at once cooler and more private on one of the rustic benches in the shrubbery, but pride would not allow this. If he preferred to remain here in full view of the house, they must do so. She looked up at him with a teasing smile. 'Am I in disgrace still, Charles?'

'In disgrace? How can you think so? You must know that it is only my love for you that makes me anxious on your behalf. I am sorry if I seemed to speak sharply last night, but I had been in an agony of fear for you. To come back and find you gone — and so mysteriously gone. Henrietta, you can have no idea of what I suffered.'

'Dear Charles, I am so sorry. But let us not waste time talking about that. It is all to be forgotten now. Tell me instead what it is you have wished to say about our future.' She coloured as she spoke. Would he think it forward of her to remind him?

But he smiled down at her kindly. 'Yes, we must lose no time. These minutes alone together are too precious to be wasted. I fear you are bound to have a rush of callers today, after the talk that was going about yesterday. Indeed, I think that Miss Jenkinson had that very much in mind when she said she would come to see you.'

'Oh, you mean she too knows that I was "mysteriously gone" as you call it?'

'My poor Henrietta, I fear you must resign yourself to the fact that everybody knows it. But with Miss Jenkinson and me at your side I think you can rely on carrying it off with a high hand. That brings me though, exactly to the point I wished to make. Of course I know that these scrapes of yours are merely the result of your high spirits but, Henrietta, for my sake, I beg you will be more careful. You must know that I do not mean to remain a mere army officer forever. The tide of war has turned at last. It will be over soon, I think, and, with peace, the chance of a successful army career is, of course, slight. I mean to sell out as soon after the peace as I can.'

She interrupted him, surprised. 'Why, Charles, I thought you were to be a general!'

'Why, so I should, if the war had but lasted a while longer, but as things are going now, I do not believe Boney can hold out much beyond next spring. Then, of course, with peace will come the cry for retrenchment; the army will be cut to the bone, there will be no chance for promotion, certainly not by merit. No, no, there is no career for me there.'

'But what do you mean to do?'

'Why, go into politics, of course. With you at my side, and your father behind me, I am sure I shall have no difficulty in finding a seat. It is unfortunate that the dissolution will probably come this autumn, before I am out of the army, but we will just have to hope for a by-election. And once I am in the House, let me alone to make my mark. Now, Henrietta, I am sure you understand why I have been somewhat troubled about you. It is bad enough — you will forgive me, I know, for saying this — for your father, in his position, to have you made the subject of public comment. For me it might be fatal. You know the tag about Caesar's wife. I beg you will apply it to yourself.'

'You mean then to be First Minister, I take it?'

'With God's help — and yours. And now I know you will understand how delighted I am to find you such good friends with Miss Jenkinson. She is on the very best of terms with her cousin, Lord Liverpool, and who knows what might not come of that? But here, if I mistake not, comes the man to announce your first caller.' And indeed, a footman was floating majestically across the lawn towards them. 'Miss Jenkinson is here, Miss Marchmont,' he said, 'and the Miss Giddys.'

'Oh!' Henrietta made a face. 'What am I to say to them, Charles? Stand by me, I beg of you.'

'Of course I will. Do not trouble yourself for a moment. They cannot harm you now I am here.' And he took her arm and led her back to the house.

In the comfort of his touch, Henrietta forgot a certain disappointment she had felt in her conversation. If Charles' plans for the future had seemed just a shade cold-blooded, she must remember that all his life he had had his own way to make. And now he had her to plan for as well as himself. No wonder if the responsibility weighed him down so that the lover was somewhat lost in the man of affairs. She pressed his arm gently. 'Charles, I cannot tell you how happy it makes me to have you here.'

They found Lady Marchmont entertaining Miss Jenkinson and the three Miss Giddys, who swooped upon Henrietta with little cries of affection.

'You dear wicked creature,' said Miss Giddy, reaching up for an unwanted kiss.

'Giving us such a fright,' added Miss Letitia.

'We quite thought you had been abducted,' explained Miss Patricia.

'Fanny was positively in spasms when we told her,' said Miss Giddy.

'We thought we would have to send for dear Sir Henry,' said Miss Patricia.

'But then this morning we had the good good news that that

wicked Mr. Clinton had been captured. Hanging's too good for him, if you ask me,' concluded Miss Letitia.

Allowing them each to kiss her cheek in turn, Henrietta thought that there was one thing to be said for the Miss Giddys. They did make conversation very easy. And this time they obviously knew that they had gone too far in what they had said about her yesterday. Mr. Clinton had done her an admirable turn in getting captured when he did. In their contrition over having accused her of helping him to escape, they would forget to wonder what she had really been doing. She returned their greetings courteously and delighted them by asking after 'poor Miss Fanny'.

Poor Miss Fanny, it seemed, who had been in spasms all day yesterday, had eaten a hearty breakfast after hearing the news of Mr. Clinton's capture and had sent them out with strict instructions to bring her all the news.

'So of course we came to dear Lady Marchmont's,' said Miss Giddy.

'And see how right we were,' said Miss Letitia.

'We shall be able to tell her we found you radiant, positively radiant with happiness,' Miss Patricia told Henrietta.

'With dear Mr. Rivers at your side,' concluded Miss Giddy.

'And dearest Lady Marchmont,' added Miss Patricia.

'Only to think of our finding Miss Jenkinson here,' said Miss Giddy.

'But where is Lord Beaufrage?' asked Miss Patricia.

'Where, indeed?' said Miss Jenkinson. 'I bet him a tenner to a twilled silk that I would be here before he was up, and look, here he comes.'

And indeed, Henrietta, who had retired to the window alcove, saw Cedric leap off his horse on the carriage sweep and hurry towards the house.

Miss Jenkinson greeted him with teasing laughter and a demand for her twilled silk. 'And I shall choose it myself, mind. I'll not be fobbed off with any of your Bond Street bargains. But what is this? Have you not told your mother?'

For almost the first time, Henrietta saw Lady Marchmont looking at a loss. 'Told me what?' she asked.

'Why, of our engagement,' said Miss Jenkinson. 'Dear Lady Marchmont (as Miss Giddy would say), can it be that I am to have the happiness of breaking it to you that I am to marry your son? Cedric, you absurd creature, I told you to tell no one, but surely you knew I did not mean your mama. Dearest Lady Marchmont, will you bear with my vulgarity and my nonsense and be a mother to me?'

Lady Marchmont surprised everyone, herself included, by bursting into tears, through which came an incoherent muttering of 'So happy,' 'Dear Sally — I must call you so,' and 'Dear, dear Cedric.'

As for the Miss Giddys, their cup was running over, and they lost no time in taking their leave and hurrying off to tell the news all over town.

To Henrietta's disappointment, Rivers, too, had to leave soon in order to visit his grandparents in Wimbledon and to execute the many commissions he had undertaken to fulfil while he was in England. Henrietta longed to suggest that she give him the meeting in Wimbledon, but forbore to do so, since he did not, and spent the afternoon, instead, in devising a particularly devastating toilette for Lady Liverpool's rout. When Rivers called to escort them there he rewarded her with an admiring glance and a murmured compliment. She had the satisfaction, as they drove up in the queue of carriages to Lady Liverpool's house, of knowing that she looked almost more than her best. Happiness had given her cheeks a glow they had recently lacked, and Rivers' company was ample protection against the whims of society. For once, she found herself looking forward to an evening out with pure pleasure.

It passed all too quickly. Lord Liverpool's house was so crowded that it took all Rivers' firmness to make a way for Henrietta and her stepmother to the top of the stairs where Miss Jenkinson stood by her cousin to receive their guests. In the next room a few couples were contriving to dance their way through the crowd, and here Peveril soon claimed Lady Marchmont's hand, leaving Henrietta free to dance with Rivers. It was such happiness to meet him in the pattern of the dance, to touch his hand, and then, again, to see him returning to her through the crowded room, that she did not mind the fact that there was little opportunity for talk. There would be time enough one day. For the present, it was ample bliss just to be with him.

If there were still rumours afloat linking her with Clinton's escape, she heard nothing of them. After the months of loneliness, it was a very different matter to appear in public with Rivers at her side. He stayed with her all evening, successfully pleading a soldier's rights to any partner who sought her for the dance. It was he who brought her cold chicken and champagne at suppertime, and he, at last, who handed her into her carriage after Lady Marchmont in the cold hours of the dawn.

She leaned down towards him. 'Shall I see you tomorrow? Today, I should say?'

'My love' — he still had her hand — 'I fear not. I would not tell you before, for fear of spoiling your evening, but I must leave town at once. My despatches are ready. It is but Lord Liverpool's kindness that has given me these few hours of happiness. Now, I must go home and change my dress and it is time to start.'

'Oh, Charles.' Her hand trembled in his.

'Good-bye, my love.' He gathered both her hands for a moment to his breath, then bent to kiss them and, very gently, disengage himself. 'Take care of yourself, I beg. And, Henrietta, for my sake, no more scrapes!'

She laughed down at him, forbidding tears. 'My darling, I promise you shall come back to find me a perfect paragon, a monument of the dullest virtue. Oh, Charles' — she echoed him — 'do you be careful too.'

But the horses were getting restless. 'Lady Marchmont's carriage blocks the way,' cried a footman in stentorian tones. Rivers bowed low and stepped back, the coachman whipped up his horses, and Henrietta sank back, sobbing, in her corner. It was only then, so absorbed had she been in her thoughts of Charles, that she realised Lady Marchmont had, inevitably, witnessed the whole scene. She was sitting now, very silent in her own corner. For a moment, Henrietta was tempted to go to her, to break down the barrier between them, so that they might share their tears.

Lady Marchmont forestalled her. 'A very touching scene,' she said dryly. 'I am glad you have made your peace with Charles so easily.' But her voice betrayed her. For the first time, Henrietta, in the flush of her own happiness, realised what her stepmother must be suffering. But there was nothing to be said. In the face of Lady Marchmont's grief, she could only be silent and admit that her own sorrow was but the mask of a deep happiness. Charles was hers now. The quarrel was over. It was but to wait his return and all would be well. She slept that night, sweet and deeply, as, it seemed, she had not for weeks, and woke to believe in happiness.

To her relief, Lady Marchmont, too, contrived to present at least an appearance of content next morning. She was full of plans for Cedric's wedding, which was to take place as soon as possible.

'In October at the very latest,' said Lady Marchmont. 'I am sorry your father cannot be here for it, my love, but he seems fixed with the Czar for the duration of the war. Lord Liverpool was telling me only the other day that we owe the new agreement between the Allies entirely to his negotiations.' She sighed. 'I am almost tempted to wish he had been less successful, if it means he must stay still longer from home. But as for dear Cedric's wedding, I am sure you will agree with me that it would be foolish to allow of any delay.'

Henrietta smiled and agreed. Lady Marchmont, she knew, was prey to a gnawing fear that Miss Jenkinson would change her mind. For herself, she thought this unlikely. She was very fond of Sally Jenkinson by now, and gave her credit for being admirably clear about her own intentions. If she had decided to have Cedric, she would do so, come what might. Henrietta's real anxiety was for Lady Marchmont herself. Deprived of Cedric, as well as of Rivers and her husband, how would she contrive to go on? It was a curious thing, but despite all the reasons she had to distrust and even hate her stepmother, she found herself, these days, increasingly pitying her. She seemed, somehow, so lost, so helpless. What could be the matter with her?

She was growing thin and losing her gay young looks. Peveril and Stanmore came to the house more rarely, and when she and Henrietta rode in the park, it was often alone. The young idlers about town had found themselves other interests. Lady Marchmont was being relegated, whether she liked it or not, to middle age.

Increasingly anxious about her stepmother's altered looks, Henrietta frequently debated with herself whether she ought to say anything to her about little Caroline, who was at last beginning to bloom and thrive at Miss Gilbert's school. Presumably, Mrs. Muggeridge must have reported that the child was lost, and Henrietta sometimes wondered if Lady Marchmont's drawn appearance could possibly be due to anxiety on her behalf. But how could this be so? According to Miss Muggeridge, Lady Marchmont had certainly acquiesced in if not encouraged, the diabolical project of the 'accident'. Why, then, should she peak and pine at the news that it had been successfully accomplished? No; Henrietta hardened her heart. What had been planned once, might be again. For the child's own sake she dared not let Lady Marchmont know of her whereabouts. She wondered, sometimes, what Cedric thought of the affair. Did he take it for granted that, having failed to enlist his assistance, she had given up all idea of trying to rescue little Caroline? Did he, too, believe that the child was genuinely lost? She did not know and did not mean to ask. Cedric, anyway, was at home so little these days that she seldom saw him. He was more deeply involved in Sally's life and was even, at her instigation, spending a good deal of time at her different properties, being instructed by her patient managers in the ways of business.

Sally told Henrietta that Cedric was making an extremely favourable impression. 'I told you,' she said triumphantly, one hot September morning, 'that he was only extravagant because he had nothing else to do. We shall see him a man of affairs yet. And one thing I will say for him — he has no false pride about turning businessman. I was afraid he might not like to be talking about hides in Birmingham and pottery in Manchester, but he takes it all as the greatest joke in the world. I believe he and I will do very well, Henrietta.'

Henrietta thought so too, and was able to agree with her friend wholeheartedly. There was no doubt about it, Cedric was a different creature these days. After a few painful sessions with Sally's lawyers, he had been freed for the first time from his burden of debt, and confided to Henrietta what an astonishing change he found it to be able to look the world in the eye without fear of a dun. 'I am a reformed character, believe me.'

She did believe him and, more important still, began to think that his gratitude to his betrothed, who had handled the whole affair with the greatest tact and generosity, was developing, without his realising it himself, into a stronger feeling. 'Truly, Henrietta, she is the best girl in the world!' He had gone on more surprisingly still. 'And do you not think that she is developing into quite a beauty now she has got a little town bronze?'

Henrietta privately doubted whether her short and freckled friend would ever come within a mile of beauty, but was delighted to find that Cedric's affection for her was beginning to overpower his judgment. She temporised and turned instead to praise of Sally's disposition.

The wedding was celebrated with all possible pomp. Lord Liverpool gave away the bride. Lady Marchmont, every inch the matron in plum-coloured satin and a turban, sobbed discreetly into her pocket handkerchief. Henrietta, carrying the bride's bouquet of hothouse flowers, wished Charles was there and blessed Sally in her heart for her thoughtfulness in inviting Simon. Society was her friend again these days, having lost interest in her and turned instead in full cry after Lady Caroline Lamb, who had recently, so the Miss Giddys said, attempted suicide at an evening party. Henrietta, whose indiscretions certainly paled in comparison to this, nevertheless found herself increasingly weary of her position as an engaged young lady without a fiancé. It was a very pleasant change to have Simon at her elbow, glad to dance with her, ready to hold her fan or fetch her gloves, ready even, at her request, to perform similar errands for Lady Marchmont.

He was in tearing spirits, and after the happy couple had driven off in a shower of rose petals and good wishes he seized a quiet moment in the ebb of the party to tell Henrietta why.

'Is it not famous?' He led her to a quiet corner of the emptying room, 'My grandfather has agreed at last. I am to leave Oxford and come to London with Matt Gurney to try our hand as clerks in his father's bank. Mr. Gurney says it is the best possible start for a businessman. We are to begin at the very bottom, and if we show promise — and work hard, of course — he will find us openings later on. And to think that I owe it all to you, Miss Marchmont.'

'To me?'

'Why, yes. I did not like to tell you before, because I was afraid it would trouble you, but old inkhorn — my tutor — spotted me when I was climbing back into college after we went to Shrovebridge that day. There was the devil to pay, I can tell you, with lecturings and gatings and letters to my grandfather — and the long and the short of it was that they decided between them I am not cut out to be a clergyman. Which is what I have been telling them these three years past or more. So you see that I really owe it all to you.'

Henrietta was horrified 'What! You have been in all this trouble for my sake, and never even let me know? I might at least have spoken to your grandfather on your behalf.'

'But you could not,' he pointed out, 'since the reason for your going to Shrovebridge was a secret. And that reminds me, now that I am a free man at last, I contrived to ride down there yesterday to see how little miss was doing.'

'Did you really? How *good* you are, Mr. Rivers.'

He coloured. 'Not at all. I promised her I would, poor little thing, and have felt guilty not to have done so sooner. They tell me she still does not speak.'

'No, the poor lamb. Miss Gilbert begins to fear there may be some congenital deficiency, but I still hope it is but the result of what she has suffered. If you had but *seen* the place and the people I rescued her from.'

'I can well imagine it. I tell you, Miss Marchmont, there is so much suffering, so much to be done in the world that I do not know how I can bear to lose time as a clerk. I met a man called Shelley the other day — he was up at Oxford for a while, but was sent down last year — and you should just hear his plans for improving the world! He is to found an ideal community, with everyone equal and all working in common for what they need. Pantisocracy, he calls it. I tell you, I was sorely tempted to throw in my lot with him.'

'But you did not?'

'Why, no.' Again he coloured. 'To tell truth, I was not sure that it would work. Dreams are all very well, and when one listened to him talk it seemed possible enough, but I do not believe one can reform things so suddenly. No, I mean to go the slow way about it. First I must make a place for myself in the world, then, perhaps, I can do some good. Besides, I am afraid I am selfish enough after all. I want to marry some day and have children, and I do not see how I could support them if I lived in Mr. Shelley's ideal community. It is all very well for him: His father is a baronet, and I suppose he has always had money, but you know my case is quite different. What there is must go to Charles with the title and I will have only what I can earn. But that is nothing — only look what your father has achieved. I cannot tell you what an inspiration he has been to me.'

Henrietta smiled and sympathised, but could not help a feeling of dismay at the idea of Simon with a wife. It was natural enough, she told herself. She was practically his sister and as such could feel how very long it must be before he could possibly afford to marry. But the party, she saw, was now breaking up fast and Lady Marchmont was looking about for her. She rose and left Simon pausing first to make him promise that he would come often to see her now that he was settled in London. 'I shall be lonelier than ever,' she said, 'now that my dear Sally is married. You must promise to be a comfortable brother to me, Mr. Rivers.'

When had she used that phrase before? She could not remember.

## CHAPTER FOURTEEN

In the inevitable letdown after Cedric's wedding, Henrietta had time to take stock of her position. Outwardly, at least, it was immeasurably improved. Society seemed to have accepted her at last. The Miss Giddys fawned on her and even went so far as to hurry to her with sympathy when they heard the news of British successes in North America and, more particularly, of the taking of the American *Shannon* by the British *Chesapeake*.

The tide of public opinion was against this unnecessary war by now and Henrietta's position was so much the easier. But there was more to it, she thought, than that. With a grudging respect for its percipience, she admitted to herself that society must have sensed something wrong, before, about her engagement to Charles. It was his brief visit and their appearance in public as an unmistakably affianced couple that had finally set her right in the eyes of the world.

His letters were the focal point of her days. Wellington had taken San Sebastián now and was fighting his way towards the French frontier, and though Charles wrote gaily and lovingly, it was impossible to miss the strain that underlay his words. 'To you alone can I say it,' he wrote once. 'I find I am not cut out for a soldier. Now that I have so much to hope for, and so much to lose, I can no longer look upon a battle as if it were some sort of a cricket match. I fear you have ruined me for the army, Henrietta.'

That letter lay under her pillow every night, and yet it filled her with a kind of superstitious terror. Now that he no longer enjoyed fighting, would he still bear the charmed life of which Simon had spoken? Her anxiety on his account was exacerbated by her fears for her father, who wrote brief, hurried letters, sometimes to her and sometimes to her stepmother, dated often from the travelling carriage in which he journeyed to and fro between the different Allied headquarters. To his relief, Bonaparte's surprise victory at Dresden had served merely to consolidate the alliance against him and plans were well forward for an advance upon France. It was only, he said, over and over again, a matter of time and then with victory, and peace, he would be home at last. Increasingly, a note of homesickness sounded between the lines of his letters and, with it, one of anxiety for his wife. She did not sound to be in spirits, he said in one of his letters to Henrietta. He hoped that she had not overtired herself with the arrangements for Cedric's wedding. He relied on Henrietta to do her best to lessen the blow that losing Cedric must be to her.

In the same post as this appeal Henrietta received a letter from Sally, who was still on a honeymoon tour of her various properties. She and Cedric, she said, had been thinking about Henrietta all alone in Marchmont House with her stepmother. Could she not come and pay them a long visit until it was time for them to return to town? They would dearly love, she said, to have her.

It was an invitation that Henrietta had half hoped to receive. She was tired of London, tired of Marchmont house, tired of her stepmother's company. And yet, now that it came to the point, she sat down at once to write an affectionate and grateful refusal. Lady Marchmont, she knew, had wisely decided not to visit the young couple until the honeymoon was over; she would not leave her alone in town. Her father's letter had only confirmed her own anxiety about her stepmother. Lady Marchmont was pale and listless these days. She spent long hours alone in her own room, reading, Henrietta suspected, the most depressing kind of revivalist literature. Even a visit from the Miss Giddys, full of rumours of an engagement for Princess Chalotte, failed to interest her, and she amazed them and Henrietta alike by reading them a lecture on the iniquitousness of gossip.

Only when the post came did she rouse herself, and Henrietta could not decide whether it was anxiety for her husband or for Charles Rivers that inspired her almost frenzied interest in her letters. Sometimes, though, letters from both of them would leave the hectic flush still on her cheek, her hand still shaking. What else, Henrietta wondered, could she be waiting for?

The servants, she knew, were beginning to comment on the change in their mistress. Rose spoke of her maid Fenner's anxiety about her. She did not sleep these nights, it seemed, but paced up and down her room till dawn.

'And then the strange people that come to see her,' said Rose. 'Gypsies and beggars and I don't know what all. Truly, miss, I don't know what's come to my lady.'

A few days later Henrietta was sitting at her embroidery in the morning room, battling with her conscience, which told her she should have accompanied her stepmother on a round of morning visits, when a footman announced Miss Gilbert.

She expected to see the elder Miss Gilbert, who had recently returned to town after a prolonged autumn visit to her sister at Shrovebridge. Instead, it was Patience Gilbert herself who hurried anxiously into the room, exclaiming at her good fortune in finding Henrietta at home and alone.

'Truly,' she went on breathlessly, 'I could not decide what to do for the best, but knowing how fond you were of the poor child, I thought I would just chance it and bring her to you.'

'Bring her? What? You have brought Caroline?'

'I do hope I have done right. I left her in the carriage for fear you would not approve. But I must explain. You will think me out of my mind, coming to you like this, but in truth this disaster has been too much for me.'

'What disaster? Dear Miss Gilbert, I beg you will sit down and compose yourself.'

Miss Gilbert did so, wringing her hands. 'The smallpox. Poor little Johnny Erith is dying, the doctor says, and I fear Blanche Savernake is marked for life. But you must understand, Miss Marchmont, Caroline has not been exposed. I had taken her to the seaside for a few days, hoping that alone with me she might perhaps begin to speak. But all to no avail . . . except that it has saved her from the smallpox. I must go back at once. Poor Miss Harris, whom I left in charge, is nearly out of her mind with worry, but I thought that since little Caroline had not been exposed I would bring her to you in the hope that you might keep her until the danger is past.'

Henrietta put her hand to her brow. 'Miss Gilbert, I do not know what to say. Let me but think a minute. But in the meanwhile, do, I beg you let us have the child in. She will be tired and hungry after her long journey.' She rang for a footman and ordered cakes and a glass of milk, then hurried out with Miss Gilbert to the carriage, where they found little Caroline curled up asleep in a corner.

At once Henrietta regretted her suggestion. The child was well enough where she was — and suppose Lady Marchmont were to return and find her in the house? But she had gone to call, among other people on the Miss Giddys, who had recently returned from visiting Cedric and Sally. It seemed impossible that she should be home for at least another hour. And Caroline, as they watched her, stirred, woke and began to cry with fatigue and hunger. They took her indoors and Henrietta fed her milk and cakes while racking her brain as to what to do, and trying to fend off Miss Gilbert's apologies for her intrusion. What in the world was she to do with the child? Approach Lady Marchmont after all? But she had already decided against that. And besides, there was a new difficulty. Under Miss Gilbert's care Caroline's face had grown plump and rosy, losing its fine-boned likeness to Lady Marchmont. Even those haunting blue eyes no longer looked so like her mother's. Lady Marchmont might simply refuse to acknowledge her. After all, Henrietta had no proof whatever.

Her thoughts were interrupted by a scream from the doorway. She looked up to see Lady Marchmont, white as a sheet, clinging to the doorpost.

'Caroline!' She held out her arms.

'Mamma!' The child jumped down from Henrietta's lap and ran across the room into the arms held out to her. 'Mamma,' she said again through her sobs. 'Mamma, Mamma.'

For a few minutes there was amazed silence in the room, broken only by Lady Marchmont's incoherent murmurings over the child. Then Patience Gilbert rose to her feet.

'I must go,' she said. 'You will forgive me, I hope, Miss Marchmont. I had no intention, no idea . . . Naturally, I shall not say a word.' And with a half-blind curtsey to Lady Marchmont, to whom she had not even been introduced, she hurried from the room.

Her thoughts in a turmoil, Henrietta let her go. Bitterly angry with herself, she realised that she had been wrong in everything she had thought about Lady Marchmont and the child. It was all too clear, now, what had been the matter with Lady Marchmont and why such strange people had been visiting her. She had been suffering, pining, searching everywhere for her vanished child. Now, over Caroline's head, she looked up at Henrietta.

'I do not understand it,' she said. 'Where did you find her? Oh, my darling, my precious.' She bent once more over the child. 'I have found you at last. I will never let you go again.'

And again, with that miraculously discovered voice, little Caroline murmured her only word, 'Mamma, Mamma.'

Haltingly, Henrietta began to explain, her sense of guilt deepening as Lady Marchmont listened, exclaimed and shuddered.

'But why did you not come to me?' she asked.

It was unanswerable. Henrietta blushed and was silent.

Her silence itself was an answer. Lady Marchmont coloured angrily in her turn. 'Henrietta! You cannot have thought ... My own child, my Caroline,' and speech was lost in a flood of tears. Alarmed by this, little Caroline for her part burst into a fresh paroxysm of weeping, clinging anew to her mother. Lady Marchmont was calm at once. 'We will talk about it later,' she said. 'For the moment, the child must rest. Come my precious, you shall lie down on Mamma's bed and sleep your troubles away.'

When she returned, it was with an air of determination. 'I do not care what comes of it,' she said. 'I mean to keep the child with me.'

'To keep her?' Henrietta did not try to conceal her amazement. 'But, dear madam, have you considered?'

'I have considered everything. I know it may mean ruin, but I do not care. The child needs me; nobody else does. You know well enough, Henrietta, that if he ever does come home, your father could go on perfectly well without me. As it is, he spends most of his time in the House of Lords or at his club. If he had ever needed me more everything might have been different. No, I have quite made up my mind. I shall tell him the whole story. He has the right to know. And if he will not allow me to keep the child here, well, I shall simply have to leave him. It was another matter, of course, before Cedric was established in the world, but now, who have I to consider but myself — and Caroline? Do you realize that the sight of me made her speak at last? Henrietta, how can I part from her again? No, if your father proves adamant, as he well may, and indeed I could hardly blame him, Caroline and I will retire to the country and live together like the Ladies of Llangollen. You will come and see us I know, Henrietta, and so will Cedric and Sally. For the rest of the world, why should I care? I have served it long enough to know how barren are its rewards.'

Henrietta could not help sympathising. 'Of course I would come and see you,' she said. 'But I hope it will not come to that. Let us put our heads together and decide how the child may best be explained to the world. It will be much easier for my father to accept her if society has done so already.'

'Yes,' agreed Lady Marchmont. 'I have been thinking that very thing. And the more I think about it, Henrietta, the more it seems to me that we must stick to your original story.'

'My story?'

'Yes, of finding her straying in Richmond park and taking pity on her. Why not? It is impossible for slander to connect her with you, since everybody knows that you were not in this country when she was born. Henrietta, I know I have not always behaved to you as a stepmother should, but on my knees I beg that you will do this for me. Consider, you are known already as something of a rebel. What more in character than this impulsive adoption of a child? And what more logical than that I should join you in it? After all, you have concerned yourself so far already in little Caroline's affairs. How can you fail her now? Think! If, after having found me at last, she is snatched away again, to however good a school, what must be the effect on her? I fear not only for her speech, but for her reason.'

'Yes.' Henrietta was afraid it might well be true. 'But, ma'am, I am afraid Charles might not be best pleased. He has warned me already against doing anything out of line.'

'Charles!' Lady Marchmont gave her a quick, strange look. 'Yes. Charles . . . We must think what's best to say to him.'

'Dear madam.' Henrietta spoke hesitantly. 'Are you sure — forgive me — but are you sure the father would not help?'

'The father! Henrietta, think a little. If I did not sanction the "accident" to the child . . .'

'You're right, of course.' It was, indeed, unanswerable.

Everything that Miss Muggeridge had told her had suggested that someone was known to want the child out of the way. So — if not Lady Marchmont . . . 'Very well,' she said at last, reluctantly. 'That shall be our story. I must send for Simon and warn him to be ready to be cross-questioned on it. At least he is safe down from Oxford, so there is no need to fear getting him into trouble there. But there is one other thing: You must let me write a full explanation both to my father and to Charles. I owe them that.'

Lady Marchmont agreed at once, only stipulating that her own letter to her husband must go off first. 'And we must write, too, to dear Cedric and Sally. Their support will be vital in the first shock of public opinion. And tell me, when does your friend Mr. Brummel return to town? If he will but back us, we can snap our fingers at the rest of them.'

'I hope you are right,' said Henrietta, 'but I fear Mr. Brummel's quarrel with the Prince Regent goes deeper than it first seemed. I am anxious for him, to tell truth. I do not think he quite understands how seriously he has affronted the prince. But he is a good friend. He will do what he can for us. If my father will but accept the child, though, that will be half the battle. I wish we could wait to hear from him, but I do not see how that can be contrived.'

'No,' said Lady Marchmont. 'It cannot, for part with Caroline again is what I will not do. Oh, Henrietta' — she crossed the room to take her hand — 'this kindness of yours is more than I deserve. I have been I cannot bear to think how guilty towards you in the past. I can only say I will endeavour to deserve your goodness in the future.' And to Henrietta's embarrassment she burst into tears. Soothing her as best she might, Henrietta thought that indeed they had come a long way from the day when her stepmother had tried to destroy the papers proving her birth. But what was the use of remembering that now? They were to be friends at last, and she was glad of it. She changed the subject.

'I must write a note to Simon Rivers at once,' she said. 'May I invite him to dinner tonight? I think he gets but short commons at his lodgings, and Caroline, I know, will welcome him as a friend. She liked him very much better than she did me that day we took her down to Shrovebridge.'

Simon arrived in admirable spirits, but turned grave and shook his head when Henrietta, who had made a point of being down ahead of Lady Marchmont to receive him, told him what they had planned.

'I hope you know what you are doing,' he said. 'Of course, you can count on me to back you up in any story you choose to tell, but I do not like to think what Lord Marchmont, and, for that matter, what Charles will say. It is not at all the kind of thing that he will like, you know. Cannot Lady Marchmont take the responsibility for "discovering" Caroline? After all . . .' It was the nearest he had come to a reference to Caroline's parentage.

'That's just it.' Henrietta, too, spoke indirectly. 'Everyone knows how recently I am come from America . . . I did ask whether the father — '

'The father?' He gave her a quick look. 'And what did Lady Marchmont say?'

'That it is out of the question. Besides, she loves the child. When you see them together you will understand.'

'I just hope for your sake, Henrietta, that Charles will. But where is my little friend? Am I not to see her?'

'Of course you shall.' Henrietta led him upstairs and tapped gently on the door of Lady Marchmont's room where a couple of amazed servants had installed a truckle bed for the child. The maid Fenner opened the door with the look of acid disapproval she had worn all day and admitted them reluctantly.

Lady Marchmont had already completed her toilet and was sitting by the little bed, dressing a doll for Caroline. She stopped and smiled her greeting 'Come in, Mr. Rivers, and let me thank you.'

But Caroline had already recognised him. She stretched out her arms to him. 'Rivers,' she said. It was her second word.

Fenner left that same day, more in dudgeon, Henrietta thought, at not being admitted into the secret of Caroline's birth than for her ostensible reason of 'never staying where there was children'. Lady Marchmont saw her go with relief and confessed to Henrietta that she had long distrusted her and had, indeed, suspected her of making a very good thing of commissions from the various tradespeople she had employed. Henrietta, who remembered various suggestive remarks of Madame Bégué's, thought this all too likely, but worried a little about the harm Fenner might contrive to do to her former mistress. Still, there was no use fretting about that, and she had enough to think about in drafting her letters to her father and to Charles.

In neither of them did she refer to little Caroline's parentage. Both men she thought, could be relied on to read between the lines where that was concerned. 'Lady Marchmont has taken an enormous fancy to the child,' was as near as she got. 'It makes her very happy to have her here.' It should be enough, to anyone who knew Lady Marchmont as these two men did. But where she found the letter to her father easy enough, that to Charles proved unexpectedly difficult. She kept hearing Simon's voice, grave, warning: 'It is not at all the kind of thing that he will like . . .' After writing and re-writing it, she sent the letter off at last in a spirit more of despair than optimism, and she and Lady Marchmont settled down to await the two men's reactions, and the world's.

The world, for once, was kind. Henrietta and Lady Marchmont had planned little Caroline's introduction to society almost as if it was a military campaign, and it succeeded as if it had Lord Wellington in command. Henrietta had fired the opening gun by telling Mr. Brummel their agreed version of the story when she met him at a dress party on the night of the child's arrival.

He had looked at her with his wise and worldly eyes, taken snuff, and thought for a moment. 'Hmm,' he said at last. 'You might even get away with it, Miss Marchmont. Always provided that Lady Caroline Lamb continues to provide a diversion with her rumpuses . . . and, of course, that the child does not look too much like anybody.'

Henrietta opened wide eyes. 'Look like anybody? But why should she, Mr. Brummel?'

He laughed. 'Why indeed? It would be most inconsiderate of her, would it not? But I am your friend, and dumb, Miss Marchmont. Only, perhaps, I might suggest that Lady Marchmont should discourage the child from calling her "Mamma" too publicly.'

'Good heavens, Mr. Brummel. Had you then heard of it already?'

'Of course I had. What do you think Lady Marchmont's maid has been doing since she left her but spreading the most damaging kind of slanders about her late mistress? Truly, I think you two conspirators have much to thank her for. Society does not like a talebearer, particularly not one in the lower walk of life. I think you will find she has done you more good than harm with her libels.'

The Miss Giddys, calling early the next morning, proved the soundness of this conjecture. They had come, according to the eldest, 'to see the dear little girl'.

'So romantic,' sighed Miss Patricia.

'So generous,' said Miss Letitia.

'So like our dear impulsive Miss Marchmont,' said Miss Giddy.

'And to think that the little dear is quite a daughter to you already.' Miss Letitia was addressing Lady Marchmont now. 'It seems like the hand of providence, does it not, now when my lord is so sadly and unavoidably absent. And when poor dear Miss Marchmont, too, has so little to interest her in life. How pleased dear Lord Marchmont and dear, dear Mr. Rivers must be to think you have found yourselves so interesting an occupation.'

Receiving no answer to this all too pertinent hint, she changed the subject. 'But we must tell you, dear Lady Marchmont, of the strangest imposition to which we were subjected yesterday.'

'Yes.' Miss Giddy took up the tale. 'Only to think of your woman Fenner —'

'Having the effrontery to come to see us,' chimed in Miss Patricia.

'With the most amazing tale of a cock and a bull,' said Miss Giddy. 'Which we will not sully your ears by repeating,' summed up Miss Giddy, much to Henrietta's relief.

'We soon sent her about her business, I can tell you.' It was Miss Letitia again.

'And with a flea in her ear, too,' added Miss Patricia.

'I hope it will be some time before she goes around uttering such libels again,' said Miss Giddy.

'And as for finding her a place,' said Miss Letitia, 'I hope we knew better than that. She will find that she has spoiled her market with a vengeance.'

'It's a foolish bird that fouls its own nest,' said Miss Patricia.

'As she will find to her cost,' added Miss Giddy.

They were interrupted in their diatribe by the arrival of Rose with little Caroline and spent the rest of their visit in enthusiastic cooings over the child. Luckily, she had already added 'Hetta' to her small store of words which made it seem slightly less odd that she continued to address Lady Marchmont as 'Mamma.'

'She takes you for her lost mother.' Miss Giddy gave the cue to her sisters.

'Most remarkable,' said Miss Patricia.

'Most touching,' said Miss Letitia.

And they turned to a serious discussion of the child's probable age, in which Lady Marchmont and Henrietta took part with the best composure they could muster. Rising, at last, to go, they gave the adoption their final blessing.

'We are going now to dear Lady Melbourne's,' said Miss Giddy.

'We shall tell her how happy we found you,' said Miss Letitia.

'And all about the little stranger,' concluded Miss Patricia.

And they took their leave in a perfect whirlwind of kisses and congratulations. Lady Marchmont smiled at Henrietta over little Caroline's fair head. 'So much for the world,' she said.


## CHAPTER FIFTEEN


Foggy November wore into cold December and still they had had no answer to their letters to Lord Marchmont and to Charles Rivers. The posts to Spain were always erratic in the winter months and according to the latest despatches Lord Wellington had now forced the French lines between Bayonne and the Pyrenees. The guns had fired on a cold November afternoon to celebrate this, and again when news came of the Allies' capture of Dresden. Rivers was doubtless fighting his way into France with Wellington, Lord Marchmont busy maintaining concord among the Allied sovereigns. At home, there was nothing to do but play with little Caroline and wait.

Marchmont House was a different place these days. The servants, dubious at first about the child, had been quick to take their cue from society and welcome her as a member of the family. The maids all spoiled her, and the footmen rode her pig-a-back round the servants' hall and caught her at the bottom when she slid down the banisters of the front stairs. And every day added its group of new words to her vocabulary. She had names for everyone in the household by now and was welcomed wherever she went, but still her fondest love was reserved for Lady Marchmont and for Simon Rivers, who was a frequent visitor these days, bringing always some entertaining story of city life for Lady Marchmont and Henrietta, and a new toy, made by his own clever hands, for Caroline.

It was evident from everything he said that he had thrown himself enthusiastically into his new life as a man of business and Henrietta thought that he was just as certainly making a success of it. He seemed to be a frequent and welcome visitor at the Gurneys' house in the Strand and Henrietta felt an odd qualm of — what was it? — when on several occasions she met him riding in the park with the Miss Gurneys. But then, she told herself, her anxiety for him was natural enough. He should look higher for a wife than one of the plain Miss Gurneys, however well dowered they might be.

She suspected, too, that he was still hankering after a political career, and indeed, he told her that he had gone with Matt Gurney to several meetings of the London Hampden Club, had heard Sir Francis Burdett speak, and had even tried his hand, on more than one informal occasion, at speaking himself. Henrietta sympathised too deeply with his passionate desire for an improvement in the lot of the working classes to remind him that he had once told her his coming out as a Whig might kill his grandfather. Fortunately, Lord and Lady Queensmere had been in Scotland all autumn so she hoped there was no need for them to know of their grandson's activities.

Christmas came, and with it, at last, letters from Lord Marchmont in answer to those he had received from his wife and Henrietta about the child. He had justified Henrietta's confidence in him. She never knew what he had said to his wife; only that Lady Marchmont stayed in her room all afternoon and appeared at last with red eyes to embrace Henrietta and vow that she would do her utmost to be worthy of so much goodness.

There was a letter, too, from Charles for Henrietta, who opened it with a shaking hand, only to realise, from the date, that he could not possibly have received hers about Caroline when he wrote. She read his protestations of undying love with an odd sensation of doom postponed, and turned with relief to his news of the war. 'We have them on the run now, sweetheart,' he wrote. 'It is but a question of time.' Her father, too, wrote hopefully, and London was full of rumours of peace. The Miss Giddys hurried in, a few days before Christmas, with the news that Princess Charlotte was engaged at last to the Prince of Orange. 'Young Frog they call him,' said Miss Letitia, 'I hope it will do.' They had more important news too: positive information, they said, that Bonaparte had accepted the Allies' terms. Even Simon, reporting that consols had risen to seventy, was hopeful for a day or two. But nothing came of it; there was still no answer from Charles; and December ended in a cold fog that combined with her continuing anxiety to reduce Henrietta's spirits to a nadir. A prey to unreasoning gloom, she could hardly rouse herself to share little Caroline's amazed delight at her New Year's presents.

And the weather grew worse and worse. As January wore into February, the fog lifted at last, but the cold remained intense. The Thames froze over, and enterprising businessmen built stalls on it and sold savoury pies, gin and gingerbread to the warmly dressed crowds who danced there to the music of the Pandean pipes. But Henrietta huddled at home over the fire, sick with cold and an undefined apprehension. She was roused at last by a visit from Simon, just returned from escorting his grandparents back from Scotland. He brought bad news. The cold had struck even sooner and more fiercely in the North. Lord Queensmere had caught a chill riding about his estates and had grown rapidly worse on the journey back to London, which he had refused to postpone.

'He is dying, Henrietta, and knows it,' Simon told her. 'And, what I know must please you, except for the reason, he has sent for Charles.'

'What?'

'Yes. He wrote some weeks ago, both to Charles and to Lord Wellington, asking that Charles might be sent home. There is much, I collect, to be settled about the estate. I think there is no question but that Charles will get leave to come. Whether he will find my grandfather alive is another matter. I cannot tell you how loath I was to leave him, and my poor grandmother, upon whom the whole burden of his illness falls, but to tell truth, Henrietta, there is not much that I can do for my grandfather. He has not, I fear, forgiven me for my refusal to go into the church and has also, I think, got wind of my political activities. But what can I do? I know it must grieve him deeply, but there is so much to be done, and so few to do it. I do not see how I can turn back now. And yet it's so sad, Henrietta. We used to be such good friends, he and I, and now he just turns away from me and asks over and over again for Charles.'

Henrietta was trying to think of something to say that was at once true and consoling when little Caroline danced into the room.

'Simon!' she cried. 'You are back at last.' And flung herself upon him.

Lifted at once to his shoulder, she beamed down upon Henrietta from her perch. '*Now* can we go skating?'

Henrietta sighed and smiled. The child had been begging ever since the freeze began to be taken skating on the Thames. Henrietta had rashly admitted that she had learned to skate as a child in Boston and nothing would satisfy the child but that she should be taught too. But Henrietta had put her off. In her present state of depression, she was in no mood for such an outing and had pointed out that they had no one to escort them. When Mr. Rivers returned ... perhaps ...

Simon shifted the child to the other shoulder. 'How well she talks these days,' he said. 'I think she deserves the treat, do not you, Henrietta? And it would do you good, too. You look a trifle peaked, if I may take a brother's liberty to say so.'

In the end, Henrietta yielded to their joint persuasions and was glad she had done so when she saw the animated scene on the river. The sky, which had for days been a sullen grey, threatening snow, had cleared miraculously and the sun shone through, picking out here a touch of scarlet, there of white, against the silver-grey background of ice. At the end of a happy hour or so, she turned her flushed and laughing face to Simon.

'How happy I am,' she cried impulsively. 'I had forgotten what it was like to be alive.' And she turned to flash away from him on her quicksilver skates, fetched a whirligig pattern on the ice and returned at such speed that Caroline let out a cry of dismay and Simon let go her hand to steady Henrietta with both of his. She clung to him for a moment, laughing and breathless, then dropped his hands to catch hold of Caroline, who was dangerously unsteady on her feet. 'It is too much happiness,' she said. 'All this — and Charles coming home. Are you not delighted, Simon?'

'Of course.' He said it so shortly that she looked at him for a minute in puzzlement. Used, by now, to all his moods, she was surprised to miss his usual quick response to hers. Then an explanation struck her.

'Oh, Simon,' she exclaimed, 'how selfish I am. I forgot all about your poor grandfather, and we have kept you far too long from him and your work. Come, Caroline it is time to go home.'

It was a subdued little party that returned to the carriage. Simon continued oddly silent and surprised Henrietta by agreeing at once to her suggestion that they set him down near his place of business. But Caroline, whose teeth were chattering with cold, set up a wail of disappointment when he left them, and grizzled all the way home. Perhaps because of this, Henrietta too found her bright spirits oddly dimmed. And yet, she had so much cause for rejoicing. Charles was coming home at last. And if, as seemed probable, he arrived to find himself Lord Queensmere and a man of property, the main barrier to their marriage would be removed. Why, then, was she not happier? What was the matter with her these days? Hurrying little Caroline almost crossly to bed, she told herself that she was suffering from a schoolgirl's imaginary terrors. Charles' return would soon sweep these megrims away.

Happily for her, Cedric and Sally returned to town that week. They had beeen staying, since Christmas, at Sally's house in Leicestershire in the hopes that Cedric might be able to put in some hunting with the Quorn, but the continued frost had finally driven them back to London.

Hurrying round to visit them, at Lord Liverpool's, where they were staying, Henrietta found Sally alone, looking, she thought, paler and quieter than usual. Cedric, she explained, was out looking at a house that was for sale in Grosvenor Square.

Henrietta was delighted. 'You are thinking, then, of settling in town?'

'I believe so; for the greater part of the time at least. After all, one must be in town for the season, and it will be so much more convenient to have a base from which we may visit my properties. And, besides' — suddenly she was the old outspoken Sally — 'to tell truth, I do not find that Cedric likes life in the

Midlands. There is neither the society nor the conversation that he has been used to. And what is the use of having money if we do not use it to make ourselves happy?'

While entirely agreeing with this sentiment, Henrietta could not help wondering what had become of Sally's hopes that Cedric would take over the management of her business interests. Too tactful to refer to these, she asked instead how they had gone on at Melton Mowbray.

'Oh, well enough,' Sally replied. 'If it had not been so bitter cold. Poor Cedric had but one day's hunting all the time we were there, and if that was not bad enough, the friends of his we had asked cried off at the last moment — at the news of the frost, I imagine — so we were left high and dry with only each other to talk to. Let me tell you, Henrietta, that I find a honeymoon a grossly overrated institution. I like society, plenty of it, and so does Cedric. To shut us up alone together is almost cruelty. Why, it got so that he was falling asleep over his port after dinner while I shivered over the fire in the drawing room and pretended to entertain myself with *Childe Harold* until I could decently get myself warm in bed. If you will take my advice, Henrietta, when you marry Rivers you will take him on a round of bridal visits at once, where you may entertain yourselves with company and show off your trousseau at the same time.'

Henrietta was surprised and grieved at this speech. It was true, she had never thought that Cedric and Sally had very much in common besides a certain open good temper, but she had certainly not expected to see their marriage running into tedium so soon.

She was silent for a moment, wondering what to say, and Sally went on. 'Of course, I am a disapointment to Cedric. He bet Mark Stanmore a pony that he would have an heir before Ascot, and I fear he is to lose his money. I show no sign of breeding, and how should I when he sleeps all night over his port?'

To Henrietta's relief, these painful disclosures were interrupted by the arrival of Cedric himself, who greeted Henrietta warmly and told her he had just missed her at Marchmont House where he had been visiting his mother.

'And I met that protégée of yours, Henrietta, like Caroline. I confess, she does you credit. She was talking away nineteen to the dozen. Making up for lost time, I suppose. But, what, pray, does Rivers think of this charity of yours? Does he relish the idea of beginning married life with a daughter ready made?'

Everything in this speech grated on Henrietta's nerves. That Cedric, who knew perfectly well whose child Caroline was, should yet pretend, to her and to his wife, that she was Henrietta's protégée rather than his mother's was intolerable. And, besides, there was something about the tone of his reference to Rivers that she could not like.

'You are mistaken, Cedric,' she said. 'My father has already agreed, in the kindest of letters, that Caroline shall remain with him and Lady Marchmont. She will, I am sure, be the greatest comfort to them. As for Charles, I have not yet heard from him on the subject, but I rely entirely on his trust in me.'

'I am glad to hear it,' said Cedric unpleasantly. 'Otherwise you might perhaps be asking yourself how he will take your flirtations with his brother.'

'My flirtations with Simon: Cedric, what in the world are you talking about?'

'Only what all the world is, your constant escort by Simon Rivers. A cit, too, without a penny to bless himself with. I had thought you had more sense, Henrietta.'

She was angry now. 'That is enough, Cedric. Simon is Charles' brother and has done me a brother's service these last months by keeping me company. I know that Charles will be as grateful to him as I am. And as for his being a cit, you are surely not to be scoffing at him for that. Sally will forgive me, I know, if I ask where else the money comes from with which you are now buying houses? Let us not start casting that kind of stone, Cedric, or who knows where we shall finish?'

Back at Marchmont House, Henrietta gave way for once to despair. All her world seemed out of joint. Charles was far away and, worse still, she was not sure that she wanted him any nearer. She had taken Cedric roundly to task for his remarks about her friendship with Simon, but was she, in fact, so sure that Charles would approve of it? If it had really become a subject for gossip, could she rely on him to take her part? But surely, she told herself, he could not look on her friendship with his own brother as another of the scrapes he had warned her against. She would not injure him by such a suspicion. Having come to this wise decision, she lay down on her bed and burst into tears.

She was roused by Rose tapping on her door with a message

from Lady Marchmont. Caroline, who had been fretful and ailing for some days with a chill caught, Henrietta feared, on their skating expedition, had taken a turn for the worse. Hurrying to her room, Henrietta found Lady Marchmont bending anxiously over the little bed, on which Caroline tossed and turned in the grip of a raging fever. Always emotional, Lady Marchmont had given way already to complete despair and it was Henrietta who sent for the doctor and gave the orders necessary to turn the child's bedroom into a sickroom.

The doctor, when he came, was gloomy. The child, he said, was still too frail to withstand the fever that shook her. It was only a question of days, of hours perhaps ... He shook his head sadly and murmured something to himself about a 'merciful dispensation.' Fortunately, Lady Marchmont, sobbing by the bed, did not hear him, but Henrietta did, and led him to the door with a sudden, fierce courtesy that reminded him formidably of her father. Having got rid of him, she rolled up her sleeves and sent for Rose, whose red eyes showed that they were already mourning for Caroline in the servants' hall.

'Nonsense,' said Henrietta, in answer to her first lachrymose remark. 'It is merely a question of nursing.' And she sent her off with a list of commissions beginning with Dr. James' powders and ending with hot bricks and water gruel. That done, she managed to persuade Lady Marchmont to go to bed and prepared, herself, to sit up all night with the child.

Morning brought little comfort. Caroline had slept fitfully, Henrietta hardly at all, fearing that the child might uncover herself in her restless tossings and leave the bitter night air to administer the *coup de grâce*. Lady Marchmont's early appearance in the sickroom did more harm than good. She would do nothing but sob over the child's bed, convinced, apparently, that this illness was somehow the result of her own neglect. Inevitably, her tears were the signal for Caroline's. At last Henrietta banished her entirely and arranged that she and Rose, who was proving a tower of strength, should take turns to nurse and sit up with the child. Three days passed like this, days in which Henrietta seemed cut off from the world. It was, in a way, restful. Below, in the garden, snow still lay white on the ground. The cold remained intense and one of Henrietta's main anxieties was to keep the room warm enough, since it was almost impossible to keep Caroline covered through her spells of restless delirium.

From time to time, Lady Marchmont would come whispering to the door, with enquiries for the invalid and news of the world outside. Genuinely racked with anxiety for the child, she had yet not found it quite possible to give up her social round. After all, as she explained to Henrietta, one of them must make an appearance in society. Too busy to comment, even to herself, Henrietta simply agreed and listened passively while Lady Marchmont detailed her morning callers. One name, she noticed, was oddly absent. Where was Simon? She had been sure he would call the morning after their skating party to enquire after Caroline. But several days had passed, and still Lady Marchmont had not mentioned him. Was this, perhaps, because he was practically a member of the family — his name not worth mentioning? On the fourth morning of Caroline's illness, she asked, as casually as she could, if Lady Marchmont had not seen him.

'Why, no, not this age,' was the answer. 'Have you contrived to affront him, Henrietta? I confess I had begun to think he was here a little too often, but I have missed him strangely these last few days. I had not quite noticed how we had got in the way of giving him commissions.'

'Well then,' said Henrietta with an attempt at philosophy, 'perhaps he is grown tired of running our errands.' But she found herself oddly restless all day and amazed Rose by nearly losing her temper when Caroline spilled her gruel.

That was the day when Caroline, about whom Henrietta had secretly almost despaired, took a visible turn for the better. The results, for her nurses, were not altogether happy. In danger of her life, she had tossed and turned, slept and waked, muttered deliriously and slept again. Nursing her had been a matter, in the main, of mere physical endurance. Now, with the first return of strength and consciousness, she was fretful, restless and in need of constant entertainment. Too tired, almost, to think, Henrietta found this the greatest strain of all and turned hopefully to Lady Marchmont for help.

The experiment was not a success. A devoted enough mother according to her lights, Lady Marchmont unfortunately found her sick daughter merely tedious, and showed it. Henrietta returned from too brief a nap to find Caroline wailing fretfully while Lady Marchmont paced about the room in distracted irritation. Caroline, it seemed, wanted to be told a story. 'And you know I can no more tell stories than the man in the moon.'

She made her escape as fast as possible, while Henrietta, privately remembering how prolific she was with social fictions, set to work to pacify Caroline, who had become hot and feverish again in the course of that fatal hour of boredom.

To Henrietta's despair, all her usual wiles, her stories of life in America, her chains of cut paper dolls and black silhouettes proved useless. Still Caroline's head moved restlessly on the pillow, still she wailed for 'something else'. Then, all of a sudden her fretful wishes focused themselves. 'I want Simon,' she wailed. '*He* tells me stories.'

It was quite true. Simon had an inexhaustible supply of stories — about giants, about fairies, or just about his own comic misadventures at Harrow. But Simon was busy — at work, Henrietta explained. How could she ask him to come when he had so obviously neglected them?

Caroline turned her face into the pillow. 'I want Simon,' she cried again.

As the slow evening wore on, Henrietta tried in vain to distract her, but it was only too obvious that she was working herself up into a new bout of fever. At last, desperate and hardly admitting she was glad to the excuse — Henrietta sat down and wrote a hurried note to Simon, explaining the situation. 'I know it is late,' she concluded, 'but, Simon, if you *can*, I beg you will come to us.'

Told that Simon had been sent for, Caroline quieted a little and Henrietta was able to snatch a moment to run a comb through her disordered curls and repine at her crumpled reflection in the looking glass. Then Caroline's demands began again. Where was Simon? Why did he not come? Henrietta forgot all about her own appearance in her efforts to keep the child calm. When she heard the stir of an arrival belowstairs she sighed thankfully. She had known Simon would come. Caroline, too, had heard the bustle and perked up in her bed. 'There he is,' she said. 'Fetch him quick, Hetta, before Mamma makes him talk to her.'

Henrietta laughed ruefully and hurried out on to the landing. Looking down over the graceful balusters, she saw the footman in the act of admitting a man well muffled against the cold. 'Simon,' she called softly. 'At last.'

The visitor turned, in the act of being relieved of his heavy greatcoat, and looked up.

Henrietta's hand went to her heart. 'Charles!' She hurried

down the stairs towards him, her hands outstretched her tongue faltering over words of explanation.

He cut them short. 'Gossip seems to have been in the right of it,' he said. 'Again.' And then, with a warning look at the man in attendance, he took her hand and would have led her into one of the small saloons.

She held back. 'Charles. I am overjoyed to see you at last, but I cannot remain for more than a moment. The child — Caroline is ill. I must return to her straightway.' Her look, her touch, her tone pleaded with him to understand, to be patient.

'Ah, yes.' He raised fair eyebrows over those piercing blue eyes. 'I had almost forgot. The child.' His tone was chill.

She was beginning another attempt at an explanation; a promise that she would be with him again directly, when the footman hurried once more to the doorway. As he admitted Simon, Henrietta was alarmed by Caroline's voice from above. 'I want Simon,' she wailed. 'I want Hetta.'

Looking up, Henrietta saw with horror that the child had got out of bed and come out on to the landing in her night-dress. 'I must go,' she said. 'The child will kill herself with cold. Simon, explain to Charles.' And gathering up her skirts, she ran up the stairs, picked up the shivering child and carried her back to her bed. Then, at last, there was time to ring for Rose, who arrived at once, since it was almost her time to take over the night watch. With a quick explanation, a promise to Caroline that Simon would come to her soon, and one swift desponding glance at the haggard face in the glass, Henrietta hurried downstairs again.

She found Charles and Simon standing, apparently in silence, and not, by the look of it too friendly a one, by the library fire.

'You keep late hours,' was Charles' greeting.

'Yes.' She was determined not to lose her head. 'You must think us all run quite mad, Charles, but Simon will have explained, I am sure. This illness of Caroline's has put us quite at sixes and sevens. And that puts me in mind, Simon, that I promised her you would tell her one of your stories. I would be eternally grateful . . .'

'Of course.' He moved, with evident relief, to the door, then turned. 'Charles, Henrietta is worn out with nursing.' He reddened, looked as if he would like to say more and left them.

Alone with Henrietta, Charles looked at her for a moment in silence. Then, 'So it is Simon and Henrietta, is it?'

'Why, yes.' She looked at him in surprise. 'We are to be brother and sister, after all.'

'Yes.' He took a silent turn about the room, then came back to face her. 'Henrietta, I will be plain with you. I do not like these late night visits.'

'Oh?' For a moment she was tempted to remind him of how, once, he had visited Lady Marchmont.

Perhaps luckily, he did not give her time to speak. 'I hope you have not been encouraging Simon in these mad schemes of his,' he went on. 'He seems to have thrown his bonnet over the windmill with a vengeance. I only wish I knew where it would end. Are you aware that he has practically committed himself to the Whigs? It is no wonder my grandfather is ill. If he dies, I shall look on it as Simon's fault. To have a grandson of his talking universal suffrage, and abolition and I know not what other balderdash — I wonder the old man did not have a seizure on the spot.'

'But I believe Simon has been very careful not to flaunt his opinions in front of Lord Queensmere.' Henrietta felt bound to defend him. 'And, surely, Charles, you of all people cannot blame him for fighting for what he thinks right. I know he has suffered greatly over his decision to throw in his lot with the Whigs, since he is aware how much it must grieve both you and your grandfather, but how can he fly in the face of his convictions? You will find, I think, Charles, that he is much changed since you last saw him. Whatever you may say against it, life in the city has made a man of him.'

'A cit,' Charles sneered. 'And your dearest friend, it seems. I tell you again, I do not like these late visits.'

'Oh, Charles' — she was near losing her temper now — 'you must try to understand. The child was calling for him. She has been at death's door these last few days. Thank God she is recovering now.'

'Thanks to your nursing, Simon tells me.' And then, before she had time to take it as a compliment: 'Surely, Henrietta, there was someone in the house more suitable to look after the child.'

'More suitable? But, Charles, I love her.'

'So it seems,' he said dryly, 'since you have chosen to bring her here and flaunt her in the face of the world.'

'But what else could I have done?' And forgetting her embarrassment at the subject in her anxiety to make all right with him, she poured out the story of Miss Muggeridge's visit and disclosure of her mother's frightful plan.

He listened with a disapproving frown. 'Nonsense,' he said at last. 'I had thought better of your good sense, Henrietta, than to find you taken in by such a tale of a cock and a bull. Of course Miss Muggeridge was angling for a good bribe to protect the child. They are all alike, her kind: anything for money.'

'But, Charles, that is all the more reason for removing Caroline from their care. You cannot imagine how she is improved now that she is living here. And it give Lady Marchmont such pleasure, too. Oh, pray, do not be angry with me on the child's account, Charles. I promise you, we have contrived it almost without scandal.'

He shrugged his shoulders. 'Yes, I confess that by all reports you have handled it cleverly enough, though why you should have taken upon yourself the responsibility of the child's "discovery" passes my understanding. I should have thought Lady Marchmont was the person to do that.'

'But that was the way it happened. And besides, do you not see that it is impossible for any scandal to attach to me in the matter. I was not even in this country when Caroline was born.'

'Oh, very well.' He seemed to dismiss the subject, then returned to it. 'But I wish it clearly understood, Henrietta, that we are not going to have the child foisted upon us when we are married. You are not going to carry your softheartedness to that pitch. She is Lady Marchmont's responsibility, and Lady Marchmont's she must remain.'

'You need not trouble yourself for that. Lady Marchmont would not part with her if you went to her on your bended knees.'

'And what will your father say to that, I wonder?'

'Why, everything that is kind. We heard from him some time past. Oh, I was proud of him, Charles!' Aware that she was on precarious ground, she hurried to change the subject. 'But you have told me nothing of yourself. Are you truly home for good?'

'It seems so. My grandfather wrote to Lord Wellington in such terms that he had no choice but to release me. And it is true that there will be much to be done in settling the estate, though I confess it galled me to come away in the moment of victory. Bonaparte is beat, there is no question of it. It is but a matter of time now, and I doubt if there will be much more opportunity for distinction. I am probably better off at home, with a chance to look about me before the great ruck of retired officers come home with their way to make in the world. Thank God my grandfather's is an Irish title and will not immobilise me in the House of Lords. And that reminds me: When does your father come home? We must begin to look about for a seat for me.'

'I am not sure.' She was reluctant to disappoint him. 'But I fear he intends to stay with the Czar until they reach Paris.'

He uttered an impatient exclamation. 'Then we shall have to think again. How is your friend Sally these days? Is she still hand in glove with Lord Liverpool now that she is Lady Beaufrage?'

'I think they remain good friends. At least, I know she and Cedric stayed with the Liverpools when they first came to town. But I am afraid they are not very happy, Charles.'

'Happy? Whoever thought they would be? Not I, for one. But what's that to the question? You are still friends with her, I hope?'

'Oh, yes.' She was glad to be able to reassure him.

'Good. Then you must set about contriving for me to meet her. I cannot go into society while my grandfather is so ill, but there are a thousand ways you can arrange for us to meet and then let me alone to persuade her that I am the very man her cousin needs for his next safe seat.' He took her hand. 'And then when I am Lord Queensmere, as I fear I shall be all too soon, and a member of Parliament as well, how can your father refuse to let us be married? That is what I am working for; that is the goal that shines before me. To win something so precious as you, what toil would I not endure?'

Gently, irresistibly, he was pulling her towards him. But why did she want to resist? What was the matter with her? His lips found hers, demanding as never before. His hands gripped her bare shoulders with a bruising intensity. 'Henrietta' — the blue eyes burned down on her — 'let us be married soon.'

With a little sob (could it be of relief?) she pulled away from him. 'Charles, there is someone coming.'

For a moment, as he let her go, there was naked fury in his eyes. Then, 'Simon, no doubt,' he said dryly. 'We will talk more of this in the morning, Henrietta.'

## CHAPTER SIXTEEN

To Henrietta's surprised relief, the morning brought only a brief, passionate note from Charles. His grandfather, he wrote, had taken a turn for the worse and could not be left. After protesting his bitter disappointment at being unable to visit her, Charles concluded: 'Think, my love, about what I said to you last night. I cannot wait long for such a treasure. When the time comes, be ready for me.' They were the words of an accepted lover, words he had every right to use. Why, then, did they strike such a chill about her heart?

She lingered at home that morning, half hoping that Simon, to whom she had hardly spoken the night before, would call to ask how Caroline did. Instead, she received an early call from Mr. Gurney. Apologising for troubling her at so barbarous an hour, he explained that he had done so on purpose, in the hope of having a few words with her alone.

'Of course.' Henrietta was polite, if puzzled.

'Thank you.' He paused for a moment, then plunged in. 'I hope I am doing right in coming to you, Miss Marchmont, but you are fond, I think, of my Mr. Rivers.'

To her fury she felt herself colour to the roots of her hair. 'Why, yes,' she said, 'we are to be brother and sister, you know.'

'Precisely. That is just why I am come to you. Your influence, I collect, with Mr. Charles Rivers must be paramount. If you will but say a word to him on his brother's behalf, he cannot fail to listen to you.'

'Me? Speak to Charles about Simon? I am afraid I do not understand you, Mr. Gurney.'

'What? Has Simon not told you: I took it for certain he would have, but it is like him not to. You will have to bear with me then, Miss Marchmont, while I explain. Simon has been doing, as I am sure you are aware, admirably well in my house. I only wish my Matt had his head for business. But what interests me in some ways still more is the political turn Simon has taken. Some of the speeches he has made at the Hampden Club have been quite out of the way ... Of course I realise that I can hardly expect your father's daughter to sympathise with his politics, but for him personally I hope I can persuade you to feel.'

'Why, of course,' she said again. 'I am very fond of Simon. But I still do not understand what you would be at, Mr. Gurney.'

'Why, just this. I have had an opportunity, through friends in the inner councils of the Whig Party, of offering Simon the chance of a safe seat at Marchalsea where there is to be a by-election shortly. The Duke of Devonshire is prepared to use his influence on his behalf and that, you know, will do the business. But naturally, there are financial considerations involved. He cannot hope to be returned without a considerable outlay; it will be necessary for him to be able to guarantee one thousand pounds at least. It is the chance of a lifetime, Miss Marchmont, and it is idle to hope, as I believe he does, that it may recur. I only wish I could make the money available to him myself, but you know I have a houseful of daughters who must be launched in the world. There remains his family. Surely you can persuade Mr. Charles Rivers that, whatever he may think of his brother's change of party, this is an opportunity not to be missed.'

'I see.' Her father's daughter, she saw at once what a chance this was. 'But, surely, Lord Queensmere?' she asked.

'Is beyond business, I am told. And, besides, Simon is understandably reluctant to approach him in the matter, since he knows how deeply his change of party must affect him.'

'I see,' Henrietta said again. But what she really saw was the two brothers standing, last night, facing each other, silent and hostile, across the fireplace. In her heart she knew that to appeal to Charles would be useless. 'Mr. Gurney, I do not know what to say.'

He rose at once to his feet. 'I am sorry to have troubled you. Miss Marchmont.'

'No, no. I beg you will be seated. It is just ... Mr. Gurney, I am sorry to have to say it to you, but I do not believe Charles will help.'

'Oh. I see.' She was afraid that he saw far too much. 'Then I am afraid that my friend Simon must just say good-bye to his chance.'

Once again he rose to go, but she stopped him with an impulsive gesture. 'If only my father were here. I know he would help.' There was a little pause before she went on. 'Mr. Gurney, I — I do not know how to say this. But' — once again she paused, then, in a rush — 'I am my father's heiress. Could I not borrow the money?'

'On your expectations? Miss Marchmont, you are a true friend, but you must not be going to the moneylenders, which, I am sure is something your father would never forgive.' It was his turn to pause for a moment, thoughtfully. Then, 'But if you are sure of yourself, and will guarantee the money, by your own note to me, I will advance it to Simon.'

'Oh, thank you. Only tell me what I must write, and, Mr. Gurney, on no account must Simon know.' Or Charles either, she told herself, as, their business completed, Mr. Gurney took his leave with many protestations of friendly satisfaction.


There followed a strange, twilight time for Henrietta. Charles continued at Wimbledon, writing her, every day, short, passionate notes of which the theme was always the same. He longed for her; he was maddened by his inability to visit her; they must marry as soon as his grandfather showed the slightest sign of recovery. 'Otherwise' he wrote, 'we may find ourselves compelled to wait out the period of mourning for him, and that, my love, I could not bear.'

In her answers, she temporised, but in her heart, she despaired. What in the world had happened to her? Had Charles changed, or had she? Had she ever really loved him? Love at first sight, indeed! A girl's infatuation. Enthralled by that magic, skilful touch of his, she had loved, not Charles, but her own image of him. Time and again, when she had been shaken in her allegiance, he had drawn her into his compelling, expert arms, and she had been his slave again. Now, painfully, irrevocably, she found herself free. But what could she do? How could she tell him, now, when he had so much to trouble him, that she had changed her mind?

If only her father would come home. He would help her. And yet it was her father's absence that provided her best excuse for postponing the wedding. Her only consolation, those cold days when winter lingered on and spring would not come, was little Caroline's continued recovery. But there, too, was a drawback. A fretful and, inevitably, a spoiled convalescent, Caroline kept asking for Simon, and still Simon did not come. Pride would not let Henrietta write again and ask him to visit them, but, missing him herself more than she had imagined possible, she found it hard to keep her temper when Caroline fretted for him.

News of him, at least, she had. He had thrown himself with enthusiasm into contesting his by-election and seemed, she thought, to be making an admirable job of it.

The Miss Giddys, of course, were gloomy. 'So Mr. Simon Rivers is become a flaming radical,' said Miss Letitia.

'Drinking at the Crown and Anchor with Sir Francis Burdett,' said Miss Patricia.

'Plotting, no doubt, at the King's Arms to overset Government and bring us all to ruin,' added Miss Giddy.

'And such a well-spoken young man, too,' said Miss Letitia.

'I would never have thought it of him,' said Miss Patricia.

Henrietta, who had been controlling her temper with difficulty, could stand no more. 'I believe it to be true that Mr. Simon Rivers has joined the Whigs,' she said, 'but I am yet to learn that it necessarily means he is planning to overthrow the Government. I collect that Mr. Rivers is entitled to his opinions as much as anybody else.'

'Even if they kill his grandfather?' asked Miss Giddy.

'But of course we defer to your great knowledge, Miss Marchmont,' said Miss Letitia.

'Naturally, you would know more about Mr. Simon Rivers than most people,' said Miss Giddy.

'My dears, we must be taking our leave,' said Miss Patricia.

'To call upon dear Lady Beaufrage,' explained Miss Giddy.

'We owe her a duty for her new mother's sake,' said Miss Letitia to Lady Marchmont. 'Is it true that they are to buy a house in town and quite cut her manufacturing interests? I had hoped it might mean an interesting event . . .' She let the sentence trail off hopefully.

When Lady Marchmont did not respond, Miss Giddy took up the tale. 'They have been married these five months or more.'

'I believe dear Lord Beaufrage is quite the man about town again,' said Miss Patricia.

'His friends must be glad to see him back at Watiers,' said Miss Letitia.

'And why not?' asked Henrietta, who found this new teasing of her stepmother harder even to bear than their attacks on herself. 'I have yet to learn that a man must do nothing but stay at home and match his wife's wools, just because he is married.'

'Of course not,' agreed Miss Giddy warmly.

'What an understanding wife our dear Miss Marchmont will make,' said Miss Letitia.

'Mr. Rivers is a lucky man,' said Miss Patricia.

'Mr. *Charles* Rivers,' explained Miss Letitia.

'Such a *good* young man,' said Miss Giddy.

'So devoted a grandson,' added Miss Patricia.

'And to think of his even finding time to comfort dear, lonely Lady Beaufrage.' Miss Letitia let the sentence hang, obviously waiting to be questioned on it. But Henrietta and Lady Marchmont exchanged one long, thoughtful glance and said nothing. Deprived of the reaction they had hoped for, the Miss Giddys rose at last and took their leave.

'You must not mind them, my love,' said Lady Marchmont, when they were really gone. 'They only do it to tease you. You should not let them see that they have succeeded.'

'I know it,' Henrietta said ruefully. 'But they are beyond bearing sometimes.' Neither of them thought fit to refer to Miss Letitia's remark about Charles Rivers and Sally Beaufrage, but Henrietta thought about it a good deal in the days that followed.

The Miss Giddys, however, soon had something better to do than gossip about Henrietta. All of a sudden, with the first spring weather good news from Europe came thick and fast. Wellington had defeated Soult and taken Bordeaux, while in the North the Allied armies were advancing rapidly on Paris. And as if it was not enough delight for the Miss Giddys to run from house to house comparing and passing on the latest news, they had an ample source of scandal at home too. The quarrel between the Prince Regent and his wife had achieved new heights of vulgar publicity and he was being greeted wherever he went with shouts of, 'Where's your wife, Georgie?' Henrietta's affairs paled in comparison to this, and, to her relief, she was spared a visit from the Miss Giddys for several days.

Caroline was getting steadily better, but Charles' daily notes from Wimbledon reported no improvement in his grand-father's condition and no early hope of getting into town to see her. Instead, his notes urged, on a rising note of passion, that as soon as he could be spared from his grandfather's bedside, they should be secretly married. 'If you were but mine, I could bear everything,' he wrote. Wondering what, exactly, he meant by 'everything', Henrietta admitted to herself, at last, that she did not trust him. He was not stupid. He must be aware, by now, that her feeling towards him had changed. His reaction, it seemed, was to make sure of her. Increasingly aware of the false note in his passion, she yet found that his tone of the confident and accepted lover made it extraordinarily difficult for her to take the initiative and break their engagement. Her only comfort was that he did not come to press his suit in person, but this, she knew, was a relief that could not last.

But what could she do? It was April now and she sat at her bedroom window, nibbling at her pen, trying to think of an answer to his latest note of love and devotion, and gazing instead out at the garden, green and gold with daffodils. Suddenly she jumped to her feet. The guns were firing. Could it be victory at last? Hurrying downstairs, she met Lady Marchmont in the hall and they ran together out into Park Lane. Crowds were gathering already, and rumours passing from mouth to mouth. Bonaparte had committed suicide; Paris was in flames; the Czar of Russia had been elected King of France — No, it was Wellington, and he was to be President.

They returned to the house little the wiser, but soon a footman came back with firm news. Paris had fallen and Bonaparte had abdicated at last. All through the Easter week-end the news kept coming in and *Gazette* followed *Gazette*. By Sunday, the supply of newspapers was exhausted and the newspaper horns did not blow. But the news got about just the same. Bonaparte was to be exiled to Elba; the Allied sovereigns had made their ceremonial entry into Paris; the war was over. Most important of all, for Henrietta, was a short note from her father, dated from Paris, and announcing that he would be home next week. Crying quietly with relief, Henrietta told herself that he would free her from Charles. She had come a long way from that first encounter in a Devonshire lane.

On Monday, London was to be illuminated in celebration of the peace, and at breakfast that morning Lady Marchmont bewailed that they had no escort to take them to see the decorations, which were expected to be something quite out of the ordinary. At luncheon, she was triumphant. 'I have secured us a gallant for this evening,' she announced.

'Oh?' Henrietta looked up quickly. 'Who?'

'Why, who but Simon Rivers?'

'Simon? Are you out of your mind?'

'But why not, my love? I know he has somewhat neglected us of late, but that is only because he has had his electors at Marchalsea to consider. It can do him nothing but good to been seen out, this evening, with you and me. And since Charles, as we know, is unable to escort us, what more suitable than for his brother to do so? I cannot think why I did not hit on him sooner, for I tell you frankly I would not miss this spectacle for the world. So I just sat myself down and wrote him a little note, in both our names, asking him to come for us this evening, and have had the most polite of answers. I can tell you, my love, he is an escort these days that anyone could be proud to be seen with. I never saw such a change in anyone as there has been in him since he came to town. I declare, I quite took him for Charles the other day when I met him in the park with those plump Miss Gurneys.'

Henrietta ground her teeth silently. The damage was done: to protest further would only make matters worse. And, besides, Simon had agreed to come. Impossible to repress a leap of happiness at the idea of seeing him. And perhaps she might learn at last why he had kept away from them for so long. For she could not accept Lady Marchmont's easy explanation that he had been busy at Marchalsea, and had racked her brain during many a sleepless night as to how she could have offended him.

The afternoon dragged interminably; dinner had never seemed so long; but at last Simon appeared, looking, Henrietta thought tired, thin and pale. And surely there was a note of constraint in his greeting? She must have offended him: but how? For once, she was grateful for Lady Marchmont's ready flow of talk, glad enough to sit silently by, studying Simon's face and listening as he answered her stepmother's questions about Marchalsea. He did so readily enough, but as soon as politeness allowed, suggested that they set forward to look at the illuminations, which had already, he said, drawn great crowds. He was anxious, Henrietta told herself, to get the outing over with.

It was with mixed feelings and an infuriating tendency to tremble that she found herself leaning on his familiar arm once more. With Lady Marchmont chattering away on his other arm, he led them down Pall Mall to look at the lamps decorating the pillars of Carlton House. Returning, Lady Marchmont insisted, despite the rapidly thickening crowds, on stopping to look down St. James's Street, where each of the clubs had its gay decoration of candles, outlining every architectural nook and cranny.

As they paused to gaze at the brilliant scene, a flash of lightning suddenly put lamps and candles alike to shame. It was followed almost at once by a long, threatening roll of thunder. The crowd stirred uneasily. All day the weather had been oppressive, now the first large drops of rain began to fall. As the candles went out, one by one, the crowd began to move, hurriedly now, for shelter. The rain came faster, and another flash of lightning heralded a downpour. A woman's scream somewhere in the thick of the crowd touched off panic. Simon, who had Lady Marchmont on his inner arm, tried to guide her and Henrietta to a doorway where they could wait out panic and storm alike, but the crowd was too thick and too unreasoningly desperate. Henrietta on the outside, was torn from his protective arm and carried away in the chattering, screaming tide.

Aware that to struggle would be dangerous, she let herself go with the crowd, ignoring the rain that soaked her light muslin, and concentrating on keeping upright. To fall, she realised, might be fatal. After a day of jubilation and gin, the crowd had become an animal thing, ruthless in its panic hurry. Mercifully, in St. James's Square, the pressure eased a little and she was able to edge her way towards the central gardens and at last stand, under a tree, ignoring the beat of the rain as the crowd surged past her. When it had thinned a little she ventured out and started across the square towards Piccadilly and home. There was no hope, she was sure, of finding Simon and Lady Marchmont, nor did she dare venture back to where she had been separated from them. No doubt they, too, would make the best of their way home.

Unluckily for her, the rain now began to slacken and with it the crowd's concentration on finding shelter. At once, Henrietta became aware of how conspicuous she must be, in her drenched and clinging muslin, alone at this time of night. As she crossed the square, a man detached himself from the crowd and put his arm around her.

'All alone, my pretty?' His breath stank of gin and his voice was thick with it. 'We must do sommat about that.' And he pulled her towards him for a kiss.

Dodging his hot mouth at the last moment, Henrietta struck him a sharp blow in the face and twisted free, grateful, as she trembled in the sheltering darkness, for his fuddled state that made him incapable of following her. After that, she went more carefully, keeping, where she could, in the shadows, hurrying furtively across patches of light where the flambeaux outside the houses she passed had been relit since the rain.

She was accosted several more times before she reached Piccadilly, but managed to dodge or joke off her assailants. With the improvement in the weather, the crowd's temper, too, was improving. Quick-witted as always, she managed to convince several would-be gallants that her own escort was just behind her in the crowd. But it was an anxious business enough and it was with heartfelt relief that she saw a familiar face at the corner of Piccadilly. It was Miss Muggeridge, dressed to kill in her Sunday best of purple satin, with an equally flamboyant female friend on either arm. They looked like angels of mercy to Henrietta, who lost no time in stopping them and making her plight known.

'A golden guinea to see you home?' said Miss Muggeridge. 'I should rather think we will.' And she took Henrietta's arm in hers and turned the little party in the direction of Marchmont House. 'To tell truth,' she went on, breathing gin into Henrietta's face, 'you are most happily met. I have had it on my (hic!) conscience this long time past that I have let such a freehanded young lady be took in by a sharper. Engaged to Mr. Rivers, is it? You never told me that, or I'd a' told you a thing or two. You as was so queasy over little Caroline. Why d'you think my Ma was so agin her, but that Mr. Rivers, who promised to, never paid her shot? And that stepma of yours with never a feather to fly with, nothing but promises and tears ... But even so, I don't think my Ma would have planned nothing if it hadn't been for Mr. Rivers. He let it show clear enough what he wanted. An accident, no questions, and Ma could name her price. Not but what she'd a' been lucky to get it, from what I've been hearing. Queer Street for him and no mistake if that grandpa of his don't die precious quick. Or he don't marry you. Ah, that gets to you, don't it? Miss, dear, you don't want no truck with the likes of him. But here we is, safe and sound, and trusting (hic!) that you won't take offence at a few words spoke from the heart, and two golden guineas it was, waren't it now?'

Henrietta could not speak. Charles. It has been Charles all the time. Of course Cedric had lied to her. What else could he have done? And she had believed him, poor fool, because she wanted to. Charles ... Caroline. Those blue eyes in the thin little face. Charles' eyes, but she had refused to recognise them. Still speechless with a kind of slow, cold, growing horror, she handed Miss Muggeridge three guineas, was blessed for an openhanded young lady, and turned in at the gates of Marchmont House. As she did so, the front door of the house opened and she saw Simon's figure silhouetted against the light. His hair was plastered against his head with rain, his face distracted with worry. Then the door shut behind him and he was hurrying towards her through the dark.

'Simon.' She went to meet him. 'Do not look so. I am here, quite safe.'

'Henrietta!' He came to her, arms outstretched, and without thinking, she went into them. His lips found hers in the darkness and they stood there for a timeless moment of ecstasy before he let her go.

'Henrietta, we are gone mad.'

'Or come to our senses.'

'No, no, it is impossible. I cannot betray Charles so. Why do you think I have kept away from you since that day ... That day on the ice when I realised I loved you. Oh, Henrietta, why are you so beautiful, so alive?' He broke off and stood there for a moment, his hands still holding hers, silent in the merciful darkness, then, 'I have fought so hard against it, tried to pretend, even to myself, that what I felt for you was merely a brother's love, but it is no use. Henrietta — my love — we must not meet again.'

'Simon!'

'What else can we do?' Promise you will try to forget ... And I — I will go away. I must. Charles is my brother, your affianced bridegroom. Henrietta, I shall always love you, I cannot help it, but I promise I will never see you again.' And then, before she could find words, he had kissed her once, gently, finally, on the forehead, and left her shivering there in the dark.

# CHAPTER SEVENTEEN

Henrietta dreamed all night of Simon and woke determined not to despair. They loved each other. At last, this was certain, and she did not propose to let any fine-drawn scruples stand in the way of their happiness. As for Charles, he was beyond the pale, the would-be murderer of his own child. Not for an instant did she doubt the truth of what Miss Muggeridge had told her. It carried its own appalling conviction, and she was only amazed that she had contributed to be blind for so long to what, now, seemed so obvious. And yet, loving him, or thinking she did, how could she have believed it?

By the time she was dressed, her mind was clear. Charles must be given his dismissal as swiftly and as firmly as possible, and Simon must be made to understand — here she boggled. Here was the difficulty. She loved Simon too well, respected him too deeply, not to realise that it would be hard work to persuade him to return to her. If only her father were here ... Of course, he would be soon, but soon might so easily be too late. From Simon's whole character, and from his behaviour last night, she was convinced that he would do something drastic — and at once. There was no time to be lost if she did not want him to emigrate to America or do something equally desperate and final.

Her mind worked rapidly. She must have help. Not Lady Marchmont. She was out of the question for all kinds of reasons. Having finished a scanty and silent breakfast, she rang the bell, ordered her carriage and had herself driven to the Beaufrages' new house.

Sally, who looked pale and tired, greeted her, she thought, with the slightest tinge of embarrassment. Encouraged by this, which confirmed much that she had suspected, Henrietta came straight to the point.

'I am come to ask your help,' she said.

'My help?'

'Yes. We promised to be friends, did we not? Now you must do me a friend's office, for I never needed one more. I am in a sad quandary, Sally.' Best out with it at once. 'I have engaged myself to the wrong brother.'

'Truly?' Sally's colour came and went. 'Do you really mean it, Henrietta? Oh, I have never been so relieved in my life. I have been so troubled, so perplexed . . .'

'Ah,' said Henrietta. 'So the Miss Giddys were right, for once. Charles has been visiting you.'

'Yes, he has. Believe me, Henrietta, I did not know what to do for the best.'

Henrietta laughed. 'My poor Sally, were you afraid I would scratch your eyes out? I only hope he has been making desperate love to you. I cannot tell you how frantic I am for an expedient to be rid of him — and one that will satisfy Simon, too.'

Sally burst into one of her great fits of laughter. 'And to think that I have been wondering how in the world to break it to you that Charles is false. Yes, indeed, he has been making love to me — or trying to, and very well he does it, too. I could have enjoyed it from anyone else, circumstanced as I am, for you must have seen long since that Cedric and I are not as happy as I had hoped. As for Charles Rivers, of course it is my money he is after, not my beautiful person. I have it from my men of business that his circumstances are desperate. If his grandfather lingers on much longer he will be forced to fly the country to escape his creditors. He has been making enquiries, I should tell you, my love, about your circumstances, and has found, I think, your father to be too well in control of your fortune for his purposes. Anyway, to make a long story short, I think he has decided a wealthy mistress would suit him admirably — and I am to be she.'

Henrietta laughed. 'I hope you are properly flattered, Sally.'

'Oh, immoderately. But, come, my dearest creature, if this good news is true and you really wish to be rid of him, let us put our heads together and see what we can contrive, for, to tell truth, I have an axe of my own to grind in this business. There is not only your Simon to be thought of, but my Cedric. Let us see if we cannot turn Charles Rivers to good use for once in his life. He has been urging me, I should tell you, this age, to give him the meeting secretly. Well, I think he shall have his wish. It is Lady Laskerville's masked ball tomorrow is it not? And she has those three gloomy conservatories where nobody goes. Well, listen . . .'

Listening, Henrietta could have wished her part in the business a more active one, but she had to admit the soundness of Sally's plan. If anything could serve their purpose, it must be this. She went home to prepare her domino. Impossible, when she got there not to hope that there might, contrary to all expectation, be some word from Simon. And when she actually saw the familiar handwriting on a little package, her hand shook so that she could hardly open it. Inside she found a bunch of primroses and the briefest of notes. 'I picked these for you this morning. Farewell.' And the familiar, curly 'S'.

Pinning the primroses against her heart with a hand that would not stop trembling, she prayed that Simon would obey the anonymous note he was to receive. But how could he fail to do so, when it spoke in such terms both of herself and of Charles? And at least his message told her that he had not yet left town. After all, she consoled herself, it took some time to emigrate.

Lady Laskerville's masked ball, given on the spur of the moment to celebrate the Allied victory, was one of the most splendid Henrietta could remember. Indeed, when she saw the crowds that thronged the entrance hall, her heart sank for a moment. Suppose the conservatories, too, were crowded? Their scheme would be ruined. But it was a mild spring evening and the long windows of Lady Laskerville's public rooms stood open to her gardens, where the Pandean pipes played for the more intrepid dancers. Gradually, as the crowded rooms grew warmer, more and more couples drifted out into the gardens, and by the time the third waltz was playing — the signal agreed upon between her and Sally — she found it easy enough to slip through the crowd of masked figures and make her way to the end of the house where Lord Laskerville had built his orangery. Neglected since his death, these three communicating conservatories were dank and gloomy enough to discourage even the most amorous couple. Henrietta was relieved to find them empty and made her way with silent expedition to the inner of the three rooms, where a sadly drooping palm tree hid her entirely from view. Sally, she saw, had been right, only the central room was lighted, and that but dimly. So far, all went well.

Then came the worst part of all, the waiting. She did not care particularly whether Cedric obeyed his instructions or not, but suppose Simon did not come? Since everyone was masked, it had been impossible even to discover whether he was at the ball. Still, she would know soon enough. And with this thought she settled herself as comfortably as possible on a somewhat clammy rustic bench under the palm tree and composed herself to wait. Simon's instructions had been that he must conceal himself in the conservatory at the end of the third waltz. Cedric, if he came at all, would come still later. They had taken no risk of accidental meetings, Sally and she, planning their campaign like a couple of Peninsula generals.

The waltz music, faintly whispering from the other side of the house, swirled to its close at last and soon Henrietta, intently listening, breathlessly silent, was rewarded by the sound of cautious movement in the further room. Surely that must be Simon! As the silence fell once more, she found herself a prey to a new set of anxieties. Perhaps it was not Simon after all, or, if it was, suppose he did not have the patience to await the event of this odd assignation? But there was nothing she could do but wait and pray.

She never heard Cedric come, but this did not surprise her, since his position was to be in the main conservatory, closest to the scene that was to be played there. And, at last, she saw that it was about to begin. Sally entered the conservatory in the costume they had agreed upon — that of a nun — her veil closely drawn about her face. Almost immediately she was joined by a man in the costume of a brown friar. He, too, had his cowl pulled well around his face, but it was clear from the way he approached the nun that he expected and knew her. He took the hand she held out to him and bent low to kiss it.

'At last we are alone,' said Charles Rivers.

The nun withdrew her hand from his. 'Mr. Rivers,' she began, 'I have consented to meet you this once — '

He interrupted her. 'No names, I beg, my dearest life. You do not know what I have risked to come to you here. My grandmother thinks me indisposed. Recognition might mean my ruin.'

Sally gave her deep, unmistakable laugh behind her veil. 'Let us not talk of ruin, friar,' she said. 'Tell me instead why you have so begged and blandished me for this private interview, which, I must tell you, I grant with the greatest reluctance and have no wish to prolong.'

He snatched her hand again. 'My dearest creature, how can you be so cruel? You know all too well how I pine, how I suffer, how I die for love of you. All I ask is the opportunity to give up everything for your sake: career, fortune, title, what do I care for them if I cannot have you? Lady Beaufrage — Sally — may I not call you beloved? Only tell me that you are not altogether indifferent to my devotion, my passion, my adoration.'

The nun stood very still. 'Have you forgotten, reverend father, that I have a husband, and you a betrothed who is my dearest friend?'

'Forgotten? No. How could I, when I regret it every day of my life? But let us for once be honest with ourselves, you and I. You do not love your husband. It is not possible for a woman of your calibre to care for a gambling wastrel such as he. As for my betrothed; you have long known that it is to be the merest marriage of convenience on my part, and I am beyond that now. Without you, I cannot live. With you, the world would be paradise, exile an Eden. Sally, my love, say you will fly with me.'

'That is enough, Mr. Rivers.' A new note in her voice now. 'I have heard you patiently. Now it is my turn to speak. I owe you, I collect, an apology in some sort, since I have purposely led you on to see how far you would go. It is far indeed. So you would, for the sake of my fortune — for I do not flatter myself with any belief in your passion — no, no, for my fortune only you would blandish me into betraying my husband and my friend, both of whom I love. Do I see you start, friar? Does it surprise you to hear that I love the man you have been pleased to call a gambling wastrel — and who is worth ten of you, Mr. Rivers. It would take greater powers of persuasion than you are master of to make me false to him — particularly since I am to bear his child. You would look a fine fool, would you not, escorting an increasing mistress round the lesser courts of Europe. For that, I take it, is the life you had mapped out for me. That is the Eden you have to offer. I cannot think how you came to take me for such a fool. I am no green girl to be caught with a languishing look and a romantic tale. I have had an eye to you this long time now, and I find your proposals as unflattering as they are expected. You forgot, I collect, that I am a businesswoman, with informants everywhere. Now I see you flinch. Yes, I am aware that you have so mortgaged your expectations from your grandfather that if he does not oblige you with a speedy death you face certain ruin. I am aware, too, that he has been so inconsiderate, these last few days, as to take a turn for the better. No wonder you are mad for love of me. Since you must inevitably flee the country, and since my friend Miss Marchmont has more sense than to go with you, I can see that I and my moneybags might make you admirable companions. Well, I am sorry to disappoint you, but I have taken my goods to a happier market. I think you and I have played our last scene of pretty passion.'

With an oath, he raised his hand to strike her. Henrietta was about to start forward to her defence when a man's figure appeared from the back of the conservatory.

'Villain!' Cedric Beaufrage had him by the collar. 'Touch my wife at your peril.'

'I thank you, Cedric.' Sally's voice had lost none of its composure. 'You are arrived most happily. Perhaps you would be so good as to see Mr. Rivers to the door. I think he will go without protest. He wishes a scandal still less than we do. And if you are thinking of fighting him for my sake, my love, I wish you will think again. He is not worth it. Henrietta' — she raised her voice slightly — 'have you anything to say to Mr. Rivers before he takes his leave?'

Henrietta came forward. 'Yes,' she said. 'One word. Here is your ring, Charles, and good-bye.'

'What a romantic scene,' said a voice from the doorway.

'Quite a little drama,' added another.

'For all the world like Covent Garden,' said a third.

The voices were unmistakable, and the three Miss Giddys, elegantly, if unsuitably garbed as the Three Graces, swept into the conservatory. For once, Henrietta was glad to see them. Their arrival broke up the scene as nothing else could have done. Without another word, Charles turned and left the conservatory. Cedric paused for the merest moment, took his wife's hand and held it in a strangely moving gesture against his cheek, then turned and followed Charles. Left to face the Miss Giddys, Sally took Henrietta's hand in silent warning.

'I fear we have intruded,' said the first Grace.

'On a most interesting scene,' said the second.

'Dear Lady Beaufrage,' said the third.

'And Lord Beaufrage, of course,' said the first. 'Such touching devotion.'

'But as for your charming companion —' All three turned masked faces to look in blind question at Henrietta.

'And hers.' The third Grace, turned for a moment to look towards the door through which Rivers had vanished.

'Dear Lady Beaufrage, you must be so good as to enlighten us. You know how our poor dear Fanny frets over a mystery.'

'She will make herself ill.' Henrietta had by now identified the first Grace as Miss Giddy herself.

'My dear ladies' — Sally took the hands of two of the Graces — 'you cannot, surely, be suggesting that I betray the secrets of the masquerade? What? Am I, a mere nobody, to be instructing you in the manners of the *ton*? My companion, as you can see, wishes to remain nameless, and so does hers. But, come, I know your discretion so well . . .' And she bent and whispered something into the nearest eagerly offered ear. The Miss Giddy thus favoured let out a little shriek and whispered in her turn to the sister on the other side of her, who turned with a gasp to the third and last Grace. Then all three moved towards Henrietta, dropped her the deepest of curtseys and hurried, still passionately whispering, out into the crowded rooms.

Henrietta could not help laughing. 'Sally,' she said, 'what in the world did you tell them?'

'Why, that you were royalty, of course. They are convinced that they have seen Princess Charlotte meeting — who knows? Not Young Frog, I am sure. It will be all over town tomorrow, and by the time the Miss Giddys discover that Princess Charlotte was safe at the opera tonight they will be too deeply embroiled to trouble us further. But, look, here comes Cedric full of ardour and devotion. You will find, my dear, that married quarrels are even more interesting than those of lovers. Ah' — she turned to greet Cedric — 'here you are, love. What do you say? Shall we dance together and confound the gossips?'

He took her hand. 'My dearest, I am yours, always, to command. But tell me — is it really true?' He led her away towards the dancers.

Left alone, Henrietta stood for a moment in silence. Then, 'Simon?' she whispered.

'Henrietta!' He emerged from the further conservatory. 'I . . . I do not know what to say.'

She laughed and held out her hand to him. 'Then say nothing, but take me out into the garden instead, for, I tell you, I am heartily sick of the smell of dead leaves and mould.' And then, as they moved, still hand in hand, out and down terraced steps to a rose garden: 'Tell me, did you ever see anything more like a scene from one of Mr. Sheridan's comedies? Did not Sally play her part to perfection?'

'Play it? You mean — Henrietta, you know?'

'Yes. All that — and more.' She gave a little sigh, her hand settling more closely in his. 'Simon dear, I have been jilted. I shall be the butt of society. The Miss Giddys will have their way with me at last. I hope' — she turned to look up at him — 'I hope you are going to come to my rescue.'

He smiled down at her. 'I should not wish to see you suffer, Henrietta.' His hand on hers made her a more passionate answer.

'No? You think, perhaps, you will take pity on my lamentable condition?'

He was laughing now. 'Oh, Henrietta, you are incorrigible. Who but you — ' To finish the sentence he pulled her into his arms. Around them the garden stirred gently into life. Moonlight was fading and a bird tried out its morning song. From the house, the sounds of a last waltz died away. At last he let her go. 'Come, my love, it is time to be unmasking. Morning is here.' Very gently he untied the strings of her mask, then, removing his, bent to kiss her again.

'Good heavens,' said a familiar voice.

'Why, 'tis Miss Marchmont,' said another.

'And Mr. Rivers,' said a third. 'Mr. *Simon* Rivers,' it added reproachfully.

Gently, Simon released Henrietta, sharing as his lips left hers, a little laugh of purest happiness. 'Yes,' he turned to face the avid Miss Giddys, his arm still protectively round Henrietta. 'Miss Marchmont has made me the happiest of men. Come, my love, we must tell your mother our good news.'

'And her father,' said Miss Giddy.

'Lord Marchmont is this instant arrived from Paris,' said Miss Letitia.

'I wonder what he will say to this strange news,' said Miss Patricia.

But they were left to wonder alone. Simon had taken Henrietta across the dew-drenched lawn and up the terrace steps to the door of the main ballroom. Indoors, the lights of the chandeliers looked tawdry after the cool dawn glow outside. The dancing was over now and the rooms nearly empty. Only, here and there, a masked couple still laughed together, prolonging the night's merriment into the dawn. In the room beyond, Henrietta saw Sally and Cedric talking to Lady Marchmont and a tall man in travelling dress — her father.

He turned as they approached. 'Henrietta, my dearest child.'

In an instant she was in his arms. Letting her go at last, he looked from her to Simon. 'So the Miss Giddys were right for once, and I am delighted to hear it. You'll never be the wrong Mr. Rivers to me, Simon.' He shook him warmly by the hand. 'It's the best news since Paris fell, even if it does mean that I am to have a radical for a son-in-law.' He laughed. 'You see, I have had my informants, too, and more reliable ones than those Three Graces. Mr. Gurney wrote to me the other day.' This with a quizzical glance for Henrietta. 'He's a good friend.' To Simon, who looked puzzled. 'He spoke in the highest terms of your prospects. You know' — back again to Henrietta — 'I always thought you would make an admirable wife for a politician yet always wondered about those rebel American notions of yours. You'll suit a Whig much better than a Tory. But you'll have to keep an eye on your wife, Simon, or she will be out there on the hustings beside you, preaching rights for women and I don't know what else.'

'Sir' — Simon took Henrietta's hand — 'beside me is just where I want her.'

# ONE WAY TO VENICE

## JANE AIKEN HODGE

Taunting, teasing, full of hate, the anonymous letters bring back the misery of Julia Rivers' brief marriage, which had been destroyed by some unknown enemy who sought her death. Now she must relive all that pain, and follow the trail set by the letters, in order to save the threatened life of her child, Dominic. The journey to Venice brings a new friendship, an old confrontation and, above all, danger. But there is also the hope of happiness, if Julia can fight her way out of the web of conspiracy surrounding her.

'Jane Aiken Hodge captures interest from the start. A good holiday read — in Venice or anywhere'.

*EVENING STANDARD*

**CORONET BOOKS**

# THE ADVENTURERS

## JANE AIKEN HODGE

As Napoleon's army retreats through Germany, a group of stragglers plunder the von Hugel estate, leaving Sonia von Hugel apparently alone in the castle. Her father has been killed, her governess wounded, all seems lost. But then there appears a mysterious stranger called Charles Vincent, who leads Sonia and her wounded friend into safety, and from there into further adventure.

'A mixture of high adventure and romance which makes a most readable story'.

*BRITISH BOOKS*

**CORONET BOOKS**

## MASTERFUL NOVELS FROM
## JANE AIKEN HODGE

*All these books are available at your local bookshop or newsagent, or can be ordered direct from the publisher. Just tick the titles you want and fill in the form below.*
Prices and availability subject to change without notice.

......................................................................................................................

CORONET BOOKS, P.O. Box 11, Falmouth, Cornwall.

Please send cheque or postal order, and allow the following for postage and packing:

U.K.—One book 25p plus 10p per copy for each additional book ordered, up to a maximum of £1.05.

B.F.P.O. and EIRE—25p for the first book plus 10p per copy for the next 8 books, thereafter 5p per book.

OTHER OVERSEAS CUSTOMERS—40p for the first book and 12p per copy for each additional book.

Name ..............................................................................

Address ..........................................................................

........................................................................................